CRITICAL ACCLAIM FOR THE NOVELS OF

STEVEN PRESSFIELD

GATES OF FIRE

"Vivid and exciting... Pressfield gives the reader a perspective no ancient historian offers, a soldier's-eye view... remarkable."
—*New York Times Book Review*

"Pressfield's powerful, historically accurate novel explores Spartan society and the nature of courage without ever losing its narrative momentum." —*New Yorker*

"Impressive... vivid." —*USA Today*

"Majestic... monumental... epic... once begun, almost impossible to put down." —*New York Daily News*

"*Gates of Fire* lives up to its billing as an epic novel.... His Greeks and Persians come across as the real thing."
—*San Francisco Chronicle*

"Rich with historical detail, hot action and crafty storytelling... Riveting." —*Publishers Weekly* (starred review)

"Monumental... [a story] told with extraordinary authority and insight." —*Fort Worth Star-Telegram*

"Steven Pressfield brings the battle of Thermopylae to brilliant life, and he does for that war what Charles Frazier did for the Civil War in *Cold Mountain*." —Pat Conroy

"An incredibly gripping, moving, and literate work of art. Rarely does an author manage to re-create a moment in history with such mastery, authority, and psychological insights." —Nelson DeMille

P9-CDE-236

"A timeless epic of man and war... Pressfield has created a new classic deserving of a place beside the very best of the old."
—Stephen Coonts

"Giving voices and shapes and lives to some of the 300 Spartans who fought at Thermopylae is one of the best ideas for an historical novel I've seen in years. Anyone who enjoys military history will find *Gates of Fire* irresistible—a riveting book." —Thomas Fleming

"*Gates of Fire* is that rarity of a novel: it combines a first-rate storyteller with a first-rate story to tell. It is truly epic... a book for everyone, not just military history buffs." —Margaret George

THE VIRTUES OF WAR

"Wonderfully imagined... Stunningly graphic, intense and extraordinary." —Nelson DeMille

"Sharp and colorful... An extravagant exercise of the imagination."
—*Washington Post Book World*

"Simply superb... An absolutely gripping read."
—*Seattle Times*

"A tale as magnificent as Alexander, Warrior Supreme."
—W.E.B. Griffin

LAST OF THE AMAZONS

"Pressfield's attention to military detail fuels the action in this fantastical novel." —*Book Magazine*

"Pressfield evocatively re-creates the Greek city-state of Athens in 1250 B.C." —*Washington Post Book World*

"[A] splendid tale of valor, honor and comradeship memorializes those women whose lives and deeds have faded into the mists of legend. Highly recommended." *—Library Journal*

TIDES OF WAR

"Pressfield's battlefield scenes rank with the most convincing ever written." *—USA Today*

"On every page are color, splendor, sorrow, the unforgiving details of battle. . . . Pressfield produces an even greater spectacle—and, in its honest, incremental way, an even greater heart-tugger—than in his acclaimed tale of the battle of Thermopylae, *Gates of Fire*."

—Kirkus Reviews

By Steven Pressfield

FICTION

The Profession

Killing Rommel

The Afghan Campaign

The Virtues of War

Last of the Amazons

Tides of War

Gates of Fire

The Legend of Bagger Vance

NONFICTION

Turning Pro

The Warrior Ethos

Do The Work

The War of Art

GATES OF FIRE

AN EPIC NOVEL OF THE BATTLE OF THERMOPYLAE

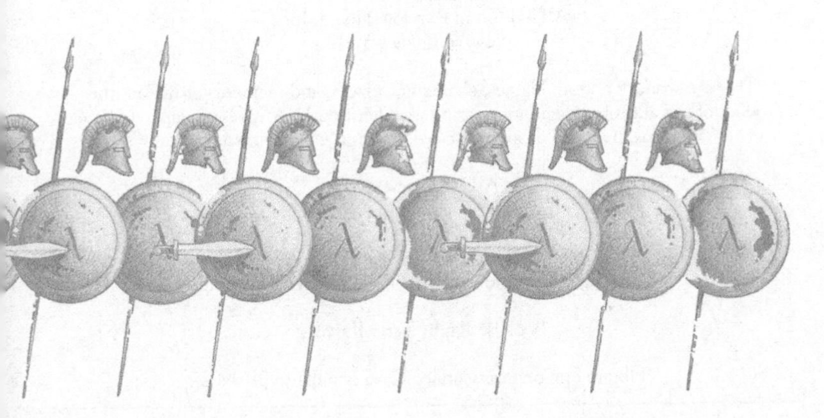

STEVEN PRESSFIELD

BANTAM BOOKS

GATES OF FIRE
A Bantam Book

PUBLISHING HISTORY
Doubleday hardcover edition published October 1998
Bantam mass market edition published September 1999
Bantam trade paperback edition / October 2005

Published by
Bantam Dell
A Division of Random House, Inc.
New York, New York

This is a work of fiction. Names, characters, places, and incidents either are the product of the author's imagination or are used fictitiously. Any resemblance to actual persons, living or dead, events, or locales is entirely coincidental.

All rights reserved
Copyright © 1998 by Steven Pressfield
Cover art by Alan Ayers
Maps copyright © 1998 by David Cain
Title page illustration copyright © 1998 by David Cain

Book design by Terry Karydes

Library of Congress Catalog Card Number: 98-19902

Bantam Books and the rooster colophon are registered trademarks of Random House, Inc.

ISBN 978-0-553-38368-3

Printed in the United States of America
Published simultaneously in Canada

www.bantamdell.com

BVG 30 29 28 27 26

FOR MY MOTHER AND FATHER

MACEDONIA
MT. OLYMPUS
THESSALY
Skiatho
Artemisium
Thermopylae
AKARNANIA
ITHAKA
Astakos
Delphi
PHOKIS
EUBOEA
BOEOTIA
Thebes
Plataea
Antirhion
Rhion
Gulf of Corinth
ATTIKA
Marath
Athe
Elis
Corinth
Salamis
PELOPONNESE
Olympia
Argos
Mantinea
Tegea
MESSENIA
Eurotas River
MT. PARNON
Selassia
Sparta
LAKEDAEMON
MT. TAYGETOS
GREECE
AND THE AEGEAN
480 B.C.

THRACE
Byzantium
Propontis
Hellespont
LYDIA
Sardis
IONIA
Ephesus
KARIA
Hallikarnassos
Rhodes
RHODES
RETE

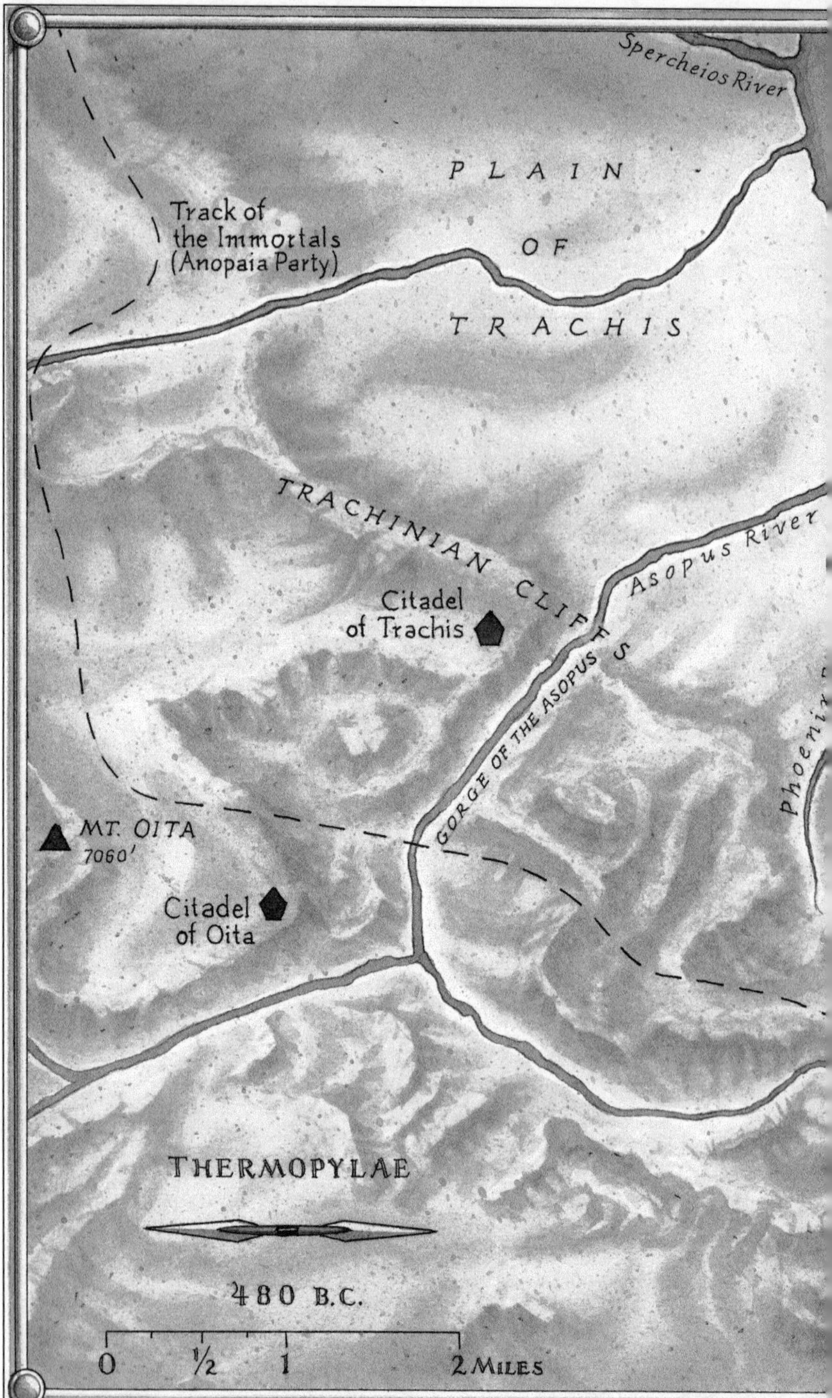

Spercheios River

PLAIN OF TRACHIS

Track of the Immortals (Anopaia Party)

TRACHINIAN CLIFFS

Asopus River

Citadel of Trachis

GORGE OF THE ASOPUS

MT. OITA 7060′

Citadel of Oita

THERMOPYLAE

480 B.C.

0 ½ 1 2 MILES

Malian Gulf
West Gate
BATTLEFIELD
NARROWS
Antheia
Hot Springs
PHOKIAN
WALL
Middle Gate
Road
East Gate
Alpenoi
Road
South
1399′
1374′
KALLIDROMOS

HISTORICAL NOTE

In 480 B.C. *the forces of the Persian Empire under King Xerxes, numbering according to Herodotus two million men, bridged the Hellespont and marched in their myriads to invade and enslave Greece.*

In a desperate delaying action, a picked force of three hundred Spartans was dispatched to the pass of Thermopylae, where the confines between mountains and sea were so narrow that the Persian multitudes and their cavalry would be at least partially neutralized. Here, it was hoped, an elite force willing to sacrifice their lives could keep back, at least for a few days, the invading millions.

Three hundred Spartans and their allies held off the invaders for seven days, until, their weapons smashed and broken from the slaughter, they fought "with bare hands and teeth" (as recorded by Herodotus) before being at last overwhelmed.

The Spartans and their Thespaian allies died to the last man, but the standard of valor they set by their sacrifice inspired the Greeks to rally and, in that fall and spring, defeat the Persians at Salamis and Plataea and preserve the beginnings of Western democracy and freedom from perishing in the cradle.

Two memorials remain today at Thermopylae. Upon the modern one, called the Leonidas monument in honor of the Spartan king who fell there, is engraved his response to Xerxes' demand that the Spartans lay down their arms. Leonidas' reply was two words, Molon labe. *"Come and get them."*

The second monument, the ancient one, is an unadorned stone engraved with the words of the poet Simonides. Its verses comprise perhaps the most famous of all warrior epitaphs:

Go tell the Spartans, stranger passing by,
that here obedient to their laws we lie.

Although extraordinary valor was displayed by the entire corps of Spartans and Thespaians, yet bravest of all was declared the Spartan Dienekes. It is said that on the eve of battle, he was told by a native of Trachis that the Persian archers were so numerous that, when they fired their volleys, the mass of arrows blocked out the sun. Dienekes, however, quite undaunted by this prospect, remarked with a laugh, "Good. Then we'll have our battle in the shade."

—HERODOTUS, *THE HISTORIES*

The fox knows many tricks;
the hedgehog one good one.

—ARCHILOCHUS

BOOK ONE

XERXES

BY ORDER OF HIS MAJESTY, *Xerxes son of Darius, Great King of Persia and Media, King of Kings, King of the Lands; Master of Libya, Egypt, Arabia, Ethiopia, Babylonia, Chaldea, Phoenicia, Elam, Syria, Assyria and the nations of Palestine; Ruler of Ionia, Lydia, Phrygia, Armenia, Cilicia, Cappadocia, Thrace, Macedonia and the trans-Caucasus, Cyprus, Rhodes, Samos, Chios, Lesbos and the islands of the Aegean; Sovereign Lord of Parthia, Bactria, Caspia, Sousiana, Paphlagonia and India; Lord of all men from the rising to the setting sun, His Most Holy, Reverend and Exalted, Invincible, Incorruptible, Blessed of God Ahura Mazda and Omnipotent among Mortals. Thus decreeth His Magnificence, as recorded by Gobartes the son of Artabazos, His historian:*

That, following the glorious victory of His Majesty's forces over the arrayed Peloponnesian foe, Spartans and allies, at the pass of Thermopylae, having extinguished the enemy to the last man and erected trophies to this valorous conquest, yet was His Majesty in His God-inspired wisdom desirous of further intelligence, both of certain infantry tactics employed by the enemy which proved of some effect against His Majesty's troops, and of the type of foemen these were who, though unbound by liege law or servitude, facing insuperable odds and certain death, yet chose to remain at their stations, and perished therein to the final man.

His Majesty's regret having been expressed at the dearth of knowledge and insight upon these subjects, then did intercede God Ahura Mazda on His Majesty's behalf. A survivor of the Hellenes (as the Greeks call themselves) was discovered, grievously wounded and in a state of extremis, beneath the wheels of a battle waggon, being unseen theretofore due to the presence of numerous corpses of men, horses and beasts of transport being heaped upon the site. His Majesty's surgeons being summoned and charged under pain of death to spare no measure to preserve the captive's life, God yet granted His Majesty's desire. The Greek survived the night and the morning following. Within ten days the man had recovered speech and mental faculty and, though yet confined to a litter and under direct care of the Royal Surgeon, was able not only at last to speak but to express his fervent desire to do so.

Several unorthodox aspects of the captive's armor and raiment were noted by the detaining officers. Beneath the man's battle helmet was found not the traditional felt cawl of the Spartan hoplite, but the dogskin cap associated with the race of helots, the Lakedaemonian slave class, serfs of the land. In contrast inexplicable to His Majesty's officers, the prisoner's shield and armor were of the finest bronze, etched with rare Hibernian cobalt, while his helmet bore the transverse crest of a full Spartiate, an officer.

In preliminary interviews, the man's manner of speech proved to be a compound of the loftiest philosophical and literary language, indicative of a deep familiarity with the epics of the Hellenes, intermingled with the coarsest and most crude gutter argot, much of which was uninterpretable even to His Majesty's most knowledgeable translators. The Greek, however, willingly agreed to translate these himself, which he did, utilizing scraps of profane Aramaic and Persian which he claimed to have acquired during certain sea travels beyond Hellas. I, His Majesty's historian, seeking to preserve His Majesty's ears from the foul and often execrable language employed by the captive, sought to excise the offensive material before His Majesty was forced to endure hearing it. Yet did His Majesty in His God-inspired wisdom instruct His servant so to translate the man's speech as to render it in whatever tongue and idiom necessary to duplicate the precise effect in Greek. This have I attempted to do. I pray that His Majesty recall the charge He imparted and hold His servant blameless for those portions of the following transcription which will and must offend any civilized hearer.

Inscribed and submitted this sixteenth day of Ululu, Fifth Year of His Majesty's Accession.

ONE

Third day of Tashritu, Fifth Year of His Majesty's Accession, south of the Lokrian border, the Army of the Empire having continued its advance unopposed into central Greece, establishing an encampment opposite the eastern fall of Mount Parnassus, the sum of whose watercourses, as numerous others before upon the march from Asia, failed and was drunk dry by the troops and horses.

The following initial interview took place in His Majesty's campaign tent, three hours after sunset, the evening meal having been concluded and all court business transacted. Field marshals, advisors, household guards, the Magi and secretaries being present, the detaining officers were instructed to produce the Greek. The captive was brought in upon a litter, eyes cloth-bound so as to dissanction sight of His Majesty. The Magus performed the incantation and purification, permitting the man to speak within the hearing of His Majesty. The prisoner was instructed not to speak directly toward the Royal Presence but to address himself to the officers of the household guard, the Immortals, stationed upon His Majesty's left.

The Greek was directed by Orontes, captain of the Immortals, to identify himself. He responded that his name was Xeones the son of Skamandridas of Astakos, a city in Akarnania. The man Xeones stated that he wished first to thank His Majesty for preserving his life and to express his gratitude for and admiration of the skill of the Royal Surgeon's staff. Speaking from his litter, and yet struggling with weakness of breath from several as-yet-unhealed wounds of the lungs and thoracic organs, he offered the following disclaimer to His Majesty, stating that he was unfamiliar with the Persian style of discourse and further stood unfortunately lacking in the gifts of poesy and story-spinning. He declared that the tale he could tell would not be of generals or kings, for the political machinations of the great, he said, he was and had been in no position to observe. He could only relate the story as he himself had lived it and witnessed it, from the vantage of a youth and squire of the heavy infantry, a servant of the battle train. Perhaps, the captive declared, His Majesty would discover little of interest in this narrative of the ordinary warriors, the "men in the line," as the prisoner expressed it.

His Majesty, responding through Orontes, Captain of the Immortals, asserted to the contrary that this was precisely the tale he wished most to hear. His Majesty was, He declared, already possessed of abundant intelligence of the intriguings of the great; what He desired most to hear was this, "the infantryman's tale."

What kind of men were these Spartans, who in three days had slain before His Majesty's eyes no fewer than twenty thousand of His most valiant warriors? Who were these foemen, who had taken with them to the house of the dead ten, or as some reports said, as many as twenty for every one of their own fallen? What were they like as men? Whom did they love? What made them laugh? His Majesty knew they feared death, as all men. By what philosophy did their minds embrace it? Most to the point, His Majesty said, He wished to acquire a sense of the individuals themselves, the real flesh-and-blood men whom He had observed from above the battlefield, but only indistinctly, from a distance, as indistinguishable identities concealed within the blood- and gore-begrimed carapaces of their helmets and armor.

Beneath his cloth-bound eyes, the prisoner bowed and offered a prayer of thanksgiving to some one of his gods. The story His Majesty wished to hear, he asserted, was the one he could truly tell, and the one he most wished to.

It must of necessity be his own story, as well as that of the warriors he had known. Would His Majesty be patient with this? Nor could the telling confine itself exclusively to the battle, but must proceed from events antecedent in time, for only in this light and from this perspective would the lives and actions of the warriors His Majesty observed at Thermopylae be given their true meaning and significance.

His Majesty, field marshals, generals and advisors being satisfied, the Greek was given a bowl of wine and honey for his thirst and asked to commence where he pleased, to tell the story in whatever manner he deemed appropriate. The man, Xeones, bowed once upon his litter and began:

. . .

I had always wondered what it felt like to die.

There was an exercise we of the battle train practiced when we served as punching bags for the Spartan heavy infantry. It was called the Oak because we took our positions along a line of oaks at the edge of the plain of Otona, where the Spartiates and the Gentleman-Rankers ran their field exercises in fall and winter. We would line up ten deep with body-length wicker shields braced upon the earth and they would hit us, the shock troops, coming across the flat in line of battle, eight deep, at a walk, then a pace, then a trot and finally a dead run. The shock of their interleaved shields was meant to knock the breath out of you, and it did. It was like being hit by a mountain. Your knees, no matter how braced you held them, buckled like saplings before an earthslide; in an instant all courage fled our hearts; we were rooted up like dried stalks before the ploughman's blade.

That was how it felt to die. The weapon which slew me at Thermopylae was an Egyptian hoplite spear, driven in beneath the plexus of the ribcage. But the sensation was not what one would have anticipated, not being pierced but rather slammed, like we sparring fodder felt beneath the oaks.

I had imagined that the dead would be detached. That they would look upon life with the eyes of objective wisdom. But the experience proved the opposite. Emotion ruled. It seemed nothing remained but emotion. My heart ached and broke as never it could on earth. Loss encompassed me with a searing, all-mastering pain. I saw my wife and children, my dear cousin Diomache, she whom I loved. I saw Skamandridas, my father, and Eunike, my mother, Bruxieus, Dekton and "Suicide," names which mean nothing to His Majesty to hear, but which to me were dearer than life and now, dying, dearer still.

Away they flew. Away I flew from them.

I was keenly conscious of the comrades-in-arms who had fallen with me. A bond surpassing by a hundredfold that which I had known in life bound me to them. I felt a sense of inexpressible relief and realized that I had feared, more than death, separation from them. I apprehended that excruciating war survivor's torment, the sense of isolation and self-betrayal experienced by those who had elected to cling yet to breath when their comrades had let loose their grip.

That state which we call life was over.

I was dead.

And yet, titanic as was that sense of loss, there existed a keener one which I now experienced and felt my brothers-in-arms feeling with me. It was this.

That our story would perish with us.

That no one would ever know.

I cared not for myself, for my own selfish or vainglorious purposes, but for them. For Leonidas, for Alexandros and Polynikes, for Arete bereft by her hearth and, most of all, for Dienekes. That his valor, his wit, his private thoughts that I alone was privileged to share, that these and all that he and his companions had achieved and suffered would simply vanish, drift away like smoke from a woodland fire, this was unbearable.

We had reached the river now. We could hear with ears that were no longer ears and see with eyes that were no longer eyes the stream of Lethe and the hosts of the long-suffering dead whose round beneath the earth was at last drawing to a period. They were returning to life, drinking of those waters which would efface all memory of their existence here as shades.

But we from Thermopylae, we were aeons away from drinking of Lethe's stream. We remembered.

A cry which was not a cry but only the multiplied pain of the warriors' hearts, all feeling what I, too, felt, rent the baleful scene with unspeakable pathos.

Then from behind me, if there can be such a thing as "behind" in that world where all directions are as one, came a glow of such sublimity that I knew, we all knew at once, it could be nothing but a god.

Phoebus Far Darter, Apollo himself in war armor, moved there among the Spartiates and Thespaians. No words were exchanged; none were needed. The Archer could feel the men's agony and they knew without speech that he, warrior and physician, was there to succor it. So quickly that surprise was impossible I felt his eye turn toward me, me the last and least who could expect it, and then Dienekes himself was beside me, my master in life.

I would be the one. The one to go back and speak. A pain beyond all previous now seized me. Sweet life itself, even the desperately sought chance to tell the tale, suddenly seemed unendurable alongside the pain of having to take leave of these whom I had come so to love.

But again, before the god's majesty, no entreaty was possible.

I saw another light, a sicklier, cruder, more coarse illumination, and knew that it was the sun. I was soaring back. Voices came to me through physical ears. Soldiers' speech, in Egyptian and Persian, and leather-gauntleted fists pulling me from beneath a sheaf of corpses.

The Egyptian marines told me later that I had uttered the word *lokas*, which in their tongue meant "fuck," and they had laughed even as they dragged my shattered body out into the light of day.

They were wrong. The word was *Loxias*—the Greek title of respect for Apollo the Cunning, or Apollo Crabwise, whose oracles arise ever elusive and oblique—and I was half crying to him, half cursing him for laying this terrible responsibility on me who had no gift to perform it.

As poets call upon the Muse to speak through them, I croaked my inarticulate grunt to the Striker From Afar.

If indeed you have elected me, Archer, then let your fine-fletched arrows spring from my bow. Lend me your voice, Far Darter. Help me to tell the tale.

TWO

Thermopylae is a spa. The word in Greek means "hot gates," from the thermal springs and, as His Majesty knows, the narrow and precipitous defiles which form the only passages by which the site may be approached—in Greek, *pylae* or *pylai,* the East and West Gates.

The Phokian Wall around which so much of the most desperate fighting took place was not constructed by the Spartans and their allies in the event, but stood in existence prior to the battle, erected in ancient times by the inhabitants of Phokis and Lokris as defense against the incursions of their northern neighbors, the Thessalians and Macedonians. The wall, when the Spartans arrived to take possession of the pass, stood in ruins. They rebuilt it.

The springs and pass themselves are not considered by the Hellenes to belong to the natives of the area, but are open to all in Greece. The baths are thought to possess curative powers; in summer the site teems with visitors. His Majesty beheld the charm of the shaded groves and pool houses, the oak copse sacred to Amphiktyon and that pleasantly meandering path bounded by the Lion's Wall, whose stones are said to have been set in place by Herakles himself. Along this in peacetime are customarily arrayed the gaily colored tents and booths used by the vendors from Trachis, Anthela and Alpenoi to serve whatever adventurous pilgrims have made the trek to the mineral baths.

There is a double spring sacred to Persephone, called the Skyllian fountain, at the foot of the bluff beside the Middle Gate. Upon this site the Spartans established their camp, between the Phokian Wall and the hillock where the final tooth-and-nail struggle took place. His Majesty knows how little drinking water is to hand from other sources in the surrounding mountains. The earth between the Gates is normally so parched and dust-blown that servants are employed by the spa to oil the walkways for the convenience of the bathers. The ground itself is hard as stone.

His Majesty saw how swiftly that marble-hard clay was churned into muck by the contending masses of the warriors. I have never seen such mud and of such depth, whose moisture came only from the blood and terror-piss of the men who fought upon it.

When the advance troops, the Spartan rangers, arrived at Thermopylae prior to the battle, a few hours before the main body which was advancing by forced march, they discovered, incredibly, two parties of spa-goers, one from Tiryns, the other from Halkyon, thirty in all, men and women, each in their separate precincts, in various states of undress. These pilgrims were startled, to say the least, by the sudden appearance in their midst of the scarlet-clad armored Skiritai, all picked men under thirty, chosen for speed of foot as well as prowess in mountain fighting. The rangers cleared the bathers and their attendant perfume vendors, masseurs, fig-cake and bread sellers, bath and oil girls, strigil boys and so forth (who had ample intelligence of the Persian advance but had thought that the recent down-valley storm had rendered the northern approaches temporarily impassable). The rangers confiscated all food, soaps, linens and medical accoutrements and in particular the spa tents, which later appeared so grimly incongruous, billowing festively above the carnage. The rangers reerected these shelters at the rear, in the Spartan camp beside the Middle Gate, intending them for use by Leonidas and his royal guard.

The Spartan king, when he arrived, refused to avail himself of this shelter, deeming it unseemly. The Spartiate heavy infantry likewise rejected these amenities. The tents fell, in one of the ironies to which those familiar with war are accustomed, to the use of the Spartan helots, Thespaian, Phokian and Opountian Lokrian slaves and other attendants of the battle train who suffered wounds in the arrow and missile barrages. These individuals, too, after the second day refused to accept shelter. The brightly colored spa tents of Egyptian linen, now in tatters, came as His Majesty saw to protect only the beasts of transport, the mules and asses supporting the commissariat, who became terrorized by the sights and smells of the battle and could not be held by their teamsters. In the end the tents were torn to rags to bind the wounds of the Spartiates and their allies.

When I say Spartiates, I mean the formal term in Greek, *Spartiatai*, which refers to Lakedaemonians of the superior class, full Spartans—the *homoioi*—Peers or Equals. None of the class called Gentleman-Rankers or of the *perioikoi*, the secondary Spartans of less than full citizenship, or those enlisted from the surrounding Lakedaemonian towns, fought at the Hot Gates, though toward the end when the surviving Spartiates became so few that they could no longer form a fighting front, a certain "leavening element," as Dienekes expressed it, of freed slaves, armor bearers and battle squires, was permitted to fill the vacated spaces.

His Majesty may nonetheless take pride in knowing that his forces defeated the flower of Hellas, the cream of her finest and most valiant fighting men.

As for my own position within the battle train, the explanation may require a certain digression, with which I hope His Majesty will be patient.

I was captured at age twelve (or, more accurately, surrendered) as a *heliokekaumenos*, a Spartan term of derision which means literally "scorched by the sun." It referred to a type of nearly feral youth, burned black as Ethiopians by their exposure to the elements, with which the mountains abounded in those days preceding and following the first Persian War. I was cast originally among the Spartan helots, the serf class that the Lakedaemonians had created from the inhabitants of Messenia and Helos after they in centuries past had conquered and enslaved them. These husbandmen, however, rejected me because of certain physical impairments which rendered me useless for field labor. Also the helots hated and mistrusted any foreigner among them who might prove an informer. I lived a dog's life for most of a year before fate, luck or a god's hand delivered me into the service of Alexandros, a Spartan youth and protege of Dienekes. This saved my life. I was recognized at least ironically as a freeborn and, evincing such qualities of a wild beast as the Lakedaemonians found admirable, was elevated to the status of *parastates pais*, a sort of sparring partner for the youths enrolled in the *agoge*, the notorious and pitiless thirteen-year training regimen which turned boys into Spartan warriors.

Every heavy infantryman of the Spartiate class travels to war attended by at least one helot. *Enomotarchai*, the platoon leaders, take two. This latter was Dienekes' station. It is not uncommon for an officer of his rank to select as his primary attendant, his battle squire, a freeborn foreigner or even a young *mothax*, a noncitizen or bastard Spartan still in *agoge* training. It was my fortune, for good or ill, to be chosen by my master for this post. I supervised the care and transport of his armor, maintained his kit, prepared his food and sleeping site, bound his wounds and in general performed every task necessary to leave him free to train and fight.

My childhood home, before fate set me upon the road which found its end at the Hot Gates, was originally in Astakos in Akarnania, north of the Peloponnese, where the mountains look west over the sea toward Kephallinia and, beyond the horizon, to Sikelia and Italia.

The island of Ithaka, home of Odysseus of lore, lay within sight across the straits, though I myself was never privileged to touch the hero's sacred soil, as a boy or later. I was due to make the crossing, a treat from my aunt and uncle, on the occasion of my tenth birthday. But our city fell first, the males of my clan were slaughtered and females sold into slavery, our ancestral land taken, and I cast out, alone save my cousin Diomache, without family or home, three days before the start of my tenth year to heaven, as the poet says.

THREE

We had a slave on my father's farm when I was a boy, a man named Bruxieus, though I hesitate to use the word "slave," because my father was more in Bruxieus' power than the other way round. We all were, particularly my mother. As lady of the house she refused to make the most trifling domestic decision—and many whose scope far exceeded that—without first securing Bruxieus' advice and approval. My father deferred to him on virtually all matters, save politics within the city. I myself was completely under his spell.

Bruxieus was an Elean. He had been captured by the Argives in battle when he was nineteen. They blinded him with fiery pitch, though his knowledge of medicinal salves later restored at least a poor portion of his sight. He bore on his brow the ox-horn slave brand of the Argives. My father acquired him when he was past forty, as compensation for a shipment of hyacinth oil lost at sea.

As nearly as I could tell, Bruxieus knew everything. He could pull a bad tooth without clove or oleander. He could carry fire in his bare hands. And, most vital of all to my boy's regard, he knew every spell and incantation necessary to ward off bad luck and the evil eye.

Bruxieus' only weakness as I said was his vision. Beyond ten feet the man was blind as a stump. This was a source of secret, if guilty, pleasure to me because it meant he needed a boy with him at all times to see. I spent weeks never leaving his side, not even to sleep, since he insisted on watching over me, slumbering always on a sheepskin at the foot of my little bed.

In those days it seemed there was a war every summer. I remember the city's drills each spring when the planting was done. My father's armor would be brought down from the hearth and Bruxieus would oil each rim and joint, rewarp and reshaft the "two spears and two spares" and replace the cord and leather gripware within the *hoplon*'s oak and bronze sphere. The drills took place on a broad plain west of the potters' quarter, just below the city walls. We boys and girls brought sunshades and fig cakes, scrapped over the best viewing positions on the wall and watched our fathers drill below us to the trumpeters' calls and the beat of the battle drummers.

This year of which I speak, the dispute of note was over a proposal made by that session's *prytaniarch*, an estate owner named Onaximandros. He wanted each man to efface the clan or individual crest on his shield and replace it with a uniform *alpha*, for our city Astakos. He argued that Spartan shields all bore a proud *lambda*, for their country, Lakedaemon. Fine, came the derisive response, but we're no Lakedaemonians. Someone told the story of the Spartiate whose shield bore no crest at all, but only a common housefly painted life-size. When his rankmates made sport of him for this, the Spartan declared that in line of battle he would get so close to his enemy that the housefly would look as big as a lion.

Every year the military drills followed the same pattern. For two days enthusiasm reigned. Every man was so relieved to be free of farm or shop chores, and so delighted to be reunited with his comrades (and away from the children and women around the house), that the event took on the flavor of a festival. There were sacrifices morning and evening. The rich smells of spitted meat floated over everything; there were wheaten buns and honey candies, fresh-rolled fig cakes, and bowls of rice and barley grilled in sweet new-pressed sesame oil.

By the third day the militiamen's blisters started. Forearms and shoulders were rubbed raw by the heavy *hoplon* shields. The warriors, though most were farmers or grovers and supposedly of stout seasoned limb, had in fact passed the bulk of their agricultural labor in the cool of the counting room and not out behind a plough. They were getting tired of sweating. It was hot under those helmets. By the fourth day the sunshine warriors were presenting excuses in earnest. The farm needed this, the shop needed that, the slaves were robbing them blind, the hands were screwing each other silly. "Look at how straight the line advances now, on the practice field," Bruxieus would chuckle, squinting past me and the other boys. "They won't step so smartly when heaven starts to rain arrows and javelins. Each man will be edging to the right to get into his rankmate's shadow." Meaning the shelter of the shield of the man on his right. "By the time they hit the enemy line, the right wing will be overlapped half a *stade* and have to be chased back into place by its own cavalry!"

Nonetheless our citizen army (we could put four hundred heavy-armored hoplites into the field on a full call-up), despite the potbellies and wobbly shins, had acquitted itself more than honorably, at least in my short lifetime. That same *prytaniarch*, Onaximandros, had two fine span of oxen, got from the Kerionians, whose countryside our forces allied with the Argives and Eleuthrians had plundered ruthlessly three years running, burning a hundred farms and killing over seventy men. My uncle Tenagros had a stout mule and a full set of armor got in those seasons. Nearly every man had something.

But back to our militia's maneuvers. By the fifth day, the city fathers were thoroughly exhausted, bored and disgusted. Sacrifices to the gods redoubled, in the hope that the immortals' favor would make up for any lack of *polemike techne*, skill at arms, or *empeiria*, experience, on the part of our forces. By now there were huge gaps in the field and we boys had descended upon the site with our own play shields and spears. That was the signal to call it a day. With much grumbling from the zealots and great relief from the main body, the call was issued for the final parade. Whatever allies the city possessed that year (the Argives had sent their *strategos autokrater*, that great city's supreme military commander) were marshaled gaily into the reviewing stands, and our reinvigorated citizen-soldiers, knowing their ordeal was nearly over, loaded themselves up with every ounce of armor they possessed and passed in glorious review.

This final event was the greatest excitement of all, with the best food and music, not to mention the raw spring wine, and ended with many a farm cart bearing home in the middle watch of the night sixty-five pounds of bronze armor and a hundred and seventy pounds of loudly snoring warrior.

This morning, which initiated my destiny, came about because of ptarmigan eggs.

Among Bruxieus' many talents, foremost was his skill with birds.

He was a master of the snare. He constructed his traps of the very branches his prey favored to roost upon. With a pop! so delicate you could hardly hear it, his clever snares would fire, imprisoning their mark by the "boot" as Bruxieus called it, and always gently.

One evening Bruxieus summoned me in secrecy behind the cote. With great drama he lifted his cloak, revealing his latest prize, a wild ptarmigan cock, full of fight and fire. I was beside myself with excitement. We had six tame hens in the coop. A cock meant one thing—eggs! And eggs were a supreme delicacy, worth a boy's fortune at the city market.

Sure enough, within a week our little banty had become the strutting lord of the walk, and not long thereafter I cradled in my palms a clutch of precious ptarmigan eggs.

We were going to town! To market. I woke my cousin Diomache before the middle watch was over, so eager was I to get to our farm's stall and put my clutch up for sale. There was a *diaulos* flute I wanted, a double-piper that Bruxieus had promised to teach me coot and grouse calls on. The proceeds from the eggs would be my bankroll. That double-piper would be my prize.

We set out two hours before dawn, Diomache and I, with two heavy sacks of spring onions and three cheese wheels in cloth loaded on a half-lame female ass named Stumblefoot. Stumblefoot's foal we had left home tied in the barn; that way we could release mama in town when we unloaded, and she would make a beeline on her own, straight home to her baby.

This was the first time I had ever been to market without a grown-up and the first with a prize of my own to sell. I was excited, too, by being with Diomache. I was not yet ten; she was thirteen. She seemed a full-grown woman to me, and the prettiest and smartest in all that countryside. I hoped my friends would fall in with us on the road, just to see me on my own beside her.

We had just reached the Akarnanian road when we saw the sun. It was bright flaring yellow, still below the horizon against the purple sky. There was only one problem: it was rising in the north.

"That's not the sun," Diomache said, stopping abruptly and jerking hard on Stumblefoot's halter. "That's fire."

It was my father's friend Pierion's farm.

The farm was burning.

"We've got to help them," Diomache announced in a voice that brooked no protest, and, clutching my cloth of eggs in one hand, I started after her at a fast trot, hauling the bawling gimpy-foot ass. How can this happen before fall, Diomache was calling as we ran, the fields aren't tinder-dry yet, look at the flames, they shouldn't be that big.

We saw a second fire. East of Pierion's. Another farm. We pulled up, Diomache and I, in the middle of the road, and then we heard the horses.

The ground beneath our bare feet began to rumble as if from an earthquake. We saw the flare of torches. Cavalry. A full platoon. Thirty-six horses were thundering toward us. We saw armor and crested helmets. I started running toward them, waving in relief. What luck! They would help us! With thirty-six men, we'd have the fires out in—

Diomache yanked me back hard. "Those aren't our men."

They came past at a near gallop, looking huge and dark and ferocious. Their shields had been blackened, soot smeared on the blazes and stockings of their horses, their bronze greaves caked with dark mud. In the torchlight I saw the white beneath the soot on their shields. Argives. Our allies. Three riders reined in before us; Stumblefoot bawled in terror and stamped to break; Diomache held the halter fast.

"What you got there, girlie?" the burliest of the horsemen demanded, wheeling his lathered, mud-matted mount before the onion sacks and the cheeses. He was a wall of a man, like Ajax, with an open-faced Boeotian helmet and white grease under his eyes for vision in the dark. Night raiders. He leaned from his saddle and made a lunging swipe for Stumblefoot. Diomache kicked the man's mount, hard in the belly; the beast bawled and spooked.

"You're burning our farms, you traitorous bastards!"

Diomache slung Stumblefoot's halter free and slapped the fear-stricken ass with all her strength. The beast ran like hell and so did we.

I have sprinted in battle, racing under arrow and javelin fire with sixty pounds of armor on my back, and countless times in training have I been driven up steep broken faces at a dead run. Yet never have my heart and lungs labored with such desperate necessity as they did that terror-filled morning. We left the road at once, fearing more cavalry, and bolted straight across country, streaking for home. We could see other farms burning now. "We've got to run faster!" Diomache barked back at me. We had come beyond two miles, nearly three, on our trek toward town, and now had to retrace that distance and more across stony, overgrown hillsides. Brambles tore at us, rocks slashed our bare feet, our hearts seemed like they must burst within our breasts. Dashing across a field, I saw a sight that chilled my blood. Pigs. Three sows and their litters were scurrying in single file across the field toward the woods. They didn't run, it wasn't a panic, just an extremely brisk, well-disciplined fast march. I thought: those porkers will survive this day, while Diomache and I will not.

We saw more cavalry. Another platoon and another, Aetolians of Pleuron and Kalydon. This was worse; it meant the city had been betrayed not just by one ally but by a coalition. I called to Diomache to stop; my heart was about to explode from exertion. "I'll leave you, you little shit!" She hauled me forward. Suddenly from the woods burst a man. My uncle Tenagros, Diomache's father. He was in a nightshirt only, clutching a single eight-foot spear. When he saw Diomache, he dropped the weapon and ran to embrace her. They clung to each other, gasping. But this only struck more terror into me. "Where's Mother?" I could hear Diomache demanding. Tenagros' eyes were wild with grief. "Where's *my* mother?" I shouted. "Is my father with you?"

"Dead. All dead."

"How do you know? Did you see them?"

"I saw them and you don't want to."

Tenagros retrieved his spear from the dirt. He was breathless, weeping; he had soiled himself; there was liquid shit on the inside of his thighs. He had always been my favorite uncle; now I hated him with a murderous passion. "You ran!" I accused him with a boy's heartlessness. "You showed your heels, you coward!"

Tenagros turned on me with fury. "Get to the city! Get behind the walls!"

"What about Bruxieus? Is he alive?"

Tenagros slapped me so hard he bowled me right off my feet. "Stupid boy. You care more about a blind slave than your own mother and father."

Diomache hauled me up. I saw in her eyes the same rage and despair. Tenagros saw it too.

"What's that in your hands?" he barked at me.

I looked down. There were my ptarmigan eggs, still cradled in the rag in my palms.

Tenagros' callused fist smashed down on mine, shattering the fragile shells into goo at my feet.

"Get into town, you insolent brats! Get behind the walls!"

FOUR

His Majesty has presided over the sack of numberless cities and has no need to hear recounted the details of the week that followed. I will append the observation only, from the horror-benumbed apprehension of a boy shorn at one blow of mother and father, family, clan, tribe and city, that this was the first time my eyes had beheld those sights which experience teaches are common to all battles and all slaughters.

This I learned then: there is always fire.

An acrid haze hangs in the air night and day, and sulphurous smoke chokes the nostrils. The sun is the color of ash, and black stones litter the road, smoking. Everywhere one looks, some object is afire. Timber, flesh, the earth itself. Even water burns. The pitilessness of flame reinforces the sensation of the gods' anger, of fate, retribution, deeds done and hell to pay.

All is the obverse of what it had been.

Things are fallen which had stood upright. Things are free which should be bound, and bound which should be free. Things which had been hoarded in secret now blow and tumble in the open, and those who had hoarded them watch with dull eyes and let them go.

Boys have become men and men boys. Slaves now stand free and freemen slaves. Childhood has fled. The knowledge of my mother and father's slaughter struck me less with grief for them or fear for myself than with the imperative to assume at once their station. Where had I been on the morn of their murder? I had failed them, trotting off on my boyish errand. Why had I not foreseen their peril? Why was I not standing at my father's shoulder, armed and possessed of a man's strength, to defend our hearth or die honorably before it, as he and my mother had?

Bodies lay in the road. Mostly men, but women and children too, with the same dark blot of fluid sinking into the pitiless dirt. The living trod past them, grief-riven. Everyone was filthy. Many had no shoes. All were fleeing the slave columns and the roundup which would be starting soon. Women carried infants, some of them already dead, while other dazed figures glided past like shades, bearing away some pitifully useless possession, a lamp or a volume of verse. In peacetime the wives of the city walked abroad with necklaces, anklets, rings; now one saw none, or it was secreted somewhere to pay a ferryman's toll or purchase a heel of stale bread. We encountered people we knew and didn't recognize them. They didn't recognize us. Numb reunions were held along roadsides or in copses, and news was traded of the dead and the soon to be dead.

Most piteous of all were the animals. I saw a dog on fire that first morning and ran to snuff his smoking fur with my cloak. He fled, of course; I couldn't catch him, and Diomache snatched me back with a curse for my foolishness. That dog was the first of many. Horses hamstrung by sword blades, lying on their flanks with their eyes pools of numb horror. Mules with entrails spilling; oxen with javelins in their sides, lowing pitifully yet too terrified to let anyone near to help. These were the most heartbreaking: the poor dumb beasts whose torment was made more pitiful by their lack of faculty to understand it.

Feast day had come for crows and ravens. They went for the eyes first. They peck a man's asshole out, though God only knows why. People chased them off at first, rushing indignantly at the blandly feeding scavengers, who would retreat as far only as necessity dictated, then hop back to the banquet when the coast was clear. Piety demanded that we bury our fallen countrymen, but fear of enemy cavalry pushed us on. Sometimes bodies would be dragged into a ditch and a few pitiful handfuls of dirt cast over them, accompanied by a miserable prayer. The crows got so fat they could barely fly a foot off the ground.

We did not go into the city, Diomache and I.

We had been betrayed from within, she instructed me, speaking slowly as one would to a simpleton, to make sure I understood. Sold out by our own citizens, some faction seeking power, then they themselves had been double-crossed by the Argives. Astakos was a port, a poor one, but a western harbor nonetheless, which Argos had long coveted. Now she had it.

We found Bruxieus on the morn of the second day. His slave brand had saved him. That, and his blindness, which the conquerors mocked even as he cursed and swung at them with his staff. "You're free, old man!" Free to starve or beg from his belly's necessity for the victor's yoke.

The rain came that evening. This, too, seems a constant coda to slaughter. What had been ash was now gray mud, and the stripped bodies which had not been reclaimed by sons and mothers now glistened a ghastly white, cleansed by the gods in their remorseless way.

Our city no longer existed. Not alone the physical site, the citizens, the walls and farms. But the very spirit of our nation, the *polis* itself, that ideal of mind called Astakos that, yes, had been smaller than a *deme* of Athens or Corinth or Thebes, that, yes, had been poorer than Megara or Epidauros or Olympia, but that existed as a city nonetheless. Our city, my city. Now it was effaced utterly. We who called ourselves Astakiots were effaced with it. Without a city, who were we? What were we?

A dislocation of the faculties seemed to unman all. No one could think. A numb shock possessed our hearts. Life had become like a play, a tragedy one had seen enacted on the stage—the fall of Ilium, the sack of Thebes. Only now it was real, performed by actors of flesh and blood, and those actors were ourselves.

East of the Field of Ares, where the fallen in battle were buried, we came upon a man digging a grave for an infant. The baby, wrapped in the man's cloak, lay like a grocer's bundle at the edge of the pit. He asked me to hand it down to him. He was afraid the wolves would get it, he said, that's why he had dug the hole so deep. He didn't know the child's name. A woman had handed it to him during the flight from the city. He had carried the babe for two days; on the third morning it died. Bruxieus wouldn't let me hand the little body down; it was bad luck, he said, for a living young spirit to handle a dead one. He did it himself. We recognized the man now. He was a *mathematikos*, a tutor of arithmetic and geometry, from the city. His wife and daughter emerged from the woods; we realized they had been hiding till they knew we brought no harm. They had all lost their minds. Bruxieus had instructed Diomache and me in the signs. Madness was contagious, we must not linger.

"We needed Spartans," the teacher declared, speaking softly behind his sad watery eyes. "Just fifty would have saved the city."

Bruxieus was nudging us to go.

"See how numb we are?" the man continued. "We glide about in a daze, disconnected from our reason. You'll never see Spartans in such a state. This"—he gestured to the blackened landscape—"is their element. They move through these horrors with clear eyes and unshaken limbs. And they hate the Argives. They are their bitterest enemies."

Bruxieus pulled us away.

"Fifty of them!" the man still shouted, while his wife struggled to tug him back to the safety of the trees. "Five! One would have saved us!"

We recovered Diomache's mother's body, and my mother's and father's, on the eve of the third day. A squad of Argive infantry had set up camp around the gutted ruins of our farmhouse. Already surveyors and claims markers had arrived from the conquering cities. We watched, hidden, from the woods as the officials marked off the parcels with their measuring rods and scrawled upon the white wall of my mother's kitchen garden and sign of the clan of Argos whose lands ours would now become.

An Argive taking a piss spotted us. We took to flight but he called after us. Something in his voice convinced us that he and the others intended no harm. They had had enough of blood for now. They waved us in, gave us the bodies. I sponged the mud and blood off my mother's corpse, using the singlet she had made for me, for my promised passage to Ithaka. Her flesh was like cold wax. I did not weep, neither shrouding her form in the burial robe she had woven with her own hands and which in its cupboard chest remained miraculously unstolen, nor interring her bones and my father's beneath the stone that bore our ancestors' blazon and signia.

It was my place to know the rites, but I had not been taught them, awaiting my initiation to the tribe when I turned twelve. Diomache lit the flame, and the Argives sang the *paean*, the only sacred song any of them knew.

Zeus Savior, spare us
Who march into your fire

Grant us courage to stand
Shield-to-shield with our brothers

Beneath your mighty aegis
We advance

Lord of the Thunder
Our Hope and our Protector

When the hymn was over, the men raped her.

I didn't understand at first what they intended. I thought she had violated some portion of the rite and they were going to beat her for it. A soldier snatched me by the scalp, one hairy forearm around my neck to snap it. Bruxieus found a spear at his throat and the point of a sword pricking the flesh of his back. No one said a word. There were six of them, armorless, in sweat-dark corselets with their rank dirty beards and the rain-sodden hair on their chests and calves coarse and matted and filthy. They had been watching Diomache, her smooth girl's legs and the start of breasts beneath her tunic.

"Don't harm them," Diomache said simply, meaning Bruxieus and me.

Two men took her away behind the garden wall. They finished, then two more followed, and the last pair after that. When it was over, the sword was lowered from Bruxieus' back, and he crossed to carry Diomache away in his arms. She wouldn't let him. She stood to her feet on her own, though she had to brace herself against the wall to do it, both her thighs dark with blood. The Argives gave us a quarter-skin of wine and we took it.

It was clear now that Diomache could not walk. Bruxieus took her up in his arms. Another of the Argives pressed a hard bread into my hands. "Two more regiments will be coming from the south tomorrow. Get into the mountains and go north, don't come down till you're out of Akarnania." He spoke kindly, as if to his own son. "If you find a town, don't bring the girl in or this will happen again."

I turned and spat on his dark stinking tunic, a gesture of powerlessness and despair. He caught my arm as I turned away. "And get rid of that old man. He's worthless. He'll only wind up getting you and the girl killed."

FIVE

They say that ghosts sometimes, those that cannot let go their bond to the living, linger and haunt the scenes of their days under the sun, hovering like substanceless birds of carrion, refusing Hades' command to retire beneath the earth. That is how we lived, Bruxieus, Diomache and I, in the weeks following the sack of our city. For a month and more, for most of that summer we could not quit our vacated *polis*. We roamed the wild country above the *agrotera*, the marginal wastes surrounding the cropland, sleeping in the day when it was warm, moving at night like the shades we were. From the ridgelines we watched the Argives move in below, repopulating our groves and farmsteads with the excess of their citizenry.

Diomache was not the same. She would wander away by herself, into the dark glades, and do unspeakable things to her womanly parts. She was trying to dispatch the child that might be growing inside her. "She thinks she has given offense to the god Hymen," Bruxieus explained to me when I broke in upon her one day and she chased me with curses and a hail of stones. "She fears that she may never be a man's wife now but only a slave or a whore. I have tried to tell her this is foolishness, but she will not hear it, coming from a man."

There were many others like us in the hills then. We would run into them at the springs and try to resume the fellow-feeling we had shared as Astakiots. But the extinction of our *polis* had severed those happy bonds forever. It was every man for himself now; every clan, every kin group.

Some boys I knew had formed a gang. There were eleven of them, none more than two years older than I, and they were holy terrors. They carried arms and boasted that they had killed grown men. They beat me up one day when I refused to join them. I wanted to, but couldn't leave Diomache. They would have taken her in too, but I knew she would never go near them.

"This is our country," their boy-lord warned me, a beast of twelve who called himself Sphaireus, "Ball Player," because he had stuffed in hide the skull of an Argive he had slain, and now kicked about with him the way a monarch bears a *skeptron*. He meant his gang's country, the high ground above the city, beyond the reach of Argive armor. "If we catch you trespassing here again, you or your cousin or that slave, we'll cut out your liver and feed it to the dogs."

At last in fall we put our city behind us. In September when Boreas, the North Wind, begins to blow. Without Bruxieus and his knowledge of roots and snares, we would have starved.

Before, on my father's farm, we had caught wild birds for our cote, or to make breeding pairs, or just to hold for an hour before returning them to freedom. Now we ate them. Bruxieus made us devour everything but the feathers. We crunched the little hollow bones; we ate the eyes, and the legs right down to the boot, discarding only the beak and the unchewable feet. We gulped eggs raw. We choked down worms and slugs. We wolfed grubs and beetles and fought over the last lizards and snakes before the cold drove them underground for good. We gnawed so much fennel that to this day I gag at a whiff of that anisey smell, even a pinch flavoring a stew. Diomache grew thin as a reed.

"Why won't you talk to me anymore?" I asked her one night as we tramped across some stony hillside. "Can't I put my head in your lap like we used to?"

She began to cry and would not answer me. I had made myself an infantryman's spear, stout ash and fire-hardened, no longer a boy's toy but a weapon meant to kill. Visions of revenge fed my heart. I would live among the Spartans. I would slay Argives one day. I practiced the way I had seen our warriors do, advancing as if on line, an imaginary shield before me at high port, my spear gripped strong above the right shoulder, poised for the overhand strike. I looked up one dusk and there stood my cousin, observing me coldly. "You will be like them," she said, "when you grow."

She meant the soldiers who had shamed her.

"I will not!"

"You will be a man. You won't be able to help yourself."

One night when we had tramped for hours, Bruxieus inquired of Diomache why she had held herself so silent. He was concerned for the dark thoughts that might be poisoning her mind. She refused to speak at first. Then, at last relenting, told us in a sweet sad voice of her wedding. She had been planning it in her head all night. What dress she would wear, what style of garland, which goddess she would dedicate her sacrifice to. She had been thinking for hours, she told us, of her slippers. She had all the strapping and beadwork worked out in her mind. They would be so beautiful, her bridal slippers! Then her eyes clouded and she looked away. "This shows what a fool I have become. No one will marry me."

"I will," I proffered at once.

She laughed. "You? A fair chance of that!"

Foolish as it sounds to recount, to my boy's heart these careless words stung like no others in my life. I vowed that I would marry Diomache one day. I would be man enough and warrior enough to protect her.

For a time in autumn we tried surviving on the seacoast, sleeping in caves and combing the sloughs and marshes. You could eat there at least. There were shellfish and crabs, mussels and spinebacks to be prised from rocks; we learned how to take gulls on the wing with stakes and nets. But the exposure was brutal as winter came on. Bruxieus began to suffer. He would never let his weakness show to Diomache and me when he thought we were looking, but I would watch his face sometimes when he slept. He looked seventy. The elements were hard on him in his years; all the old wounds ached, but more than that he was donating his substance to preserve ours, Diomache's and mine. Sometimes I would catch him looking at me, studying a tilt to my face or the tone of something I had said. He was making sure I hadn't gone crazy or feral.

As the cold came on, it became more difficult to find food. We must beg. Bruxieus would pick out an isolated farmstead and approach the gate alone; the hounds would converge in a clamorous pack and the men of the farm would emerge, on guard, from the fields or from some rude falling-down outbuilding; brothers and a father, their callused hands resting on the tools which would become weapons if the need arose. The hills were infested with outlaws then; the farmers never knew who would walk up to their gate and with what duplicitous intent. Bruxieus would doff his cap and wait for the woman of the house, making sure she took note of his milky eyes and beaten posture. He would indicate Diomache and me, shivering miserably in the road, and ask the mistress not for food, which would have made us beggars in the landsmen's eyes and prompted them loosing the dogs on us, but for any broken item of use that she could spare—a rake, a thrashing staff, a worn-out cloak, something we could repair and sell in the next town. He made sure to ask directions and appear eager to be moving on. That way they knew any kindness would not make us linger. Almost always the farm wives volunteered a meal, sometimes inviting us in to hear what news we bore from foreign places and to tell us their own.

It was during one of those forlorn feedings that I first heard the word "Sepeia." This is a place of Argos, a wooded area near Tiryns, where a battle had just been fought between the Argives and the Spartans. The boy who bore this tale was a farmer's visiting nephew, a mute, who communicated through signs and whom even his own family could barely comprehend. The Spartans under King Kleomenes, the boy gave us to understand, had achieved a spectacular victory. Two thousand Argives dead was one figure he had heard, though others had it at four thousand and even six. My heart exploded with joy. How I wished I could have been there! To have been a man grown, advancing in that battle line, mowing down in fair fight the men of Argos, as they had cut down by perfidy my own mother and father.

The Spartans became for me the equivalent of avenging gods. I couldn't learn enough about these warriors who had so devastatingly defeated the murderers of my mother and father, the violators of my innocent cousin. No stranger we met escaped my boyish grilling. Tell me about Sparta. Her double kings. The three hundred Knights who protected them. The *agoge* which trained the city's youth. The *syssitia*, the warriors' messes. We heard a tale of Kleomenes. Someone had asked the king why he did not raze Argos once and for all when his army had stood at the gates and the city lay prostate before him. "We need the Argives," Kleomenes responded. "Who else will our young men train on?"

In the winter hills we were starving. Bruxieus was getting weaker. I took to stealing. Diomache and I would raid a shepherd's fold at night, fighting off the dogs with sticks and snatching a kid if we could. Most of the shepherds carried bows; arrows would whiz past us in the dark. We stopped to grab them and soon had quite a cache. Bruxieus hated to see us turning into thieves. We got a bow one time, snagging it right out from under a sleeping goatherd's nose. It was a man's weapon, a Thessalian cavalry bow, so stout that neither Diomache nor I could draw it. Then came the event which changed my life and set it on the course that reached its terminus at the Hot Gates.

I got caught stealing a goose. She was a fat prize, her wings pegged for market, and I got careless going over a wall. The dogs got me. The men of the farm dragged me into the mud of the livestock pen and nailed me to a hide board the size of a door, driving tanning spikes through both my palms. I was on my back, screaming in agony, while the farm men lashed my kicking, flailing legs to the board, vowing that after lunch they would castrate me like a sheep and hang my testicles upon the gate as a warning to other thieves. Diomache and Bruxieus crouched, hidden, up the hillside; they could hear everything . . .

Here the captive drew up in his narration. Fatigue and the ordeal of his wounds had taken severe toll of the man, or perhaps, his listeners imagined, it was memory of the instance he was recounting. His Majesty, through the captain Orontes, inquired of the prisoner if he required attention. The man declined. The hesitation in the tale, he declared, arose not from any incapacity of its narrator, but at the prompting of the god by whose inner direction the order of events was being dictated, and who now commanded a momentary alteration of tack. The man Xeones resettled himself and, granted permission to wet his throat with wine, resumed.

. . .

Two summers subsequent to this incident, in Lakedaemon, I witnessed a different kind of ordeal: a Spartan boy beaten to death by his drill instructors.

The lad's name was Teriander, he was fourteen; they called him Tripod because no one of his age-class could take him down in wrestling. Over the succeeding years I looked on in attendance as two dozen other boys succumbed beneath this same trial, each like Tripod disdaining so much as a whimper in pain, but he, this lad, was the first.

The whippings are a ritual of the boys' training in Lakedaemon, not in punishment for stealing food (at which exploit the boys are encouraged to excel, to develop resourcefulness in war), but for the crime of getting caught. The beatings take place alongside the Temple of Artemis Orthia in a narrow alley called the Runway. The site is beneath plane trees, a shaded and quite pleasant space in less grisly circumstances.

Tripod was the eleventh boy whipped that day. The two *eirenes*, drill instructors, who administered the beatings, had already been replaced by a fresh pair, twenty-year-olds just out of the *agoge* and as powerfully built as any youths in the city. It worked like this: the boy whose turn it was grasped a horizontal iron bar secured to the bases of two trees (the bar had been worn smooth by decades, some said centuries, of the ritual) and was flogged with birch rods, as big around as a man's thumb, by the *eirenes* taking turns. A priestess of Artemis stood at the boy's shoulder, presenting an ancient wooden image which must, tradition dictated, receive the spray of human blood.

Two of the boy's mates from his training platoon kneel at each shoulder to catch the lad when he falls. At any time the boy may terminate the ordeal by releasing the bar and pitching forward to the dirt. Theoretically a boy would only do this when thrashed to unconsciousness, but many pitched simply when they could no longer bear the pain. Between a hundred and two hundred looked on this day: boys of other platoons, fathers, brothers and mentors and even some of the boys' mothers, keeping discreetly to the rear.

Tripod kept taking it and taking it. The flesh of his back had been torn through in a dozen places; you could see tissue and fascia, rib-cage and muscle and even the spine. He would not go down. "Pitch!" his two comrades kept urging between blows, meaning let go of the bar and fall. Tripod refused. Even the drill instructors began hissing this between their teeth. One look in the boy's face and you could see he had passed beyond reason. He had made up his mind to die rather than raise the hand for quarter. The *eirenes* did as they were instructed in such cases: they prepared to wallop Tripod so hard in four rapid successive blows that the impact would knock him unconscious and thus preserve his life. I will never forget the sound those four blows made upon the boy's back. Tripod dropped; the drill instructors immediately declared the ordeal terminated and summoned the next boy.

Tripod managed to lift himself upon all fours. Blood was sheeting from his mouth, nose and ears. He could not see or speak. He managed somehow to turn about and almost stand, then he sank slowly to his seat, held there a moment and then dropped, hard, into the dirt. It was clear at once that he would never rise.

Later that evening when it was over (the ritual was not suspended on account of Tripod's death but continued for another three hours), Dienekes, who had been present, walked apart with his protege, the boy Alexandros whom I mentioned earlier. I served Alexandros at this time. He was twelve but looked no older than ten; already he was a wonderful runner, but extremely slight and of a sensitive disposition. Moreover he had shared a bond of affection with Tripod; the older boy had been a sort of guardian or protector; Alexandros was devastated by his death.

Dienekes walked with Alexandros, alone except for his own squire and myself, to a spot beneath the temple of Athena Protectress of the City, immediately below the slope from the statue of Phobos, the god of fear. At that time Dienekes' age was, I would estimate, thirty-five years. He had already won two prizes of valor, at Erythrae against the Thebans and at Achillieon against the Corinthians and their Arkadian allies. As nearly as I can recall, this is how the older man instructed his protege:

First, in a gentle and loving tone, he recalled his own first sight, when he was a lad in years younger even than Alexandros, of a boy comrade whipped to death. He recounted several of his own ordeals in the Runway, beneath the rod.

Then he began the sequence of query and response which comprises the Lakedaemonian syllabus of instruction.

"Answer this, Alexandros. When our countrymen triumph in battle, what is it that defeats the foe?"

The boy responded in the terse Spartan style, "Our steel and our skill."

"These, yes," Dienekes corrected him gently, "but something more. It is that." His gesture led up the slope to the image of Phobos.

Fear.

Their own fear defeats our enemies.

"Now answer. What is the source of fear?"

When Alexandros' reply faltered, Dienekes reached with his hand and touched his own chest and shoulder.

"Fear arises from this: the flesh. This," he declared, "is the factory of fear."

Alexandros listened with the grim concentration of a boy who knows his whole life will be war; that the laws of Lykurgus forbid him and every other Spartan to know or pursue a trade other than war; that his term of obligation extends from age twenty to age sixty, and that no force under heaven will excuse him from soon, very soon, assuming his place in line of battle and clashing shield-to-shield, helmet-to-helmet with the enemy.

"Now answer again, Alexandros. Did you observe today in the manner of the *eirenes* delivering the beating any sign or indication of malice?"

The boy answered no.

"Would you characterize their demeanor as barbarous? Did they take pleasure in dealing agony to Tripod?"

No.

"Was their intention to crush his will or break his spirit?"

No.

"What was their intention?"

"To harden his mind against pain."

Throughout this conversation the older man maintained a voice tender and solicitous with love. Nothing Alexandros could do would ever make this voice love him less or abandon him. Such is the peculiar genius of the Spartan system of pairing each boy in training with a mentor other than his own father. A mentor may say things that a father cannot; a boy can confess to his mentor that which would bring shame to reveal to his father.

"It was bad today, wasn't it, my young friend?"

Dienekes then asked the boy how he imagined battle, real battle, compared with what he had witnessed today.

No answer was required or expected.

"Never forget, Alexandros, that this flesh, this body, does not belong to us. Thank God it doesn't. If I thought this stuff was mine, I could not advance a pace into the face of the enemy. But it is not ours, my friend. It belongs to the gods and to our children, our fathers and mothers and those of Lakedaemon a hundred, a thousand years yet unborn. It belongs to the city which gives us all we have and demands no less in requital."

Man and boy moved on, down the slope to the river. They followed the path to that grove of double-boled myrtle called the Twins, sacred to the sons of Tyndareus and to the family to which Alexandros belonged. It would be to this spot, on the night of his final ordeal and initiation, that he would repair, alone save his mother and sisters, to receive the salve and sanction of the gods of his line.

Dienekes sat upon the earth beneath the Twins. He gestured to Alexandros to take the place beside him.

"Personally I think your friend Tripod was foolish. What he displayed today contained more of recklessness than true courage, *andreia*. He cost the city his life, which could have been spent more fruitfully in battle."

Nonetheless it was clear Dienekes respected him.

"But to his credit he showed us something of nobility today. He showed you and every boy watching what it is to pass beyond identification with the body, beyond pain, beyond fear of death. You were horrified to behold his *agonisma*, but it was awe that struck you truly, wasn't it? Awe of that boy or whatever *daimon* animated him. Your friend Tripod showed us contempt for this." Again Dienekes indicated the flesh. "A contempt which approached the stature of the sublime."

From my spot, above on the bank, I could see the boy's shoulders shudder as the grief and terror of the day at last purged themselves from his heart. Dienekes embraced and comforted him. When at last the boy had recomposed himself, his mentor gently released him.

"Have your instructors taught you why the Spartans excuse without penalty the warrior who loses his helmet or breastplate in battle, but punish with loss of all citizenship rights the man who discards his shield?"

They had, Alexandros replied.

"Because a warrior carries helmet and breastplate for his own protection, but his shield for the safety of the whole line."

Dienekes smiled and placed a hand upon his protege's shoulder.

"Remember this, my young friend. There is a force beyond fear. More powerful than self-preservation. You glimpsed it today, in a crude and unself-aware form, yes. But it was there and it was genuine. Let us remember your friend Tripod and honor him for this."

I was screaming upon the hide board. I could hear my cries bounce off the walls of the livestock enclosure and shriek off, multiplied, up the hillsides. I knew it was disgraceful but I could not stop.

I begged the farm men to release me, to end my agony. I would do anything, and I described it all at the top of my lungs. I cried out to the gods in a shameful little boy's voice piping up the mountainside. I knew Bruxieus could hear me. Would his love for me impel him to dash in and be nailed alongside me? I didn't care. I wanted the pain to end. I begged the men to kill me. I could feel the bones in both hands shattered by the spikes. I would never hold a spear or even a gardening spade. I would be a cripple, a clubfist. My life was over and in the meanest, most dishonorable way.

A fist shattered my cheek. "Shut your pipehole, you sniveling little shitworm!" The men set the tanning board upright, angled against a wall, and there I squirmed, impaled, for the sun's endless crawl across the sky. Urchins from the up-valley farms clustered to watch me scream. The girls tore my rags and poked at my privates; the boys pissed on me. Dogs snuffed my bare soles, emboldening themselves to make a meal of me. I only stopped wailing when my throat could cry no longer. I was trying to tear my palms free right through the spikes, but the men lashed my wrists tighter so I couldn't move. "How does that feel, you fucking thief? Let's see you pick off another prize, you night-creeping little rat."

When at last their own growling bellies drove my tormentors indoors for supper, Diomache slipped down from the hill and cut me free. The spikes would not come out of my palms; she had to blade the wood off the frame with her dagger. My hands came away with the tanning nails still through them. Bruxieus carried me off, as he had borne Diomache earlier, after her violation.

"Oh God," my cousin said when she saw my hands.

SIX

That winter, Bruxieus said, was the coldest he could remember. Sheep froze in the high pastures. Twenty-foot drifts sealed the passes. Deer were driven so desperate with hunger that they straggled down, skeleton-thin and blind from starvation, all the way to the shepherds' winter folds, where they presented themselves for slaughter, point-blank before the herdsmen's bows.

We stayed in the mountains, so high up that martens' and foxes' fur grew white as the snow. We slept in dugouts that shepherds had abandoned or in ice caves we chopped out with stone axes, lining their floors with pine boughs and huddling together beneath our triple cloaks in a pile like puppies. I begged Bruxieus and Diomache to abandon me, let me die in peace in the cold. They insisted that I allow them to carry me down to a town, to a physician. I refused absolutely. Never again would I place myself before a stranger, any stranger, without a weapon in my hand. Did Bruxieus imagine that doctors possessed a more exalted sense of honor than other men? What payment would some hill-town quack demand? What profitable turn would he discover in a slave and a crippled boy? What use would he make of a starving thirteen-year-old girl?

I had another reason for refusing to go to a town. I hated myself for the shameless way I had cried out, and could not make myself stop, during the hours I was put to the trial. I had seen my own heart and it was the heart of a coward. I despised myself with a blistering, pitiless scorn. The tales I had cherished of the Spartans only made me loathe myself more. None of them would beg for his life as I had, absent every scrap of dignity. The dishonor of my parents' murder continued to torment me. Where was I in their hour of desperation? I was not there when they needed me. In my mind I imagined their slaughter again and again, and always myself absent. I wanted to die. The only thought that lent me solace was the certainty that I would die, soon, and thereby exit this hell of my own dishonored existence.

Bruxieus intuited these thoughts and tried in his gentle way to disarm them. I was only a child, he told me. What prodigies of valor could be expected from a lad of ten? "Boys are men at ten in Sparta," I declared.

This was the first and only time I saw Bruxieus truly, physically angry. He seized me by both shoulders and shook me violently, commanding me to face him. "Listen to me, boy. Only gods and heroes can be brave in isolation. A man may call upon courage only one way, in the ranks with his brothers-in-arms, the line of his tribe and his city. Most piteous of all states under heaven is that of a man alone, bereft of the gods of his home and his *polis*. A man without a city is not a man. He is a shadow, a shell, a joke and a mockery. That is what you have become now, my poor Xeo. No one may expect valor from one cast out alone, cut off from the gods of his home."

He drew up then; his eyes broke away in sorrow. I saw the slave brand upon his brow. I understood. Such was the state he had endured, all these years, in the house of my father. "But you have acted the man, little old uncle," I said, employing the fondest Astakiot term of affection. "How have you done it?"

He looked at me with sad, gentle eyes. "The love I might have given my own children, I gave to you, little nephew. That was my answer to the unknowable ways of God. But it seems the Argives are dearer to Him than I. He has let them rob me of my life not once, but twice."

These words, intended to bring comfort, only reinforced further my resolve to die. My hands had swollen now to twice their normal size. Pus and poison oozed from them, then froze in a hideous icy mass that I had to chip away each morning to reveal the mangled flesh beneath. Bruxieus did everything he could with salves and poultices, but it was no use. Both central metacarpals had been shattered in my right hand. I could not close the fingers nor form a fist. I would never hold a spear nor grip a sword. Diomache sought to comfort me by equating my ruin to hers. I scorned her bitterly. "You can still be a woman. What can I do? How can I ever take my place in the line of battle?"

At night, bouts of fever alternated with fits of teeth-rattling ague. I curled contorted in Diomache's arms, with Bruxieus' bulk enwrapping us both for warmth. I called out again and again to the gods but received no whisper in reply. They had abandoned us, it was clear, now that we no longer possessed ourselves or were possessed by our *polis*.

One fever-racked night, perhaps ten days after the incident at the farmstead, Diomache and Bruxieus wrapped me in skins and set off foraging. It had begun to snow and they hoped to use the silence, perhaps with luck to take unawares a hare or a gone-to-ground covey of grouse.

This was my chance. I resolved to take it. I waited till Bruxieus and Diomache had moved off beyond sight and sound. Leaving cloak and furs and foot wraps behind for them, I set out barefoot into the storm.

I climbed for what seemed like hours but was probably no more than five minutes. The fever had me in its grip. I was blind like the deer, yet guided by an infallible sense of direction. I found a place amid a stand of pines and knew this was my spot. A profound sense of decorum possessed me. I wanted to do this properly and, above all, to be no trouble to Bruxieus and Diomache.

I picked out a tree and settled my back against it so that its spirit, which touched both earth and sky, would conduct mine safely out of this world. Yes, this was the tree. I could feel Sleep, brother of Death, advancing up from the toes. Feeling ebbed from my loins and midsection. When the numbness reaches the heart, I imagined, I will pass over. Then a terrifying thought struck me.

What if this is the wrong tree? Perhaps I should be leaning against that one. Or that other, over there. A panic of indecision seized me. I was in the wrong spot! I had to get up but could no longer command my limbs to move. I groaned. I was failing even in my own death. Just as my panic and despair reached their apex, I was startled to discover a man standing directly above me in the grove!

My first thought was that he could help me move. He could

advise me. Help me decide. Together we would pick out the correct tree and he would place my back against it. From some part of my mind the numb thought arose: what is a man doing up here at this hour, in this storm?

I blinked and tried with all my failing power to focus. No, this was not a dream. Whoever this was, he was really here. The thought came foggily that he must be a god. It occurred to me that I was acting impiously toward him. I was giving offense. Surely propriety demanded that I respond with terror or awe, or prostrate myself before him. Yet something in his posture, which was not grave but oddly whimsical, seemed to say, Don't give yourself the bother. I accepted this. It seemed to please him. I knew he was going to speak, and that whatever words came forth would be of paramount importance for me, in this my earthly life or the life I was about to pass into. I must listen with all my faculties and forget nothing.

His eyes met mine with a gentle, amused kindness.

"I have always found the spear to be," he spoke with a quiet majesty that could be nothing other than the voice of a god, "a rather inelegant weapon."

What a queer thing to say, I thought.

And why "inelegant"? I had the sense that the word was absolutely deliberate, the one precise term the god sought. It seemed to carry significance for him in level upon level, though I myself had no idea what this meaning could be. Then I saw the silver bow slung over his shoulder.

The Archer.

Apollo Far Striker.

In a flash that was neither thunderbolt nor revelation but the plainest, least adorned apprehension in the world, I understood all that his words and presence implied. I knew what he meant, and what I must do.

My right hand. Its severed sinews would never produce the warrior's grasp upon the shank of a spear. But its forefingers could catch and draw the twined gut of a bowstring. My left, though ever denied power to close upon the gripcord of a *hoplon* shield, could yet hold stable the handpiece of a bow and extend it to full stretch.

The bow.

The bow would preserve me.

The Archer's eyes probed mine, gently, for one final instant. Had I understood? His glance seemed to inquire not so much "Will you now serve me?" as to confirm the fact, unknown to me heretofore, that I had been in his service all my life.

I felt warmth returning to my midsection and the blood surging like a tide into my legs and feet. I heard my name being called from below and knew it was my cousin, she and Bruxieus in alarm, scouring the hillside for me.

Diomache reached me, scrabbling over the snowy crest and lurching into the grove of pines. "What are you doing up here all alone?" I could feel her slapping my cheeks, hard, as if to bring me around from a vision or transport; she was crying, clutching and hugging me, tearing off her cloak to wrap about me. She called back to Bruxieus, who in his blindness was clambering as fast as he could up the slope below.

"I'm all right," I heard my voice assuring her. She slapped me again and then, weeping, cursed me for being such a fool and scaring them so to death. "It's all right, Dio," I heard my voice repeating. "I'm all right."

SEVEN

I beg His Majesty's patience with this recounting of the events following the sack of a city of which he has never heard, an obscure *polis* without fame, spawner of no hero of legend, without link to the greater events of the present war and of the battle which His Majesty's forces fought with the Spartans and their allies at the pass of Thermopylae.

My intent is simply to convey, through the experiences of two children and a slave, some poor measure of the soul terror and devastation which a vanquished population, any population, is forced to endure in the hour of its nation's extinction. For though His Majesty has commanded the sack of empires, yet, if one may speak plainly, he has witnessed the sufferings of their peoples only at a remove, from atop a purple throne or mounted on a caparisoned stallion, protected by the gold-pommeled spears of his royal guard.

Over the following decade more than six score battles, campaigns and wars were fought between and among the cities of Greece. At least forty *poleis*, including such inpregnably founded citadels as Knidos, Arethusa, Kolonaia, Amphissa and Metropolis, were sacked in whole or in part. Numberless farms were torched, temples burned, warships sunk, men-at-arms slaughtered, wives and daughters carried off into slavery. No Hellene, however mighty his city, could state with certainty that even one season hence he would still find himself above the earth, with his head still upon his shoulders and his wife and children slumbering in safety by his side. This state of affairs was unexceptional, neither better nor worse than any era in a thousand years, back to Achilles and Hektor, Theseus and Herakles, to the birth of the gods themselves. Business as usual, as the *emporoi*, the merchants, say.

Each man of Greece knew what defeat in war meant and knew

that sooner or later that bitter broth would complete its circuit of the table and settle at last before his own place.

Suddenly, with the rise of His Majesty in Asia, it seemed that hour would be sooner.

Terror of the sack spread throughout all Greece as word began coming, from the lips of too many to be disbelieved, of the scale of His Majesty's mobilization in the East and his intent to put all Hellas to the torch.

So all-pervasive was this dread that it had even been given a name.

Phobos.

The Fear.

Fear of you, Your Majesty. Terror of the wrath of Xerxes son of Darius, Great King of the Eastern Empire, Lord of all men from the rising to the setting sun, and the myriads all Greece knew were on the march beneath his banner to enslave us.

Ten years had passed since the sack of my own city, yet the terror of that season lived on, indelible, within me. I was nineteen now. Events which will in their course be related had parted me from my cousin and from Bruxieus and carried me, as was my wish, to Lakedaemon and there, after a time, into the service of my master, Dienekes of Sparta. In this capacity I was dispatched (myself and a trio of other squires) in attendance upon him and three other Spartiate envoys—Olympieus, Polynikes and Aristodemos—to the island of Rhodes, a possession of His Majesty's empire. It was there that these warriors, and I myself, glimpsed for the first time a fraction of the armored might of Persia.

The ships came first. I had been given the afternoon free and, making use of the time to learn what I could of the island, had attached myself to a company of Rhodian slingers in their practice. I watched as these ebullient fellows hurled with astonishing velocity their lead sling bullets thrice the size of a man's thumb. They could drill these murderous projectiles through half-inch pine planks at a hundred paces and strike a target the size of a man's chest three times out of four. One among them, a youth my own age, was showing me how the slingers carved with their dagger points into the soft lead of their bullets whimsical greetings—"Eat this" or "Love and kisses"—when another of the platoon looked up and pointed out to the horizon, toward Egypt. We saw sails, perhaps a squadron, at least an hour out. The slingers forgot them and continued their drill. What seemed like moments later, the same fellow sang out again, this time with startlement and awe. All drew up and stared. Here came the squadron, triple-bankers with their sails brailed up for speed, already turning the cape and bearing fast upon the breakwater. None had ever seen vessels of such size moving so fast. They must be skimmers, someone said. Racing shells. No full-size ship, and certainly no man-of-war, could slice the water at speeds like that.

But they were warships. Tyrian triremes so tight to the surface that the swells seemed to crest no more than a handbreadth beneath their thalamites' benches. They were racing each other for sport beneath His Majesty's banner. Training for Greece. For war. For the day their bronze-sheathed rams would send the navies of Hellas to the bottom.

That evening Dienekes and the other envoys made their way on foot to the harbor at Lindos. The warships were drawn up upon the strand, within a perimeter manned by Egyptian marines. These recognized the Spartans by their scarlet cloaks and long hair. A wry scene ensued. The captain of the marines motioned the Spartiates forward, calling them forth with a smile from the throng who had assembled to gawk at the vessels and taking them through a full inspecting admiral's tour. The men speculated, through an interpreter, about how soon they would be at war with each other, and whether fate would bring them again face-to-face across the line of slaughter.

The Egyptian marines were the tallest men I had ever seen and burned nearly black by the sun of their desert land. They were under arms, in doeskin boots, with bronze fish-scale cuirasses and ostrich-plume helmets detailed with gold. Their weapons were the pike and scimitar. They were in high spirits, these marines, comparing the muscles of their buttocks and thighs with those of the Spartans, while each laughed in his tongue unintelligible to the other.

"Pleased to meet you, you hyena-jawed bastards." Dienekes grinned at the captain, speaking in Doric and clapping the fellow warmly upon the shoulder. "I'm looking forward to carving your balls and sending them home in a basket." The Egyptian laughed uncomprehending and replied, beaming, with some foreign-tongued insult no doubt equally menacing and obscene.

Dienekes asked the captain's name, which the man replied was Ptammitechus. The Spartan tongue was defeated by this and settled upon "Tommie," which seemed to please the officer just as well. He was asked how many more warships like these the Great King numbered in his navy. "Sixty" came the translated response.

"Sixty ships?" asked Aristodemos.

The Egyptian loosed a brilliant smile. "Sixty squadrons."

The marines conducted the Spartans upon a more detailed examination of the warships, which, hauled up on the sand, had been canted onto careening beams, exposing the undersides of their hulls for cleaning and sealing, which chores the Tyrian seamen were now enthusiastically performing. I smelled wax. The sailors were greasing the boats' bellies for speed. The vessels' planks were butted end-to-end with mortise-and-tenon joinery of such precision that it seemed the work not of shipwrights, but of master cabinetmakers. The conjoining plates between the ram and the hull were glazed with speed-enhancing ceramic and waxed with some kind of naphtha-based oil which the mariners applied molten, with paddles. Alongside these speedsters, the Spartan state galley *Orthia* looked like a garbage scow. But the items which commanded the most animated attention bore no bearing to concerns of the sea.

These were the mail loincloths worn by the marines to protect their private parts.

"What are these, diapers?" Dienekes inquired, laughing and tugging at the hem of the captain's corselet.

"Be careful, my friend," the marine responded with a mock-theatric gesture, "I have heard about you Greeks!"

The Egyptian inquired of the Spartans why they wore their hair so long. Olympieus replied, quoting the lawmaker Lykurgus, "Because no other adornment makes a handsome man more comely or an ugly one more terrifying. And it's free."

The marine next began teasing the Spartans about their notoriously short *xiphos* swords. He refused to believe that these were the actual weapons the Lakedaemonians carried into battle. They must be toys. How could such diminutive apple-corers possibly work harm to an enemy?

"The trick is"—Dienekes demonstrated, pressing himself chest-to-chest to the Egyptian Tommie—"to get nice and cozy."

When they parted, the Spartans presented the marines with two skins of Phalerian wine, the finest they had, a gift intended for the Rhodian consulate. The marines gave each Spartan a gold daric (a month's pay for a Greek oarsman) and a sack apiece of fresh Nile pomegranates.

The mission returned to Sparta unsuccessful. The Rhodians, as His Majesty knows, are Dorian Hellenes; they speak a dialect similar to the Lakedaemonians and call their gods by the same Doric-derived names. But their island had been since before the first Persian War a protectorate of the Empire. What option other than submission did the Rhodians possess, their nation lying as it does within the very shadow of the masts of the imperial fleet? The Spartan embassy had sought, against all expectation, to detach through ancient bonds of kinship some portion of the Rhodian navy from service to His Majesty. It found no takers.

Nor had there been, our embassy learned upon its return to the mainland, from simultaneous missions dispatched to Crete, Cos, Chios, Lesbos, Samos, Naxos, Imbros, Samothrace, Thasos, Skyros, Mykonos, Paros, Tenos and Lemnos. Even Delos, birthplace of Apollo himself, had offered tokens of submission to the Persian.

Phobos.

This terror could be inhaled in the air of Andros, where we touched upon the voyage home. One felt it like a sweat on the skin at Keos and Hermione, where no harbor inn or beaching ground lacked for ship's masters and oarsmen with terror-inspiring tales of the scale of mobilization in the East and eyewitness reports of the uncountable myriads of the enemy.

Phobos.

This stranger accompanied the embassy as it landed at Thyrea and began the dusty, two-day hump across Parnon to Lakedaemon. Trekking up the eastern massif, the envoys could see landsmen and city folk evacuating their possessions to the mountains. Boys drove asses laden with sacks of corn and barley, protected by the men of the family under arms. Soon the old ones and the children would follow. In the high country, clan groups were burying jars of wine and oil, building sheepfolds and carving crude shelters out of the cliffsides.

Phobos.

At the frontier fort of Karyai, our party fell in with an embassy from the Greek city of Plataea, a dozen men including a mounted escort, headed for Sparta. Their ambassador was the hero Arimnestos of Marathon. It was said that this gentleman, though well past fifty, had in that famous victory ten years past waded in full armor into the surf, slashing with his sword at the oars of the Persian triremes as they backed water, fleeing for their lives. The Spartans loved this sort of thing. They insisted on Arimnestos' party joining ours for supper and accompanying us on the remaining march to the city itself.

The Plataean shared his intelligence of the enemy. The Persian army, he reported, comprised of two million men drawn from every nation of the Empire, had assembled at the Great King's capital, Susa, in the previous summer. The force had advanced to Sardis and wintered there. From this site, as the greenest lieutenant could not fail to project, the myriads would proceed north along the coast highways of Asia Minor, through Aeolis and the Troad, crossing the Hellespont by either bridge of boats or massive ferrying operation, then proceed west, traversing Thrace and the Chersonese, southwest across Macedonia and then south into Thessaly.

Greece proper.

The Spartans recounted what they had learned at Rhodes; that the Persian army was already on the march from Sardis; the main body stood even now at Abydos, readying to cross the Hellespont.

They would be in Europe within a month.

At Selassia a messenger from the ephors in Sparta awaited my master with an ambassadorial pouch. Dienekes was to detach himself from the party and proceed at once to Olympia. He took his leave at the Pellana road and, accompanied by myself alone, set out at a fast march, intending to cover the fifty miles in two days.

It is not uncommon upon these treks to have fall in with one as he tramps various high-spirited hounds and even half-wild urchins of the vicinity. Sometimes these carefree comrades remain on the troop all day, trotting in merry converse at the trekker's heels. Dienekes loved these ranging strays and never failed to welcome them and take cheer in their serendipitous companionship. This day, however, he sternly dismissed all we encountered, canine as well as human, striding resolutely onward, glancing neither left nor right.

I had never seen him so troubled or so grave.

An incident had occurred at Rhodes which I felt certain lay at the source of my master's disquiet. This event transpired at the harbor, immediately after the Spartans and Egyptian marines had completed their exchange of gifts and were making ready to take leave of one another. There arose then that interval when strangers often discard that formality of intercourse with which they have heretofore conversed and speak instead man-to-man, from the heart. The captain Ptammitechus had clearly taken to my master and the *polemarch* Olympieus, Alexandros' father. He summoned these now aside, declaring that he had something be wished to show them. He led them into the naval commander's campaign tent, erected there upon the strand, and with this officer's permission produced a marvel the like of which the Spartans, and of course I myself, had never beheld.

This was a map.

A geographer's representation not merely of Hellas and the islands of the Aegean but of the entire world.

The chart spread in breadth nearly two meters, of consummate detail and craftsmanship and inscribed upon Nile papyrus, a medium so extraordinary that though held to the light one could see straight through it, yet even the strongest man's hands could not rend it, save by first opening a tear with the edge of a blade.

The marine rolled the map out upon the squadron commander's table. He showed the Spartans their own homeland, in the heart of the Peloponnese, with Athens 140 miles to the north and east, Thebes and Thessaly due north of there, and Mounts Ossa and Olympus at the northernmost extremity of Greece. West of this the mapmaker's stylus had depicted Sikelia, Italia and all the leagues of sea and land clear to the Pillars of Herakles. Yet the bulk of the chart had barely begun to be unfurled.

"I wish only to impress upon you, for your own preservation, gentlemen," Ptammitechus addressed the Spartans through his interpreter, "the scale of His Majesty's Empire and the resources he commands to bring against you, that you may make your decision to resist or not, based upon fact and not fancy."

He unrolled the papyrus eastward. Beneath the lamplight arose the islands of the Aegean, Macedonia, Illyria, Thrace and Scythia, the Hellespont, Lydia, Karia, Cilicia, Phoenicia and the Ionic cities of Asia Minor. "All these nations the Great King controls. All these he has compelled into his service. All these are coming against you. But is this Persia? Have we reached yet the seat of Empire . . ."

Out rolled more leagues of landmass. The Egyptian's hand swept over the outlines of Ethiopia, Libya, Arabia, Egypt, Assyria, Babylonia, Sumeria, Cappadocia, Armenia and the trans-Caucasus. The fame of each of these kingdoms he recited, quoting the numbers of their warriors and the arms and armaments they carried.

"A man traveling fast may traverse all the Peloponnese in four days. Look here, my friends. Merely to get from Tyre to Susa, the Great King's capital, is three months' march. And all that land, all its men and wealth, belong to Xerxes. Nor do his nations contend one against the other as you Hellenes love so to do, nor disunite into squabbling alliances. When the King says assemble, his armies assemble. When he says march, they march. And still," he said, "we have not reached Persepolis and the heart of Persia."

He rolled the map out farther.

Into sight arose yet more lands covering yet more leagues and called by yet more curious names. The Egyptian reeled off more numbers. Two hundred thousand from this satrapy, 300,000 from that. Greece, in the West, was looking punier and punier. She seemed to be shriveling into a microcosm in contrast to the endless mass of the Persian Empire. The Egyptian spoke now of outlandish beasts and chimera. Camels and elephants, wild asses the size of draught horses. He sketched the lands of Persia herself, then Media, Bactria, Parthia,

Caspia, Aria, Sogdiana and India, nations of whose names and existence his listeners had never even heard.

"From these vast lands His Majesty draws more myriads of warriors, men raised under the blistering sun of the East, inured to hardships beyond your imagining, armed with weapons you have no experience in combating and financed by gold and treasure beyond counting. Every article of produce, every fruit, grain, pig, sheep, cow, horse, the yield of every mine, farm, forest and vineyard belongs to His Majesty. And all of it he has poured into the mounting of this army which marches now to enslave you.

"Listen to me, brothers. The race of Egyptians is an ancient one, numbering the generations of its fathers by the hundreds into antiquity. We have seen empires come and go. We have ruled and been ruled. Even now we are technically a conquered people, we serve the Persians. Yet regard my station, friends. Do I look poor? Is my demeanor dishonored? Peer here within my purse. With all respect, brothers, I could buy and sell you and all you own with only that which I bear upon my person."

At that point Olympieus called the Egyptian short and demanded that he speak to his point.

"My point is this, friends: His Majesty will honor you Spartans no less than us Egyptians, or any other great warrior people, should you see wisdom and enlist yourselves voluntarily beneath his banner. In the East we have learned that which you Greeks have not. The wheel turns, and man must turn with it. To resist is not mere folly, but madness."

I watched my master's eyes then. Clearly he perceived the Egyptian's intent as genuine and his words proffered out of friendship and regard. Yet he could not stop anger from flushing his countenance.

"You have never tasted freedom, friend," Dienekes spoke, "or you would know it is purchased not with gold, but steel." He contained his anger swiftly, reaching to rap the Egyptian's shoulder like a friend and to meet his eyes with a smile.

"And as for the wheel you speak of," my master finished, "like every other, it turns both ways."

We arrived at Olympia on the afternoon of the second day from Pellana. The Olympic Games, sacred to Zeus, are the holiest of all Hellenic festivals; during the weeks of their celebration no Greek may take up arms against another, or even against an alien invader. The Games would be held this very year, within weeks; in fact the Olympic grounds and dormitories were already teeming with athletes and trainers from all the Greek cities, preparing on-site as prescribed by heaven's law. These competitors, in their youthful prime and peerless in speed and prowess, surrounded my master on the instant of his arrival, clamorous for intelligence of the Persian advance and torn by the Olympic proscription from bearing arms. It was not my place to inquire of my master's mission; one could only surmise, however, that it entailed a request for dispensation from the priests.

I waited outside the precinct while Dienekes conducted his business within. Several hours of daylight remained when he finished; our two-man party, unescorted as it was, should have turned about and pushed on for Sparta at once. But my master's troubled mood continued; he seemed to be working something out in his mind. "Come on," he said, leading toward the Avenue of the Champions, west of the Olympic stadium, "I'll show you something for your education."

We detoured to the steles of honor, where the names and nations of champions of the Games were recorded. There my own eye located the name of Polynikes, one of my master's fellow envoys to Rhodes, graven twice for successive Olympiads, victor in the armored *stadion* race. Dienekes pointed out the names of other Lakedaemonian champions, men now in their thirties and forties whom I knew by sight from the city, and others who had fallen in battle decades and even centuries past. Then he indicated a final name, four Olympiads previous, in the victors' lists for the pentathlon.

Iatrokles
Son of Nikodiades
Lakedaemonian

"This was my brother," Dienekes said.

That night my master took shelter at the Spartan dormitory, a cot being vacated for him within and space set aside for me beneath the porticoes. But his mood of disquiet had not abated. Before I had even settled on the cool stones, he appeared from within fully dressed and motioned me to follow. We traversed the deserted avenues to the Olympic stadium, entering via the competitors' tunnel and emerging into the vast and silent expanse of the agonists' arena, purple and brooding now in the starlight. Dienekes mounted the slope above the judges' station, those seats upon the grass reserved during the Games for the Spartans. He selected a sheltered site beneath the pines at the crest of the slope overlooking the stadium, and there he settled.

I have heard it said that for the lover the seasons are marked in memory by those mistresses whose beauty has enflamed his heart. He recalls this year as the one when, moonstruck, he pursued a certain beloved about the city, and that year, when another favorite yielded at last to his charms.

For the mother and father, on the other hand, the seasons are numbered by the births of their children—this one's first step, that one's initial word. By these homely ticks is the calendar of the loving parent's life demarcated and set within the book of remembrance.

But for the warrior, the seasons are marked not by these sweet measures nor by the calendared years themselves, but by battles. Campaigns fought and comrades lost; trials of death survived. Clashes and conflicts from which time effaces all superficial recall, leaving only the fields themselves and their names, which achieve in the warrior's memory a stature ennobled beyond all other modes of commemoration, purchased with the holy coin of blood and paid for with the lives of beloved brothers-in-arms. As the priest with his *graphis* and tablet of wax, the infantryman, too, has his scription. His history is carved upon his person with the stylus of steel, his alphabet engraved with spear and sword indelibly upon the flesh.

Dienekes settled upon the shadowed earth above the stadium. I began now, as was my duty as his squire, to prepare and apply the warm oil, laced with clove and comfrey, which were required by my master, and virtually every other Peer past thirty years, simply to settle himself upon the earth in sleep. Dienekes was far from an old man, barely two years past forty, yet his limbs and joints creaked like an ancient's. His former squire, a Scythian called "Suicide," had instructed me in the proper manner of kneading the knots and loaves of scar tissue about my master's numerous wounds, and the little tricks in arming him so that his impairments would not show. His left shoulder could not move forward past his ear, nor could that arm rise at the elbow above his collarbone; the corselet had to be wrapped first about his torso, which he would support by pinning it with his elbows while I set the shoulder leathers and thumb-bolted them into place. His spine would not bend to lift his shield, even from its position of rest against his knee; the bronze sleeve had to be held aloft by me and jockeyed into place over the forearm, in the standing position. Nor could Dienekes flex his right foot unless the tendon was massaged until the flow of the nerves had been restored along their axis of command.

My master's most gruesome wound, however, was a lurid scar, the width of a man's thumb, that ran in jagged course across the entire crown of his brow, just below the hairline. This was not visible normally, covered as it was by the fall of his long hair across his forehead, but when he bound his hair to accept the helmet, or tied it back for sleep, this livid gash re-presented itself. I could see it now in the starlight. Apparently the curiosity in my expression struck my master as comical, for he chuckled and lifted his hand to trace the line of the scar.

"This was a gift from the Corinthians, Xeo. An ancient one, picked up around the time you were born. Its history, aptly enough, tells a tale of my brother."

My master glanced away, down the slope that led toward the Avenue of the Champions. Perhaps he felt the proximity of his brother's shade, or the fleeting shards of memory, from boyhood or battle or the *agon* of the Games. He indicated that I might pour for him a bowl of wine, and that I may take one for myself.

"I wasn't an officer then," he volunteered, still preoccupied. "I wore a banty hat instead of a curry brush." Meaning the front-to-back-crested helmet of the infantry ranker, instead of the transverse-crested helm of a platoon leader. "Would you like to hear the tale, Xeo? As a bedtime story."

I replied that I would, very much. My master considered. Clearly he was debating in his mind if such a retelling constituted vanity or excessive self-revelation. If it did, he would break it off at once. Apparently, however, the incident contained an element of instruction, for, with a barely perceptible nod, my master gave himself permission to proceed. He settled more comfortably against the slope.

"This was at Achilleion, against the Corinthians and their Arkadian allies. I don't even remember what the war was about, but whatever it was, those sons of whores had found their courage. They were putting the steel to us. The line had broken down, the first four ranks were scrambled, it was man against man across the entire field. My brother was a platoon leader and I was a third." Meaning he, Dienekes, commanded the third squad, sixteen positions back in order of march. "So that when we deployed into line by fours, I came up to my third's position beside my brother at the head of my squad. We fought as a *dyas*, Iatrokles and I; we had trained in the pairs since we were children. Only there was none of that sport now, it was pure blood madness.

"I found myself across from a monster of the enemy, six and a half feet tall, a match for two men and a horse. He was dismasted, his spear had been shivered, and he was so raging with possession he didn't have the presence of mind to go for his sword. I said to myself, man, you better get some iron into this bastard fast, before he remembers he's got that daisy-chopper on his hip.

"I went for him. He met me with his shield as a weapon, swinging it, edge-on like an axe. His first blow splintered my own shield. I had my eight-footer by the haft, trying to uppercut him, but he splintered the shaft clean through with a second blow. I was now bronze-naked in front of this demon. He swung that shield like a relish plate. Took me right here, square above the eye sockets.

"I could feel the crown of the helmet tear up and off, shearing half my skull with it. The bottom lip of the eyehole had opened the muscles beneath the brow, so that my left eye was sheeted with blood.

"I had that helpless feeling you get when you're wounded, when you know it's bad but you don't know how bad, you think you may be dead already but you're not sure. Everything is happening slowly, as in a dream. I was down on my face. I knew this giant was over me, aiming some blow to send me to hell.

"Suddenly he was there beside me. My brother. I saw him take a step and sling his *xiphos* like a throwing blade. It hit this Corinthian Gorgon right below the nose; the iron smashed the fellow's teeth, blew right through the bone of the jaw and into his throat, lodging there with the grip sticking out before his face."

Dienekes shook his head and released a dark chuckle, the kind one summons recalling a tale at a distance, knowing how close he had come to annihilation and in awe before the gods that he had somehow survived. "It didn't even slow this dick-stroker down. He came right back at Iatrokles, with bare hands and that pig-poker buried square in his jaw. I took him low and my brother took him high. We dropped him like a wrestler. I drove the blade end of my eight-footer that was now a one-footer into his guts, then grabbed the butt-spike end of someone's discarded eight from the dirt and laid all my weight on it, right through his groin all the way into the ground, nailing him there. My brother had grabbed the bastard's sword and hacked half the top of his head off, right through the bronze of his helmet. He still got up. I had never seen my brother truly terrified but this time it was serious. 'Zeus Almighty!' he cried, and it was not a curse but a prayer, a piss-down-your-leg prayer."

The night had grown cool; my master draped his cloak around his shoulders. He took another draught of wine.

"He had a squire, my brother did, from Antaurus in Scythia, of whom you may have heard. This man was called by the Spartans 'Suicide.' "

My expression must have betrayed startlement, for Dienekes chuckled in response. This fellow, the Scythian, had been Dienekes' squire before me; he became my own mentor and instructor. It was all new to me, however, that the man had served my master's brother before him.

"This reprobate had come to Sparta like you, Xeo, on his own, the crazy bastard. Fleeing bloodguilt, a murder; he had killed his father or father-in-law, I forget which, in some hill-tribe dispute over a girl. When he arrived in Lakedaemon, he asked the first man he met to dispatch him, and scores more for days. No one would do it, they feared ritual pollution; finally my brother took him with him to battle, promising he'd get him polished off there.

"The man turned out a holy terror. He wouldn't keep to the rear like the other squires, but waded right in, unarmored, seeking death, crying out for it. His weapon, as you know, was the javelin; he crafted his own, sawed-off specimens no longer than a man's arm, which he called 'darning needles.' He carried twelve of them, in a quiver like arrows, and threw them by the clutch of three, one after the other, at the same man, saving the third for the close work."

This indeed described the man. Even now, what must be twenty years later, he remained fearless to the point of madness and utterly reckless of his life.

"Anyway here he came now, this Scythian lunatic. Hoom, hoom, hoom, he put two darning needles through that Corinthian monster's liver and out his back, and added one for good measure right where the man's fruit hung. That did it. The titan looked straight at me, bellowed once, then dropped like a sack off a waggon. I realized later that half my skull was showing through to the sun, my face a mass of blood, and the whole right side of my beard and chin had been hacked off."

"How did you get out of the battle?" I asked.

"Get out? We had to fight across another thousand yards before the enemy finally turned the creases and it was over. I couldn't tell the state I was in. My brother wouldn't let me touch my face. 'You've got a few scratches,' he said. I could feel the breeze on my skull; I knew it was bad. I remember only this ghoulish surgeon, our friend Suicide, stitching me up with sailor's twine while my brother held my head and cracked jokes. 'You're not going to be too pretty after this one. I won't have to worry any more about you stealing my bride.' "

Here Dienekes drew up, his expression going suddenly sober and solemn. He declared that the story at this point proceeded into the province of the personal. He must put a period to it.

I begged him to continue. He could see the disappointment on my face. Please, sir. You must not carry the tale this far, only to discard it by the wayside.

"You know," he offered in wry admonishment, "what happens to squires who spread tales out of school." He took a draught of wine and, after a thoughtful moment, resumed.

"You are aware that I am not my wife's first husband. Arete was married to my brother first."

I had known this, but never from my master's lips.

"It created a grievous rift in my family, because I habitually declined to share a meal at his home, I always found some excuse. My brother was deeply wounded by this, thinking I disrespected his wife or had found some fault in her which I would not divulge. He had taken her from her family very young, when she was just seventeen, and this overhaste I know troubled him. He wanted her so much he couldn't wait, he was afraid another would claim her. So when I avoided his house, he thought I found fault with him for this.

"He went to our father and even to the ephors over it, seeking to force me to accept his invitations. One day we wrestled in the *palaistra* and he nearly strangled me (I was never half a match for him) and ordered me that evening to present myself at his home, in my best dress and manners. He swore he would break my back if I gave offense once more.

"It was just getting to be evening when I spotted him approaching me again, beside the Big Ring, as I was finishing training. You know the lady Arete and her tongue. She had had a talk with him. 'You are blind, Iatrokles,' she had said. 'Can't you see that your brother has feelings for me? That is why he declines all invitations to visit with us. He feels shame to experience these passions for his brother's wife.'

"My brother asked me straight out if this was true. I lied like a dog, but he saw through me as he always did. You could see he was profoundly troubled. He stood absolutely still, in a way he had since he was a boy, considering the matter. 'She will be yours when I am slain in battle,' he declared. That seemed to settle the matter for him.

"But not for me. Within a week I found excuse to get myself out of the city, assisting on an embassy overseas. I managed to keep away for the whole winter, returning only when the Herakles regiment was called up for Pellene. My brother was killed there. I didn't even know it in the advance, not until the battle was won and we remustered. I was twenty-four years old. He was thirty-one."

Dienekes' countenance grew even more solemn. All effect of the wine had fled. He hesitated for long moments, as if considering whether to continue or break off the tale at this point. He scrutinized my expression until at last, seeming to satisfy himself that I was listening with the proper attention and respect, he dumped the dregs of his bowl and continued.

"I felt it was my doing, my brother's death, as if I had willed it in secret and the gods had somehow responded to this shameful prayer. It was the most painful thing that had ever happened to me. I felt I couldn't go on living, but I didn't know how honorably to end my life. I had to come home, for my father and mother's sake and for the funeral games. I never went near Arete. I intended to leave Lakedaemon again as soon as the games were over, but her father came to me. 'Aren't you going to say one word to my daughter?' He had no clue of my feelings for her, he simply meant the courtesy of a brother-in-law and my obligation as *kyrios* to see that Arete was given to a proper husband. He said that husband should be myself. I was Iatrokles' only brother, the families were already profoundly intertwined and since Arete had as yet borne no children, mine with hers would be as if they were my brother's as well.

"I declined.

"This gentleman could make no guess of the real reason, that I couldn't embrace the shame of satisfying my deepest self-interest over the bones of my own brother. Arete's father could not understand; he was deeply hurt and insulted. It was an impossible situation, spawning suffering and sorrow in every quarter. I had no idea how to set it right. I was at wrestling one afternoon, just going through the motions, plagued by internal torment, when there came a commotion at the *Gymnasion* gate. A woman had entered the precinct. No female, as all know, may intrude upon those grounds. Murmurs of outrage were building. I myself arose from the pit—*gymnos* as all were, naked—to join the others in throwing the interloper out.

"Then I saw. It was Arete.

"The men parted before her like grain before the reapers. She stopped right beside the lanes, where the boxers were standing naked waiting to enter the ring.

" 'Which of you will have me as his wife?' she demanded of the entire assembly, who were by now gaping slack-jawed, dumbstruck as calves. Arete is a lovely woman still, even after four daughters, but then, yet childless and barely nineteen, she was as dazzling as a goddess. Not a man didn't desire her, but they were all too paralyzed to utter a peep. 'Will no man come forward to claim me?'

"She turned and marched then, right up in front of me. 'Then you must make me your wife, Dienekes, or my father will not be able to bear the shame.'

"My heart was wrenched by this, half numb at the sheer brass and temerity of this woman, this girl, to attempt such a stunt, the other half moved profoundly by her courage and wit."

"What happened?" I asked.

"What choice did I have? I became her husband."

Dienekes related several other tales of his brother's prowess in the Games and his valor in battle. In every field, in speed and wit and beauty, in virtue and forbearance, even in the chorus, his brother eclipsed him. It was clear Dienekes revered him, not merely as a younger brother will his elder, but as a man, in sober assessment and admiration. "What a pair Iatrokles and Arete made. The whole city anticipated their sons. What warriors and heroes their combined lines would produce."

But Iatrokles and Arete had had no children, and the lady's with Dienekes had all been girls.

Dienekes gave it no voice, but one could readily perceive the sorrow and regret upon his face. Why had the gods granted him and Arete only daughters? What could it be but their curse, that divinely apportioned requital for the crime of selfish love in my master's heart? Dienekes rose from this preoccupation, or what I felt certain was this preoccupation, and gestured down the slope toward the Avenue of the Champions.

"Thus you see, Xeo, how courage before the enemy may perhaps come more easily to me than to others. I hold the example of my brother before me. I know that no matter what feat of valor the gods permit me to perform, I will never be his equal. This is my secret. What keeps me humble."

He smiled. An odd, sad sort of smile.

"So now, Xeo, you know the secrets of my heart. And how I came to be the handsome fellow you see before you." I laughed, as my master had wanted. All merriment, however, had fled his features.

"And now I am tired," he said, shifting upon the earth. "If you will excuse me, it's time to deflower the straw maiden, as they say."

And with that he curled upon his reed groundbed and settled at once into sleep.

BOOK TWO

ALEXANDROS

EIGHT

The preceding interviews were transcribed over the course of several evenings as His Majesty's forces continued their still-unopposed advance into Hellas. The defenders at Thermopylae having been vanquished, the Hellenic fleet suffering further severe losses of ships and men at the naval battle fought simultaneously opposite Artemisium, all Greek and allied units, army and navy, now fled the field. The Hellenic land forces retreated south toward the Isthmus of Corinth, across which they and the armies now massing from the other Greek cities, including the forces of Sparta under a full call-up, were constructing a wall to defend the Peloponnese. The sea elements withdrew around Euboea and Cape Sounion to unite with the main body of the Hellenic fleet at Athens and Salamis in the Gulf of Saronika.

His Majesty's army put all Phokis to the torch. Imperial troops burned to the ground the cities of Drymus, Charada, Erochus, Tethronium, Amphikaea, Neon, Pedies, Trites, Elateia, Hylampolis and Parapotamii. All temples and sanctuaries of the Hellenic gods, including that of Apollo at Abae, were razed and their treasuries looted.

As for His Majesty Himself, the Royal Person's time now became consumed, nearly twenty hours a day, with urgent matters military and diplomatic. These demands notwithstanding, yet did His Majesty's desire remain undiminished to hear the continuation of the captive Xeones' tale. He ordered the interviews to proceed in His absence, their verbatim record to be transcribed for His Majesty's perusal at such hours as He found free.

The Greek responded vigorously to this order. The sight of his native Hellas being reduced by the overmastering numbers of the imperial forces caused the man severe distress and seemed to fire his will to commit to record as much of his tale as he could, as expeditiously as possible. Dispatches relating the overrunning of the Temple of the Oracle of Apollo at Delphi seemed only to increase the prisoner's grief. Privately he stated his concern that His Majesty was growing impatient with the tale of his own and other individuals' personal histories and becoming anxious to move on to the more apposite topics of Spartan tactics, training and military philosophy. The Greek begged His Majesty's patience, stating that the tale seemed to be "telling itself" at the god's direction and that he, its narrator, could only follow where it led.

We began again, His Majesty absent, on the evening of the ninth day of Tashritu, in the tent of Orontes, captain of the Immortals.

His Majesty has requested that I recount some of the training practices of the Spartans, particularly those relating to the youth and their rearing under the Lykurgan warrior code. A specific incident may be illustrative, not only to impart certain details but to convey also the flavor of the thing. This event was in nowise atypical. I report it both for its informative value and because it involved several of the men whose heroism His Majesty witnessed with his own eyes during the struggle at the Hot Gates.

This incident took place some six years prior to the battle at Thermopylae. I was fourteen at the time and not yet employed by my master as his battle squire; in fact I had at that time barely dwelt in Lakedaemon two years. I was serving as a *parastates pais*, a sparring partner, to a Spartiate youth of my own age named Alexandros. This individual I have mentioned once or twice in other contexts. He was the son of the *polemarch*, or war leader, Olympieus, and at that time, aged fourteen, the protege of Dienekes.

Alexandros was a scion of one of the noblest families of Sparta; his line descended on the Eurypontid side directly from Herakles. He was, however, not constitutionally suited to the role of warrior. In a gentler world Alexandros might have been a poet or musician. He was easily the most accomplished flute player of his age-class, though he barely touched the instrument to practice. His gifts as a singer were even more exceptional, both as a boy alto and later as a man when his voice stabilized into a pure tenor.

It chanced, unless the hand of a god was at work in it, that he and I when we were thirteen were flogged simultaneously, for separate offenses, on different sides of the same training field. His transgression related to some breach within his *agoge boua*, his training platoon; mine was for improperly shaving the throat of a sacrificial goat.

In our separate whippings, Alexandros fell before I did. I mention this not as cause for pride; it was simply that I had taken more beatings. I was more accustomed to it. The contrast in our deportment, unfortunately for Alexandros, was perceived as a disgrace of the most egregious order. As a means of rubbing his nose in it, his drill instructors assigned me permanently to him, with instructions that he fight me over and over until he could beat the hell out of me. For my part, I was informed that if I was even suspected of going easy on him, out of fear of the consequences of harming my better, I would be lashed until the bones of my back showed through to the sun.

The Lakedaemonians are extremely shrewd in these matters; they know that no arrangement could be more cunningly contrived to bind two youths together. I was keenly aware that, if I played my part satisfactorily, I would continue in Alexandros' service and become his squire when he reached twenty and took his station as a warrior in line of battle. Nothing could have suited me more. This was why I had come to Sparta in the first place—to witness the training close-up and to endure as much of it as the Lakedaemonians would permit.

The army was at the Oaks, in the Otona valley, a blistering late summer afternoon, on an eight-nighter, what they call in Lakedaemon, the only city which practices it, an *oktonyktia*. These are regimental exercises normally, though in this case it involved a division. An entire *mora*, more than twelve hundred men with full armor and battle train including an equal number of squires and helots, had marched out into the high valleys and drilled in darkness for four nights, sleeping in the day in open bivouac, by watches, at full readiness with no cover, then drilling day and night for the following three days. Conditions were deliberately contrived to make the exercise as close as possible to the rigor of actual campaign, simulating everything except casualties. There were mock night assaults up twenty-degree slopes, each man bearing full kit and *panoplia*, sixty-five to eighty pounds of shield and armor. Then assaults down the hill. Then more across. The terrain was chosen for its boulder-strewn aspect and the numerous gnarled and low-branched oaks which dotted the slopes. The skill was to flow around everything, like water over rocks, without breaking the line.

No amenities whatever were brought. Wine was at half-rations the first four days, none the second two, then no liquid at all, including water, for the final two. Rations were hard linseed loaves, which Dienekes declared fit only for barn insulation, and figs alone, nothing hot. This type of exercise is only partially in anticipation of night action; its primary purpose is training for surefootedness, for orientation by feel within the phalanx and for action without sight, particularly over uneven ground. It is axiomatic among the Lakedaemonians that an army must be able to dress and maneuver the line as skillfully blind as sighted, for, as His Majesty knows, in the dust and terror of the *othismos*, the initial battlefield collision and the horrific scrum that ensues, no man can see more than five feet in any direction, nor hear even his own cries above the din.

It is a common misconception among the other Hellenes, and one deliberately cultivated by the Spartans, that the character of Lakedaemonian military training is brutal and humorless in the extreme. Nothing could be further from the fact. I have never experienced under other circumstances anything like the relentless hilarity that proceeds during these otherwise grueling field exercises. The men bitch and crack jokes from the moment the *sarpinx*'s blare sounds reveille till the final bone-fatigued hour when the warriors curl up in their cloaks for sleep, and even then you can hear cracks being muttered and punchy laughter breaking out in odd corners of the field for minutes until sleep, which comes on like a hammerblow, overtakes them.

It is that peculiar soldiers' humor which springs from the experience of shared misery and often translates poorly to those not on the spot and enduring the same hardship. "What's the difference between a Spartan king and a mid-ranker?" One man will lob this query to his mate as they prepare to bed down in the open in a cold driving rain. His friend considers mock-theatrically for a moment. "The king sleeps in that shithole over there," he replies. "We sleep in this shithole over here."

The more miserable the conditions, the more convulsing the jokes become, or at least that's how it seems. I have witnessed venerable Peers of fifty years and more, with thick gray in their beards and countenances as distinguished as Zeus', dropping helpless with mirth onto hands and knees, toppling onto their backs and practically pissing down their legs they were laughing so hard. Once on an errand I saw Leonidas himself, unable to get to his feet for a minute or more, so doubled over was he from some otherwise untranslatable wisecrack. Each time he tried to rise, one of his tent companions, grizzled captains in their late fifties but to him just boyhood chums he still addressed by their *agoge* nicknames, would torment him with another variation on the joke, which would reconvulse him and drop him back upon his knees.

This, and other like incidents, endeared Leonidas universally to the men, not just the Spartiate Peers but the Gentleman-Rankers and *perioikoi* as well. They could see their king, at nearly sixty, enduring every bit of misery they did. And they knew that when battle came, he would take his place not safely in the rear, but in the front rank, at the hottest and most perilous spot on the field.

The purpose of an eight-nighter is to drive the individuals of the division, and the unit itself, beyond the point of humor. It is when the jokes stop, they say, that the real lessons are learned and each man, and the *mora* as a whole, make those incremental advances which pay off in the ultimate crucible. The hardship of the exercises is intended less to strengthen the back than to toughen the mind. The Spartans say that any army may win while it still has its legs under it; the real test comes when all strength is fled and the men must produce victory on will alone.

The seventh day had come and gone now, and the army had reached that stage of exhaustion and short-temperedness that the eight-nighter was contrived to produce. It was late afternoon; the men were just rousing themselves from some pitifully inadequate catnap, parched and filthy and stink-begrimed, in anticipation of the final night's drill. Everyone was hungry and tired and drained utterly of fluid. A hundred variations were spun out on the same joke, each man's wish for a real war so he could finally get more than a half hour's snooze and a bellyful of hot chow. The men were dressing their long sweat-matted hair, griping and bitching, while their squires and helots, as miserable and dehydrated as they, handed them the last dry fig cake, without wine or water, and readied them for the sunset sacrifice, while their stacked arms and *panoplia* waited in perfect order for the night's work to begin.

Alexandros' training platoon was already awake and in formation, with eight others of the fourth age-class, boys thirteen and fourteen under their twenty-year-old drill instructors, on the lower slopes below the army's camp. These *agoge* platoons were regularly exposed to the sight of their elders and the rigors they endured, as a means of rousing their emulative instincts to even greater levels of exertion. I had been dispatched to the upper camp with a message stick when the commotion came from back down across the plain.

I turned and saw Alexandros singled out at the edge of his platoon, with Polynikes, the Knight and Olympic champion, standing before him, raging. Alexandros was fourteen, Polynikes twenty-three; even at a range of a hundred yards you could see the boy was terrified.

This warrior Polynikes was no man to be trifled with. He was a nephew of Leonidas, with a prize of valor already to his name, and utterly pitiless. Apparently he had come down from the upper camp on some errand, had passed the boys of the *agoge* in their lineup and spotted some breach of discipline.

Now the Peers on the slope above could see what it was.

Alexandros had neglected his shield, or to use the Doric term, *etimasen*, "defamed" it. Somehow he had allowed it to lie outside his grasp, facedown, untended on the ground with its big concave bowl pointing at the sky.

Polynikes stood in front of him. "What is this I see in the dirt before me?" he roared. The Spartiates uphill could hear every syllable. "It must be a chamber pot, with its bowl peeking up so daintily."

Is it a chamber pot? he demanded of Alexandros. The boy answered no.

Then what is it?

It is a shield, lord.

Polynikes declared this impossible.

"It can't be a shield, I'm certain of that." His voice carried powerfully up the amphitheater of the valley. "Because not even the dumbest bum-fucked shitworm of a *paidarion* would leave a shield lying facedown where he couldn't snatch it up in an instant when the enemy came upon him." He towered above the mortified boy.

"It is a chamber pot," Polynikes declared. "Fill it."

The torture began.

Alexandros was ordered to piss into his shield. It was a training shield, yes. But Dienekes knew as he looked down with the other Peers from the slope above that this particular *aspis*, patched and repatched over decades, had belonged to Alexandros' father and grandfather before him.

Alexandros was so scared and so dehydrated, he couldn't raise a drop.

Now a second factor entered the equation. This was the tendency among the youths in training, those who were not for the moment the object of their superiors' rage, to convulse with perverse glee at the misery of whatever luckless mate now found himself spitted above the coals. Up and down the line of boys, teeth sank into tongues seeking to suppress this fear-inspired hilarity. One lad named Ariston, who was extremely handsome and the fastest sprinter of the fourth class, something of a younger version of Polynikes himself, could not contain himself. A snort escaped his clamped jaws.

Polynikes turned upon him in fury. Ariston had three sisters, all what the Lakedaemonians call "two-lookers," meaning they were so pretty that one look was not enough, you had to look twice to appreciate them.

Polynikes asked Ariston if he thought this was funny.

"No, lord," the boy replied.

"If you think this is funny, wait till you get into combat. You'll think that's hysterical."

"No, lord."

"Oh yes you will. You'll be giggling like your goddam sisters." He advanced a pace nearer. "Is that what you think war is, you fucking come-spot?"

"No, lord."

Polynikes pressed his face inches from the boy's, glowering into his eyes with a look of blistering malice. "Tell me. Which do you think will be the bigger laugh: when you take an enemy spear eighteen inches up the dogblossom, or when your psalm-singing mate Alexandros takes one?"

"Neither, lord." Ariston's face was stone.

"You're afraid of me, aren't you? That's the real reason you're laughing. You're so fucking happy it wasn't you I singled out."

"No, lord."

"What? You're not afraid of me?"

Polynikes demanded to know which it was. Because if Ariston was afraid of him, then he was a coward. And if he wasn't, he was reckless and ignorant, which was even worse.

"Which is it, you miserable mound of shit? 'Cause you'd better fucking well be afraid of me. I'll put my dick in your right ear, pull it out your left and fill that chamber pot myself."

Polynikes ordered the other boys to take up Alexandros' slack. While their pathetic dribbles of urine splotched onto the wood and leather-padded frame, over the good-luck talismans that Alexandros' mother and sisters had made and that hung from the inner frame, Polynikes returned his attention to Alexandros, querying him on the protocol of the shield, which the boy knew and had known since he was three.

The shield must stand upright at all times, Alexandros declaimed at the top of his voice, with its forearm sleeve and handgrip at the ready. If a warrior stand at the rest, his shield must lean against his knees. If he sit or lie, it must be supported upright by the *tripous basis*, a light three-legged stand which all bore inside the bowl of the concave *hoplon*, in a carrying nest made for that purpose.

The other youths under Polynikes' orders had now finished urinating as best they could into the hollow of Alexandros' shield. I glanced at Dienekes. His features betrayed no emotion, though I knew he loved Alexandros and wished for nothing more than to dash down the slope and murder Polynikes.

But Polynikes was right. Alexandros was wrong. The boy must be taught a lesson.

Polynikes now had Alexandros' *tripous basis* in his hand. The little tripod was comprised of three dowels joined at one end by a leather thong. The dowels were the thickness of a man's finger and about eighteen inches long. "Line of battle!" Polynikes bellowed. The platoon of boys formed up. He had them all lay their shields, defamed, facedown in the dirt, exactly as Alexandros had done.

By now twelve hundred Spartiates up the hill were observing the spectacle, along with an equal number of squires and helot attendants.

"Shields, port!"

The boys lunged for their heavy, grounded *hopla*. As they did, Polynikes lashed at Alexandros' face with the tripod. Blood sprung. He swatted the next boy and the next until the fifth at last wrestled his twenty-pound, unwieldy shield off the ground and up into place to defend himself.

He made them do it again and again and again.

Starting at one end of the line, then the other, then the middle. Polynikes, as I have said, was an Agiad, one of the Three Hundred Knights and an Olympic victor besides. He could do anything he liked. The drill instructor, who was just an *eirene*, had been brushed aside, and could do nothing but look on in mortification.

"This is hilarious, isn't it?" Polynikes demanded of the boys. "I'm beside myself, aren't you? I can hardly wait to see combat, which will be even more fun."

The youths knew what was coming next.

Tree fucking.

When Polynikes tired of torturing them here, he would have their drill instructor march them over to the edge of the plain, to some particularly stout oak, and order them, in formation, to push the tree down with their shields, just the way they would assault an enemy in battle.

The boys would take station in ranks, eight deep, the shield of each pressed into the hollow of the boy's back before him, with the leading boy's shield mashed by their combined weight and pressure against the oak. Then they would do *othismos* drill.

They would push.

They would strain.

They would fuck that tree for all they were worth.

The soles of their bare feet would churn the dirt, heaving and straining until a rut had been excavated ankle-deep, while they crushed each other's guts humping and hurling, grinding into that unmoveable trunk. When the front-rank boy could stand no more, he would assume the position of the rearmost and the second boy would move up.

Two hours later Polynikes would casually return, perhaps with several other young warriors, who had themselves been through this hell more than once during their own *agoge* years. These would observe with shock and disbelief that the tree was still standing. "By God, these dog-strokers have been at it half the watch and that pitiful little sapling is still right where it was!"

Now effeminacy would be added to the list of the lads' crimes. It was unthinkable that they be allowed to return to the city while this tree yet defied them; such failure would disgrace their fathers and mothers, brothers, sisters, aunts, uncles and cousins, all the gods and heroes of their line, not to mention their hounds, cats, sheep and goats and even the rats in their helots' barns, who would hang their heads and have to slink off to Athens or some other rump-split *polis* where men were men and knew how to put out a respectable fucking.

That tree is the enemy!

Fuck the enemy!

On it would go, into all-night shield drill which by mid second watch would have reduced the boys to involuntary regurgitation and defecation; they would be puking and shitting themselves, their bodies shattered utterly from exhaustion, and then, when the dawn sacrifices at last brought clemency and reprieve, the boys would fall in for another full day of training without a minute's sleep.

This torment, the boys knew now as they stood under Polynikes face-lashing, was yet to come. This was what they had to look forward to.

By this point every nose in the formation had been broken. Each boy's face was a sheet of blood. Polynikes was just taking a breath (he had tired his arm with all that swatting) when Alexandros thoughtlessly reached with a hand to the side of his blood-begrimed face.

"What do you think you're doing, buttfuck?" Polynikes turned instantly upon him.

"Wiping the blood, lord."

"What are you doing that for?"

"So I can see, lord."

"Who the fuck told you you had a right to see?"

Polynikes continued his blistering mockery. Why did Alexandros think the division was out here, training at night? Was it not to learn to fight when they couldn't see? Did Alexandros think that in combat he would be allowed to pause to wipe his face? That must be it. Alexandros would call out to the enemy and they would halt politely for a moment, so the boy could pluck a nosenugget from his nostril or wipe a turdberry from his crease. "I ask you again, is this a chamber pot?"

"No, lord. It is my shield."

Again Polynikes' dowels blasted the boy across the face. " 'My'?" he demanded furiously. " 'My'?"

Dienekes looked on, mortified, from where he stood at the edge of the upper camp. Alexandros was excruciatingly aware that his mentor was watching; he seemed to summon his composure, rally all his senses. The boy stepped forward, shield at high port. He straightened to attention before Polynikes and enunciated in his loudest, clearest voice:

"This is my shield.
I bear it before me into battle,
but it is not mine alone.
It protects my brother on my left.
It protects my city.

I will never let my brother
out of its shadow
nor my city out of its shelter.
I will die with my shield before me
facing the enemy."

The boy finished. The last of his words, shouted at the top of his voice, echoed for a long moment around the valley walls. Twenty-five hundred men stood listening and watching.

They could see Polynikes nod, satisfied. He barked an order. The boys resumed formation, each now with his shield in proper place, upright against its owner's knees.

"Shields, port!"

The boys lunged for their *hopla*.

Polynikes swung the tripod.

With a crack that could be heard across the valley, the slashing sticks struck the bronze of Alexandros' shield.

Polynikes swung again, at the next boy and next. All shields were in place. The line protected.

He did it again from the right and from the left. Now all shields leapt into the boys' grips, all swiftly into place before them.

There.

With a nod to the platoon's *eirene*, Polynikes stepped back. The boys held fast at attention, shields at high port, with the blood beginning to cake dry on their empurpled cheekbones and shattered noses.

Polynikes repeated his order to the drill instructor, that these sheep-stroking sons of whores would do tree-fucking till the end of the second watch, then shield drill till dawn.

He walked once down the line, meeting each boy's eye. Before Alexandros, he halted.

"Your nose was too pretty, son of Olympieus. It was a girl's nose." He tossed the boy's tripod into the dirt at his feet. "I like it better now."

NINE

One of the boys died that night. His name was Hermion; they called him "Mountain." At fourteen he was as strong as any in his age-class or the class above, but dehydration in combination with exhaustion overcame him. He collapsed near the end of the second watch and fell into that state of convulsive torpor the Spartans call *nekrophaneia*, the Little Death, from which a man may recover if left alone but will die if he tries to rise or exert himself. Mountain understood his extremity but refused to stay down while his mates kept their feet and continued their drill.

I tried to make the platoon take water, I and my helot mate Dekton, whom they later called "Rooster." We snuck a skin to them around the middle of the first watch, but the boys refused to accept it. At dawn they carried Mountain in on their shoulders, the way the fallen in battle are borne.

Alexandros' nose never did heal properly. His father had it broken again, twice, and reset by the finest battle surgeons, but the seam where the cartilage meets the bone never mended quite right. The airway would constrict involuntarily, triggering those spasms of the lungs called by the Greeks *asthma*, which were excruciating simply to watch and must have been unbearable to endure. Alexandros blamed himself for the death of the boy called Mountain. These fits, he was certain, were the retribution of heaven for his lapse of concentration and unwarrior-like conduct.

The spasms enfeebled Alexandros' endurance and made him less and less a match for his age-mates within the *agoge*. Worse still was the unpredictability of the attacks. When they hit, he was good for nothing for minutes at a stretch. If he could not find a way to reverse this condition, he could not when he reached manhood be made a warrior; he would lose his citizenship and be left to choose between living on in some lesser state of disgrace or embracing honor and taking his own life.

His father, gravely concerned, offered sacrifice again and again and even sent to Delphi for counsel from the Pythia. Nothing helped.

Aggravating the situation further was the fact that, despite what Polynikes had said about the boy's broken nose, Alexandros remained "pretty." Nor did his breathing difficulties, for some reason, affect his singing. It seemed somehow that fear, rather than physical incapacity, was the trigger for these attacks.

The Spartans have a discipline they call *phobologia*, the science of fear. As his mentor, Dienekes worked with Alexandros privately on this, after evening mess and before dawn, while the units were forming up for sacrifice.

Phobologic discipline is comprised of twenty-eight exercises, each focusing upon a separate nexus of the nervous system. The five primaries are the knees and hams, lungs and heart, loins and bowels, the lower back, and the girdle of the shoulders, particularly the trapezius muscles, which yoke the shoulder to the neck.

A secondary nexus, for which the Lakedaemonians have twelve more exercises, is the face, specifically the muscles of the jaw, the neck and the four ocular constrictors around the eye sockets. These nexuses are termed by the Spartans *phobosynakteres*, fear accumulators.

Fear spawns in the body, *phobologic* science teaches, and must be combated there. For once the flesh is seized, a *phobokyklos*, or loop of fear, may commence, feeding upon itself, mounting into a "runaway" of terror. Put the body into a state of *aphobia*, fearlessness, the Spartans believe, and the mind will follow.

Under the oaks, in the still half-light before dawn, Dienekes practiced alone with Alexandros. He would tap the boy with an olive bough, very lightly, on the side of the face. Involuntarily the muscles of the trapezius would contract. "Feel the fear? There. Feel it?" The older man's voice crooned soothingly, like a trainer gentling a colt. "Now. Drop your shoulder." He popped the boy's cheek again. "Let the fear bleed out. Feel it?"

Man and boy worked for hours on the "owl muscles," the

ophthalmomyes surrounding the eyes. These, Dienekes instructed Alexandros, were in many ways the most powerful of all, for God in His wisdom made mortals' keenest defensive reflex that which protects the vision. "Watch my face when the muscles constrict," Dienekes demonstrated. "What expression is this?"

"*Phobos*. Fear."

Dienekes, schooled in the discipline, commanded his facial muscles to relent.

"Now. What does this expression indicate?"

"*Aphobia*. Fearlessness."

It seemed effortless when Dienekes did it, and the other boys in their training were practicing and mastering this too. But for Alexandros, nothing of the discipline came easy. The only time his heart beat truly without fear was when he mounted the choral stand and stood, solitary, to sing at the *Gymnopaedia* and the other boy's festivals.

Perhaps his true guardians were the Muses. Dienekes had Alexandros sacrifice to them and to Zeus and Mnemosyne. Agathe, one of the "two-looker" sisters of Ariston, made a charm of amber to Polyhymnia, and Alexandros carried it with him, pended from the crosshatch within his shield.

Dienekes encouraged Alexandros in his singing. The gods endow each man with a gift by which he may conquer fear; Alexandros', Dienekes felt certain, was his voice. Skill in singing in Sparta is counted second only to martial valor and in fact is closely related, through the heart and lungs, within the discipline of the *phobologia*. This is why the Lakedaemonians sing as they advance into battle. They are schooled to open the throat and gulp the air, work the lungs till the accumulators relent and break the constriction of fear.

There are two running courses within the city: the Little Ring, which begins at the *Gymnasion* and follows the Konooura road beneath Athena of the Brazen House, and the Big Ring, which laps all five villages, past Amyklai, along the Hyakinthian Way and across the slopes of Taygetos. Alexandros ran the big one, six miles barefoot, before sacrifice and after dinner mess. Extra rations were slipped him by the helot cooks. By unspoken compact the boys of his *boua* protected him in training. They covered for him when his lungs betrayed him, when it seemed he might be singled out for punishment. Alexandros responded with a secret shame which propelled him to even greater exertions.

He began to train in the "all-in," that type of no-holds-barred boys' brawling unique to Lakedaemon, in which the competitor may kick, bite, gouge the eyes, do anything but raise the hand for quarter. Alexandros hurled himself barefoot up the Therai watercourse and bare-handed against the *pankratist*'s bag; he ran weighted sprints, he pounded his fists into the trainer's boxes of sand. His slender hands became scarred and knuckle-busted. His nose broke again and again. He fought boys from his own platoon and others, and he fought me.

I was growing fast. My hands were getting stronger. Every athletic action Alexandros performed, I could do better. In the fighting square it was all I could do not to break up his face even more. He should have hated me, but it was not in him. He shared his surplus rations and worried that I would be whipped for going easy on him.

We talked for hours in secret on the pursuit of *esoterike harmonia*, that state of self-composure which the exercises of the *phobologia* are designed to produce. As a string of the *kithera* vibrates purely, emitting only that note of the musical scale which is its alone, so must the individual warrior shed all which is superfluous in his spirit, until he himself vibrates at that sole pitch which his individual *daimon* dictates. The achievement of this ideal, in Lakedaemon, carries beyond courage on the battlefield; it is considered the supreme embodiment of virtue, *andreia*, of a citizen and a man.

Beyond *esoterike harmonia* lies *exoterike harmonia*, that state of union with one's fellows which parallels the musical harmony of the multistringed instrument or of the chorus of voices itself. In battle *exoterike harmonia* guides the phalanx to move and strike as one man, of a single mind and will. In passion it unites husband to wife, lover to lover, in wordless perfect union. In politics *exoterike harmonia* produces a city of concord and unity, in which each individual, securing his own noblest expression of character, donates this to each other, as obedient to the laws of the commonwealth as the strings of the *kithera* to the immutable mathematics of music. In piety *exoterike harmonia* produces that silent symphony which most delights the ears of the gods.

At the height of that summer there was a war with the Antirhionians. Four of the army's twelve *lochoi* were mobilized (reinforced by elements of the Skiritai, the mountain rangers who comprised their own main-force regiment) to a call-up of the first ten age-classes, twenty-eight hundred in all. This was no force to be taken lightly, all-Lakedaemonian, commanded by the king himself; the battle train alone would be half a mile long. It would be the first full-scale campaign since the death of Kleomenes and the third in which Leonidas would assume command as king.

Polynikes would go as a Knight of the king's bodyguard, Olympieus with the Huntress battalion in the Wild Olive *lochos* and Dienekes as a platoon commander, an *enomotarch*, in the Herakles. Even Dekton, my half-breed friend, would be mobilized as herd boy for the sacrificial beasts.

The entire Deukalion mess in which Alexandros "stood-to," meaning acted as occasional cupbearer and server so he could observe his elders and learn, was called up except the five eldest men, between forty and sixty. For Alexandros, though he was six years too young to go, the mobilization seemed to plunge him even more deeply under his cloud. The uncalled-up Peers twitched about with their own brand of frustration. The air was touchy and ripe for explosiveness.

Somehow an all-in match got started one evening between Alexandros and me, outdoors behind the mess. The Peers gathered eagerly; the action was just what they needed. I could hear Dienekes' voice, cheering the brawl on. Alexandros seemed full of fire; we were bare-handed and his smallish fists flew fast as darts. He kicked me hard, to the temple, and followed with a solid elbow to the gut; I dropped. It was a true fall, I was really hurt, but the Peers had seen Alexandros' friends cover for him so frequently that they now thought I was tanking it. Alexandros did too.

"Get up, you outlander piece of shit!" He straddled me in the dirt and hit me again when I rose. For the first time I heard real killer instinct in his voice. The Peers heard it too and raised a shout of delight. Meanwhile the hounds, of whom there were never fewer than twenty after chow time, howled and bounded from every quarter in the turf-skimming fever that their masters' excited voices now drove them to.

I got up and hit Alexandros. I knew I could beat him easily, despite his crowd-impelled fury; I tried to pull my punch, just slightly so that no one would notice. They did. A howl of outrage rose from the Peers of the mess and others from adjacent *syssitia*, who had now clustered, forming a ring from which neither Alexandros nor I could escape.

Men's fists cuffed me hard about the ears. "Fight him, you little fucker!" The pack instinct had seized the hounds; they were at the verge of losing themselves to their animal nature. Suddenly two burst into the ring. One got in a nip at Alexandros before the men's sticks sent him scampering. That was it.

A spasm of the lungs seized Alexandros; his throat constricted, he began to choke. My punch hesitated. A three-foot switch burned my back. "Hit him!" I obeyed; Alexandros dropped to one knee. His lungs had frozen, he was helpless. "Pound him, you whore's son!" a voice shouted from behind me. "Finish him!"

It was Dienekes.

His switch lashed me so hard it drove me to my knees. The delirium of voices overwhelmed the senses, all calling for me to polish Alexandros off. It was not anger at him. Nor were they rooting for me. The Peers could not have cared less about me. It was for him, to teach him, to make him eat the thousandth bitter lesson of the ten thousand more he would endure before they hardened him into the rock the city demanded and allowed him to take his place as an Equal and a warrior. Alexandros knew it and rose with the fury of desperation, choking for breath; he charged like a boar. I felt the lash. I swung with everything I had. Alexandros spun and dropped, face-first into the dirt, blood and spittle slinging from the side of his mouth.

He lay there, motionless as a dead man.

The Peers' shouting ceased instantly. Only the ungodly racket of the hounds continued at its maddening shrill pitch. Dienekes stepped across to the fallen form of his protege and knelt to feel his heart. In unconsciousness Alexandros' breath returned. Dienekes' hand scraped the sputum from the boy's lips.

"What are you gaping at!" he barked at the circling Peers. "It's over! Let him be!"

The army marched out next morning for Antirhion. Leonidas strode at the fore, in full *panoplia* including slung shield, with his brow wreathed and his plumeless, unadorned helmet riding the rolled battle pack atop his scarlet cloak, his long steel-colored hair immaculately dressed and falling to his shoulders. About him marched the companion guard of the Knights, a half call-up, a hundred and fifty, with Polynikes in the forerank of honor beside six other Olympic victors. They marched not rigidly nor in grim silent lockstep, but at ease, talking and joking with one another and their families and friends along the roadside. Leonidas himself, were it not for his years and station of honor, could easily have been mistaken for a common infantryman, so unprepossessing was his armament, so nonchalant his demeanor. Yet all the city knew that this march-out, as the two previous beneath his command, was driven by his will and his will alone. It was aimed at the Persian invasion the king knew would come, perhaps not this year, perhaps not five years from now, but surely and inevitably.

The twin ports of Rhion and Antirhion commanded the western approach to the Gulf of Corinth. This avenue threatened the Peloponnese and all of central Greece. Rhion, the near-side port, stood already within the Spartan hegemony; she was an ally. But Antirhion across the strait remained haughtily aloof, thinking herself beyond the reach of Lakedaemonian power. Leonidas meant to show her the error of her ways. He would bring her to heel and bottle up the gulf, protecting central Hellas from Persian sea assault, at least from the northwest.

Alexandros' father, Olympieus, marched past at the head of the Wild Olive regiment, with Meriones, the fifty-year-old battle captive and former Potidaean captain, beside him as his squire. This gentle fellow possessed a grand beard, white as snow; he used to secrete little treasures within its bushy nest and pluck them forth, as surprise gifts, for Alexandros and his sisters when they were children. He did this now, straying to the roadside, to place in Alexandros' hand a tiny iron charm in the shape of a shield. Meriones clasped the boy's hand with a wink and moved on.

I stood in the crowd before the Hellenion with Alexandros and the other boys of the training platoons, the women and children, the whole city drawn up beneath the acacias and cypresses, singing the hymn to Castor, as the regiments trooped out along the Going-Away Street with their shields slung and spears at the slope, helmets lashed athwart the shoulders of their crimson cloaks, bobbing atop their *polemothylakioi*, the battle packs which the Peers bore now for show but which, like their armor, would be transferred, with all kit save spears and swords, to the shoulders of their squires when the army assumed column of march and stripped for the long, dusty hump north.

Alexandros' beautiful broken face remained a mask as Dienekes strode into view, flanked by his squire, Suicide, at the head of his platoon of the Herakles *lochos*. The main body of troops passed on. Leading and accompanying each regiment trudged the pack animals laden with the supplies of the commissariat and thwacked merrily on the rumps by the switches of their helot herd boys. The train of armament waggons passed next, already obscured within a churning storm of road dust; then followed the tall victualry waggons with their cargo of oil pots and wine jars, sacks of figs, olives, leeks, onions, pomegranates and the cooking pots and ladles swinging on hooks beneath them, banging into each other musically in the dust of the mules' tread, contributing a ringing metronomic air to the cacophony of cracking whips and squalling wheel rims, teamsters' bawls and groaning axles.

Behind the provisions bearers came the portable forges and armorers' kits with their spare *xiphos* blades and butt-spikes, "lizard-stickers" and long iron spear blades, then the spare eight-footers, uncured ash and cornel shafts lashed lengthwise along the waggon rails. Helot armorers strode in the cloud alongside, clad in their dog-skin caps and aprons, forearms crisscrossed with the burn scars of the smithy.

Last of all trooped the sacrificial goats and sheep, with their horns wrapped and leashes held by the helot herd urchins, led by Dekton in his already road-begrimed altar-boy white, trailering a haltered ass laden with feed grain and two victory roosters in cages, one on either side of the cargo frame. He grinned when he passed, a little flash of contempt escaping his otherwise impeccably pious demeanor.

I was deep into slumber that night, on the stone of the portico behind the ephorate, when I felt a hand shake me awake. It was Agathe, the Spartan girl who had made Alexandros' charm to Polyhymnia. "Get up, you!" she hissed, so as not to alert the score of other youths of the *agoge* asleep and on watch around these public buildings. I blinked around. Alexandros, who had been asleep beside me, was gone. "Hurry!"

The girl melted at once into shadow. I followed her swiftly through the dark streets to that copse of the double-boled myrtle they called Dioscuri, the Twins, just west of the start of the Little Ring.

Alexandros was there. He had snuck away from his platoon without me (which would have put both of us, if caught, in line for a merciless whipping). He stood now, wearing his black *pais*' cloak and battle pack, confronted by his mother, the lady Paraleia, one of their male house helots and his two younger sisters. Hard words flew. Alexandros intended to follow the army to battle. "I'm going," he declared. "Nothing will stop me."

I was ordered by Alexandros' mother to knock him down.

I saw something flash in his fist. His *xyele*, the sicklelike weapon all the boys carried. The women saw it too, and the deadly-grim look in the lad's eye. For a long moment, every form froze. The preposterousness of the situation was becoming more and more apparent, as was the adamantine resolution of the boy.

His mother straightened before him.

"Go, then," the lady Paraleia addressed her son at last. She didn't need to add that I would go with him. "And may God preserve you in the lashing you receive when you return."

TEN

It was not hard to follow the army. The track along the Oenous was churned to dust, ankle-deep. At Selassia the *perioikic* Stephanos regiment had joined the expedition. Alexandros and I, arriving in the dark, could still make out the trodden-bare marshaling ground and the freshly dried blood upon the altar where the sacrifices had been performed and the omens taken. The army itself was half a day ahead; we could not stop for sleep, but pushed on all night.

At dawn we came upon men we recognized. A helot armorer named Eukrates had broken his leg in a fall and was being helped home by two of his fellows. He informed us that at the frontier fort of Oion fresh intelligence had reached Leonidas. The Antirhionians, far from rolling over and playing dead as the king had hoped, had sent envoys in secret, appealing for aid to the *tyrannos* Gelon in Sikelia. Gelon could appreciate as well as Leonidas and the Persians the strategic indispensability of the port of Antirhion; he wanted it too. Forty Syrakusan ships bearing two thousand citizen and mercenary heavy infantry were on their way to reinforce the Antirhionian defenders. It would be a real battle after all.

The Spartan force pressed on through Tegea. The Tegeates, member allies of the Peloponnesian League and obligated to "follow the Spartans whithersoever they should lead," reinforced the army with six hundred of their own heavy infantry, swelling its fighting total to beyond four thousand. Leonidas had not been seeking *parataxis*, a pitched battle, with the Antirhionians. Rather he had hoped to overawe them with a show of such force that they would perceive the folly of defiance and enroll themselves of their own free will in the alliance against the Persians. Among Dekton's herd was a wrapped bull, brought in anticipation of celebration, of festive sacrifice in honor of this new addition to the League. But the Antirhionians, perhaps bought by Gelon's gold, inflamed by the rhetoric of some glory-hungry demagogue or betrayed by a lying oracle, had chosen to make a fight of it.

When Alexandros spoke to the helots on the road, he had queried them for intelligence on the specific makeup of the Syrakusan forces: which units, under which commanders, reinforced by which auxiliaries. The helots didn't know. In any army other than the Spartan, such ignorance would have provoked a fierce tongue-lashing or worse. Yet Alexandros let it go without a thought. Among the Lakedaemonians, it is considered a matter of indifference of whom and in what the enemy consists.

The Spartans are schooled to regard the foe, any foe, as nameless and faceless. In their minds it is the mark of an ill-prepared and amateur army to rely in the moments before battle on what they call *pseudoandreia*, false courage, meaning the artificially inflated martial frenzy produced by a general's eleventh-hour harangue or some peak of bronze-banging bravado built to by shouting, shield-pounding and the like. In Alexandros' mind, which already at age fourteen mirrored that of the generals of his city, one Syrakusan was as good as the next, one enemy *strategos* no different from another. Let the foe be Mantinean, Olynthian, Epidaurian; let him come in elite units or hordes of shrieking rabble, crack citizen regiments or foreign mercenaries hired for gold. It made no difference. None was a match for the warriors of Lakedaemon, and all knew it.

Among the Spartans the work of war is demystified and depersonalized through its vocabulary, which is studded with references both agrarian and obscene. Their word which I translated earlier as "fuck," as in the youths' tree-fucking, bears the connotation not so much of penetration as of grinding, like a miller's stone. The front three ranks "fuck" or "mill" the enemy. The verb "to kill," in Doric *theros*, is the same as "to harvest." The warriors in the fourth through sixth ranks are sometimes called "harvesters," both for the work they do on the trampled enemy with the butt-spike "lizard-stickers" of their eight-footers and for that pitiless threshing stroke they make with the short *xiphos* sword, which itself is often called a "reaper." To decapitate a man is to "top him off" or "give him a haircut." Chopping off a hand or arm is called "limbing."

Alexandros and I arrived at Rhion, at the bluff overlooking the army's embarkation port, a little after midnight of the third day. The port lights of Antirhion shone, clearly visible across the narrow strait. The embarkation beaches were already packed with men and boys, women and children, a thronging festive mob gathered to watch the spectacle of the fleet of galleys and coasters, conscripted merchantmen, ferries and even fishing boats assembled in advance by the allied Rhionians to transport the army in darkness west along the coast, out of sight of Antirhion, then across the gulf where it stood widest, some five miles down. Leonidas, respecting the sea-fighting reputation of the Antirhionians, had elected to make this passage at night.

Among the blufftop farewell-bawlers Alexandros and I located a boy our age whose father, he claimed, owned a fast smack and would not be averse to pocketing the wad of Attic drachmas clutched in Alexandros' fist in exchange for a swift silent crossing, no questions asked. The boy led us down through the crush of spectators and merrymakers to an obscure launching beach called the Ovens, behind an unlighted breakwater. Not twenty minutes after the last Spartan transport had cast off, we were on the water too, trailing the fleet out of sight to the west.

I fear the sea anytime, but never more than on a moonless night and in the hands of strangers. Our captain had insisted on bringing along his two brothers, though a man and a boy could easily handle the light swift craft. I have known these coasters and man jacks and mistrust them; the brothers, if indeed that's what they were, were hulking louts barely capable of speech, with beards so dense they began just below the eyeline and extended thick as fur to the matted pelts of their chests.

An hour passed. The smack was making far too much speed; across the dark water the plash of the transports' oarblades and even the creaking of looms against tholepins carried easily. Alexandros ordered the pirate twice to retard his progress, but the man tossed it off with a laugh. We were downwind, he said, no one could hear us, and even if they did they would take us for part of the convoy, or one of the spectator boats, trailing to catch the action.

Sure enough, as soon as the belly of the coastline had swallowed the lights of Rhion behind us, a Spartan cutter emerged out of the black and made way to intercept us. Doric voices hailed the smack and ordered her to heave-to. Suddenly our skipper demanded his money. When we land, Alexandros insisted, as agreed. The beards clamped oars in their fists like weapons. Cutter's getting closer, boys. How will it go with you if you're caught?

"Give him nothing, Alexandros," I hissed.

But the boy perceived the precariousness of our predicament. "Of course, Captain. It will be my pleasure."

The pirate accepted his fare, grinning like Charon on the ferry to hell. "Now, lads. Over the side with you."

We were smack in the middle of the widest part of the gulf.

Our boatman indicated the Spartan cutter bearing swiftly down. "Catch a line and keep under the stern while I feed these lubbers a yard of shit." The beards loomed. "Soon as we talk these fools off, we'll haul you back aboard none the worse for wear."

Over we went. Up came the cutter. We heard the scrape of a knife blade through rope.

The line came off in our hands.

"Happy landings, lads!"

In a flash the smack's steering oar bit deep into the swell, the two worthless brutes suddenly showed themselves anything but. Three swift heaves on the driving oars and the smack shot off like a sling bullet.

We were cast adrift in the middle of the channel.

The cutter came up, calling after the smack as she sped from sight. The Spartans still hadn't seen us. Alexandros clamped my arm. We must not sing out, that would mean dishonor.

"I agree. Drowning's a lot more honorable."

"Shut up."

We held silent, treading water while the cutter quartered the area, scanning for other craft that might be spies. Finally she showed her stern and rowed off. We were alone beneath the stars.

As vast as the sea can look from the deck of a ship, it looks even bigger from a single handbreadth above the surface.

"Which shore do we make for?"

Alexandros gave me a look as if I had lost my senses. Of course we would go forward.

We paddled for what seemed like hours. The shore had not crawled one spear-length closer. "What if the current's against us? For all we know we're stuck here in place, or even drifting backward."

"We're closer," Alexandros insisted.

"Your eyes must be better than mine."

There was nothing to do but paddle and pray. What monsters of the sea prowled at this moment beneath our feet, ready to snare our legs in their horrible coils, or shear us off at the kneecaps? I could hear Alexandros gulp water, fighting an asthmatic fit. We pulled closer together. Our eyes were gumming up from the salt; our arms felt like lead.

"Tell me a story," Alexandros said.

For a moment I feared he was going mad.

"To encourage each other. Keep our spirits up. Tell me a story."

I recited some verses from the *Iliad* which Bruxieus had made Diomache and me commit to memory, our second summer in the hills. I was getting the hexameters out of order but Alexandros didn't care; the words seemed to fortify him greatly.

"Dienekes says the mind is like a house with many rooms," he said. "There are rooms one must not go into. To anticipate one's death is one of those rooms. We must not allow ourselves even to think it."

He instructed me to continue, selecting only verses of valor. He declared that we must under no circumstances give thought to failure. "I think the gods may have dropped us here on purpose. To teach us about those rooms."

We paddled on. Orion the Hunter had stood overhead when we began; now his arc descended, halfway down the sky. The shore stood as far off as ever.

"Do you know Agathe, Ariston's sister?" Alexandros asked out of nowhere. "I'm going to marry her. I've never told anyone that."

"Congratulations."

"You think I'm joking. But my thoughts have kept coming back to her for hours, or however long we've been out here." He was serious. "Do you think she'll have me?"

It made as much sense to debate this in the middle of the ocean as anything else. "Your family outranks hers. If your father asks, hers will have to say yes."

"I don't want her that way. You've watched her. Tell me the truth. Will she have me?"

I considered it. "She made you that amber charm. Her eyes never leave you when you sing. She comes out to the Big Ring with her sisters when we run. She pretends to be training, but she's really sneaking looks at you."

This seemed to cheer Alexandros mightily. "Let's make a push. Twenty minutes as strong as we can, and see how far we can get."

When we hit twenty, we decided to try for another.

"You have a girl you love too, don't you?" Alexandros asked as we paddled. "From your city. The girl you lived in the hills with, your cousin who went to Athens."

I said it was impossible that he could know all that.

He laughed. "I know everything. I hear it from the girls and the goat boys and from your helot friend Dekton." He said he wanted to know more about "this girl of yours."

I told him I wouldn't tell him.

"I can help you to see her. My great-uncle is *proxenos* for Athens. He can have her found, and brought to the city if you wish."

The swells were getting bigger; a cold wind had gotten up. We were going nowhere. I supported Alexandros again as another choking fit attacked him. He stuck his thumb between his teeth and bit through the flesh till it bled. The pain seemed to steady him. "Dienekes says that warriors advancing into battle must speak steadily and calmly to each other, each man encouraging his mate. We have to keep talking, Xeo."

The mind plays tricks in conditions of such extremity. I cannot tell how much I spoke aloud to Alexandros over the succeeding hours and how much simply swam before memory's eye as we labored endlessly toward the shore that refused to come closer.

I know I told him of Bruxieus. If my knowledge of Homer were worthy, all credit lay with this fortune-cursed man, sightless as the poet himself, and his fierce will that I and my cousin not grow to adulthood wild and unlettered in the hills.

"This man was mentor to you," Alexandros pronounced gravely, "as Dienekes is to me." He wished to hear more. What was it like to lose mother and father, to watch your city burn? How long did you and your cousin remain in the hills? How did you get food, and how protect yourself from the elements and wild beasts?

In gulps and snatches, I told him.

By our second summer in the mountains, Diomache and I had become such accomplished hunters that not only did we no longer need to descend to town or farm for food, we no longer wished to. We were happy in the hills. Our bodies were growing. We had meat, not once or twice a month or on festival occasions only, as in our fathers' houses, but every day, with every meal. Here was our secret. We had found dogs.

Two puppies to be exact, runts of a disowned litter. Arkadian shepherd's hounds we had discovered shivering and suckling-blind, abandoned by their mother, who had untimely given birth in midwinter. We named one Happy and the other Lucky, and they were. By spring both had legs to run, and by summer their instincts had made them hunters. With those dogs our hungry days were over. We could track and kill anything that breathed. We could sleep with both eyes closed and know that nothing could take us unawares. We became such a proficient hunting team, Dio and I and the hounds, that we actually passed up opportunities, came upon game and let it go with the benevolence of gods. We feasted like lords and viewed the sweating valley farmers and plodding highland goatherds with contempt.

Bruxieus began to fear for us. We were growing wild. Cityless. In evenings past, Bruxieus had recited Homer and made it a game how many verses we could repeat without a slip. Now this exercise took on a deadly earnestness for him. He was failing, we all knew it. He would not be with us much longer. Everything he knew, he must pass on.

Homer was our school, the *Iliad* and *Odyssey* the texts of our curriculum. Over and over Bruxieus had us recite the verses upon Odysseus' return, when, clad in rags and unrecognizable as the rightly lord of Ithaka, the hero of Troy seeks shelter at the hut of Eumaeus, the swineherd. Though Eumaeus has no idea that the traveler at his gate is his true king, and thinks him only another cityless beggar, yet out of respect to Zeus, who protects the wayfarer, he invites the wanderer kindly in and shares with him his humble fare.

This was humility, hospitality, graciousness toward the stranger; we must imbibe it, sink it deep within our bones. Bruxieus tutored us relentlessly in compassion, that virtue which he saw diminishing each day within our mountain-hardened hearts. We were made to recite the tent scene at the close of the *Iliad*, when Priam of Troy kneels before Achilles to kiss in supplication the hand of the man who has slain his sons, including the mightiest and dearest to him, Hektor, hero and protector of Ilium. Then Bruxieus grilled us upon it. What would we have done were we Achilles? Were we Priam? Was each man's action proper and pious in the eyes of the gods?

We must have a city, Bruxieus declared.

Without a city we were no better than the wild brutes we hunted and killed.

Athens.

There, Bruxieus insisted, was where Dio and I must go. The city of Athena was the only truly open city in Hellas, her freest and most civilized. The love of wisdom, *philosophia*, was esteemed in Athens beyond all other pursuits; the life of the mind was cultivated and honored, invigorated by a high culture of theater, music, poetry, architecture and the arts. Nor were the Athenians inferior to any city in Hellas in the practice of war.

The Athenians welcomed immigrants. A bright strong boy like me could take a trade, indenture himself in a shop. And Athens had a fleet. Even with my crippled hands I could pull an oar. With my skill with the bow I could become a *toxotes*, a marine archer, distinguish myself in war and exploit that service to advance my position.

Athens, too, was where Diomache must go. As a well-spoken freeborn, and with her blooming beauty, she could find service in a respected house and attract no shortage of admirers. She was at just the right age for a bride; it was far from a stretch to imagine her securing betrothal to a citizen. As the wife even of a *metik*, a resident alien, she could protect me, aid me in securing employment. And we would have each other.

As Bruxieus' strength diminished with the passing weeks, his conviction intensified that we follow his will in these matters. He made us swear that when his time came, we would go down from the hills and make for Attika, to the city of Athena.

In October of that second year Dio and I hunted one long cold-coming day and killed nothing. We tramped back into camp, grumbling at each other, anticipating a mean porridge of mixed pulse and mountain peas and, worse, the sight of Bruxieus, whose slackening constitution was each day becoming more painful to behold, maintaining that all was well with him; he did not need meat. We saw his smoke and watched the dogs bound up the hill as they loved to, sprinting to their friend to receive his hugs and homecoming roughhouse.

From the trail's turn below the camp we heard their barking. Not the usual squeals of play, but something keener, more insistent. Happy scrambled into view a hundred feet above us. Diomache looked at me and we both knew.

It took an hour to build Bruxieus' pyre. When his gaunt slave-branded body lay at last within the purifying flame, I lit a pitched arrow from the hollow above his heart and loosed it, flaming, with all my strength, arcing like a comet down the dark valley.

. . . then aged Nestor, peerless in
wisdom among the flowing-haired Achaeans,
laid himself down in the fullness of years
and closed his eyes as if in sleep,
slain by Artemis' gentle darts.

Ten dawns later Diomache and I stood at the Three-Cornered Way, on the frontier of Attika and Megara, where the Athens road breaks off to the east, the Sacred Road to Delphi and the west and the Corinthian southwest, to the Isthmus and the Peloponnese. No doubt we looked like the most savage pair of ragamuffins, barefoot, faces scorched by the sun, our long hair tied in horsetails behind us. Both of us carried daggers and bows, and the dogs loped beside us, as burr-coated and filthy as we were.

Traffic lumbered through the Three Corners, the predawn vehicles, freighters and produce waggons, firewood haulers, farm urchins on their way to market with their cheeses and eggs and sacks of onions, just as Dio and I had started out for Astakos that morning that seemed so long ago and yet was only two winters by the calendar. We halted at the crossroads and asked directions. Yes, a teamster pointed, Athens was that way, two hours, no more.

My cousin and I had barely spoken on the weeklong tramp down from the mountains. We were thinking of cities and what our new life would be like. I watched the other travelers when they passed on the highway, how they eyed her. The need was on her to be a woman. "I want babies," she said out of the blue, the last day as we marched. "I want a husband to care for and to care for me. I want a home. I don't care how humble, just someplace I can have a little garden, put flowers on the sill and make it pretty for my husband and our children." This was her way of being kind to me, of drawing a distance beforehand, so I would have time to absorb it. "Can you understand, Xeo?"

I understood. "Which dog do you want?"

"Don't be cross with me. I'm only trying to tell you how things are, and how they must be."

We decided she would take Lucky, and I would keep Happy.

"We can stay together in the city," she thought out loud as we walked. "We'll tell the people we're brother and sister. But you must understand, Xeo, if I find a decent man, someone who will treat me with respect . . ."

"I understand. You can stop talking now."

Two days before, a gentlewoman of Athens had passed us on the highway, traveling by coach with her husband and a merry party of friends and servants. The lady had been taken by the sight of this wild girl, Diomache, and insisted upon having her serving women bathe and oil her and dress her hair. She wanted to do mine too, but I wouldn't let them near me. Their whole party stopped by a shaded stream and entertained themselves with cakes and wine while the maids took Dio away and groomed her. When my cousin emerged, I didn't recognize her. The Athenian lady was beside herself with delight; she couldn't stop praising Dio's charms, nor anticipating the stir her blossoming beauty would create among the young bloods of the city. The lady insisted that Dio and I proceed straight to her husband's home the moment we arrived in Athens; she would look to our employment and the continuation of our schooling. Her manservant would await us at the Thriasian Gates. Just ask anyone.

We tramped on, that last long day. On the freighters that passed now we could read the words "Phaleron" and "Athens" scrawled on the destination bands of serried wine jars and crated merchandise. Accents were becoming Attic. We stopped to watch a troop of Athenian cavalry, out on a lark. Four seamen marched past, heading for the city, each balancing his oar upon his shoulder and carrying his strap and cushion. That would be me before long.

Always in the hills Dio and I had slept in each other's arms, not as lovers, but for warmth. These final nights on the road, she wrapped herself in her own cloak and took her sleep apart. At last we arrived at dawn before the Three Corners. I had stopped and was watching a freight waggon pass. I could feel my cousin's eyes upon me.

"You're not coming, are you?"

I said nothing.

She knew which fork I would be taking.

"Bruxieus will be angry with you," she said.

Dio and I had learned, from the dogs and on the hunt, how to communicate with just a look. I told her good-bye with my eyes and begged her to understand. She would be well cared for in this city. Her life as a woman was just beginning.

"The Spartans will be cruel to you," Diomache said. The dogs paced impatiently at our feet. They did not yet know that they were parting too. Dio took my hands in both of hers. "And will we never sleep in each other's arms again, cousin?"

It must have seemed a queer spectacle to the teamsters and farm boys passing, the sight of these two wild children embracing upon the roadside, with their slung bows and daggers and their cloaks bound into traveler's rolls upon their backs.

Diomache took her road and I took mine. She was fifteen. I was twelve.

How much of this I imparted to Alexandros in those hours in the water, I cannot say. Dawn had still not shown her face when I finished. We were clinging to a miserable floating spar, barely big enough to support one, and too exhausted to swim another stroke. The water was getting colder. *Hypothermia* gripped our limbs; I heard Alexandros cough and sputter, struggling for the strength to speak.

"We have to quit this spar. If we don't, we'll die."

My eyes strained toward the north. Peaks could be made out, but the shore itself remained invisible. Alexandros' cold hand clasped mine.

"Whatever happens," he swore, "I will not abandon you."

He let go of the spar. I followed.

An hour later we collapsed like Odysseus on a rock beach beneath a bawling rookery. We gulped fresh water from a cliff-wall spring, washed the salt from our hair and eyes and knelt in thanksgiving for our deliverance. For half the morning we slept like the dead. I climbed for eggs, which we wolfed raw from the shell, standing on the sand in the rags of our garments.

"Thank you, my friend," Alexandros said very quietly.

He extended his hand; I took it.

"Thank you too."

The sun stood near its zenith; our salt-stiff cloaks had dried upon our backs.

"Let's get moving," Alexandros said. "We've lost half a day."

E L E V E N

The battle took place on a dusty plain to the west of the city of Antirhion, within bowshot of the beach and immediately beneath the citadel walls. A desultory stream, the Akanathus, meandered across the plain, bisecting it at the midpoint. Perpendicular to this watercourse, along the seaward flank, the Antirhionians had thrown up a crude battle wall. Rugged hills sealed the enemy's left. A portion of the plain adjacent the wall was occupied by a maritime junkyard; rotting craft lay littered at all angles, extending halfway across the field, amid tumbledown work shacks and stinking mounds of debris squalled over by wheeling flocks of gulls. In addition the enemy had strewn boulders and driftwood to break up the flat over which Leonidas and his men must advance. Their own side, the foe's, had been cleared smooth as a schoolmaster's desk.

When Alexandros and I scurried breathless and tardy upon the site, the Spartan Skiritai rangers had just finished setting the enemy refuse yards ablaze. The armies yet stood in formation, two-fifths of a mile apart, with the burning hulks between them. All native merchantmen and fishing craft had been withdrawn by the enemy, either hauled to safety within the fortified portion of the anchorage or standing offshore beyond the invaders' reach. This did not deter the Skiritai from torching the wharves and warehouses of the harbor. The timbers of the ship sheds the rangers had saturated with naphtha; already they blazed in ruins to the waterline. The defenders of Antirhion, as Leonidas and the Spartans well knew, were militiamen, farmers and potters and fishermen, summertime soldiers like my father. The devastation of their harbor was meant to unnerve them, to dislocate their faculties unaccustomed to such sights and sear into their unseasoned senses the stink and scourge of coming slaughter. It was morning, about market time, and the shore breeze had gotten up. Black smoke from the careened wrecks began to obscure the field; the pitch and encaustic of their timbers blazed with fury, abetted by the wind, which turned the debris-pile smudge burns into howling bonfires.

Alexandros and I had secured a vantage along the landward bluff, no more than a furlong above the site where the massed formations must clash. The smoke was already gagging us. We made our way across the slope. Others had claimed the site before us, boys and older men of Antirhion, armed with bows, slings and missile weapons they meant to hurl down upon the Spartans as they advanced, but these light-armed forces had been cleared early by the Skiritai, whose comrades below would advance as always from their position of honor on the Lakedaemonian left. The rangers took possession of half the face, driving the enemy skirmishers back where their slings and shafts were outranged and could work no harm to the army.

Directly beneath us, an eighth of a mile away, the Spartans and their allies were marshaling into their ranks. Squires armed the warriors from the feet up, starting with the heavy oxhide soles which could tread over fire; then the bronze greaves, which the squires bent into place around the shins of their masters, securing them at the rear of the calf by the flex of the metal alone. We could see Alexandros' father, Olympieus, and the white beard of his squire, Meriones.

The troops bound their private parts next, accompanied by obscene humor as each warrior mock-solemnly saluted his manhood and offered a prayer that he and it would still be acquainted when the day was over.

This process of arming for battle, which the citizen-soldiers of other *poleis* had practiced no more than a dozen times a year in the spring and summer training, the Spartans had rehearsed and rerehearsed, two hundred, four hundred, six hundred times each campaigning season. Men in their fifties had done this ten thousand times. It was as second-nature to them as oiling or dusting their limbs before wrestling or dressing their long hair, which they, fitted now with the linen *spolas* corselet and bronze breastplate, proceeded to do with elaborate care and ceremony, assisting one another like a regiment of dandies preparing for a dress ball, all the while radiating an eerie presence of calm and nonchalance.

Finally the men scribed their names or signs upon *skytalides*, the improvised twig bracelets they called "tickets," which would distinguish their bodies should they, falling, be maimed too hideously to be identified. They used wood because it was valueless as plunder by the enemy.

Behind the massing men, the omens were being taken. Shields, helmets and foot-long spearpoints had been burnished to a mirror's gleam; they flashed brilliantly in the sun, investing the massed formation with the appearance of some colossal milling machine, made not so much of men as of bronze and iron.

Now the Spartans and Tegeates advanced to their positions in the line. First the Skiritai, on the left, forty-eight shields across and eight deep; next the Selassian Stephanos, the Laurel regiment, eleven hundred *perioikic* hoplites. To the right of these massed the six hundred heavy infantry of Tegea; then the *agema* of the Knights in the line's center, Polynikes prominent among them, thirty shields across and five deep, to fight around and protect the person of the king. Right of these, dressing their line, moved into place the Wild Olive regiment, a hundred and forty-four across, with the Panther battalion adjacent the Knights, then the Huntress with Olympieus in the forerank, and the Menelaion. On their right, already to their marks, massed the battalions of the Herakles, another hundred and forty-four across, with Dienekes clearly visible at the head of his thirty-six-man *enomotia*, dividing now into four nine-man files, or *stichoi*, anchoring the right. The total, excluding armed squires ranging as auxiliaries, exceeded forty-five hundred and extended wing to wing across the plain for nearly six hundred meters.

From our vantage, Alexandros and I could see Dekton, as tall and muscular as any of the warriors, unarmored in his altar-boy white, leading two she-goats swiftly out to Leonidas, who stood garlanded with the battle priests before the formation in readiness for the sacrifice. Two goats were needed in case the first bled inpropitiously. The commanders' postures, like those of the massed warriors, projected an air of absolute insouciance.

Across from these the Antirhionians and their Syrakusan allies had massed in their numbers, the same width as the Spartans but six or more shields deeper. The scrapyard hulks had now burned down to ashy skeletons, spewing a blanket of smoke across the field. Beyond these, the stones of the harbor sizzled black in the water, while the spikes of burned-black wharf timbers protruded from the flotsam-choked surface like burial stones; a clotted ash-colored haze obscured what was left of the waterfront.

The wind bore the smoke upon the enemy, upon the massed individuals, the sinews of whose knees and shoulders shivered and quaked beneath the weight of their unaccustomed armor, while their hearts hammered in their breasts and the blood sang in their ears. It took no diviner's gift to discern their state of agitation. "Watch their spearpoints," Alexandros said, pointing to the massed foe as they jostled and jockeyed into their ranks. "See them tremble. Even the plumes on their helmets are quaking." I looked. In the Spartan line the iron-bladed forest of eight-footers rose solid as a spike fence, each shaft upright and aligned, dressed straight as a geometer's line and none moving. Across among the enemy, shafts wove and wobbled; all save the Syrakusans in the center were misaligned in rank and file. Some shafts actually clattered against their neighbors', chattering like teeth.

Alexandros was tallying the battalions in the Syrakusans' ranks. He made their total at twenty-four hundred shields, with twelve to fifteen hundred mercenaries and an additional three thousand citizen militiamen from the city of Antirhion herself. The enemy's numbers totaled half again that of the Spartans'. It was not enough and the foe knew it.

Now the clamor began.

Among the enemy's ranks, the bravest (or perhaps the most fear-stricken) began banging the ash of their spear shafts upon the bronze bowls of their shields, creating a tumult of *pseudoandreia* which reverberated across and around the mountain-enclosed plain. Others reinforced this racket with the warlike thrusting of their spearpoints to heaven and the loosing of cries to the gods and shouts of threat and anger. The roar multiplied threefold, then five, and ten, as the enemy rear ranks and flankers picked the clamor up and contributed their own bluster and bronze-banging. Soon the entire fifty-four hundred were bellowing the war cry. Their commander thrust his spear forward and the mass surged behind him into the advance.

The Spartans had neither moved nor made a sound.

They waited patiently in their scarlet-cloaked ranks, neither grim nor rigid, but speaking quietly to each other words of encouragement and cheer, securing the final preparation for actions they had rehearsed hundreds of times in training and performed dozens and scores more in battle.

Here came the foe, picking up the pace of his advance. A fast walk. A swinging stride. The line was extending and fanning open to the right, "winging out" as men in fear edged into the shadow of the shield of the comrade on their right; already one could see the enemy ranks stagger and fall from alignment as the bravest surged forward and the hesitant shrank back.

Leonidas and the priests still stood exposed out front.

The shallow stream yet waited before the enemy. The foe's generals, expecting the Spartans to advance first, had formed their lines so that this watercourse stood midway between the armies. In the enemy's plan, no doubt, the sinuous defile of the river would disorder the Lakedaemonian ranks and render them vulnerable at the moment of attack. The Spartans, however, had outwaited them. As soon as the bronze-banging began, the enemy commanders knew they could not restrain their ranks longer; they must advance while their men's blood was up, or all fervor would dissipate and terror flood inevitably into the vacuum.

Now the river worked against the enemy. His foreranks descended into the defile, yet a quarter mile from the Spartans. Up they came, their already disordered dress and interval disintegrating further. They were again on the flat now, but with the river to their rear, the most perilous place it could be in the event of a rout.

Leonidas stood patiently watching, flanked by the battle priests and Dekton with his goats. The enemy was now a fifth of a mile off and accelerating the pace of his advance. The Spartans still hadn't moved. Dekton handed over the first she-goat's leash. We could see him glancing apprehensively as the plain began to thunder from the pounding of the enemy's feet and the air commenced to ring with their fear- and rage-inspired cries.

Leonidas performed the *sphagia,* crying aloud to Artemis Huntress and the Muses, then piercing with his own sword the throat of the sacrificial goat whose haunches he pinned from behind with his knees, his left hand hauling the beast's jaw exposed as the blade thrust through its throat. No eye in the formation failed to see the blood gush and spill into Gaia, maternal earth, splattering as it fell Leonidas' bronze greaves and painting crimson his feet in their oxhide battle soles.

The king turned, with the life-fled victim yet clamped between his knees, to face the Skiritai, Spartiates, *perioikoi* and Tegeates, who still held, patient and silent, in their massed ranks. He extended his sword, dark and dripping the blood of holy sacrifice, first heavenward toward the gods whose aid he now summoned, then around, toward the fast-advancing enemy.

"Zeus Savior and Eros!" his voice thundered, eclipsed but not unheard in that cacophonous din. "Lakedaemon!"

The *sarpinx* sounded "Advance!," trumpeters sustaining the ear-drum-numbing note ten paces after the men had stepped off, and now the pipers' wail cut through, shrill notes of their *auloi* piercing the melee like the cry of a thousand Furies. Dekton heaved the butchered goat and the live one over his shoulders and scampered like hell for the safety of the ranks.

To the beat the Spartans and their allies advanced, eight-footers at the upright, their honed and polished spearpoints flashing in the sun. Now the foe broke into an all-out charge. Leonidas, displaying neither haste nor urgency, fell into step in his place in the front rank as it advanced to envelop him, with the Knights flowing impeccably into position upon his right and left.

Now from the Lakedaemonian ranks rose the *paean,* the hymn to Castor ascending from four thousand throats. On the climactic beat of the second stanza,

Heaven-shining brother
Skyborne hero

the spears of the first three ranks snapped from the vertical into the attack.

Words cannot convey the impact of awe and terror produced upon the foe, any foe, by this seemingly uncomplex maneuver, called in Lakedaemon "spiking it" or "palming the pine," so simple to perform on the parade ground and so formidable under conditions of life and death. To behold it executed with such precision and fearlessness, no man surging forward out of control nor hanging back in dread, none edging right into the shadow of his rankmate's shield, but all holding solid and unbreakable, tight as the scales on a serpent's flank, the heart stopped in awe, the hair stood straight up upon the neck and shivers coursed powerfully the length of the spine.

As when some colossal beast, brought to bay by the hounds, wheels in his fury, bristling with rage and baring his fangs, and plants himself in the power and fearlessness of his strength, so did the bronze and crimson phalanx of the Lakedaemonians now snap as one into its mode of murder.

The left wing of the enemy, eighty across, collapsed even before the shields of their *promachoi*, the front-rankers, had come within thirty paces of the Spartans. A cry of dread rose from the throats of the foe, so primal it froze the blood, and then was swallowed in the tumult.

The enemy left broke from within.

This wing, whose advancing breadth had stood an instant earlier at forty-eight shields, abruptly became thirty, then twenty, then ten as panic flared like a gale-driven fire from terror-stricken pockets within the massed formation. Those in the first three ranks who turned in flight now collided with their comrades advancing from the rear. Shield rim caught upon shield rim, spear shaft upon spear shaft; a massive tangle of flesh and bronze ensued as men bearing seventy pounds of shield and armor stumbled and fell, becoming obstacles and impediments to their own advancing comrades. You could see the brave men stride on in the advance, crying out in rage to their countrymen as these abandoned them. Those who still clung to courage pushed past those who had forsaken it, calling out in outrage and fury, trampling the forerankers, or else, as valor deserted them too, jerked free and fled to save their own skins.

At the height of the foe's confusion the Spartan right fell upon them. Now even the bravest of the enemy broke. Why should a man, however valorous, stand and die while right and left, fore and rear, his fellows deserted him? Shields were flung, spears cast wildly to the turf. Half a thousand men wheeled on their heels and stampeded in terror. At that instant the center and right of the enemy's line crashed shields-on into the central corps of the Spartans.

That sound which all warriors know but which to Alexandros' and my youthful ears had been heretofore unknown and unheard now ascended from the clash and collision of the *othismos*.

Once, at home when I was a child, Bruxieus and I had helped our neighbor Pierion relocate three of his stacked wooden beehives. As we jockeyed the stack into place upon its new stand, someone's foot slipped. The stacked hives dropped. From within those stoppered confines yet clutched in our hands arose such an alarum, neither shriek nor cry, growl nor roar, but a thrum from the netherworld, a vibration of rage and murder that ascended not from brain or heart, but from the cells, the atoms of the massed *poleis* within the hives.

This selfsame sound, multiplied a hundred-thousandfold, now rose from the massed compacted crush of men and armor roiling beneath us on the plain. Now I understood the poet's phrase the "mill of Ares" and apprehended in my flesh why the Spartans speak of war as work. I felt Alexandros' fingernails dig into the flesh of my arm.

"Can you see my father? Do you see Dienekes?"

Dienekes waded into the rout below us; we could see his cross-crested "curry brush" at the right of the Herakles, in the fore of the third platoon. As disordered as were the ranks of the enemy, so held the Spartans' intact and cohesive. Their forerank did not charge wildly upon the foe, flailing like savages, nor did they advance with the stolid precision of the parade ground. Rather they surged, in unison, like a line of warships on the ram. I had never appreciated how far beyond the interleaved bronze of the *promachoi*'s shields the murderous iron of their eight-footers could extend. These punched and struck, overhand, driven by the full force of the right arm and shoulder, across the upper rim of the shield; not just the spears of the front-rankers but those of the second and even the third, extending over their mates' shoulders to form a thrashing engine that advanced like a wall of murder. As wolves in a pack take down the fleeing deer, so did the Spartan right fall upon the defenders of Antirhion, not in frenzied shrieking rage, lip-curled and fang-bared, but predator-like, cold-blooded, applying the steel with the wordless cohesion of the killing pack and the homicidal efficiency of the hunt.

Dienekes was turning them. Wheeling his platoon to take the enemy in flank. They were in the smoke now. It became impossible to see. Dust rose in such quantities beneath the churning feet of the men, commingling with the screen of smoke from the tindered hulks, that the entire plain seemed afire, and from the choking cloud arose that sound, that terrible indescribable sound. We could sense rather than see the Herakles *lochos*, directly beneath us where the dust and smoke were thinner. They had routed the enemy left; their front ranks now surged into the business of cutting down those luckless bastards who had fallen or been trampled or whose panic-unstrung knees could not find strength to bear them swiftly enough from their own slaughter.

On the center and right, along the whole line the Spartans and Syrakusans clashed now shield-to-shield, helmet-to-helmet. Amid the maelstrom we could catch only glimpses, and those primarily of the rear-rankers, eight deep on the Lakedaemonian side, twelve and sixteen deep on the Syrakusan, as they thrust the three-foot-wide bowls of their *hoplon* shields flush against the backs of the men in file before them and heaved and ground and shoved with all their strength, the soles of their footgear churning up trenches in the plain and slinging yet more dust into the already choking air.

No longer was it possible to distinguish individual men, or even units. We could see only the tidal surge and back-surge of the massed formations and hear without ceasing that terrible, blood-stilling sound.

As when a flood descends from the mountains and the wall of water crashes down the dry courses, smashing into the stone-founded stakes and woven brush of the husbandman's dam, so did the Spartan line surge against the massed weight of the Syrakusans. The dam's bulk, founded as firmly against the flood as fear and forethought may devise, seems itself to dig in and hold, to plant its force fiercely into the earth, and for long moments displays no sign of buckling. But then, as the anxious planter watches, before his eyes a surge begins to capsize one deep-sunken stake, another rush undermines a stacked stone revetment. Into each fraction of a breach, the force and weight of the downrushing wave thrusts itself irresistibly, hammering deeper, tearing and gouging, widening the gap and exploiting it with each successive ripping surge.

Now the dam wall which had cracked only a handbreadth splits to a foot and then a yard. The mass of the plunging flood builds upon itself, as ton upon ton plummets in from the courses above, adding its weight to the irresistible ever-mounting tide. Along the banked margins of the watercourse, sheets of earth calve into the churning, boiling torrent. So now did the Syrakusan center, pounded and hammered by the Tegeate heavy infantry, the king and the Knights and the massed battalions of the Wild Olive, begin to peel and founder.

The Skiritai had routed the enemy right. From the left the battalions of the Herakles rolled up the enemy flank. Each Syrakusan wingman forced to wheel to defend his unshielded side meant another drawn off from the forward push against the frontally advancing Spartans. The sound of the keening struggle seemed to rise for a moment, then went dead silent as desperate men summoned every reserve of valor from their shrieking, exhausted limbs. An eternity passed in the time it takes to draw a dozen breaths, and then, with the same sickening sound made by the mountain dam as it gives way unable to withstand the onrushing torrent, the Syrakusan line cracked and broke.

Now in the dust and fire of the plain the slaughter began.

A shout, half of joy and half of awe, sprung from the throats of the crimson-tunicked Spartans. Back the Syrakusan line fell, not in rout and riot as their allies the Antirhionians had done, but in still-disciplined squads and bunches, held yet by their officers, or whatever brave men had taken it upon themselves to act as officers, maintaining their shields to the fore and closing ranks as they retreated. It was no use. The Spartan front-rankers, men of the first five age-classes, were the cream of the city in foot speed and strength, none save the officers over twenty-five years old. Many, like Polynikes in the van among the Knights, were sprinters of Olympic and near-Olympic stature with garland after garland won in games before the gods.

These now, loosed by Leonidas and driven on by their own lust for glory, pressed home the sentence of steel upon the fleeing Syrakusans.

When the trumpeters had blown the *sarpinx* and its mind-numbing wail sounded the call to still the slaughter, even the rawest untrained eye could read the field like a book.

There, on the Spartan right where the Herakles regiment had routed the Antirhionians, one saw the turf unchurned and the field beyond littered with enemy shields and helmets, spears and even breastplates, flung aside by the stampeding foe in his flight. Bodies lay scattered at intervals, facedown, with the shameful gashes of death delivered upon their fleeing backs.

On the right where the stronger troops of the enemy had held longer against the Skiritai, the carnage spread thicker and more dense, the turf chewed more fiercely; along the battle wall which the foe had erected to anchor its flank, clumps of corpses could be seen, slain as they, trapped by their own wall, had struggled in vain to scale it.

Then the eye found the center, where the slaughter had achieved its most savage concentration. Here the earth was rent and torn as if a thousand span of oxen had assaulted it all day with the might of their hooves and the steel of their ploughs' deep-churning blades. The chewed-up dirt, dark with piss and blood, extended in a line three hundred meters across and a hundred deep where the feet of the contending formations had heaved and strained for purchase upon the earth. Bodies sprawled like a carpet upon the earth, mounded in places two and three deep. To the rear, across the plain where the Syrakusans had fled, and along the riven walls of the watercourse, more corpses could be seen in scattered perimeters manned by two and three, five and seven, where these in their flight had closed ranks and made their stand, doomed as castles of sand against the tide. They fell with wounds of honor, facing their Spartan foe, cut down from the front.

A wail arose from the hillsides where the watching Antirhionian skirmishers now looked down upon their comrades' vanquishment, while from the walls of the citadel itself wives and daughters keened in grief as must have Hekube and Andromache upon the battlements of Ilium.

The Spartans were hauling bodies off the stacks of the dead, seeking friend or brother, wounded and clinging yet to life. As each groaning foeman was flung down, a *xiphos* blade held him captive at the throat. "Hold!" Leonidas cried, motioning urgently to the trumpeters to resound the call to break off. "Attend them! Attend the enemy too!" he shouted, and the officers relayed the order up and down the line.

Alexandros and I, pounding pell-mell down the slope, had reached the plain now. We were on the field. I sprinted two strides behind as the boy ranged in mortal urgency among the blood- and gore-splattered warriors, whose flesh seemed yet to burn with the furnace heat of fury and whose breath appeared to our eyes to steam upon the air.

"Father!" Alexandros cried in the exigency of dread, and then, ahead, he glimpsed the cross-crested officer's helmet and then Olympieus himself, upright and unwounded. The expression of shock upon the *polemarch*'s face was almost comical when he beheld his son sprinting toward him out of the carnage. Man and boy embraced with wide-flung arms. Alexandros' fingers searched his father's corselet and breastplate, probing to confirm that all four limbs stood intact and no unseen punctures yet leaked dark blood.

Dienekes emerged from the still-seething throng; Alexandros flew into his arms. "Are you all right? Did they wound you?" I raced up. Suicide stood there beside Dienekes, "darning needle" javelins in hand, his own face sprayed with the sling of enemy blood. A knot of staring men had clustered; I saw at their feet the torn and motionless form of Meriones, Olympieus' squire.

"What are you doing here?" Olympieus demanded of his son, his tone turning to anger as he realized the peril the boy had put himself in. "How did you get here?"

Around us other faces reacted with equal wrath. Olympieus swatted his son, hard, across the skull. Then the boy saw Meriones. With a cry of anguish he dropped to his knees in the dirt beside the fallen squire.

"We swam," I announced. A heavy fist cuffed me, then another and another.

"What is this to you, a lark? You come to sightsee?"

The men were furious, as well they should have been. Alexandros, unhearing in his concern for Meriones, knelt over the man, who lay upon his back with a warrior crouched at each side, his helmetless head pillowed upon a *hoplon* shield and his bushy white beard clotted with blood, snot and sputum. Meriones, as a squire, had no cuirass to shield his breast; he had taken a Syrakusan eight-footer right through the bone of the chest. A seeping wound pooled blood into the bowl of his sternum; his tunic bunched up sodden with the dark, already clotting fluid; we could hear the hissing of air as his sucking lungs fought for breath and inhaled blood instead.

"What was he doing in the line?" Alexandros' voice, cracking with grief, demanded of the gathered warriors. "He's not supposed to be there!"

The boy barked for water. "Bearer!" he shouted, and shouted again. He tore his own tunic and, doubling the linen, pressed it as a dressing against his fallen friend's air-sucking chest. "Why don't you bind him?" his youth's voice cried to the encircled, gravely watching men. "He's dying! Can't you see he's dying?" He bellowed again for water, but none came. The men knew why, and now, watching, it became clear to Alexandros too, as it was already to Meriones.

"I've got one foot in the ferry, little old nephew," the ancient fighter's leaking air pipes managed to croak.

Life was ebbing fast from the warrior's eyes. He was, as I said, not a Spartan but a Potidaean, an officer in his own country, taken captive long years past and never permitted to see his home again. With an effort that was pitiful to behold, Meriones summoned strength to lift one hand, black with blood, and placed it gently upon the boy's. Their parts reversed, the dying man comforted the living youth.

"No happier death than this," his leaking lungs wheezed.

"You will go home," Alexandros vowed. "By all the gods, I will carry your bones myself."

Olympieus knelt now too, taking his squire's hand in his own. "Name your wish, old friend. The Spartans will bear you there."

The old man tried to speak but the pipes of his throat would not obey him. He struggled weakly to elevate his head; Alexandros restrained him, then gently cradled the veteran's neck and lifted it. Meriones' eyes glanced to the front and the sides where, amid the churned and liquid turf, the scarlet cloaks of other fallen warriors could be seen, each surrounded by a knot of comrades and brothers-in-arms. Then, with an effort which seemed to consume all his remaining substance, he spoke:

"Where these lie, plant me there. Here is my home. I ask none better."

Olympieus swore it. Alexandros, kissing Meriones' forehead, seconded the vow.

A dark peace seemed to settle upon the man's eyes. A moment passed. Then Alexandros lifted his own clear pure tenor in the Hero's Farewell:

> "*That* daimon *which* God
> *breathed into me at birth*
> *I with glad heart*
> *return now to Him.*"

In victory Dekton brought to Leonidas the rooster which would be sacrificed as thank-offering to Zeus and Nike. The boy himself was flushed with the triumph; his hands shook violently, wishing they had been permitted to hold a shield and spear and stand in the line of battle.

For my own part I could not stop staring about at the faces of the warriors I had known and watched in drill and training but until now had never looked upon in the blood and horror of battle. Their stature in my mind, already elevated beyond the men of any other city I had known, now rose close to that of heroes and demigods. I had witnessed the mere sight of them utterly rout the not-unvaliant Antirhionians, fighting before their own walls in defense of their homes and families, and overcome within minutes the crack troops of the Syrakusans and their mercenaries, trained and equipped by the tyrant Gelon's limitless gold.

Nowhere in all the field had these Spartans faltered. Now even in the hot blood aftermath their discipline maintained them chaste and noble, above all vaunting and boasting. They did not strip the bodies of the slain, as the soldiers of any other city would eagerly and gloatingly do, nor did they erect trophies of vainglory and conceit from the arms of the vanquished. Their austere thank-offering was a single cock, worth less than an obol, not because they disrespected the gods, but because they held them in awe and deemed it dishonorable to overexpress their mortal joy in this triumph that heaven had granted them.

I watched Dienekes, re-forming the ranks of his platoon, listing their losses and summoning aid for the wounded, the *traumatiai*. The Spartans have a term for that state of mind which must at all costs be shunned in battle. They call it *katalepsis*, possession, meaning that derangement of the senses that comes when terror or anger usurps dominion of the mind.

This, I realized now watching Dienekes rally and tend to his men, was the role of the officer: to prevent those under his command, at all stages of battle—before, during and after—from becoming "possessed." To fire their valor when it flagged and rein in their fury when it threatened to take them out of hand. That was Dienekes' job. That was why he wore the transverse-crested helmet of an officer.

His was not, I could see now, the heroism of an Achilles. He was not a superman who waded invulnerably into the slaughter, single-handedly slaying the foe by myriads. He was just a man doing a job. A job whose primary attribute was self-restraint and self-composure, not for his own sake, but for those whom he led by his example. A job whose objective could be boiled down to the single understatement, as he did at the Hot Gates on the morning he died, of "performing the commonplace under uncommonplace conditions."

The men were collecting their "tickets" now. These, to which I alluded earlier, are the wooden-twig bracelets tied with twine which each man makes for himself before battle, to identify his corpse if necessary in the aftermath. A man writes or scratches his name twice, once on each end of the twig, then breaks it down the middle. The "blood half" he ties with string around his left wrist and wears with him into battle; the "wine half" stays behind in a basket maintained with the train in the rear. The halves are broken off jaggedly on purpose, so that even if the blood name were effaced or defiled in some other way, its twin would still fit in an unequivocally recognizable manner. When the battle is over, each man retrieves his ticket. Those remaining unclaimed in the basket number and identify the slain.

When the men heard their names called and came forward to take their tickets, they could not stop their limbs from quaking.

All up and down the line, one beheld warriors clustering in groups of twos and threes as the terror they had managed to hold at bay throughout the battle now slipped its bonds and surged upon them, overwhelming their hearts. Clasping their comrades by the hand, they knelt, not from reverence alone, though that element was abundant, but because the strength had suddenly fled from their knees, which could no longer support them. Many wept, others shuddered violently. This was not regarded as effeminate, but termed in the Doric idiom *hesma phobou*, purging or "fear-shedding."

Leonidas strode among the men, letting all see that their king lived and moved unwounded. The men gulped greedily their ration of strong, heavy wine and made no shame to drink water as well and plenty of it. The wine went down fast and produced no effect whatever. Some of the men tried to dress their hair, as if thereby to induce a return to normalcy. But their hands trembled so badly they could not do it. Others would chuckle knowingly at the sight, the veteran warriors who knew better than to try; it was impossible to make the limbs behave, and the frustrated groomers would chuckle back, a dark laughter from hell.

When the tickets had all found their mates and been reclaimed by their owners, those pieces bereft within the basket identified the men who had been killed or were too badly wounded to come forward. These latter were claimed by brothers and friends, fathers and sons and lovers. Sometimes a man would take his own ticket, then another, and sometimes a third besides, weeping as he accepted them. Many returned to the basket, just to look in. In this way they could perceive the numbers of the lost.

This day it was twenty-eight.

His Majesty may set this number in comparison alongside the thousands slain in greater battles and perhaps judge it insignificant. But it seemed like decimation now.

There was a stir, and Leonidas emerged into view along the front of the assembled warriors. "Have you knelt?" He moved down the line, not declaiming like some proud monarch seeking satisfaction from the sound of his own voice, but speaking softly like a comrade, touching each man's elbow, embracing some, placing an arm around others, speaking to each warrior man-to-man, Peer-to-Peer, with no kingly condescension. Assemble, the word spread by murmur without needing to be spoken.

"Does every man have the halves of his ticket? Have your hands stopped shaking enough to fit them together?" He laughed and the men laughed with him. They loved him.

The victors formed up in no particular order, wounded and unwounded, plus squires and helots. They cleared a space for the king, those in front kneeling to allow their comrades behind to see and hear, while Leonidas himself strode informally up and down the line, presenting himself so that his voice would carry and his face be seen by all.

The battle priest, Olympieus in this case, held the basket up before the king. Leonidas took out each unclaimed ticket and read the name. He offered no eulogy. No word was spoken but the name. Among the Spartans, this alone is considered the purest form of consecration.

Alkamenes.

Damon.

Antalkides.

Lysandros.

On down the list.

The bodies, already retrieved by their squires from the field, would be cleansed and oiled; prayers would be offered and sacrifices made. Each of the fallen would be shrouded in his own cloak or that of a friend and interred here upon the site, beside his mates, beneath a mound of honor. Shield, sword, spear and armor alone would be borne home by his comrades, unless the omens declared it more honorable for his corpse to be restored and interred in Lakedaemon.

Leonidas now held up his own bracelet and slid the twin halves together into place. "Brothers and allies, I salute you. Gather, friends, and hear the words of my heart."

He paused for a moment, sober and solemn.

Then, when all stood silent, he spoke:

"When a man seats before his eyes the bronze face of his helmet and steps off from the line of departure, he divides himself, as he divides his 'ticket,' in two parts. One part he leaves behind. That part which takes delight in his children, which lifts his voice in the chorus, which clasps his wife to him in the sweet darkness of their bed.

"That half of him, the best part, a man sets aside and leaves behind. He banishes from his heart all feelings of tenderness and mercy, all compassion and kindness, all thought or concept of the enemy as a man, a human being like himself. He marches into battle bearing only the second portion of himself, the baser measure, that half which knows slaughter and butchery and turns the blind eye to quarter. He could not fight at all if he did not do this."

The men listened, silent and solemn. Leonidas at that time was fifty-five years old. He had fought in more than two score battles, since he was twenty; wounds as ancient as thirty years stood forth, lurid upon his shoulders and calves, on his neck and across his steel-colored beard.

"Then this man returns, alive, out of the slaughter. He hears his name called and comes forward to take his ticket. He reclaims that part of himself which he had earlier set aside.

"This is a holy moment. A sacramental moment. A moment in which a man feels the gods as close as his own breath.

"What unknowable mercy has spared us this day? What clemency of the divine has turned the enemy's spear one handbreadth from our throat and driven it fatally into the breast of the beloved comrade at our side? Why are we still here above the earth, we who are no better, no braver, who reverenced heaven no more than these our brothers whom the gods have dispatched to hell?

"When a man joins the two pieces of his ticket and sees them weld in union together, he feels that part of him, the part that knows love and mercy and compassion, come flooding back over him. This is what unstrings his knees.

"What else can a man feel at that moment than the most grave and profound thanksgiving to the gods who, for reasons unknowable, have spared his life this day? Tomorrow their whim may alter. Next week, next year. But this day the sun still shines upon him, he feels its warmth upon his shoulders, he beholds about him the faces of his comrades whom he loves and he rejoices in their deliverance and his own."

Leonidas paused now, in the center of the space left open for him by the troops.

"I have ordered pursuit of the foe ceased. I have commanded an end to the slaughter of these whom today we called our enemies. Let them return to their homes. Let them embrace their wives and children. Let them, like us, weep tears of salvation and burn thank-offerings to the gods.

"Let no one of us forget or misapprehend the reason we fought other Greeks here today. Not to conquer or enslave them, our brothers, but to make them allies against a greater enemy. By persuasion, we hoped. By coercion, in the event. But no matter, they are our allies now and we will treat them as such from this moment.

"The Persian!"

Suddenly Leonidas' voice rose, booming with such explosive emotion that those closest to him started from its sudden power. "The Persian is why we fought here today. His presence loomed, invisible, over the battlefield. He is why these tickets lie bereft in this basket. Why twenty-eight of the noblest men of the city will never again behold the beauty of her hills or dance again to her sweet music. I know many of you think I am half-cracked, I and Kleomenes the king before me." Laughter from the men. "I hear the whispers, and sometimes they're not such whispers." More laughter. "Leonidas hears voices the rest of us don't. He takes chances with his life in an unkingly manner and prepares for war against an enemy he has never seen and who many say will never come. All this is true . . ."

The men laughed again. "But hear this and never forget it: the Persian will come. He will come in numbers dwarfing those he sent four years ago when the Athenians and Plataeans defeated him so gloriously on the plain of Marathon. He will come tenfold, a hundredfold, mightier. And he will come soon."

Leonidas paused again, the heat in his breast making his face flush and his eyes burn with fever and conviction.

"Listen to me, brothers. The Persian is not a king as Kleomenes was to us or as I am to you now. He does not take his place with shield and spear amid the manslaughter, but looks on, safe, from a distance, atop a hill, upon a golden throne." Murmured jeers rose from the men's throats as Leonidas spoke this. "His comrades are not Peers and Equals, free to speak their minds before him without fear, but slaves and chattel. Each man, even the noblest, is deemed not an equal before God, but the King's property, counted no more than a goat or a pig, and driven into battle not by love of nation or liberty, but by the lash of other slaves' whips.

"This King has tasted defeat at the Hellenes' hands, and it is bitter to his vanity. He comes now to revenge himself, but he comes not as a man worthy of respect, but as a spoiled and petulant child, in its tantrum when a toy is snatched from it by a playmate. I spit on this King's crown. I wipe my ass on his throne, which is the seat of a slave and which seeks nothing more noble than to make all other men slaves.

"Everything I have done as king and everything Kleomenes has performed before me, every enemy courted, every confederation forged, every weak-kneed ally brought to heel, has been for this single event: the day when Darius, or one of his sons, returns to Hellas to pay us out."

Leonidas lifted now the basket which held the tickets of the fallen.

"That is why these, better men than ourselves, gave their lives here today, why they consecrated this earth with their heroes' blood. This is the meaning of their sacrifice. They have dumped their guts not in this piss-puddle war we fought today, but in the first of many battles in the greater war which God in heaven and all of you in your hearts know is coming. These brothers are heroes of that war, which will be the gravest and most calamitous in history.

"On that day," and Leonidas gestured out over the gulf, to Antirhion below and Rhion across the channel, "on that day when the Persian brings his multitudes against us via this strait, he will find not clear passage and paid-for friends, but enemies united and implacable, Hellene allies who will sally to meet him from both shores. And if he chooses some other route, if his spies report what awaits him here and he elects another passage, some other site of battle where land and sea play to our greater advantage, it will be because of what we did today, because of the sacrifice of these our brothers whose bodies we inter now within a hero's grave.

"Therefore I have not waited for the Syrakusans and the Antirhionians, our enemies this day, to send their heralds to us as is customary to entreat our permission to retrieve the bodies of their slain. I have dispatched our runners to them first, offering them truce without rancor, with generosity. Let our new allies reclaim unprofaned the armor of their fallen, let them recover undefiled the bodies of their husbands and sons.

"Let those we spared this day stand beside us in line of battle on that day when we teach the Persian once and for all what valor free men can bring to bear against slaves, no matter how vast their numbers or how fiercely they are driven on by their child-king's whip."

BOOK THREE

ROOSTER

TWELVE

At this point in the recounting of the tale, an unfortunate incident occurred regarding the Greek Xeones. A subordinate of the Royal Surgeon, during the ongoing attendance upon the captive's wounds, unwittingly informed the fellow of the fate of Leonidas, the Spartan king and commander at Thermopylae, after the battle at the Hot Gates, and what sacrilege, to the Greek's eyes, His Majesty's troops had performed upon the corpse after it was recovered from the heaps of the dead following the slaughter. The prisoner had hitherto been in ignorance of this.

The man's outrage was immediate and extreme. He forthwith refused to speak any further on the subjects to hand and in fact demanded of his immediate captors, Orontes and the officers of the Immortals, that they put him also to death, and at once. The man Xeones stood clearly in a state of extreme consternation over the beheading and crucifixion of the body of his king. All arguments, threats and blandishments failed to dislodge him from this posture of grief.

It was clear to the captain Orontes that, should His Majesty be informed of the prisoner's defiance, however much He Himself desired to hear the continuance of the man's tale, the captive Xeones must, for his insolence to the Royal Person, be put to death. The captain, truth to tell, feared as well for his own head and those of his officers, should His Majesty be frustrated by the Greek's intransigence in His desire to learn all He could about the Spartan enemy.

Orontes had become, through various informal exchanges with the fellow Xeones during the course of the interrogation, something of a confidant and even, if the word's meaning may be stretched to this point, a friend. He sought upon his own initiative to soften the captive's stance. To that end he attempted to make clear to the Greek the following:

That the physical desecration performed upon the corpse of Leonidas was regretted keenly by His Majesty almost as soon as He had ordered it.

The actual command had been issued amid the grief of the battle's aftermath, when His Majesty's blood was raging over the loss before his own eyes of thousands, by some counts as many as twenty thousand, of the Empire's finest warriors slain by the troops of Leonidas, whose defiance of God Ahura Mazda's will could only be perceived through Persian eyes as an outrage against heaven. In addition two of His Majesty's own brothers, Habrocomes and Hyperanthes, and more than thirty royal kinsmen had been sent down to the house of death by the Spartan foe and their allies.

Moreover, the captain appended, the mutilation of Leonidas' corpse was, when viewed in the apposite light, a testament to the respect and awe in which the Spartan king was held by His Majesty, for against no other commander of the enemy had He ever ordered such extreme and, to Hellenic eyes, barbarous retribution.

The man Xeones remained unmoved by these arguments and repeated his desire to be dispatched at once. He refused all food and water. It seemed that the telling of his tale would be broken off here and not resumed.

It was at this point, fearing that the situation could not be kept from His Majesty much longer, that Orontes sought out Demaratos, the deposed king of Sparta residing within the court as a guest exile and advisor, and urged his intercession. Demaratos, responding, betook himself in person to the Royal Surgeon's tent and there spoke alone with the captive Xeones for more than an hour. When he emerged, he informed the captain Orontes that the man had experienced a change of heart and was now willing to continue the interrogation.

The crisis had passed. "Tell me," the captain Orontes inquired, much relieved, "what argument and persuasion did you employ to effect this turnabout?"

Demaratos replied that of all the Hellenes the Spartans were acknowledged the most pious and held the gods most in awe. He declared it his own observation that in this regard among the Lakedaemonians, the lesser rankers and those in service, particularly the outlanders of the captive Xeones' station, were almost without exception, in Demaratos' phrase, "more Spartan than the Spartans."

Demaratos had, he said, appealed to the fellow's respect for the gods, specifically Phoebus Apollo, for whom the man clearly evinced the most profound reverence. He suggested that the prisoner pray and sacrifice to determine, as best he could, the god's will. For, he told the fellow, surely the Far Striker has assisted your tale thus far. Why would he now order its discontinuance? Did the man Xeones, Demaratos asked, place himself above the immortal gods, presuming to know their unknowable will and stopper their words at his own whim?

Whatever answer the captive received from his gods, it apparently coincided with the counsel proposed to him by Demaratos.

We picked up the tale again on the fourteenth day of the month of Tashritu.

Polynikes was awarded the prize of valor for Antirhion.

This was his second, achieved at the unheard-of age of twenty-four years. No other Peer save Dienekes had been decorated twice, and that not until he was nearly forty. For his heroism Polynikes was appointed Captain of the Knights; it would be his honor to preside over the nomination of the Three Hundred king's companions for the following year. This supremely coveted distinction, coupled with his sprinter's crown from Olympia, established Polynikes as a beacon of fame whose brilliance shone forth far beyond the borders of Lakedaemon. He was perceived as a hero of all Hellas, a second Achilles, who stood now upon the threshold of unbounded and undying glory.

To Polynikes' credit, he refused to become puffed up over this. If any swelling of the head could be discerned, it manifested itself only in a more fiercely applied self-discipline, though this zeal for virtue, as events were to tell, could spill over into excess when applied to others less spectacularly gifted than himself.

As for Dienekes, he had only been honored with inclusion in the company of Knights once, when he was twenty-six, and had declined respectfully all subsequent nominations. He liked the obscurity of a platoon commander, he said. He felt more himself among the ranks. It was his conviction that he could contribute best by leading men directly, and that only to a certain number. He refused all attempts to promote him beyond the platoon level. "I can't count past thirty-six" was his standard disclaimer. "Beyond that, I get dizzy."

I will add, from my own observation, that Dienekes' gift and vocation, more so even than warrior and officer, was that of teacher.

As all born teachers, he was primarily a student.

He studied fear, and its opposite.

But to pursue such an excursus at this time would lead us astray from the narrative. To resume at Antirhion:

On the return passage to Lakedaemon, as punishment for accompanying Alexandros in following the army, I was removed from that youth's company and forced to march in the dust at the rear of the train, with the sacrificial herd and my half-helot friend Dekton. This Dekton had acquired at Antirhion a new nickname—Rooster—from the event that, immediately following the battle, he had delivered the thank-offering cock to Leonidas half-strangled in his own fists, so frenzied was he with excitement from the battle and his own frustrated desire to have participated in it. The name stuck. Dekton *was* a rooster, bursting with barnyard belligerence and ready to scrap with anything, his own size or three times bigger. This new tag was picked up by the whole army, who began to regard the boy as something of a good-luck talisman, a mascot of victory.

This of course galled Dekton's pride beyond even its accustomed bellicose state. In his eyes the name embodied condescension, yet another reason to hate his masters and to despise his own position in their service. He declared me a blockhead for following the army.

"You should've flown," he hissed sidelong as we trudged in the choking flyblown wake of the train. "You deserve every lash you get, not for what they blame you for, but for not drowning that hymn-singer Alexandros when you had the chance—and churning your shanks straight to the temple of Poseidon." He meant that sanctuary in Tainaron to which runaways could flee and be granted asylum.

My loyalty to the Spartans was rebuked with scorn and ridicule by Dekton. I had been placed in this boy's power shortly after fate had brought me to Lakedaemon, two years earlier, when both he and I were twelve. His family worked the estate of Olympieus, Alexandros' father, who was related to Dienekes via his wife, Arete. Dekton himself was a half-breed helot, illegitimately sired, so rumor had it, by a Peer whose gravestone,

Idotychides
in war at Mantinea

lay along the Amyklaian Way, opposite the line of *syssitia*, the common messes.

This half-Spartiate lineage did nothing to advance Dekton's status. He was a helot and that was it. If anything, the youths his age, and the Peers even more so, regarded him with extra suspicion, reinforced by the fact of Dekton's exceptional strength and athletic skill. At fourteen he was built like a grown man and nearly as strong.

He would have to be dealt with someday, and he knew it.

I myself had been in Lakedaemon half a year then, a wild boy just down from the hills and consigned, since it was safer than risking ritual pollution by killing me, to the meanest of farm labor. I proved such an infuriating failure at this that my helot masters took their complaints directly to their lord, Olympieus. This gentleman took pity on me, perhaps for my free birth, perhaps because I had come into the city's possession not as a captive, but of my own uncoerced will.

I was reassigned to the goat and kid detail.

I would be a herd boy for the sacrificial animals, minding the train of beasts that serviced the morning and evening ceremonies and followed the army into the field for training exercises.

The head boy was Dekton. He hated me from the first. He saved his most blistering scorn for my tale, imprudently confessed, of receiving counsel directly from Apollo Far Striker. Dekton thought this hilarious. Did I think, did I dream, did I imagine, that an Olympian god, scion of Zeus Thunderer, protector of Sparta and Amyklai, guardian of Delphi and Delos and who knows how many other *poleis*, would piss away his valuable time swooping down to chat in the snow with a cityless *heliokekaumenos* like me? In Dekton's eyes I was the dumbest mountain-mad yokel he had ever seen.

He appointed me the herd's Chief Ass Wiper. "You think I'm going to get my back striped for handing the king a shit-caked goat? Get in there, make that puckerhole spotless!"

Dekton never missed an occasion to humiliate me. "I'm educating you, Bung Boy. These assholes are your academy. Today's lesson is the same as yesterday's: In what does the life of a slave consist? It is in being debased and degraded and having no option but to endure it. Tell me, my freeborn friend. How do you like it?"

I would make no response, but simply obey. He scorned me the more for that.

"You hate me, don't you? You'd like nothing better than to chop me down. What's stopping you? Give it a try!" He stood before me one afternoon when we and the other boys were grazing the animals in the king's pasture. "You've lain awake planning it," Dekton taunted me. "You know just how you'd do it. With that Thessalian bow of yours, if your masters would let you near it. Or with that dagger you keep hidden between the boards in the barn. But you won't kill me. No matter how much disgrace I heap on your head, no matter how miserably I degrade you."

He picked up a rock and threw it at me, point-blank, striking me so hard in the chest it almost knocked me over. The other helot boys clustered to watch. "If it was fear that stopped you, I could respect that. It would at least show sense." Dekton slung another stone that struck me in the neck, drawing blood. "But your reason is more senseless than that. You won't harm me for the same reason you won't hurt one of these miserable, stinking beasts." With that, he kicked a goat furiously in the gut, bowling it over and sending it bawling. "Because it will offend *them*." He gestured with bitter contempt across the plain to the gymnastic fields, where three platoons of Spartiates were going through spear drill in the sun. "You won't touch me because I'm their property, just like these shit-eating goats. I'm right, aren't I?"

My expression answered for me.

He glared at me with contempt. "What are they to you, moron? Your city was sacked, they say. You hate the Argives and think these sons of Herakles"—he indicated the drilling Peers, spitting the final phrase with sarcastic loathing—"are their enemies. Wake up! What do you think *they* would have done had they sacked your city? The same and worse! As they did to my country, to Messenia and to me. Look at my face. Look at your own. You've fled slavery only to become lower than a slave yourself."

Dekton was the first person I had ever met, man or boy, who had absolutely no fear of the gods. He didn't hate them as some do, or mock their antics as I had heard the impious freethinkers did in Athens and Corinth. Dekton didn't grant their existence at all. There were no gods, it was as simple as that. This struck me with a kind of awe. I kept watch, waiting for him to be felled by some hideous blow of heaven.

Now, on the road home from Antirhion, Dekton (I should say Rooster) continued the harangue I had heard from him so many times before. That the Spartans had gulled me like they gull everyone; that they exploit their chattel by permitting them the crumbs off their table, elevating one slave a fraction above another and turning each individual's miserable hunger for station into the invisible bonds which held them in chains and in thrall.

"If you hate your masters so much," I asked him, "why were you hopping like a flea during the battle, so frantic to get into the fight yourself?"

Another factor, I knew, added to Rooster's frustration. He had just got his barnfriend (as the helot boys called their illicit wenches) pregnant. Soon he would be a father. How could he flee then? He would not abandon a child, nor could he make his getaway lugging a girl and a babe.

He stomped along, cursing one of the other herd boys who had let two goats stray, chasing the urchin back after these stragglers behind the herd. "Look at me," he growled as he fell again into step beside me. "I can run as fast as any of these Spartan dick-strokers. I'm fourteen but I'll fight any twenty-year-old man-to-man and bring him down. Yet here I trudge, in this fool's nightshirt, holding the leash on a goat."

He vowed he would steal a *xyele* and cut a Spartan's throat one day.

I told him he must not speak like this in my hearing.

"What'll you do? Report me?"

I wouldn't and he knew it.

"But by the gods," I swore to him, "raise your hand once against them, any one of them, and I'll kill you."

Rooster laughed. "Pluck a sharp stick from the roadside and drive it into your sockets, my friend. It couldn't make you any blinder than you are already."

The army reached the frontier at Oion at nightfall of the second day, and Sparta herself twelve hours later. Runners had preceded the troops; the city had known for two days the identities of the wounded and the slain. Funeral games stood already in preparation; they would be celebrated within the fortnight.

That evening and the following day were consumed in decamping the battle train: cleaning and refitting weapons and armor, reshafting spears which had been shivered in combat and rewrighting the oaken hubs of the *hoplon* shields, disassembling and storing the riggings of the waggons, tending to the pack and draught animals, making sure each beast was properly watered and groomed and dispersed with their helot teamsters to their various *kleroi*, the farmsteads they worked. That second night, the Peers of the train at last returned to their messes.

This was customarily a solemn evening, in the aftermath of a battle, when fallen comrades were memorialized, acts of valor recognized and dishonorable conduct censured, when errors were reviewed and turned to instruction and the grave capital of battle stored up against future need.

The messes of the Peers are customarily havens of respite and confidentiality, sanctuaries within which all converse is privileged and private. Here after the long day friends may let down their hair among friends, speak as gentlemen the truths of their hearts and even, though never to excess, embrace the mellowing comfort of a bowl or two of wine.

This night, however, was not one for ease or conviviality. The souls of the twenty-eight perished hung heavily over the city. The secret shame of the warrior, the knowledge within his own heart that he could have done better, done more, done it more swiftly or with less self-preserving hesitation; this censure, always most pitiless when directed against oneself, gnawed unspoken and unrelieved at the men's guts. No decoration or prize of valor, not victory itself, could quell it entire.

"Well," Polynikes called the youth Alexandros forward and addressed him sternly, "how did you like it?"

He meant war.

To be there, to see it raw and entire.

The evening stood now well advanced. The hour of the *epaikla* had expired, that second course of the meal at which game meat and wheaten bread may be contributed, and now the sixteen Peers of the Deukalion mess settled, hunger satisfied, upon their hardwood couches. Now the lads who stood-to the mess for their instruction might be summoned and roasted upon the griddle.

Alexandros was made to stand forth before his elders at the position of boy's attention, hands tucked from sight beneath the folds of his cloak, eyes glued to the floor as not yet worthy of rising to meet a Peer's full in the face.

"How did you enjoy the battle?" Polynikes queried.

"It made me sick," Alexandros replied.

Under the interrogation the boy confessed that he had been unable to sleep since, neither aboard ship nor on the march home. If he closed his eyes even for a moment, he declared, he saw again with undiminished horror the scenes of slaughter, particularly the death spasm of his friend Meriones. His compassion, he acknowledged, was elicited as much by those casualties of the enemy as for the fallen heroes of his own city. Pressed hard upon this point, the boy declared the slaughter of war "barbarous and unholy."

"Barbarous and unholy, is it?" responded Polynikes, darkening with anger.

The Peers in their messes are encouraged, when they deem it useful for the instruction of youth, to single out one lad, or even another Peer, and abuse him verbally in the most stern and pitiless fashion. This is called *arosis*, harrowing. Its purpose, much like the physical beatings, is to inure the senses to insult, to harden the will against responding with rage and fear, the twin unmanning evils of which that state called *katalepsis*, possession, is comprised. The prized response, the one the Peers look for, is humor. Deflect defamation with a joke, the coarser the better. Laugh in its face. A mind which can maintain its lightness will not come undone in war.

But Alexandros possessed no gift for the wisecrack. It wasn't in him. All he could do was answer in his clear pure voice with the most excruciating candor. I watched him from my service station at the left of the mess entrance, beneath the carven plaque—

Exo tes thyras ouden,

"Out this door nothing"—meaning no word spoken within these precincts may be repeated elsewhere.

It was a form of high courage which Alexandros displayed, to stand up to the Peers' hammering without a joke or a lie. At any time during a harrowing, the object boy may signal and call a stop. This is his right under the laws of Lykurgus. Pride, however, prevented Alexandros from exercising this option, and everyone knew it.

You wanted to see war, Polynikes began. What did you imagine it would be?

Alexandros was required to answer in the Spartan style, at once, with extreme brevity.

Your eyes were horror-stricken, your heart aggrieved at the sight of the manslaughter. Answer this:

What did you think a spear was for?

A shield?

A *xiphos* sword?

Questions of this kind would be put to the boy not in a harsh or abusive tone, which would have been easier to bear, but coldly, rationally, demanding a concisely expressed reasoned response. Alexandros was made to describe the wounds an eight-footer could produce and the types of deaths that would ensue. Should an overhand thrust be aimed at the throat or the chest? If the tendon of a foeman's calf be severed, should you pause to finish him off or press forward with the advance? If you plunge a spear into the groin above a man's testicles, should it be pulled straight out or ripped upward, blade vertical, to eviscerate the man's bowels? Alexandros' face flushed, his voice quaked and broke. Would you like to stop, boy? Is this instruction too much for you?

Answer concisely:

Can you envision a world without war?

Can you imagine clemency from an enemy?

Describe the condition of Lakedaemon without her army, without her warriors, to defend her.

Which is better, victory or defeat?

To rule or be ruled?

To make a widow of the enemy's wife or to have one's own wife widowed?

What is the supreme virtue of a man? Why? Whom of all in the city do you admire most? Why?

Define the word "mercy." Define "compassion." Are these the virtues of war or of peace? Of men or of women? Are they virtues at all?

Of the Peers who harrowed Alexandros this evening, Polynikes did not on the surface seem the most relentless or display the harshest severity. He did not lead the *arosis*, nor was his interrogation overtly cruel or malicious. He just wouldn't let it stop. In the tone of the other men's voices, no matter how ruthlessly they grilled Alexandros, resided at bottom the unspoken fundament of inclusion. Alexandros was of their blood, he was one of them; everything they did tonight and every other night was not to break his spirit or crush him like a slave, but to make him stronger, to temper his will and render him more worthy of being called warrior, as they were, of taking his place as a Spartiate and a Peer.

Polynikes' harrowing was different. There was something personal about it. He hated the boy, though it was impossible to guess why. What made it even more painful, to watch as it must have been to endure, was Polynikes' supreme physical beauty.

In every aspect of his person, face as well as physique, the Knight was formed as flawlessly as a god. Naked in the *Gymnasion*, even alongside scores of youths and warriors blessed in comeliness and elevated by their training to the peak of condition, Polynikes stood out, without equal, surpassing all others in symmetry of form and faultlessness of physical structure. Clothed in white robes for the Assembly, he shone like Adonis. And armed for war, with the bronze of his shield burnished, his scarlet cloak across his shoulders and the horsehair-crested helmet of a Knight pushed back upon his brow, he shone forth, peerless as Achilles.

To watch Polynikes train on the Big Ring, in preparation for the Games at Olympia or Delphi or Nemea, to behold him in the pastel light of day's end when he and the other sprinters had finished their distance work and now, under the eyes of their trainers, donned their racing armor for the final dressed sprints, even the most hardened Peers, training in the boxing oval or the wrestling pits, would pull up from their regimens and watch.

Four runners regularly trained with Polynikes: two brothers, Malineus and Gorgone, both victors at Nemea in the *diaulos* sprint; Doreion the Knight, who could outrun a racehorse over sixty meters; and Telamonias the boxer and *enomotarch* of the Wild Olive regiment.

The five would take their marks and a trainer would clap the start. For thirty meters, sometimes as long as fifty, the elite field remained a pack of straining bronze and flesh, laboring beneath the weight of their harness, and for a span of heartbeats the watching Peers would think, maybe this once, maybe this singular time, one will best him. Then from the fore, as the runners' accelerating power began to break the bonds of their burdens, Polynikes' churning shield would emerge, twenty pounds of oak and bronze sustained upon the pumping flesh and sinew of his left forearm; you saw his helmet flash; his polished greaves extended next, flying like the winged sandals of Hermes himself, and then, with a force and power so magnificent they stopped the heart, Polynikes would catapult out of the pack, blazing with such impossible swiftness that he seemed to be naked, even winged, and not belabored by the poundage upon his arm and across his back. Around the turning pole he flew. Daylight burst between him and his pursuers. He vaulted forward to the finish, four hundred meters total, no longer in his mind competing with these lesser fellows, these pedestrian mortals, any one of whom in another city would have been the object of adoration, mobbed by throngs of admirers, but who here, against this invincible runner, were doomed to eat dust and like it. This was Polynikes. No one could touch him. He possessed in every pore those blessings of feature and physique which the gods allow to combine in a single mortal only once in a generation.

Alexandros was beautiful too. Even with the broken nose Polynikes had gifted him with, his physical perfection approached that of the peerless runner. Perhaps this, in some way, lay at the root of the hatred the man felt for the boy. That he, Alexandros, whose joy lay in the chorus and not on the athletic field, was unworthy of this gift of beauty; that it, in him, failed to reflect the manly virtue, the *andreia*, which it in Polynikes so infallibly proclaimed.

My own suspicion was that the runner's animus was inflamed further by the favor Alexandros had found in Dienekes' eyes. For of all the men in the city with whom Polynikes competed in virtue and excellence, he resented most my master. Not so much for the honors Dienekes had been granted by his peers in battle, for Polynikes, like my master, had been awarded the prize of valor twice, and he was ten or twelve years younger.

It was something else, some less obvious aspect of character which Dienekes possessed and which the city honored him by recognizing, instinctively, without prompting or ceremony. Polynikes saw it in the way the young boys and girls joked with Dienekes when he passed their *sphairopaedia*, the ball-playing fields, during the noonday break. He caught it in the tilt of a smile from a matron and her maids at the springs or an old woman passing in the square. Even the helots granted my master a fondness and respect that were withheld from Polynikes, for all the heaps of honors that were his in other quarters. It galled him. Mystified him. He, Polynikes, had even produced two sons, while Dienekes' issue were all female, four daughters who, unless Arete could produce a son, would extinguish his line altogether, while Polynikes' strapping swift lads would one day be warriors and men. That Dienekes wore the respect of the city so lightly and with such self-effacing wit was even more bitter to Polynikes.

For the runner saw in Dienekes neither beauty of form nor fleetness of foot. Instead he perceived a quality of mind, a power of self-possession, which he himself, for all the gifts the gods had lavished upon him, could not call his own. Polynikes' courage was that of a lion or an eagle, something in the blood and the marrow, which summoned itself out of its own preeminence, without thought, and gloried in its instinctual supremacy.

Dienekes' courage was different. His was the virtue of a man, a fallible mortal, who brought valor forth out of the understanding of his heart, by the force of some inner integrity which was unknown to Polynikes. Was this why he hated Alexandros? Was it why he had splintered the boy's nose that evening of the eight-nighter? Polynikes sought to break more than the youth's face now. Here in the mess he wanted to crack him, to see him come apart.

"You look unhappy, *pais*. As if the prospect of battle held for you no promise of joy."

Polynikes ordered Alexandros to recite the pleasures of war, to which the boy responded by rote, citing the satisfactions of shared hardship, of triumph over adversity, of camaraderie and *philadelphia*, love of one's comrades-in-arms.

Polynikes frowned. "Do you feel pleasure when you sing, boy?"

"Yes, lord."

"And when you flirt around with that trollop Agathe?"

"Yes, lord."

"Then imagine the pleasure that awaits you, when you clash in line of battle, shield-to-shield with an enemy burning to kill you, and you instead slay him. Can you imagine that ecstasy, you little shitworm?"

"The *pais* is trying, lord."

"Let me assist you. Close your eyes and picture it. Obey me!"

Polynikes was keenly aware of the torment this was causing Dienekes, who held himself controlled and impassive upon his bare couch, just two places down.

"To plunge a spear, blade-deep, into a man's guts is like fucking, only better. You like to fuck, don't you?"

"The boy doesn't know, lord."

"Don't toy with me, you twittering sparrow."

Alexandros, on his feet for an hour by this time, had steeled himself utterly. He answered his tormentor's questions, frozen at attention, eyes riveted to the dirt, ready in his guts to endure anything.

"Killing a man is like fucking, boy, only instead of giving life you take it. You experience the ecstasy of penetration as your warhead enters the enemy's belly and the shaft follows. You see the whites of his eyes roll inside the sockets of his helmet. You feel his knees give way beneath him and the weight of his faltering flesh draw down the point of your spear. Are you picturing this?"

"Yes, lord."

"Is your dick hard yet?"

"No, lord."

"What? You've got your spear in a man's guts and your dog isn't stiff? What are you, a woman?"

At this point the Peers of the mess began rapping their knuckles upon the hardwood, an indication that Polynikes' instruction was going too far. The runner ignored this.

"Now picture with me, boy. You feel the foe's beating heart upon your iron and you rip it forth, twisting as you pull. A sensation of joy surges up the ash of your spear, through your hand and along your arm up into your heart. Are you enjoying this yet?"

"No, lord."

"You feel like God at that moment, exercising the right only He and the warrior in combat may experience: that of dealing death, of loosing another man's soul and sending it down to hell. You want to savor it, to twist the blade deeper and pull the man's heart and guts out upon the iron point of your spear, but you can't. Tell me why."

"Because I must move on and slay the next man."

"Are you going to weep now?"

"No, lord."

"What will you do when the Persians come?"

"Slay them, lord."

"What if you stand on my right in line of battle? Will your shield protect me?"

"Yes, lord."

"What if I advance, defended by the shadow of your shield? Will you hold it high at port before me?"

"Yes, lord."

"Will you bring down your man?"

"I will."

"And the next?"

"Yes."

"I don't believe you."

At this the Peers rapped more vigorously with their knuckles upon the tables. Dienekes spoke. "This is no longer instruction, Polynikes. This is malice."

"Is it?" the runner answered, not deigning to look in the direction of his rival. "We'll inquire of its object. Have you had enough, you psalm-singing wad of shit?"

"No, lord. The boy begs the Peer to continue."

Dienekes stepped in. Gently, with compassion, he addressed the youth, his protege. "Why do you tell the truth, Alexandros? You could lie, like every other boy, and swear you reveled in the witnessing of slaughter, you savored the sight of limbs cleaved and men maimed and murdered within the jaws of war."

"I thought of that, lord. But the company would see through me."

"You're fucking right we would," confirmed Polynikes. He heard the anger in his own voice and brought it swiftly under control. "However, out of deference to my esteemed comrade"—here he turned with a mock-courteous bow to Dienekes—"I will address my next question not to this child, but to the mess as a whole." He paused, then indicated the boy at attention before them. "Who will stand with this woman on his right in the line of battle?"

"I will," Dienekes answered without hesitation.

Polynikes snorted.

"Your mentor seeks to shield you, *paidarion*. In the pride of his own prowess he imagines he may fight for two. This is recklessness. The city cannot risk his loss, because he has eyes for the comeliness of your girlish face."

"Enough, my friend." This from Medon, senior of the mess. The Peers seconded with a chorus of knuckle raps.

Polynikes smiled. "I accede to your chastisement, gentlemen and elders. Please excuse my excess of zeal. I seek only to impart to our youthful comrade some insight into the nature of reality, the state of man as the gods have made him. May I conclude his instruction?"

"With brevity," Medon admonished.

Polynikes turned again to Alexandros. When he resumed now, his voice was gentle and without malice; if anything it seemed informed with something not unlike kindness and even, odd as it sounds, sorrow.

"Mankind as it is constituted," Polynikes said, "is a boil and a canker. Observe the specimens in any nation other than Lakedaemon. Man is weak, greedy, craven, lustful, prey to every species of vice and depravity. He will lie, steal, cheat, murder, melt down the very statues of the gods and coin their gold as money for whores. This is man. This is his nature, as all the poets attest.

"Fortunately God in his mercy has provided a counterpoise to our species' innate depravity. That gift, my young friend, is war.

"War, not peace, produces virtue. War, not peace, purges vice. War, and preparation for war, call forth all that is noble and honorable in a man. It unites him with his brothers and binds them in selfless love, eradicating in the crucible of necessity all which is base and ignoble. There in the holy mill of murder the meanest of men may seek and find that part of himself, concealed beneath the corrupt, which shines forth brilliant and virtuous, worthy of honor before the gods. Do not despise war, my young friend, nor delude yourself that mercy and compassion are virtues superior to *andreia*, to manly valor." He finished, turning to Medon and the elders. "Forgive me for waxing long-winded."

The harrowing ended; the Peers dispersed. Outside beneath the oaks, Dienekes sought out Polynikes, addressing him by his praise-name Kallistos, which may be defined as "harmoniously beautiful" or "of perfect symmetry," though in the tone Dienekes employed, it expressed itself in the converse, as "pretty boy" or "angel face."

"Why do you hate this youth so much?" Dienekes demanded.

The runner replied without hesitation. "Because he does not love glory."

"And is love of glory the supreme virtue of a man?"

"Of a warrior."

"And of a racehorse and a hunting dog."

"It is the virtue of the gods, which they command us to emulate."

The others of the mess could overhear this exchange, though they affected not to, since, under the laws of Lykurgus, no matter discussed behind those doors may be carried over to these more public precincts. Dienekes, realizing this as well, brought himself under control and faced the Olympian Polynikes with an expression of wry amusement.

"My wish for you, Kallistos, is that you survive as many battles in the flesh as you have already fought in your imagination. Perhaps then you will acquire the humility of a man and bear yourself no longer as the demigod you presume yourself to be."

"Spare your concern for me, Dienekes, and save it for your boy friend. He has greater need of it."

That hour had arrived when the messes along the Amyklaian Way released their men, those over thirty to depart for their homes and wives, and the younger men, of the first five age-classes, to retire under arms to the porticoes of the public buildings, there to stand the night watches over the city or curl in their cloaks for sleep. Dienekes took these last moments to speak apart with Alexandros.

The man placed an arm about the boy's shoulder; they moved slowly together beneath the unlit oaks. "You know," Dienekes said, "that Polynikes would give his life for you in battle. If you fell wounded, his shield would preserve you, his spear would bring you safely back. And if death's blow did find you, he would swim without hesitation into the manslaughter and spend his last breath to retrieve your body and keep the enemy from stripping your armor. His words may be cruel, Alexandros, but you have seen war now and you know it is a hundred times crueler.

"Tonight was a lark. It was practice. Prepare your mind to endure its like again and again, until it is nothing to you, until you can laugh in Polynikes' face and return his insults with a carefree heart.

"Remember that boys of Lakedaemon have endured these harrowings for hundreds of years. We spend tears now that we may conserve blood later. Polynikes was not seeking to harm you tonight. He was trying to teach that discipline of mind which will block out fear when the trumpets sound and the battle pipers mark the beat.

"Remember what I told you about the house with many rooms. There are rooms we must not enter. Anger. Fear. Any passion which leads the mind toward that 'possession' which undoes men in war.

"Habit will be your champion. When you train the mind to think one way and one way only, when you refuse to allow it to think in another, that will produce great strength in battle."

They stopped beneath an oak and sat.

"Did I ever tell you about the goose we had on my father's *kleros?* This bird had formed a habit, God knows why, of pecking three times at a certain patch of turf before she waddled into the water with her brothers and sisters. When I was a boy, I used to marvel at this. The goose did it every time. It was compelled to.

"One day I got it into my head to prevent her. Just to see what she would do. I took up a station on that patch of superstitious turf—I was no more than four or five years old at the time—and refused to let that goose come near it. She became frantic. She rushed at me and beat me with her wings, pecking me bloody. I fled like a rat. At once the goose recovered composure. She pecked her little spot of turf three times and slid into the water, contented as could be."

The older Peers were departing now for their homes, the younger men and boys returning to their stations.

"Habit is a mighty ally, my young friend. The habit of fear and anger, or the habit of self-composure and courage." He rapped the boy warmly upon the shoulder; they both stood.

"Go now. Get some sleep. I promise you, before you see battle again, we'll arm you with all the handiest habits."

THIRTEEN

When the youths began dispersing to their stations, Dienekes with his squire, Suicide, moved out to the road, joining a company of other officers assembling to proceed to the *ekklesia*, where they were to assist in the organization of the coming funeral games. A helot boy approached Dienekes there, before the mess, dashing up with a message. I was on the point of departing with Alexandros for the open porches around the Square of Freedom to take up my berth for the night when a sharp whistle summoned me.

To my astonishment it was Dienekes.

I crossed to him swiftly, presenting myself respectfully upon his left, his shield side. "Are you acquainted with the location of my house?" he asked. These were the first words he had ever addressed directly to me. I replied that I did. "Go there now. This boy will lead you."

Dienekes said nothing more but turned and departed at once with the body of officers toward the Assembly. I had no idea what was required of me. I asked the boy if perhaps there was some mistake, was he sure it was I who was required? "It's you, all right, and we'd better make the pebbles fly."

The town house of Dienekes' family, in contradistinction to the farmstead their helot families worked three miles south along the Eurotas, stood two lanes off the Eventide Road, on the west end of the village of Pitana. It was not conjoined to other dwellings, as many in that quarter were, but isolated at the edge of a grove beneath ancient oaks and olives. It had itself been a farmhouse at some point in the past and possessed yet the unadorned utilitarian charm of a country *kleros*. The house itself was unassuming in the extreme, barely larger than a cottage, less prepossessing even than the house of my own father in Astakos, though its courtyard and grounds, nestled within a grove of myrtle and hyacinth, arose like a haven of refuge and charm. One arrived upon the site at the terminus of a series of flower-girt lanes, each seeming to draw one deeper into a space of serenity and seclusion, passing, as one went, the dappled clusters of other Peers' cottages, their hearths aglow in the evening chill, with the peal of children's laughter and the happy yapping of their hounds spilling over the founded walls. The site itself, and its bowered environs, could not have appeared farther removed from the precincts of training and of war, nor offered more contrast and comfort to those repairing from them.

Dienekes' eldest daughter, Eleiria, who was eleven at the time, let me in the gate. I perceived low white walls surrounding an immaculately swept courtyard of plain tile brick, decorated with flowers in earthen pots upon the sill. Jasmine bloomed along the unvarnished beams of an axe-hewn pergola; wisteria and oleander nestled trim upon the face; a stonework watercourse, no wider than a handbreadth, gurgled along the northern wall. A servant girl whom I did not recognize waited beside a plaited wicker garden seat in the shadows.

I was directed to a stone bowl and told to rinse my hands and feet. Several clean linen cloths hung upon a bar; I dried myself and rehung them scrupulously. My heart was hammering, though for the life of me I could not have said why. The maiden Eleiria ushered me inside to the hearth hall, the solitary room, other than Dienekes' and his wife Arete's bedchamber, of which the house was comprised.

All four of Dienekes' daughters were present, including a slumbering toddler and a newborn; the second-eldest, Alexa, now being joined by her sister, both of whom sat to the side and proceeded to card wool as if it were the normal activity for the middle of the night. These maidens were presided over by the lady Arete, who sat with the infant at her breast upon a low uncushioned stool adjacent the hearth.

I discerned at once, however, that it was not Dienekes' lady upon whom I was to attend. Instead, at her side, and more toward the meridian of the room, sat the lady Paraleia, Alexandros' mother, the wife of the *polemarch* Olympieus.

This mistress began without ceremony to interrogate me on the harrowing her son had received not half an hour earlier in the mess. That she knew of this event at all, and so immediately, was surprise enough. Something in her eyes warned me I must choose my words with care.

The lady Paraleia declared that she was keenly cognizant of and held in profoundest respect the proscription against revealing any exchange spoken within the precincts of a Peers' mess. Nonetheless I might, without violating the sanctity of the law, yet vouchsafe to her, a mother understandably concerned about her son's welfare and future, some indication, if not of the precise words and actions of the aforesaid event, then perhaps some portion of its tone and flavor.

She inquired by way of motivation, in the identical understated tone with which the Peers of the mess had interrogated Alexandros, who it was who governed the city. The kings and the ephors, I replied at once, and of course the Laws. The lady smiled and glanced, just for a moment, toward the mistress Arete.

"Yes," she said. "Surely this must be so."

This was her way of letting me know that the women ran the show and that if I didn't want to find myself permanently back in the farmers' shitfields, I'd better start coughing up a satisfactory dose of information. Within ten minutes she had gotten everything there was to get. I sang like a bird.

She wished, the lady Paraleia began, to know everything her son had done in the hours after he had defied her wishes in the grove of the Twins and set off to follow the army to Antirhion. She grilled me as if I were a spy. The lady Arete did not interrupt. Her eldest daughters never lifted their eyes toward me nor toward the lady Paraleia, yet they remained in their modest silence riveted to every word. This was how they learned. The lesson today was how to grill a boy in service. How a lady did it. What tone she took, what questions she asked, when her voice rose with a hint of threat and when it lowered to assume a more confidential, candor-evoking tone.

What rations had Alexandros and I taken? What arms? When our food ran out, how had we acquired more? Did we encounter strangers along the way? How did her son comport himself? How did the strangers respond? Did they show him respect worthy of a Spartan? Did her son's demeanor command it?

The lady assimilated my responses, revealing nothing herself, though it was plain at certain junctures that she disapproved of her son's conduct. Only once did she permit actual anger to invest her tone, that when I acknowledged under compulsion that Alexandros had not secured the name of the boat captain who had ferried and betrayed us. The lady's voice shook. What was wrong with the boy? What had he learned all these years at his father's table and in the common mess? Didn't he see that this reptile, this fisher captain, must be punished, executed if necessary, to teach these scoundrels the price of playing perfidy with the son of a Peer of Lakedaemon? Or if prudence dictated, that he, this boatman, could be exploited to advantage? If war with the Persian came, this blackguard, turned informer, could prove an invaluable source of intelligence for the army. Even if he attempted through falsehood to play the traitor, this could be discerned and valuable knowledge acquired. Why didn't my son find out his name?

"Your servant does not know, lady. Perhaps your son did and his servant was unaware of it."

"Call yourself 'I,' " Paraleia scolded me sharply. "You're not a slave, don't talk like one."

"Yes, lady."

"The boy needs something to wet his throat, Mother." This from the maiden Eleiria, with a giggle. "Look at him. If his face gets any redder, he'll burst like a tomato."

The grilling went on for another hour. Adding to the discomfort I felt on this hot seat was the effect of the lady Paraleia's physical appearance, which bore an uncanny resemblance to that of her son. Like him, the lady was beautiful, and like him, her beauty took the unadorned, underplayed Spartan form.

The wives and maidens of my native Astakos, and those of every other city in Hellas, routinely employ cosmetics and facial paint to enhance their comeliness. These ladies are keenly aware of the effect the artificial sheen of their curls or the pink of their lips produces upon any male within range of their charms.

None of this entered into the scheme of the lady Paraleia, nor Arete either. Her *peplos* robe was split up the side in the Spartan style, revealing her bare leg to the thigh. This in any other city would have been lewd to the point of scandalous. Yet here in Lakedaemon it was unremarkable in the extreme. This is a leg. We women possess them just like you men. For Spartan males to leer at or ogle a lady in this dress would have been unthinkable. They had beheld their mothers and sisters and daughters naked since they were old enough to open their eyes, both in the girls' and women's athletic training and in the festivals and the other women's processions.

Still these ladies, both of them, were not unaware of their personal magnetism and the effect it produced, even upon a boy in service drawn up before them. After all, wasn't Helen herself a Spartan? The wife of Menelaus, she whom Paris had carried off to Troy,

the cause of endless suffering
among Trojans and Greeks, and for
whose peerless beauty's sake so many
brave Achaeans lost their lives in Troy
far from their native country.

Spartan women surpass for beauty all others in Hellas, and not the least of their charms is that they make so little play upon it. Aphrodite is not their goddess, but Artemis Huntress. Look at the loveliness of our hair, their bearing seems to say, which reflects the lamplight not by the artifice of the cosmetician's art, but by the sheen of health and the luster of virtue. Look in our eyes which embrace a man's, neither lowering in contrived modesty nor fluttering behind dyed lashes like Corinthian whores. Our legs we groom not in the boudoir with wax and myrtle, but under the sun in the race and upon the Ring.

They were dams, these ladies, wives and mothers whose primary calling was to produce boys who would grow to be warriors and heroes, defenders of the city. Spartan women were brood mares, the pampered damsels of other cities might scoff, but if they were mares, they were racers, Olympic champions. The athletic glow and vigor which the *gynaikagoge*, the women's training discipline, produced in them was powerful stuff and they knew it.

Standing before these women now, my thoughts despite all efforts were wrung back into the past, to Diomache and to my mother. I saw in memory my cousin's bare legs flashing strong and well made when we raced after some hare or doe with our dogs sprinting ahead up some rock-strewn slope. I saw the smooth glowing flesh of her arm when she drew the bow, her eyes that shrank before nothing and the flush of youth and freedom that suffused the skin of her face when she smiled. I saw again my mother, who was only twenty-six at her death, and whose memory to my eyes was of surpassing gentleness and nobility. These thoughts were like a room in the house of the mind that Dienekes spoke of, a room I had sworn since the Three-Cornered Way never to permit myself to enter.

But now, finding myself here in this real room of this real house, before these womanly rustles and scents, the feminine auroras of these wives and mothers and daughters and sisters, six of them, so much female presence concentrated in so close a space, I was driven back in mind against my will. It took all my self-composure to conceal the effect of these memories and to answer the lady's continuing questions in good order. At last it seemed the inquisition was approaching its conclusion.

"Answer now one final question. Speak with candor. If you lie, I will know. Does my son possess courage? Evaluate his *andreia*, his manly virtue, as a youth who must soon take his place as a warrior."

It took no brains to see I was treading the thinnest of ice. How could one answer a question like that? I straightened and addressed the lady directly.

"There are fourteen hundred boys in the training platoons of the *agoge*. Only one displayed the temerity to follow the army, and that in knowing defiance of his own mother's wishes, not to say full awareness of what punishment he must endure upon his return."

The lady considered this. "It is a politic answer, but a good one. I accept it."

She rose and thanked the lady Arete for arranging this interview and for providing for its confidentiality. I was told to wait outside in the courtyard. The lady Paraleia's maidservant stood there still, smirking; no doubt she had overheard every word and would blab it to all the Eurotas valley by sunrise tomorrow. In a moment the lady herself emerged, deigning neither to look at nor speak to me, and accompanied by her maid, strode off without torchlight down the dark lane.

"Are you old enough to take wine?"

The lady Arete addressed me directly, speaking from the doorway and motioning me back within the dwelling. All four daughters slept now. The lady herself prepared a bowl for me, cut six to one as for a boy. I took a grateful swallow. Clearly this night of interviews was not over.

The lady invited me to sit. She herself settled at the mistress's station beside the hearth. She placed a chunk of *alphita* barley bread on a plate before me and brought a relish of oil, cheese and onion.

"Be patient, this night among women will soon be over. You'll be back with the men, with whom you clearly feel more comfortable."

"I am at ease, lady. Truly. It's a relief to be away from barrack life for an hour, even if it means dancing barefoot on the hot steel of the skillet."

The lady smiled at this, but it was apparent that her mind was held by a more sober subject. She drew my eyes to hers.

"Have you ever heard the name Idotychides?"

I had.

"He was a Spartiate slain in battle at Mantinea. I have seen his stone before the mess of Winged Nike on the Amyklaian Way."

"What else do you know of this man?" the lady asked. I muttered something. "What else?" she insisted.

"They say that Dekton, the helot boy called Rooster, is his bastard. By a Messenian mother, who died giving birth."

"And do you believe this?"

"I do, lady."

"Why?"

I had stuck myself in a corner now; I could see the lady perceive it. "Is it because," she answered for me, "this boy Rooster hates the Spartans so much?"

I was struck with dread that she knew this and for long moments could not find my tongue.

"Have you noticed," the lady continued in a voice that to my surprise displayed neither outrage nor anger, "that among slaves the meanest seem to bear their lot without excessive distress, while the noblest, those at the brink of freedom, chafe most bitterly? It's as if the more one in service feels himself worthy of honor, yet denied the means to achieve it, the more excruciating is the experience of subjection."

This was Rooster in a nutshell. I had never thought about it that way but, now that the lady had expressed it thus, I saw it was true.

"Your friend Rooster talks too much. And what his tongue withholds, his demeanor announces only too plainly." She quoted, virtually verbatim, several seditious statements that Dekton had spoken, in my hearing alone, I thought, on the march back from Antirhion.

I was speechless and could feel myself breaking into a sweat. The lady Arete maintained her expression inscrutable.

"Do you know what the *krypteia* is?" she asked.

I did. "It is a secret society among the Peers. No one knows who its members are, just that they are of the youngest and strongest, and they do their work at night."

"And what work is that?"

"They make men disappear." Helots, I meant. Treasonous helots.

"Now answer this, and consider before you speak." The lady Arete paused, as if to reinforce the importance of the question she was about to put. "If you were a member of the *krypteia* and you knew what I have just told you about this helot, Rooster, that he had expressed sentiments treasonous to the city and further declared his intention of taking action based upon them, what would you do?"

There could be only one answer.

"It would be my duty to kill him, were I a member of the *krypteia*."

The lady absorbed this, her expression still betraying nothing. "Now answer: if you were yourself, a friend to this helot boy, Rooster, what would you do?"

I stammered something about exculpatory circumstances, that Rooster was a hothead, he often spoke without thinking, much of what he said was bluster and everyone knew it.

The lady turned toward the shadows.

"Is this boy lying?"

"Yes, Mother!"

I spun in startlement. Both older daughters were wide awake, in their shared bed, glued to every word.

"I will answer the question for you, young man," the lady said, rescuing me from my predicament. "I think you would do this. I think you would warn this boy, Rooster, to speak no more of such things within your hearing and to take no action, however slight—or you yourself would dispatch him."

I was now utterly discomfited. The lady smiled. "You are a poor liar. It is not one of your gifts. I admire that. But you tread dangerous ground. Sparta may be the greatest city in Hellas, but it is still a small town. A mouse cannot sneeze without every cat saying God bless you. The servants and helots hear everything, and their tongues can be set a-wag for the price of a honey cake."

I considered this.

"And will mine," I asked, "be loosened for the cost of a bowl of wine?"

"The boy disrespects you, Mother!" This from Alexa, who was nine. "You must have him striped!"

To my relief the lady Arete regarded me in the lamplight with neither anger nor indignation, but calmly, studying me. "A boy in your position should rightly stand in fear of the wife of a Peer of my husband's stature. Tell me: why aren't you afraid of me?"

I hadn't realized until that moment that in fact I wasn't. "I'm not sure, lady. Perhaps because you remind me of someone."

For several moments the lady did not speak, but continued regarding me with that same intense scrutiny.

"Tell me about her," she commanded.

"Who?"

"Your mother."

I flushed again. It made me squirm to think this lady divined the contents of my heart before I even spoke them.

"Go ahead, take some wine. You don't have to play tough in front of me."

What the hell. I took it. It helped. I told the lady briefly of Astakos, of its sack and of my mother and father's murder at the hands of the night-skulking warriors of Argos.

"The Argives have always been cowards," she observed, dismissing them with a snort of contempt that endeared her, more than she realized, to me. Clearly her long ears had learned my poor story already, yet she listened attentively, seeming to respond with empathy to hearing the tale from my own lips.

"You have had an unhappy life, Xeo," she said, speaking my name for the first time. To my surprise this moved me profoundly; I had to fight not to let it show.

For my part, I was summoning every ounce of self-composure I possessed, to speak correctly, in proper Greek worthy of a freeborn, and to hold myself with respect not only for her but for my own country and my own line.

"And why," the lady asked, "does a boy of no city display so much loyalty to this alien country of Lakedaemon, of which he is not, and can never be, a part?"

I knew the answer but could not judge how much I dared entrust to her. I responded obliquely, speaking briefly of Bruxieus. "My tutor instructed me that a boy must have a city or he cannot grow to be fully a man. Since I no longer possessed a city of my own, I felt free to choose any I liked."

This was a novel point of view, but I could see the lady approved of it. "Why not, then, a *polis* of riches or opportunity? Thebes or Corinth or Athens? All that can come to you here is coarse bread and a striped back."

I replied with a proverb that Bruxieus had once quoted to Diomache and me: that other cities produce monuments and poetry, Sparta produces men.

"And is this true?" the lady inquired. "In your most candid judgment, now that you have had opportunity to study our city, its worst as well as its best?"

"It is, lady."

To my surprise these words seemed to move the lady profoundly. She averted her gaze, blinking several times. Her voice, when she summoned herself again to speak, was hoarse with affect.

"What you have heard of the Peer Idotychides is true. He was the father of your friend Rooster. He was something other as well. He was my brother."

She could see me react with surprise.

"You didn't know this?"

"No, lady."

She mastered the emotion, the grief, I now saw, that had threatened to discompose her.

"So you see," she said with a smile brought forth with effort, "that makes this young Rooster something of a nephew to me. And I an aunt to him."

I took more wine. The lady smiled.

"May I ask why the lady's family has not sponsored the boy Rooster and put him forward as a *mothax*?"

This is a special dispensation in Lakedaemon, a "stepbrother" category of youth, available to the lesser-born or bastard sons of Spartiate fathers primarily, who could despite their mean birth be sponsored and elevated, enrolled in the *agoge*. They would train alongside the sons of Peers. They could even, if they showed sufficient merit and courage in battle, become citizens.

"I have asked your friend Rooster more than once," the lady answered. "He rebuffs me."

She could see the disbelief on my face.

"With respect," she added. "Most courtly respect. But with finality."

She considered this for a moment.

"There is another curiosity of mind which one may observe among slaves, particularly those who spring from a conquered people, as this boy Rooster does, being of a Messenian mother. Those men of pride will often identify with the meaner half of their line, out of spite perhaps, or the wish not to seem to curry favor by seeking to ingratiate themselves on the better side."

This was indeed true of Rooster. He saw himself as Messenian, and fiercely so.

"I tell you this, my young friend, for your sake as well as my nephew's: the *krypteia* knows. They have watched him since he was five. They watch you too. You speak well, you have courage, you are resourceful. None of this goes unobserved and unremarked. And I will tell you something more. There is one among the *krypteia* who is not unknown to you. This is the Captain of Knights, Polynikes. He will not hesitate to slit a treasonous helot's throat, nor do I think that your friend Rooster, for all his strength and spirit, will outrun a champion of Olympia."

The girls by now had all succumbed to slumber. The house itself and the darkness beyond its walls seemed at last entirely, eerily still.

"War with the Persian is coming," the lady declared. "The city will need every man. Greece will need every man. But just as important, this war, which all agree will be the gravest in history, will afford a mighty stage and arena for greatness. A field upon which a man may display by his deeds the nobility denied him by his birth."

The lady's eyes met mine and held them.

"I want this boy Rooster alive when war comes. I want you to protect him. If your ear detects any hint of danger, the slightest rumor, you must come straightaway to me. Will you do this?"

I promised I would.

"You care for this boy, Xeo. Though he has scourged you, I see the friendship you share. I implore you in the name of my brother and his blood which flows in this boy Rooster's veins. Will you watch over him? Will you do this for me?"

I promised that what I could do, I would.

"Swear it."

I complied, by all the gods.

It seemed preposterous. How could I stand against the *krypteia* or any other force that sought to murder Rooster? Still somehow my boy's promise seemed to ease the lady's distress. She studied my face for a long moment.

"Tell me, Xeo," she said softly. "Do you ever . . . have you ever asked anything just for yourself?"

I replied that I did not understand the lady's question.

"I command one other thing of you. Will you perform it?"

I swore I would.

"I order you one day to take an action purely for your own sake and not in service to another. You will know when the time comes. Promise me. Say it aloud."

"I promise, lady."

She rose then, with the sleeping infant in her arms, and crossed to a cradle between the beds of the other girls, laying the babe down and settling it within the soft covers. This was the signal for me to take my leave. I had risen already, as respect commanded, when the lady stood.

"May I ask one question, lady, before I go?"

Her eyes glinted teasingly. "Let me guess. Is it about a girl?"

"No, lady." Already I regretted my impulse. This question I had was impossible, absurd. No mortal could answer it.

The lady had become intrigued, however, and insisted that I continue.

"It's for a friend," I told her. "I cannot answer it myself, being too young and knowing too little of the world. Perhaps you, lady, with your wisdom may be able to. But you must promise not to laugh or take offense."

She agreed.

"Or repeat this to anyone, including your husband."

She promised.

I took a breath and plunged in.

"This friend . . . he believes that once, when he was a child, alone at the point of death, he was spoken to by a god."

I pulled up, minding keenly for any sign of scorn or indignation. To my relief the lady displayed none.

"This boy . . . my friend . . . he wishes to know if such a thing is possible. Could . . . would a being of divinity condescend to speak to a boy without city or station, a penniless child who possessed no gift to offer in sacrifice and did not even know the proper words of prayer? Or was my friend hatching phantoms, fabricating empty visions out of his own isolation and despair?"

The lady asked which god it was, who had spoken to my friend.

"The archer god. Apollo Far Striker."

I was squirming. Surely the lady will scorn such temerity and presumption. I should never have opened my cheesepipe.

But she did not mock my question nor deem it impious. "You are something of an archer yourself, I understand, and far advanced for your years. They took your bow, didn't they? It was confiscated when you first appeared in Lakedaemon?"

She declared that fortune must have guided me to her hearth this night, for yes, the goddesses of the earth flew thick and near at hand. She could feel them. Men think with their minds, the lady said; women with their blood, which is tidal and flows at the discretion of the moon.

"I am no priestess. I can respond only out of a woman's heart, which intuits and discerns truth directly, from within."

I replied that this was precisely what I wished.

"Tell your friend this," the lady said. "That which he saw was truth. His vision indeed was of the god."

Without warning, fierce tears sprung to my eyes. At once emotion overwhelmed me. I buckled and sobbed, mortified at such loss of self-command and astonished at the power of passion which had sprung seemingly from nowhere to overcome me. I buried my face in my hands and wept like a child. The lady stepped to me and held me gently, patting my shoulder like a mother and uttering kind words of assurance.

Within moments I had mastered myself. I apologized for this shameful lapse. The lady would hear none of it; she scolded me, declaring that such passion was holy, inspired by heaven, and must not be repented or apologized for.

She stood now by the open doorway, through which the starlight fell and the soft babbling of the courtyard watercourse could be heard.

"I would like to have known your mother," the lady Arete said, regarding me with kindness. "Perhaps she and I will meet someday, beyond the river. We will speak of her son, and the unhappy portion the gods have set out before him."

She touched me once upon the shoulder in dismissal.

"Go now, and tell your friend this: he may come again with his questions, if he wishes. But next time he must come in person. I wish to look upon the face of this boy who has sat and chatted with the Son of Heaven."

FOURTEEN

Alexandros and I received our whippings for Antirhion the following evening. His was administered by his father, Olympieus, before the Peers of that officer's mess; I was lashed without ceremony in the fields by a helot groundsman. Rooster helped me away afterward, alone in the darkness, down to a grove called the Anvil beside the Eurotas to bathe and dress my stripes. This was a spot sacred to Demeter of the Fields and segregated by custom to the use of Messenian helots; there had once been a smithy upon the site, hence the name.

To my relief Rooster did not treat me to his customary harangue about the life of a slave, but rather limited his diatribe to the observation that Alexandros had been whipped like a boy and I like a dog. He was kind to me and, more important, possessed expertise in cleansing and dressing that unique species of ruptured laceration which is produced by the impact of the knurled birch upon the naked flesh of the back.

First water and plenty of it, bodily immersion to the neck in the icy current. Rooster supported me from behind, elbows braced beneath my armpits, since the shock of the frigid water upon the opened weals rarely fails to knock one faint. The cold numbs the flesh swiftly, and a wash of boiled nettles and Nessos' wort may be applied and endured. This stanches the flow of blood and promotes the rapid resealing of the flesh. A dressing of wool or linen at this stage would be unendurable, even applied with the gentlest touch. But a friend's bare palm, placed lightly at first, then pressed hard into the quivering flesh and held down, brings a relief whose effects approach ecstasy. Rooster had endured his own share of thrashings and knew the drill well.

Within five minutes I could stand. In fifteen my skin could take the soft sphagnum, which Rooster pressed into the blotted mass to suck out the poison and to inject its own subtle anesthetic. "By God, there's not a virgin left," he observed, meaning a space that was still God's flesh and not ruptured and reruptured scar tissue. "You won't be humping that hymn-singer's shield across this back for a month."

He was just launching into another venomous denunciation of my boy-master when a rustle came from the bank above us. We both wheeled, ready for anything.

It was Alexandros. He stepped into view beneath the plane trees, his cloak furled forward, leaving his own throttled back bare. Rooster and I froze. Alexandros would buy himself a second whipping if he was found here at this hour, and us with him.

"Here," he said, skidding down the bank to join us, "I picked the surgeon's locker for this."

It was wax of myrrh. Two fingers' worth, wrapped in green rowan leaves. He stepped into the stream beside us.

"What have you got there on his back?" he demanded of Rooster, who stepped aside with a look of blank astonishment. Myrrh was what the Peers used on wounds of battle when they could get it, which they rarely could. They would beat Alexandros half to death if they knew he'd purloined this precious portion. "Get it on him later when you peel off the moss," Alexandros directed Rooster. "Wash it off good by dawn. If anyone smells it, it'll be all our backs and more."

He placed the wrapped leaves in Rooster's hands.

"I have to be back before count," Alexandros declared. In an instant he had melted away up the bank; we could hear his footfalls vanishing softly as he sprinted in shadow back toward the boys' stations around the Square.

"Well, bend me over and root me senseless," Rooster spoke, shaking his head. "That little lark's got bigger globes than I thought."

At dawn when we fell in before sacrifice, Rooster and I were called out from our places by Suicide, Dienekes' Scythian squire. We were white with dread. Someone had peeped on us; there would be hell to pay for sure.

"You little turdnuggets must be floating under a lucky star" was all Suicide said. He conducted us to the rear of the formation. Dienekes stood there, silent, alone in the predawn shadows. We took our stations of deference on his left, his shield side. The pipers sounded; the formation moved off. Dienekes indicated that Rooster and I were to stay put.

He held stationary before us. Suicide stood on his right, with the quiver of sawed-off javelins he called "darning needles" angled nonchalantly across his back.

"I've been examining your record," Dienekes addressed me, his first words, other than the summons two nights previous to follow the serving boy to his home, ever spoken directly to me. "The helots tell me you're worthless as a field hand. I've watched you in the sacrificial train; you can't even shave the throat of a goat correctly. And it's clear from your conduct with Alexandros that you'll follow any order, no matter how mindless or absurd." He motioned me to turn, so he could examine my back. "It seems the only talent you possess is you're a fast healer."

He bent and sniffed my back. "If I didn't know better," he observed, "I'd swear these stripes had been waxed with myrrh."

Suicide kicked me around, back to face Dienekes. "You're an unwholesome influence on Alexandros," the Peer addressed me. "A boy doesn't need another boy, and certainly not a trouble collector like you; he needs a mature man, someone with the authority to stop him when he gets some reckless stunt into his head like tracking after the army. So I'm giving him my own man." His nod indicated Suicide. "I'm sacking you," he told me. "You're through."

Oh hell. Back to the shitfields.

Dienekes turned next to Rooster. "And you. The son of a Spartiate hero and you can't even hold a sacrificial cock in your fists without strangling it. You're pathetic. You've got a mouth looser than a Corinthian's asshole and it broadcasts treason every time it yawns. I'd be doing you a favor to slit your cheesepipe right here and save the *krypteia* the trouble."

He reminded Rooster of Meriones, the squire of Olympieus who had fallen so gallantly last week at Antirhion. Neither of us boys had any idea where this was going.

"Olympieus is past fifty, he possesses all the prudence and circumspection he needs. His next squire should balance him with youth. Somebody green and strong and reckless." He regarded Rooster with wry scorn. "God knows what folly has inspired him, but Olympieus has picked you. You will take Meriones' place. You will attend Olympieus. Report to him at once. You're his first squire now."

I could see Rooster blinking. This must be a trick.

"It's no joke," Dienekes said, "and you'd better not make it one. You're treading in the steps of a man better than half the Peers in the regiment. Screw it up and I'll spit you over the flame personally."

"I won't, lord."

Dienekes studied him a long, hard moment. "Shut up and get the fuck out of here."

Rooster took off after the formation at a run. I confess I was ill with envy. The first squire of a Peer, and not just that, but a *polemarch* and king's tent companion. I hated Rooster for his dumb blind luck.

Or was it? As I blanched, numb with jealousy, a picture of the lady Arete shot across the eye of my mind. She was behind this. I felt even worse and regretted bitterly that I had confided to her my vision of Apollo Far Striker.

"Let me see your back," Dienekes commanded. I turned again; he whistled appreciatively. "By God, if there were an Olympic event in back-striping, you'd be the betting man's favorite." He had me face about and stand at attention before him; he regarded me thoughtfully, his gaze seeming to pierce straight through to my spine. "The qualities of a good battle squire are simple enough. He must be dumb as a mule, numb as a post and obedient as an imbecile. In these qualifications, Xeones of Astakos, I declare your credentials impeccable."

Suicide was chuckling darkly. He tugged something from behind the quiver at his back. "Go ahead, take a look," Dienekes ordered. I raised my eyes.

In the Scythian's hand stood a bow. My bow.

Dienekes commanded me to take it.

"You're not strong enough yet to be my first squire, but if you can manage to keep your head out of your ass, you might make a half-respectable second." Into my palm Suicide placed the bow, the big Thessalian cavalry weapon that had been confiscated from me at twelve, when first I crossed the frontier into Lakedaemon.

I could not stop my hands from trembling; I felt the warm ash of the bow and the living current that coursed its length and up into my palms.

"You'll pack my rations, bedding and medical kit," Dienekes instructed me. "You'll cook for the other squires and hunt for my pot, on exercises in Lakedaemon and beyond the border on campaign. Do you accept this?"

"I do, lord."

"At home you may hunt hares and keep them for yourself, but don't flaunt your good fortune."

"I won't, lord."

He regarded me with that look of wry amusement I had observed on his face before, at a distance, and which I would come to see many times more close-up.

"Who knows," my new master said, "with luck, you might even get in a potshot at the enemy."

BOOK FOUR

ARETE

FIFTEEN

The army of Lakedaemon marched out in twenty-one different campaigns over the next five years, all in actions against other Hellenes. That pitch of enmity which Leonidas had sought since Antirhion to maintain focused upon the Persian now found itself of necessity directed against more immediate targets, those cities of Greece which tilted perfidiously toward playing the traitor, allying themselves in advance with the invader, to save their own skins.

Mighty Thebes, whose exiled aristocrats conspired ceaselessly with the Persian court, seeking to reclaim preeminence in their country by selling it out to the foe.

Jealous Argos, Sparta's most bitter and proximate rival, whose nobles treated openly with the agents of the Empire. Macedonia under Alexander had long since offered tokens of submission. Athens, too, had exiled aristocrats reclining within the Persian pavilions while they plotted for their own restoration as lords beneath the Persian pennant.

Sparta herself stood not immune from treason, for her deposed king, Demaratos, as well had taken up the exile's station among the sycophants surrounding His Majesty. What else could Demaratos' desire be, save reaccession to power in Lakedaemon as satrap and magistrate of the Lord of the East?

In the third year after Antirhion, Darius of Persia died. When news of this reached Greece, hope rekindled in the free cities. Perhaps now the Persian would abort his mobilization. With her King dead, would not the army of the Empire disband? Would not the Persian vow to conquer Hellas be set aside?

Then you, Your Majesty, acceded to the throne.

The army of the foe did not disband.

Her fleet did not disperse.

Instead the Empire's mobilization redoubled. The zeal of a prince freshly crowned burned within His Majesty's breast. Xerxes son of Darius would not be judged by history inferior to his father, nor to his illustrious forebears Cambyses and Cyrus the Great. These, who had vanquished and enslaved all Asia, would be joined in the pantheon of glory by Xerxes, their scion, who would now add Greece and Europe to the roll of provinces of the Empire.

Across all Hellas, *phobos* advanced like a sapper's tunnel. One smelled the dust of its excavation in the still of morning and felt its yard-by-yard advance rumbling beneath one in his sleep. Of all the mighty cities of Greece, only Sparta, Athens and Corinth held fast. These dispatched legation after legation to the wavering *poleis*, seeking to bind them to the Alliance. My own master was assigned in a single season to five separate overseas embassies. I puked over so many different ships' rails I couldn't recall one from the other.

Everywhere these embassies touched, *phobos* had called first. The Fear made people reckless. Many were selling all they owned; others, more heedless, were buying. "Let Xerxes spare his sword and send his purse instead," my master observed in disgust after yet another embassy had been rebuffed. "The Greeks will trample one another's bones, racing to see who first can sell his freedom."

Always upon these legations, a part of my mind kept alert for word of my cousin. Three times in my seventeenth year the service of my master brought me through the city of the Athenians; each time I inquired after the location of the home of the gentlewoman whom Diomache and I had encountered that morning on the road to the Three Corners, when that fine lady had ordered Dio to seek her town estate and take service there. I secured at last the quarter and street but never succeeded in finding the house.

Once at a salon in the Athenian Akademe a lovely bride of twenty appeared, mistress of the household, and for a moment I was certain it was Diomache. My heart began to pound so violently that I must kneel upon one knee for fear of dropping to the floor dead faint. But the lady was not she. Nor was the bride glimpsed a year later bearing water from a spring in Naxos. Nor the physician's wife encountered under cloister in Histiaea six months thereafter.

Upon one blistering summer evening, two years before the battle at the Gates, the ship bearing my master's legation touched briefly at Phaleron, a port of Athens. Our mission completed, we had two hours before tide's turn. I was granted leave and on the run at last located the house of the family of the lady of the Three Corners. The place was shuttered; *phobos* had driven the clan forth to landholdings in Iapygia, or so I was informed by a loitering squad of Scythian archers, those thugs whom the Athenians employ as city constabulary. Yes, the brutes remembered Diomache. Who could forget her? They took me for another of her suitors and spoke in the crude language of the street.

"The bird winged off," one said. "Too wild for the cage."

Another declared he had encountered her since, in the market with a husband, a citizen and sea officer. "The fool bitch," he laughed. "To knot with that salt-sucker, when she could have had me!"

Returning to Lakedaemon, I resolved to root this folly of longing from my heart, as a farmer burns out a stubborn stump. I told Rooster it was time I took a bride. He found one for me, his cousin Thereia, the daughter of his mother's sister. I was eighteen, she fifteen when we were joined in the Messenian fashion practiced by the helots. She bore a son within ten months and a daughter while I was away on campaign.

A husband now, I vowed to think no more of my cousin. I would eradicate my own impiety and dwell no longer upon fancies.

The years had passed swiftly. Alexandros completed his service as a youth of the *agoge;* he was given his war shield and assumed his station among the Peers of the army. He took to wife the maiden Agathe, just as he had promised. She bore him twins, a boy and girl, before he was twenty.

Polynikes was crowned at Olympia for the second time, victor again in the sprint in armor. His wife, Altheia, bore him a third son.

The lady Arete produced for Dienekes no more children; she had come up barren after four daughters, without producing a male heir.

Rooster's wife, Harmonia, bore a second child, a boy whom he named Messenieus. The lady Arete attended the birth, providing her own midwife and assisting at the delivery with her own hands. I myself bore the torch that escorted her home. She would not speak, so torn was she between the joy of witnessing at last from her line the birth of a male, a defender for Lakedaemon, and the sorrow of knowing that this boy-child, issue of her brother's bastard, Rooster, with all his treasonous defiance of his Spartan masters, right down to the name he had chosen for his son, would face the sternest and most perilous passage to manhood.

The Persian myriads stood now in Europe. They had bridged the Hellespont and traversed all of Thrace. Still the Hellenic allies wrangled. A force of ten thousand heavy infantry, commanded by the Spartan Euanetus, was dispatched to Tempe in Thessaly, there to make a stand against the invader at the northernmost frontier of Greece. But the site, when the army got there, proved undefendable. The position could be turned by land via the pass at Gonnus and outflanked by sea through Aulis. In disgrace and mortification the force of Ten Thousand pulled out and dispersed to its constituent cities.

A desperate paralysis possessed the Congress of the Greeks. Thessaly, abandoned, had gone over to the Persian, adding her matchless cavalry to swell the squadrons of the foe. Thebes teetered at the brink of submission. Argos was sitting it out. Dread omens and prodigies abounded. The Oracle of Apollo at Delphi had counseled the Athenians,

"Fly to the ends of the earth,"

while the Spartan Council of Elders, notoriously slow to action, yet dithered and dawdled. A stand must be made somewhere. But where?

In the end it was their women who galvanized the Spartans into action. It came about like this.

Refugees, many brides with babes, were flooding into the last of the free cities. Young mothers took flight to Lakedaemon, islanders and relations fleeing the Persian advance across the Aegean. These brides inflamed their listeners' hatred of the foe with tales of the conquerors' atrocities in their earlier passage through the islands: how the enemy at Chios and Lesbos and Tenedos had formed dragnets at one end of the territory and advanced across each island, scouring out every hiding place, hauling forth the young boys, herding the handsomest together and castrating them for eunuchs, killing every man and raping the women, selling them forth into foreign slavery. The babies' heads these heroes of Persia dashed against the walls, splattering their brains upon the paving stones.

The wives of Sparta listened with icy fury to these tales, cradling their own infants at their breasts. The Persian hordes had swept now through Thrace and Macedonia. The baby-murderers stood upon the doorstep of Greece, and where was Sparta and her warrior defenders? Blundering homeward unblooded from the fool's errand of Tempe.

I had never seen the city in such a state as in the aftermath of that debacle. Heroes with prizes of valor skulked about, countenances downcast with shame, while their women snapped at them with scorn and held themselves aloof and disdainful. How could Tempe have happened? Any battle, even a defeat, would have been preferable to none at all. To marshal such a magnificent force, garland it before the gods, transport it all that way and not draw blood, even one's own, this was not merely disgraceful but, the wives declared, blasphemous.

The women's scorn excoriated the city. A delegation of wives and mothers presented itself to the ephors, insisting that they themselves be sent out next time, armed with hairpins and distaffs, since surely the women of Sparta could disgrace themselves no more egregiously nor accomplish less than the vaunted Ten Thousand.

In the warriors' messes the mood was even more corrosive. How much longer would the Allied Congress dither? How many more weeks would the ephors delay?

I recall vividly the morning when at last the proclamation came. The Herakles regiment trained that day in a dry watercourse called the Corridor, a blistering funnel between sand banks north of the village of Limnai. The men were running impact drills, two-on-ones and three-on-twos, when a distinguished elder named Charilaus, who had been an ephor and a priest of Apollo but now functioned primarily as a senior counselor and emissary, appeared on the crest of the bank and spoke aside to the *polemarch* Derkylides, the regimental commander. The old man was past seventy; he had lost the lower half of a leg in battle years past. For him to have hobbled on his staff this far from the city could only mean something big had happened.

The patriarch and the *polemarch* spoke in private. The drills went on. No one looked up, yet every man knew.

This was it.

Dienekes' men got the word from Laterides, commander of the adjacent platoon, who passed it down the line.

"It's the Gates, lads."

The Hot Gates.

Thermopylae.

No assembly was called. To the astonishment of all, the regiment was dismissed. The men were given the whole rest of the day off.

Such a holiday had only been granted half a dozen times in my memory; invariably the Peers broke up in high spirits and made for home at the trot. This time no one budged. The entire regiment stood nailed to the site, in the sweltering confines of the dry river, buzzing like a hive.

Here was the word:

Four *morai*, five thousand men, would be mobilized for Thermopylae. The column, reinforced by four *perioikic* regiments and packing squires and armed helots two to a man, would march out as soon as the Karneia, the festival of Apollo which prohibited taking up arms, expired. Two and half weeks.

The force would total twenty thousand men, twice the number at Tempe, concentrated in a pass ten times narrower.

Another thirty to fifty thousand allied infantry would be mobilized behind this initial force, while a main force of the allied navy, a hundred and twenty ships of war, would seal the straits at Artemisium and Andros and the narrows of the Euripus, protecting the army at the Gates from flank assault by sea.

This was a massive call-up. So massive it smelled. Dienekes knew it and so did everyone else.

My master humped back to the city accompanied by Alexandros, now a full line warrior of the platoon, his mates Bias, Black Leon and their squires. A third of the way along we overtook the elder Charilaus, shambling home with painful slowness, supported by his attendant, Sthenisthes, who was as ancient as he. Black Leon led an ass of the train on a halter; he insisted the old man ride. Charilaus declined but permitted the place to his servant.

"Cut through the shit for us, will you, old uncle?" Dienekes addressed the statesman affectionately but with a soldier's impatience for the truth.

"I relay only what I'm instructed, Dienekes."

"The Gates won't hold fifty thousand. They won't hold five."

A wry expression wizened the old-timer's face. "I see you fancy your generalship superior to Leonidas'."

One fact was self-evident even to us squires. The Persian army stood now in Thessaly. That was what, ten days to the Gates? Less? In two and a half weeks their millions would sweep through and be eighty miles beyond. They'd be parked upon our threshold.

"How many in the advance party?" Black Leon inquired of the elder.

He meant the forward force of Spartans that would, as always in advance of a mobilization, be dispatched to Thermopylae now, at once, to take possession of the pass before the Persians got there and before the main force of the allied army moved up.

"You'll hear it from Leonidas tomorrow," the old man replied. But he saw the younger men's frustration.

"Three hundred," he volunteered. "All Peers. All sires."

My master had a way of setting his jaw, a fierce clamping action of the teeth, which he employed when he was wounded on campaign and didn't want his men to know how bad. I looked. This expression stood now upon his face.

An "all-sire" unit was comprised only of men who were fathers of living sons.

This was so that, should the warriors perish, their family lines would not be extinguished.

An all-sire was a suicide unit.

A force dispatched to stand and die.

My customary duties upon return from training were to clean and stow my master's gear and look to, with the servants of the mess, the preparation of the evening meal. Instead this day Dienekes asked Black Leon for his squire to do double duty. Myself he ordered on ahead, at a run, to his own home. I was to inform the lady Arete that the regiment had been dismissed for the day and that her husband would arrive at home shortly. I was to issue an invitation to her on his behalf: would she and their daughters accompany him this afternoon for a ramble in the hills?

I raced ahead, delivered this message and was dismissed to my own pursuits. Some impulse, however, made me linger.

From the hill above my master's cottage I could see his daughters burst from the gate and dash with eager enthusiasm to greet him upon the way. Arete had prepared a basket of fruit, cheese and bread. The party was all barefoot, wearing big floppy sun hats.

I saw my master tug his wife aside beneath the oaks and there speak privately with her for several moments. Whatever he said, it prompted her tears. She embraced him fiercely, both arms flung tight about his neck. Dienekes seemed at first to resist, then in a moment yielded and clamped his wife to him, holding her tenderly.

The girls clamored, impatient to be off. Two puppies squalled underfoot. Dienekes and Arete released their embrace. I could see my master lift his youngest, Ellandra, and plant her pony style astride his shoulders. He held the maiden Alexa's hand as they set off, the girls exuberant and gay, Dienekes and Arete lagging just a little.

No main-force army would be dispatched to Thermopylae; that tale was for public consumption only, to shore up the allies' confidence and put iron in their backbones.

Only the Three Hundred would be sent, with orders to stand and die.

Dienekes would not be among them.

He had no male issue.

He could not be selected.

SIXTEEN

I must now recount an incident of battle several years previous, whose consequences at this present juncture came powerfully to affect the lives of Dienekes, Alexandros, Arete and others in this narrative. This occurred at Oenophyta against the Thebans, one year after Antirhion.

I refer to the extraordinary heroism demonstrated on that occasion by my mate Rooster. Like myself at the time, he was just fifteen and had been serving, green as grass, for less than twelve months as first squire of Alexandros' father, Olympieus.

The armies' fronts had clashed. The Menelaion, Polias and Wild Olive regiments were locked in a furious struggle with the Theban left, which was stacked twenty deep instead of the customary eight and was holding its position with terrific stubbornness. To augment this peril, the foe's wing overlapped the Spartan right an eighth of a mile; these elements now began to wheel inboard and advance, taking the Menelaion in the flank. Simultaneously the enemy's right, which was taking the most grievous casualties, lost cohesion and fell back upon the massed ranks of its rearmen. The foe's right broke in panic while his left advanced.

In the midst of this melee Olympieus received a crippling lizard-sticker wound through the arch of the foot, from the butt-spike of an enemy spear. This came, as I said, at a moment of extreme dislocation upon the field, with the enemy right collapsing and the Spartans surging into the pursuit, while the foe's left wheeled in attack, supported by numbers of their cavalry coursing uncontested across the broken field.

Olympieus found himself alone upon the open "gleaning ground" to the rear of the onrolling battle, with his foot wound rendering him crippled, while his cross-crested officer's helmet provided an irresistible target for any would-be hero of the enemy's ranging horse.

Three Theban cavalrymen went after him.

Rooster, unarmed and unarmored, sprinted headlong into the fray, snatching a spear from the ground as he ran. Dashing up to Olympieus, he not only employed his master's shield to protect him from the missile weapons of the enemy but took on the attacking horsemen single-handedly, wounding and driving off two with spear thrusts and caving in the skull of the third with the man's own helmet, which he, Rooster, in the madness of the moment, had torn off the fellow's head with his bare hands as he simultaneously ripped him out of his seat. Rooster even succeeded in capturing the handsomest of the three horses, a magnificent battle mount which he used in the aftermath to draw the litter which evacuated Olympieus safely from the field.

When the army returned to Lakedaemon after this campaign, Rooster's exploit was the talk of the city. Among the Peers his prospects were debated at length. What should be done with this boy? All recalled that though his mother was a Messenian helot, his father had been the Spartiate Idotychides, Arete's brother, a hero slain in battle at Mantinea when Rooster was two.

The Spartans, as I have noted, have a grade of warrior youth, a "stepbrother" class called a *mothax*. Bastards like Rooster and even legitimate sons of Peers who through misfortune or poverty have lost their citizenship may be, if deemed worthy, plucked from their straits and elevated to this station.

This honor was now proffered to Rooster.

He turned it down.

His stated reason was that he was already fifteen. It was too late for him; he preferred to remain in service as a squire.

This rejection of their generous offer enraged the Peers of Olympieus' mess and created an outrage, as much as the affair of a helot bastard could, within the city at large. Assertions were made to the point that this headstrong ingrate was notorious for his disloyal sentiments. He was a type not uncommon among slaves, prideful and stubborn. He sees himself as Messenian. He must either be eliminated, and his family with him, or secured beyond doubt of betrayal to the Spartan cause.

Rooster eluded assassination at the hands of the *krypteia* that time, largely due to his youth and to Olympieus' intercession, man-to-man among the Peers. The affair faded for the moment, rekindling itself, however, upon subsequent campaigns when Rooster again and again proved himself the boldest and most valorous of the young squires, surpassing all in the army save Suicide, Cyclops, main man of the Olympic pentathlete Alpheus, and Polynikes' squire, Akanthus.

Now the Persians stood at the threshold of Greece. Now the Three Hundred were being selected for Thermopylae. Olympieus would be prominent among them, with Rooster at his shoulder in his service. Could this treasonous youth be trusted? With a blade in his fist and himself a handbreadth from the *polemarch*'s back?

The last thing Sparta needed at this desperate hour was trouble at home with the helots. The city could not stand a revolt, even an abortive one. Rooster by this time, aged twenty, had become a force among the Messenian laborers, farmers and vineyardmen. He was a hero to them, a youth whose courage in battle could have been exploited by him as a ticket out of his servitude. He could be wearing Spartan scarlet and lording it over his mean-birthed brothers. But this he had disdained. He had declared himself Messenian, and his fellows never forgot. Who knows how many of them followed Rooster in their hearts? How many absolutely vital craftsmen and support personnel, armorers and litter bearers, squires and victualry men? It is an ill wind, they say, that blows no one good, and this Persian invasion could be the best thing that ever happened to the helots. It could spell deliverance. Freedom. Would they stand loyal? Like the gate of a mighty citadel which turns upon a single tempered hinge, much of the Messenian sentiment focused its attention upon Rooster and stood ready to take its cue from him.

It was now the night before the proclamation of the Three Hundred. Rooster was summoned to stand-to before Olympieus' mess, the Bellerophon. There, officially and with the goodwill of all, the honor of Spartan scarlet was again offered to the youth.

Again he spurned it.

I loitered deliberately in that hour outside the Bellerophon, to see which way the issue would go. It took no imagination, hearing the murmur of outrage within and beholding Rooster's swift and silent exit, to read the gravity of the issue, and its peril. An assignment for my master detained me for the bulk of an hour. At last I found opportunity to scamper free.

Beside the Little Ring where the starter's box stands is a grove with a dry course branching in three directions. There Rooster and I and other boys used to meet and even bring girls, because if you were found, you could dash away easily in the dark down one of the three dry riverbeds. I knew he would be there now, and he was. To my amazement Alexandros was with him. They were arguing. It took only moments to see it was the clash of one who wishes to be another's friend and the other who rejects him. What was startling was that it was Alexandros who wanted to be friend to Rooster. He would be in calamitous trouble if he was caught, so immediately subsequent to his initiation as a warrior. As I skittered down into the shadows of the dry course, Alexandros was cursing Rooster and declaring him a fool.

"They'll kill you now, don't you know that?"

"Fuck them. Fuck them all."

"Stop this!" I burst down between them. I recited what all three of us knew: that Rooster's prestige among the lower orders precluded him from acting for himself alone; what he did bore repercussions for his wife, his son and daughter, his family. He had cooked himself and them with him. The *krypteia* would finish him this very night, and nothing would suit Polynikes more.

"He won't catch me if I'm not here."

Rooster had set his mind to flee, this night, to the Temple of Poseidon at Tainaron, where a helot could be granted sanctuary.

He wanted me to come. I told him he was insane. "What were you thinking when you turned them down? What they offered you is an honor."

"Fuck their honors. The *krypteia* hunts me now, in darkness, faceless as cowards. Is that honor?"

I told him his slave's pride had bought his own ticket to hell.

"Shut up, both of you!"

Alexandros ordered Rooster to his shell, that term the Spartans use to describe the mean huts of the helots. "If you're going to run, run now!"

We sprinted away down the dark watercourse. Harmonia had both children, Rooster's daughter and infant son, packed and ready. In the smoky confines of the helot's shell, Alexandros pressed into Rooster's hand a clutch of Aeginetan obols, not much, but all he had, enough to aid a runaway.

This gesture struck Rooster speechless.

"I know you don't respect me," Alexandros told him. "You think yourself my better in skill at arms, in strength and in valor. Well, you are. I have tried, as the gods are my witness, with every fiber of my being and still I'm not half the fighter you are. I never will be. You should stand in my place and I in yours. It is the gods' injustice that makes you a slave and me free."

This from Alexandros utterly disarmed Rooster. You could see the combativeness in his eyes relent and his proud defiance slacken and abate.

"You own more of valor than I ever will," the bastard replied, "for you manufacture it out of a tender heart, while the gods sat me up punching and kicking from the cradle. And you do yourself honor to speak with such candor. You're right, I did despise you. Until this moment."

Rooster glanced at me then; I could see confusion in his aspect. He was moved by Alexandros' integrity, which pulled his heart strongly to remain and even to yield. Then with an effort he broke the spell. "But you won't influence me, Alexandros. Let the Persian come. Let him grind all Lakedaemon into dust. I'll jig on its grave."

We heard Harmonia gasp. Outside, torches flared. Shadows surrounded the shell. Its blanket flap was torn open. There in the rude doorway stood Polynikes, armed and backed by four assassins of the *krypteia*. They were all young, athletes nearly on a par with the Olympian, and pitiless as iron.

They burst in and bound Rooster with cord. The infant boy wailed in Harmonia's arms; the poor girl was barely seventeen; she shuddered and wept, pulling her daughter in terror to her side. Polynikes absorbed the sight with contempt. His glance flicked over Rooster, his wife and babes and myself, to settle with scorn upon the person of Alexandros.

"I might have known we'd find you here."

"And I you," the youth responded.

On his face was written plain his hatred of the *krypteia*.

Polynikes regarded Alexandros, and his sentiments, with barely contained outrage. "Your presence here in these precincts constitutes treason. You know it and so do these others. Out of respect to your father only, I will say this once: leave now. Depart at once and nothing more will be said. The dawn will find four helots missing."

"I will not," Alexandros answered.

Rooster spat. "Kill us all, then!" he demanded of Polynikes. "Show us Spartan valor, you night-skulking cowards."

A fist smashed his teeth, silencing him.

I saw hands seize Alexandros and felt others clamp me; thongs of hide bound my wrists, a gag of linen stoppered my throat. The *krypteis* snatched Harmonia and her babes.

"Bring them all," Polynikes ordered.

SEVENTEEN

There stands a grove upslope behind the Deukalion mess, where the men and hounds customarily muster before setting off on a hunt. There within minutes a rump court stood assembled.

The site is a grisly one. Rude kennels extend beneath the oaks, with their game nets and chase harnesses hanging beneath the eaves of the feeding stations. The mess kitchen stores its slaughtering implements in several double-locked outbuildings; upon the inner doors hang hatchets and gutting knives, cleavers and bonebreakers; a blood-black chopping board for game fowl and poultry extends along the wall, where the birds' heads are whacked off and topple to the dirt for the hounds to scrap over. Piles of plucked feathers collect as high as a man's calf, rendered sodden by the blood drippings of the next luckless fowl to stretch its gullet beneath the chopper. Above these along the runway stand the bars of the butchery with their heavy iron hooks for the hanging, gutting and bleeding of game.

It was a foregone conclusion that Rooster must die, and his infant son with him. What remained yet at issue was the fate of Alexandros, and his treason which, if published throughout the city, would work grievous harm at this most peril-fraught hour, not only to himself and his station as a newly initiated warrior but to the prestige of his entire clan, his wife, Agathe, his mother, Paraleia, his father, the *polemarch* Olympieus, and, not least of all, his mentor, Dienekes. This latter pair now took their place in the shadows, along with the other sixteen Peers of the Duekalion mess. Rooster's wife wept silently, her daughter beside her; the baby squalled, muffled, in her arms. Rooster knelt in his cord bonds, on his knees in the dry high-summer dust.

Polynikes paced impatiently, wanting a decision.

"May I speak?" Rooster croaked in a throat hoarse from having been throttled on the way to this summary arraignment.

"What has scum like you to say?" Polynikes demanded.

Rooster indicated Alexandros. "This man your thugs think they 'captured' . . . they should be declaring him a hero. He took me captive, he and Xeones. That's why they were in my shell. To arrest me and bring me in."

"Of course," Polynikes replied sarcastically. "That's why they had you bound so tightly."

Olympieus addressed Alexandros. "Is this true, son? Did you indeed place the youth Rooster in custody?"

"No, Father. I did not."

All knew that this "trial" would not last long. Discovery was inevitable, even here in the shadows, by the *agoge* youths who stood sentry over the night city, their patrols doubled now for wartime. The assembly had perhaps five minutes, no more.

In two brief exchanges, as if the Peers couldn't divine it themselves, it became clear that Alexandros had at the eleventh hour attempted to persuade Rooster into rescinding his defiance and accepting the city's honor, that he had failed and that still he had taken no action against him.

This was treason pure and simple, Polynikes declared. Yet, he said, he personally had no wish to defame and punish the son of Olympieus, nor even myself, the squire of Dienekes. Let it end here. You gentlemen retire. Leave this helot and his brat to me.

Dienekes now spoke. He expressed his gratitude to Polynikes for this offer of clemency. There remained, however, an aspect of half-exoneration to the Knight's suggestion. Let us not leave it at that, but clear Alexandros' name entire. May he, Dienekes requested, speak on the young man's behalf?

The senior Medon assented, the Peers seconding him.

Dienekes spoke. "You gentlemen all know my feelings for Alexandros. All of you are aware that I have counseled and mentored him since he was a child. He is like a son to me, and a friend and brother as well. But I will not defend him out of these sentiments. Rather, my friends, consider these points.

"What Alexandros was attempting this night is nothing other than that which his father has been trying since Oenophyta, that is, to influence informally, by reason and persuasion, and out of friendly feeling, this boy Dekton called Rooster. To soften the bitterness he bears against us Spartans, who, he feels, have enslaved his countrymen, and to bring him around to the greater cause of Lakedaemon.

"In this endeavor, Alexandros has not this night and never has sought any advantage for himself. What good could come to him from enlisting this renegade beneath Spartan scarlet? His thought was alone for the good of the city, to harness to its use a young man of clearly demonstrated vigor and courage, the bastard son of a Peer and hero, my own wife's brother, Idotychides. In fact, you may hold me to blame along with Alexandros, for I more than once have referred to this boy Rooster as my by-blow nephew."

"Yes," Polynikes put in swiftly, "as a joke and term of derision."

"We do not joke here tonight, Polynikes."

There was a rustle among the leaves, and suddenly, to the astonishment of all, there into the slaughtering space advanced the lady Arete. I glimpsed a pair of barn urchins escaping into shadow; clearly these spies had witnessed the scene at Rooster's shell and dashed at once to relay it to the lady.

Now she came forward. Wearing a plain *peplos* robe, with her hair down, summoned no doubt from bedtime lullabies just moments previous. The Peers parted before her, taken so by surprise that none could momentarily find voice to protest.

"What is this," she demanded with scorn, "a skull court beneath the oaks? What august verdict will you brave warriors pronounce tonight? To murder a maiden or slit the throat of an infant?"

Dienekes sought to silence her, and the others did as well, with declamations to the effect that a woman had no business here, she must depart at once, they would hear of nothing else. Arete, however, ignored these utterly, stepping without hesitation to the side of the girl Harmonia, and there seizing Rooster's infant and taking him into her arms.

"You say my presence here can serve no purpose. On the contrary," she declared to the Peers, "I can offer most apposite assistance. See? I can tilt this child's jaw back, to make his assassination easier.

Which of you sons of Herakles will slice this infant's throat? You, Polynikes? You, my husband?"

More declarations of outrage ensued, insisting that the lady vacate at once. Dienekes himself voiced this in the most emphatic terms. Arete would not budge.

"If this young man's life were all that were at stake"—her gesture indicated Rooster—"I would obey my husband and you other Peers without hesitation. But who else will you heroes be compelled to murder in addition? The boy's half brothers? His uncles and cousins and their wives and children, all of them innocent and all assets which the city needs desperately in this hour of peril?"

It was reasserted that these issues were none of the lady's concern.

Actaeon the boxer addressed her directly. "With respect, lady, none can but see that your intention is to shield from extinction your honored brother's line," and he gestured to the squalling boy-child, "even in this, its bastard form."

"My brother has already achieved imperishable fame," the lady responded with heat, "which is more than can be said for any of you. No, it is simple justice I seek. This child you stand ready to murder is not the issue of this boy, Rooster."

This statement appeared so irrelevant as to border upon the preposterous.

"Then whose is he?" Actaeon demanded impatiently.

The lady hesitated not a moment.

"My husband's," she replied.

Snorts of incredulity greeted this. "Truth is an immortal goddess, lady," the senior Medon spoke sternly. "One would be wise to consider before defaming her."

"If you don't believe me, ask this girl, the child's mother."

The Peers plainly granted no credence whatever to the lady's outrageous assertion. Yet all eyes now centered upon the poor young housewoman, Harmonia.

"He is my child," Rooster broke in with vehemence, "and no one else's."

"Let the mother speak," Arete cut him off. Then to Harmonia: "Whose son is he?"

The hapless girl sputtered in consternation. Arete held the infant up before the Peers. "Let all see, the babe is well made, strong of limb and voice, with the cradled vigor which precedes strength in youth and valor in manhood."

She turned to the girl. "Tell these men. Did my husband lie with you? Is this child his?"

"No . . . yes . . . I don't . . ."

"Speak!"

"Lady, you terrorize the girl."

"Speak!"

"He is your husband's," the girl blurted, and began to sob.

"She lies!" Rooster shouted. He received a vicious cuff for his efforts; blood sprung from his lip, now split.

"Of course she would not tell you, her husband," the lady addressed Rooster. "No woman would. But that does not alter the facts."

With a gesture Polynikes indicated Rooster. "For the only time in his life, this villain speaks the truth. He has sired this whelp, as he says."

This opinion was seconded vigorously by the others.

Medon now addressed Arete. "I would sooner go up bare-handed against a lioness in her den than face your wrath, lady. Nor can any but commend your motive, as a wife and mother, in seeking to shield the life of an innocent. Nonetheless we of this mess have known your husband since he was no bigger than this babe here. None in the city surpasses him in honor and fidelity. We have been with him, more than once on campaign, when he has had opportunity, ample and tempting opportunity, to be faithless. Never has he so much as wavered."

This was corroborated with emphasis by the others.

"Then ask him," Arete demanded.

"We will do no such thing," Medon replied. "Even to call his honor into question would be infamous."

The Peers of the mess faced Arete, solid as a phalanx. Yet far from being intimidated, she confronted the line boldly, in a tone of order and command.

"I will tell you what you will do," Arete declared, stepping squarely before Medon, senior of the mess, and addressing him like a commander. "You will recognize this child as the issue of my husband. You, Olympieus, and you, Medon, and you, Polynikes, will then sponsor the boy and enroll him in the *agoge*. You will pay his dues. He will be given a schooling name, and that name will be Idotychides."

This was too much for the Peers to endure. The boxer Actaeon now spoke. "You dishonor your husband, and your brother's memory, even to propose such a course, lady."

"If the child were my husband's, would my argument find favor?"

"But he is not your husband's."

"If he were?"

Medon cut her short. "The lady knows full well that if a man, like this youth called Rooster, is found guilty of treason and executed, his male issue may not be allowed to live, for these, if they possess any honor whatever, will seek vengeance when they reach manhood. This is the law not merely of Lykurgus but of every city in Hellas and holds true without exception even among the barbarians."

"If you believe that, then slit the babe's throat now."

Arete stepped directly before Polynikes. Before the runner could react, her grasp sprung to his hip and snatched forth his *xiphos*. Maintaining her own hand upon the hilt, she thrust the weapon into Polynikes' hand and held the infant up, exposing its throat beneath the whetted steel.

"Honor the law, sons of Herakles. But do it here in the light where all may see, not in the darkness so beloved of the *krypteia*."

Polynikes froze. His hand sought to tug the blade back and away, but the lady's grip would not release it.

"Can't do it?" she hissed. "Let me help. Here, I'll plunge it with you . . ."

A dozen voices, led by her husband's, implored Arete to hold. Harmonia sobbed uncontrollably. Rooster looked on, still bound, paralyzed with horror.

Such a fierceness stood now in the lady's eye as must have informed Medea herself as she poised the steel of slaughter above her own babes.

"Ask my husband if this child is his," Arete demanded again. "Ask him!"

A chorus of refusal greeted this. Yet what alternative did the Peers possess? Each eye now swung to Dienekes, not so much in demand that he respond to this ridiculous accusation, as simply because they were flummoxed by the lady's temerity and did not know what else to do.

"Tell them, my husband," Arete spoke softly. "Before the gods, is this child yours?"

Arete released her hand upon the blade. She swung the babe away from Polynikes' sword and held him out before her husband.

The Peers knew the lady's assertion could not be true. Yet, if Dienekes so testified, and under oath as Arete demanded, it must be accepted by all, and by the city as well, or his holy honor would be forfeit. Dienekes understood this too. He peered for a long moment into his wife's eyes, which met his, as Medon's image had so aptly suggested, like those of a lioness.

"By all the gods," Dienekes swore, "the child is mine."

Tears welled in the lady Arete's eyes, which she at once quelled.

The Peers murmured at this defilement of the oath of honor.

Medon spoke. "Consider what you are saying, Dienekes. You defame your wife by attesting to this 'truth' and yourself by swearing to this falsehood."

"I have considered, my friend," Dienekes responded.

He restated that the child was his.

"Take him, then," Arete directed at once, advancing the final pace before her husband and placing the babe gently into his grasp. Dienekes accepted the bundle as if he'd been handed a litter of serpents.

He glanced again, for a long moment, into the eyes of his wife, then turned and addressed the Peers.

"Which of you, friends and comrades, will sponsor my son and enroll him before the ephors?"

Not a peep. It was a dreadful oath to which their brother-in-arms had sworn; would they, seconding him, be impeached by it as well?

"It will be my privilege to stand up for the child," Medon spoke. "We will present him tomorrow. His name as the lady wishes shall be Idotychides, as was her brother's."

Harmonia wept with relief.

Rooster glared at the assembly with helpless rage.

"Then it is settled," said Arete. "The child will be raised by his mother within the walls of my husband's home. At seven years he will enter the Upbringing as a *mothax* and be trained as any other blood issue of a citizen. If he proves worthy in virtue and discipline, he will when he reaches manhood receive his initiation and take his place as a warrior and defender of Lakedaemon."

"So be it," assented Medon, and the others of the mess, however reluctantly, agreed.

It was not yet over.

"This one," Polynikes indicated Rooster. "This one dies."

The warriors of the *krypteia* now hauled Rooster to his feet. None of the mess raised a hand in his defense. The assassins commenced to drag their captive toward the shadows. In five minutes he would be dead. His body would never be found.

"May I speak?"

This from Alexandros, advancing to intercept the executioners. "May I address the Peers of the mess?"

Medon, the eldest, nodded his assent.

Alexandros indicated Rooster. "There is another way to deal with this renegade which may, I suggest, prove of greater utility to the city than summarily to dispatch him. Consider: Many among the helots honor this man. His death by assassination will make him in their eyes a martyr. Those who call him friend may for the moment be cowed by the terror of his execution but later, in the field against the Persian, their sense of injustice may find an outlet opposed to the interests of Hellas and of Lakedaemon. They may prove traitor under fire, or work harm to our warriors when they are most vulnerable."

Polynikes interrupted with anger. "Why do you defend this scum, son of Olympieus?"

"He is nothing to me," Alexandros replied. "You know he holds me in contempt and considers himself a braver man than I. In this judgment he is doubtless correct."

The Peers were abashed by this candor, expressed so openly by the young man. Alexandros continued.

"Here is what I propose: Let this helot live, but go over to the Persian. Have him escorted to the frontier and cut loose. Nothing could suit his seditious purposes more; he will embrace the prospect of dealing harm to us whom he hates. The enemy will welcome a runaway slave. Them he will provide with all the intelligence he wishes about the Spartans; they may even arm him and allow him to march beneath their banner against us. But nothing he says can injure our cause, since Xerxes already has among his courtiers Demaratos, and who can give better intelligence of the Lakedaemonians than their own deposed king?

"The defection of this youth will work no harm to us, but it will accomplish something of inestimable value: it will prevent him from being viewed by his fellows in our midst as a martyr and a hero. He will be seen by them for what he is, an ingrate who was offered a chance to wear the scarlet of Lakedaemon and who spurned it out of pride and vainglory.

"Let him go, Polynikes, and I promise you this: if the gods grant that this villain come before us again on the field of battle, then you will have no need to slay him, for I will do it myself."

Alexandros finished. He stepped back. I glanced to Olympieus; his eyes glistened with pride at the case so concisely and emphatically put forward by his son.

The *polemarch* addressed Polynikes. "See to it."

The *krypteis* hauled Rooster away.

Medon broke up the assembly with orders to the Peers to disperse at once to their berths or homes and repeat nothing of what had transpired here, until tomorrow at the proper hour before the ephors. He upbraided the lady Arete sternly, admonishing her that she had tempted the gods sorely this evening. Arete, now chastened and beginning to experience that quaking of the limbs which all warriors know in the aftermath of battle, accepted the elder's chastisement without protest. As she turned her path toward home, her knees failed. She stumbled, faint, and had to be braced up by her husband, who stood at her side.

Dienekes wrapped his cloak about his wife's shoulders. I could see him regard her keenly while she struggled to reclaim her self-command. A portion of him still burned, furious at her for what she had forced him to do tonight. But another part stood in awe of her, at her compassion and audacity and even, if the word may be applied, her generalship.

The lady's equilibrium returned; she glanced up to discover her husband studying her. She smiled for him. "Whatever deeds of virtue you have performed or may yet perform, my husband, none will exceed that which you have done this night."

Dienekes appeared less than convinced.

"I hope you're right," he said.

The Peers had now departed, leaving Dienekes beneath the oaks with the babe still in the crook of his arm, about to hand it back to its mother.

Medon spoke. "Let's have a look at this little bundle."

In the starlight the elder advanced to my master's shoulder. He took the infant and passed it gently across to Harmonia. Medon examined the little fellow, extending a war-scarred forefinger, which the boy clasped in his strong infant's fist and tugged upon with vigor and pleasure. The elder nodded, approving. He caressed the babe's crown once in tender benediction, then turned back with satisfaction toward the lady Arete and her husband.

"You have a son now, Dienekes," he said. "Now you may be chosen."

My master regarded the elder quizzically, uncertain of his meaning.

"For the Three Hundred," Medon said. "For Thermopylae."

BOOK FIVE

POLYNIKES

EIGHTEEN

His Majesty read with great interest these words of the Greek Xeones which I, His historian, placed before Him in their transcribed form. The army of Persia had advanced by this date deep into Attika and made camp at that crossroads called by the Hellenes the Three-Cornered Way, two hours' march northwest of Athens. There His Majesty made sacrifice to God Ahura Mazda and distributed decorations for valor to the leading men among the Empire's forces. His Majesty had not for the preceding several days summoned into His presence the captive Xeones to hear from him in person the continuance of his tale, so consumed was He with the myriad affairs of the army and navy in the advance. Yet did His Majesty not fail to follow the narrative in His spare hours, studying it in this, the transcribed form in which His historian daily submitted it.

In fact His Majesty had not been well for the previous several nights. His sleep had been troubled; the attendance of the Royal Surgeon had been summoned. His Majesty's rest was disturbed by untoward dreams whose content He divulged to no one, save the Magi and the circle of His most trusted counselors: the general Hydarnes, commander of the Immortals and victor at Thermopylae; Mardonius, field marshal of His Majesty's land forces; Demaratos, the deposed Spartan king and now guest-friend; and the warrioress Artemisia, queen of Halicarnassus, whose wisdom in counsel His Majesty esteemed beyond all others'.

The incubus of these troublous dreams, His Majesty now confided, appeared to be His own remorse over the desecration, following the victory at the Hot Gates, of the body of the Spartan Leonidas. His Majesty reiterated his regret at the defilement of the corpse of this warrior who was, before all, a king.

The general Mardonius beseeched His Majesty to recall that He had scrupulously observed all sacred ritual prescribed to expiate the lingering vapors of blood guilt, if in fact any such had been incurred. Had not His

Majesty subsequently ordered the execution of all those of the royal party, including His own son, the prince Rheodones, who had participated in the event? What more needed doing? Yet despite all this, His Majesty declared, the royal slumber remained restless and unsound. His Majesty in wistful tone expressed the fancy that He, perhaps in induced visions or seantic trance, might acquaint Himself personally with the shade of the man Leonidas and share with him a cup of wine.

A silence of no short duration followed. "This fever," the general Hydarnes ventured at last, "has dulled Your Majesty's edge of command and compromised its keenness. I beg Your Majesty speak no more in this manner."

"Yes, yes, you're right, my friend," His Majesty replied. "As you are always."

The commanders turned their attention to matters military and diplomatic. Reports were delivered. The advance force of Persian infantry and cavalry, fifty thousand strong, had entered Athens and taken possession of the city. The Athenian citizenry had abandoned the place utterly, betaking themselves, with only those goods which they could bear upon their persons, by sail across the strait to Troezen and the island of Salamis, where they now held themselves as refugees, huddling about fires upon the hillsides and bewailing their sorrows.

The city itself had offered no resistance, save that of a small band of fanatics who occupied the High City, the Acropolis, whose precincts in ancient times had been bounded by a wooden palisade. These desperate defenders had fortified themselves in this site, placing, it seems, their faith in the oracle of Apollo which some weeks previous had declared,

". . . the wooden wall alone shall not fail you."

These lamentable remnants were routed easily by imperial archers, who slew them at a distance. So much, Mardonius decreed, for the prophecy. The bivouac fires of the Empire now burned upon the Athenian acropolis. Tomorrow His Majesty Himself would enter the city. Plans were approved for the razing of all temples and sanctuaries of the Hellenic gods and the torching of the remainder of the city. The smoke and flames, it was reported by the intelligence officer, would be visible across the strait to the

Athenian populace now cowering in the high goat pastures upon the island of Salamis. "They will have a front-row seat," the lieutenant said with a smile, "at the annihilation of their universe."

The hour had now grown late, and His Majesty had begun to display indications of fatigue. The Magus, observing, suggested that the evening might now profitably be brought to a close. All rose from their couches, prostrated themselves and made their exit, save the general Mardonius and Artemisia, whom by subtle gesture of His Majesty's hand were bade to stay. His Majesty indicated that His historian would remain as well, to record the proceedings. Clearly His Majesty's peace was troubled.

Now alone in the tent with His two closest confidants, He spoke, relaying a dream.

"I was on a battlefield, which seemed to extend to infinity, and over which the corpses of the slain spread beyond sight. Cries of victory filled the air; generals and men were vaunting triumphantly. Abruptly I espied the corpse of Leonidas, decapitated, with its head impaled upon a spike, as we had done at Thermopylae, the body itself nailed as a trophy to a single barren tree in the midst of the plain. I was seized with grief and shame. I raced toward the tree, shouting to my men to cut the Spartan down. In the dream it seemed that, if I could only reaffix the king's head, all would be well. He would revive, and even befriend me, which outcome I dearly desired. I reached to the spike, upon which the severed head sat impaled . . ."

"And the head was His Majesty's own," the lady Artemisia broke in.

"Is the dream that transparent?" His Majesty inquired.

"It is nothing and signifies nothing," the warrioress declared emphatically, continuing in a tone that deliberately made light of the matter and urged His Majesty with all speed to put it from his mind. "It means only that His Majesty, who is a king, recognizes the mortality of all kings, Himself included. This is wisdom, as Cyrus the Great Himself expressed when he spared the life of Croesus of Lydia."

His Majesty considered Artemisia's words for long moments. He wished by them to be convinced, yet, it was apparent, they had not succeeded entirely in stanching His concern.

"Victory is yours, Your Majesty, and nothing can take it from you," the general Mardonius now spoke. "Tomorrow we will burn Athens,

which was the goal of your father, Darius, and your own and the reason you have assembled this magnificent army and navy and have toiled and struggled for so long and overcome so many obstacles. Rejoice, my lord! All Greece lies prostrate before you. You have defeated the Spartans and slain their king. The Athenians you have driven before you like cattle, compelling them to abandon the temples of their gods and all their lands and possessions. You stand triumphant, Sire, with the sole of your slipper upon the throat of Greece."

So complete was His Majesty's victory, Mardonius declared, that the Royal Person need detain Itself not one hour longer here in these hellish precincts at the antipodes of the earth. "Leave the dirty work to me, Your Majesty. You yourself take ship home for Susa, tomorrow, there to receive the worship and adulation of your subjects, and to attend to the far more pressing matters of the Empire, which have been in favor of this Hellenic nuisance too long neglected. I will mop up for you. What your forces do in your name is done by you."

"And the Peloponnese?" the warrioress Artemisia put in, citing the southern peninsula of Greece, which alone of the whole country remained unsubdued. "What would you do with it, Mardonius?"

"The Peloponnese is a goat pasture," the general responded. "A desert of rocks and sheep dung, with neither riches nor spoil, nor a single port possessed of haven for more than a dozen garbage scows. It is nothing and contains nothing which His Majesty needs."

"Except Sparta."

"Sparta?" Mardonius replied contemptuously, and not without heat. "Sparta is a village. The whole stinking place would fit, with room to spare, within His Majesty's strolling garden at Persepolis. It is an up-country burg, a pile of stones. It contains no temples or treasures of note, no gold; it is a barnyard of leeks and onions, with soil so thin a man may kick through it with one strike of his foot."

"It contains the Spartans," the lady Artemisia spoke.

"Whom we have crushed," Mardonius replied, "and whose king His Majesty's forces have slain."

"We slew three hundred of them," replied Artemisia, "and it took two million of us to do it."

These words so incensed Mardonius that he seemed upon the point of rising from his couch to confront Artemisia physically.

"My friends, my friends." His Majesty's conciliating tone made to quell the momentary upset. "We are here to take counsel, not brawl with each other like schoolchildren."

Yet the lady's fervor still burned. "What is that between your legs, Mardonius, a turnip? You speak like a man with balls the size of chick-peas."

She addressed Mardonius directly, controlling her anger and speaking with precision and clarity. "His Majesty's forces have not even sighted, let alone confronted or defeated, the main force of the Spartan army, which remains intact within the Peloponnese and no doubt in full preparedness, and eagerness, for war. Yes, we have killed a Spartan king. But they, as you know, have two; Leotychides now reigns, and Leonidas' son, the boy Pleistarchus; his uncle and regent, Pausanias, who will lead the army and whom I know, is every inch the equal of Leonidas in courage and sagacity. So the loss of a king means nothing to them, other than to harden their resolve and inspire them to yet greater prodigies of valor as they seek to emulate his glory.

*"Now consider their numbers. The Spartiate Peers alone comprise eight thousand heavy infantry. Add the Gentleman-Rankers and the per-*ioikoi *and the tally multiplies by five. Arm their helots, which they most certainly will do, and the total swells by another forty thousand. To this stew toss in the Corinthians, Tegeates, Eleans, Mantineans, Plataeans and Megarians, and the Argives, whom these others will compel into alliance if they have not done so already, not to mention the Athenians, whose backs we have driven to the wall and whose hearts are primed with the valor of desperation."*

"The Athenians are ashes," Mardonius broke in. "As will be their city before tomorrow's sun sets."

His Majesty appeared of two minds, torn between the prudence of his general's counsel and the passion of the warrioress's advice. He turned to Artemisia. "Tell me, my lady, is Mardonius right? Ought I to settle myself upon pillows and take ship for home?"

"Nothing could be more disgraceful, Your Majesty," the lady replied

without hesitation, "nor more unworthy of your own greatness." She rose to her feet now and spoke, pacing before His Majesty beneath the arcing linen of His pavilion.

"Mardonius has recited the names of the Hellenic cities which have offered tokens of submission, and these I admit are not inconsiderable. But the flower of Hellas remains unplucked. The Spartans' nose we have barely bloodied, and the Athenians, though we have driven them from their lands, remain an intact polis *and a formidable one. Their navy is two hundred warships, by far the greatest in Hellas, and every vessel is manned by crack citizen crews. These may bear the Athenians anywhere in the world, where they may reestablish themselves undiminished, as potent a threat to Your Majesty's peace as ever. Nor have we depleted their manpower. Their hoplite army remains untouched, and their leaders enjoy the full respect and support of the city. We delude ourselves to underestimate these men, whom His Majesty may not know but whom I do. Themistokles, Aristides, Xanthippus the son of Ariphron; these are names of proven greatness, fired and ardent to earn more.*

"As for the poverty of Greece, what Mardonius says cannot be controverted. There is neither gold nor treasure upon these hardscrabble shores, no rich lands nor fat flocks to plunder. But are these why we came? Are these the reason Your Majesty levied and marshaled this army, the mightiest the world has ever seen? No! Your Majesty came to bring these Greeks to their knees, to compel them to offer earth and water, and this, these last defiant cities have refused and yet refuse to do.

"Put this fatigue-spawned dream from your mind, Your Majesty. It is a false dream, a phantasm. Let the Greeks degrade themselves by resort to superstition. We must be men and commanders, exploiting oracles and portents when they suit the purposes of reason and dismissing them when they do not.

"Consider the oracle which the Spartans were given, which all Hellas knows, and which they know we know. That either Sparta would lose a king in battle, which calamity had never in six hundred years befallen them, or the city herself would fall.

"Well, they have lost a king. What will their seers make of this, Your Majesty? Clearly that the city now cannot fall.

"If you retire now, Lord, the Greeks will say it was because you feared a dream and an oracle."

She drew up then, before His Majesty, and addressed these words directly to Him. "Contrary to what our friend Mardonius says, His Majesty has not yet claimed His victory. It dangles before Him, a ripe fruit waiting to be plucked. If His Majesty retires now to palaced luxury and leaves this prize to be taken by others, even those whom He most honors and holds dearest to Him, the glory of this triumph is tarnished and defamed. Victory cannot simply be declared, it must be won. And won, if I may say so, in person.

"Then, and only then, may His Majesty with honor take ship and return home."

The warrior queen finished and resumed her position upon her couch. Mardonius offered no rebuttal. His Majesty looked from one to the other.

"It seems my women have become men, and my men women."

His Majesty spoke not in rancor or disapprobation, but stretching His right hand across, He settled it with affection upon the shoulder of His friend and kinsman Mardonius, as if to reassure the general that His confidence in him remained steadfast and undiminished.

His Majesty then straightened and with forcefulness of voice and demeanor reassumed His kingly tone.

"Tomorrow," He vowed, "we will burn Athens to the ground and, following that, march upon the Peloponnese, there to overthrow the very foundation stones of Sparta, not ceasing until we have ground them, everlastingly, into dust."

NINETEEN

His Majesty did not sleep that night. Instead He ordered the Greek Xeones summoned to Him at once, intending even at this advanced hour to interrogate the man personally, seeking further intelligence of the Spartans, who now, more so even than the Athenians, had become the focus of His Majesty's fever and obsession. The warrioress Artemisia had along with Mardonius been dismissed and was at that moment taking her leave; upon hearing these orders of His Majesty she turned back and spoke with concern for Him.

"Sire, please, for the sake of the army and of those who love you, I beg you preserve the Royal Person, for godly though Your Majesty's spirit may be, yet it is contained within a mortal vessel. Get some sleep. Do not torment yourself with these cares, which are mere phantoms."

The general Mardonius seconded this with vehemence. "Why distress yourself, Lord, with this tale told by a slave? What bearing can the story of obscure officers and their petty internecine wars have upon the events of supreme moment to which we now are committed? Trouble yourself no more with this whimsy woven by a savage, who hates you and Persia with every element of his being. His story is all lies anyway, if you ask me."

His Majesty smiled at these words of his general. "On the contrary, my friend, I believe this fellow's tale is true in every regard and, though you may not yet grant it, very much to the point of matters with which we now grapple."

His Majesty indicated His campaign throne, which stood in the lamplight beneath the pinnacle of the tent. "Do you see that chair, my friends? No mortal can be lonelier or more isolated than He who sits upon it. You cannot appreciate this, Mardonius. None can who has not sat there.

"Consider: Whom can a king trust who comes into His hearing? What man enters before Him but with some secret desire, passion, grievance or

claim, which he employs all his artifice and guile to conceal? Who speaks the truth before a king? A man addresses Him either in fear for that which He may seize or in avarice for that which He may bestow. None comes before Him but as a suppliant. His heart's business the flatterer speaks not aloud, but all he obscures beneath the cloak of dissemblance and dissimulation.

"Each voice vowing allegiance, each heart declaring love, the Royal Listener must probe and examine as if He were a vendor in a bazaar, seeking the subtle indices of betrayal and deceit. How tiresome this becomes. A king's own wives whisper sweetly to Him in the darkness of the royal bedchamber. Do they love Him? How can He know, when He perceives their true passion spent in scheming and intriguing for their children's advantage or their own private gain. None speaks the truth whole to a king, not His own brother, not even you, my friend and kinsman."

Mardonius hastened to deny this, but His Majesty cut him short with a smile. "Of all those who come before me, only one man, I believe, speaks without desire for private profit. That is this Greek. You do not understand him, Mardonius. His heart yearns for one thing only: to be reunited with his brothers-in-arms beneath the earth. Even his passion to tell their story is secondary, an obligation imposed upon him by one of his gods, which is to him a burden and a curse. He seeks nothing from me. No, my friends, the Greek's words do not trouble or distress. They please. They restore."

His Majesty, standing then at the threshold of the pavilion, gestured past the guard of the Immortals to the watch fires glowing without.

"Consider the crossing at which we now stand encamped, that site the Hellenes call the Three-Cornered Way. It would be nothing to us, mere dirt beneath our feet. Yet is not this humble plot given meaning, and even charm, to recall from the prisoner's tale that he, as a child, parted here from the maiden Diomache, his cousin whom he loved?"

Artemisia exchanged a glance with Mardonius.

"His Majesty yields to sentiment," the lady addressed her King, "and fatuous sentiment at that."

At this moment the service portal of the pavilion parted and permission to enter was asked by the detention officers. The Greek was borne in, yet upon his litter, eyes cloth-bound as ever, by two subalterns of the Immortals preceded by Orontes, their captain.

"Let us see the man's face," His Majesty commanded, "and may his eyes behold ours."

Orontes obeyed. The cloth was removed.

The captive Xeones blinked several times in the lamplight, then looked for the first time upon His Majesty. So striking was the expression which then appeared upon the man's face that the captain remarked angrily upon it and demanded to know what arrogance possessed the fellow to stare so boldly at the Royal Person.

"I have looked upon His Majesty's face before," the man replied.

"Above the battle, as all the foe have."

"No, Captain. Here, in this tent. On the night of the fifth day."

"You are a liar!" Orontes struck the man in anger. For the breach to which the captive referred had in fact occurred, on the penultimate eve of battle at the Hot Gates, when a night raid of the Spartans bore a handful of their warriors within a spear's thrust of the Royal Presence, inside this very pavilion, before the intruders were driven back by the Immortals and Egyptian marines swarming to His Majesty's defense.

"I was here," the Greek responded calmly, "and would have had my skull split apart by an axe, hurled at me by a noble, had it not struck first a ridgepole of the tent and embedded itself there."

At this, the general Mardonius' face lost all color. In the west portal of the chamber, precisely where the Spartan raid had penetrated, was lodged yet an axehead, driven so deep into the cedar that it could not be extracted without splitting the pole, and so had been left in place by the carpenters, sawn off at the shaft, with the pole repaired and rewound about it with cord.

The Hellene's gaze now centered directly upon Mardonius. "This lord here threw that axe. I recognize his face as well."

The general's expression, for the moment struck dumb, betrayed the truth of this.

"His sword," the Greek continued, "severed the wrist of a Spartiate warrior, at the moment of drawing back his spear to thrust at His Majesty."

His Majesty inquired of Mardonius if this indeed was true. The general confirmed that he had in fact inflicted such a wound upon an advancing

Spartan, among numerous others delivered in those moments of confusion and peril.

"That warrior," the man Xeones declared, "was Alexandros, the son of Olympieus, of whom I spoke."

"The boy who followed the Spartan army? Who swam the channel before Antirhion?" Artemisia asked.

"Grown to manhood," the Greek confirmed. "Those officers who bore him from this tent protected by the shadows of their shields, those were the Knight Polynikes and my master, Dienekes."

All paused for several moments, absorbing this.

His Majesty spoke: "These truly were the men who penetrated here, into this tent?"

"They and others, Lord. As His Majesty saw."

The general Mardonius received this intelligence with skepticism bordering on outrage. He accused the prisoner of fabricating this tale from snatches he had overheard from the cooks or medical personnel who attended him. The captive denied this respectfully but with vehemence.

Orontes, responding to Mardonius in his capacity as Commander of the Guard, proclaimed it inconceivable that the Greek could have acquired knowledge of these events in the manner the general suggested. The captain himself had personally overseen the prisoner's sequestration. No one, either of the commissariat or of the Royal Surgeon's staff, had been allowed alone with the man, even for a moment, without the immediate supervision of His Majesty's Immortals, and these were, as all knew, without peer in scruple and attendance.

"Then he has this tale from the rumor mill of the battle," Mardonius rejoined, "from the Spartan warriors who did in fact breach His Majesty's line."

All attention now swung to the captive Xeones, who, quite undistressed by these accusations which could have produced his death upon the spot, regarded Mardonius with level gaze and addressed him without fear.

"I might have learned of these events, lord, in the manner which you suggest. But how, sir, would I know to recognize you, of all these others, as the man who hurled the axe?"

His Majesty had now crossed to the spot where the axehead was embed-

ded and with His dagger cut through the enwrapping cord to expose the weapon. Upon the steel of the axehead, His Majesty identified the double-headed griffin of Ephesus, whose corps of armorers' privilege it was to provide all edged blades and lances for Mardonius and his commanders.

"Tell me now," His Majesty addressed the general, "that no god's hand is at work here."

His Majesty declared that He and His counselors had already from the captive's tale gleaned much that was as instructive as it was unanticipated. "How much more of value may we yet learn?"

With a gesture of warmth, His Majesty motioned the man Xeones closer to Him and had the fellow's still gravely ill form propped upon a settle.

"Please, my friend, continue your tale. Tell it as you wish, in whatever manner the god instructs you."

TWENTY

I had watched the army marshal on the plain beneath Athena of the Brazen House perhaps fifty times over the previous nine years, in various strengths of call-up as it prepared to march out to one campaign or another. This one, the corps dispatched to the Hot Gates, was the slenderest ever. Not a two-thirds call-up as before Oenophyta, when nearly six thousand warriors, squires and their battle train had filled the plain, nor a half-mobilization, forty-five hundred, as before Achilleion, nor even a two-*mora*, twenty-five hundred, when Leonidas led the force to Antirhion which Alexandros and I had followed as boys.

Three hundred.

The meager tally seemed to rattle about the plain like peas in a jar. Just three dozen pack animals stood in the fore along the roadway. There were only eight waggons; the sacrificial herd was marshaled by two scared-looking goat boys. Supply trains had already been dispatched and dumps set up along the six-day route. In addition, it was anticipated, the allied cities would provide provisions along the way, as the Spartan forerunners picked up the various contingents which would complete the force and bring it to its full complement of four thousand.

An august silence pervaded the valedictory sacrifices performed by Leonidas in his role as chief priest, assisted by Olympieus and Megistias, the Theban seer who had come to Lakedaemon of his own volition, with his son, out of love not of his native city alone, but of all Hellas, to contribute without fee or reward his art in divination.

The entire army, all twelve *lochoi,* had been drawn up, not under arms because of the Karneian prohibition but yet in their scarlet cloaks, to witness the march-out. Each warrior of the Three Hundred stood garlanded, *xiphos*-armed with shield at the carry, scarlet cloak draped across his shoulders, while his squire stood at his side holding the spear until the sacrifices were completed. It was the month, as I said, of Karneius, the new year having begun at midsummer as it does in the Greek calendar, and each man was due to receive his new cloak for the year, replacing the now-threadbare one he had worn for the previous four seasons. Leonidas ordered the issue discontinued for the Three Hundred. It would be an improvident use of the city's resources, he declared, to provide new garments for men who would have use of them for so brief a time.

As Medon had predicted, Dienekes was chosen as one of the Three Hundred. Medon himself was selected. At fifty-six he was the fourth oldest, behind only Leonidas himself, who was past sixty, Olympieus and Megistias the seer. Dienekes would command the *enomotia* from the Herakles regiment. The brothers and champions of Olympia, Alpheus and Maron, were likewise selected; they would join the platoon representing the Oleaster, the Wild Olive, whose position would be to the right of the Knights, in the center of the line. Fighting as a *dyas*, the paired pentathlete and wrestler towered invincible; their inclusion greatly heartened one and all. Aristodemos the envoy was also selected. But most startling and controversial was the election of Alexandros.

At twenty he would be the youngest line warrior and one of only a dozen, including his *agoge*-mate Ariston (of Polynikes' "broken noses"), without experience of battle. There is a proverb in Lakedaemon, "the reed beside the staff," whose meaning is that a chain is made stronger by its possession of one unproven link. The tender hamstring that drives the wrestler to compensate with skill and cunning, the lisp that the orator extends his brilliance to overcome. The Three Hundred, Leonidas felt, would fight best not as a company of individual champions, but as a sort of army in miniature, of young and old, green and seasoned. Alexandros would join the platoon of the Herakles commanded by Dienekes; he and his mentor would fight as a *dyas*.

Alexandros and Olympieus were the only father and son selected for the Three Hundred. Alexandros' infant boy, also named Olympieus, would be their survivor and maintain the line. It was a sight of extreme poignancy, there along the Aphetaid, the Going-Away Street, to watch Alexandros' bride, Agathe, only nineteen years old, hold up this babe for the final farewell. Alexandros' mother, Paraleia, she who had interrogated me so masterfully after Antirhion, stood beside the girl beneath the same myrtle grove from which Alexandros and I had departed that night years ago to follow the army.

Good-byes were said on the march as the formation trooped solemnly past the rubble-walled assembly platform called the Forts, beneath the hero shrines of Lelex and Amphiareus, to the road's turn at the Running Course, above which the boys' platoons clustered at Axiopoinos, the Temple of Athena of Just Requital, Athena Tit for Tat. I watched Polynikes bid his three lads farewell; the eldest at eleven and nine stood already in the *agoge*. They straightened within their black cloaks with the gravest dignity; each would have cut off his right arm for the chance to march now with his father.

Dienekes paused before Arete on the roadside adjacent the Hellenion, whose porches stood bedecked in laurel with ribands of yellow and blue for the Karneia; she held out Rooster's boy, now named Idotychides. My master took each of his daughters in turn into his arms, lifting the younger two and kissing them with tenderness. Arete he embraced one time, setting his cheek against her neck, to smell the scent of her hair for the last time.

Two days previous to this gentle moment, the lady had summoned me in private, as she always did before a march-out. It is the Spartans' custom during the week preceding a departure for war for the Peers to pass a day neither in training nor drill, but at their ease upon the *kleroi*, the farmsteads each warrior holds under the laws of Lykurgus and from which he draws the produce which supports himself and his family as a citizen and a Peer. These "county days," as they are called, comprise a homely tradition deriving, reason must surmise, from the warrior's natural wish to revisit prior to battle, and in a sense bid farewell to, the happy scenes of his childhood. That and the more practical purpose, in the ancient days at least, of outfitting and provisioning himself from the *kleros*'s stores. A county day is a fair, one of the rare occasions when a Peer and those who serve his land may congregate as fellows and stuff their bellies with a carefree heart. In any event this was where we headed, to the farmstead called Daphneion, several mornings before the march-out to the Gates.

Two families of Messenian helots worked this land, twenty-three in all, including a pair of grandmothers, twins, so ancient they could not recall which of them was which, plus the only slightly less dotty stump-leg Kamerion, who had lost his right foot in service as Dienekes' father's squire. This toothless gaffer could outswear the foulest-tongued sailor and presided at his own insistence, and to the delight of all, as master of ceremonies for the day.

My own wife and children served this farm as well. Neighbors visited from the adjoining landholdings. Prizes were awarded in whimsical categories; there was a country dance, outdoors on the threshing floor beside the laurel grove from which the farm derived its name, and various children's games were held, before the party settled in late afternoon to a communal feast beneath the trees, at which Dienekes himself and the lady Arete and their daughters did the serving. Gifts were exchanged, quarrels and grievances patched up, claims pressed and complaints aired. If a lad of the *kleros* sought betrothal to his sweetheart from the overhill farm, he might approach Dienekes now and claim his blessing.

Invariably two or three of the sturdier helot youths and men would be slated to accompany the army, as craftsmen or armorers, battle squires or javelineers. Far from resenting or seeking to shirk these perils, the young bucks reveled in the manly attention; their sweethearts clung to them throughout the day, and many a proposal of marriage was spawned in the wine-merry amorousness of these bright country afternoons.

By the time the merry party had "put aside all desire for food and drink," as Homer says, more grain and fruit, wine and cakes and cheeses had been heaped at Dienekes' feet than he could carry into a hundred battles. He now retired to the courtyard table, with the elders of the farm, to conclude whatever details remained to set the affairs of the *kleros* in order before the march-out.

It was when the men had turned themselves to this business that the lady Arete motioned me to join her in private. We sat before a table in the farm kitchen. It was a cheerful spot, warm in the late sun that flooded through the courtyard doorway. The lad Idotychides, Rooster's boy, played outside with two other naked urchins, including my own son, Skamandridas. The lady's eyes rested for a moment, with sorrow it seemed, upon the roughhousing little fellows.

"The gods remain always a jump ahead of us, don't they, Xeo?"

This was the first hint I had received from her lips confirming that which none possessed the courage to ask: that the lady had indeed not foreseen the consequences of her action, that night of the *krypteia*, when she had saved the babe's life.

She cleared a space upon the table. Into my care the lady placed, as ever, those articles of her husband's kit which it was a wife's responsibility to provide. The surgeon's packet, bound in the thick oxhide roll that doubled as a wrap for a splint or, bound flat atop the flesh, as seal for a puncture. The three curved needles of Egyptian gold, called by the Spartans "fishhooks," with their spool of catgut twine and steel lancet, for use in the tailor's art of sewing flesh. The compresses of bleached linen, the tourniquet binders of leather, the copper "dog bites," the needle-nosed grippers for extracting arrowheads or, more often, the shards and slivers that fly from the clash of steel upon iron and iron upon bronze.

Next, money. A cache of Aeginetan obols that, as all coin or currency, the warriors were forbidden to carry but which, discovered serendipitously within a squire's pack, would come in handy at some on-route market or beside the sutler's waggon, to procure forgotten necessaries or to purchase a treat to lift the heart.

Finally those articles of purely personal significance, the little surprises and charms, items of superstition, the private talismans of love. A girl's sketch in colored wax, a riband from a daughter's hair, a charm in amber carved by a child's untutored hand. Into my care the lady placed a packet of sweets and trifles, sesame cakes and candied figs. "You may rifle your share," she said, smiling, "but save a few for my husband."

There was always something for me. This day it was a pouch of coins of the Athenians, twenty in all, tetradrachms, nearly three months' pay for a skilled oarsman or hoplite of their army. I was astonished that the lady possessed such a sum, even of her own purse, and struck dumb at her extravagant generosity. These "owls," as they were called from the image on their obverse, were good not just in the city of Athena but anywhere in Greece.

"When you accompanied my husband on embassy to Athens last month," the lady broke my dumbstruck silence, "did you find occasion to visit your cousin? Diomache. That is her name, isn't it?"

I had and she knew it. This wish of mine, long-sought, had indeed at last been fulfilled. Dienekes had dispatched me upon the errand himself. Now I glimpsed a hint of the lady's pot-stirring. I asked if it was she, Arete, who had contrived it all.

"We wives of Lakedaemon are forbidden fine gowns or jewelry or cosmetics. It would be heartless in the extreme, don't you think, to ban as well a little innocent intrigue?"

She smiled at me, waiting.

"Well?" she asked.

"Well, what?"

My wife, Thereia, was gossiping with the other farm women, out in the courtyard. I squirmed. "My cousin is a married woman, lady. As I am a married man."

The lady's eyes threw sparks of mischief. "You would not be the first husband bound by love to someone other than his wife. Nor she the first wife."

At once all teasing gaiety fled from the lady's glance. Her features became grave and shadowed, it seemed, with sorrow.

"The gods played the same trick on my husband and me." She rose, indicating the door and the courtyard beyond. "Come, let us take a walk."

The lady led barefoot up the slope to a shady spot beneath the oaks. In what country other than Lakedaemon would a noblewoman's soles be so thick with callus that they may tread upon the spiky leaves of oak and not feel their spiny barbs?

"You know, Xeo, that I was wife to my husband's brother before I was married to him."

This I did know, having learned it, as I said, from Dienekes himself.

"Iatrokles was his name, I know you have heard the story. He was killed at Pellene, a hero's death, at thirty-one. He was the noblest of his generation, a Knight and a victor at Olympia, gifted by the gods with virtue and beauty much like Polynikes in this generation. He pursued me passionately, with such impetuousness that he called me from my father's house when I was still a girl. All this the Spartans know. But I will tell you something now which no one, except my husband, knows."

The lady had reached a low bole of oak, a natural bench within the shade of the grove. She sat and indicated that I should take the place beside her.

"Down there," she said, gesturing to the open space between two outbuildings and the track that led to the threshing floor. "Right there where the path turns was where I first saw Dienekes. It was on a county day just like this. The occasion was Iatrokles' first march-out. He was twenty. My father had brought me and my brother and sisters over from our own *kleros* with gifts of fruit and a yearling goat. The boys of the farm were playing, right there, when I came, holding my father's hand, over this knoll where you and I now sit."

The lady drew up. For a moment she searched my eyes, as if to make certain of their attention and understanding.

"I saw Dienekes first from behind. Just his bare shoulders and the back of his head. I knew in an instant that I would love him and only him all my life."

Her expression grew sober before this mystery, the summons of Eros and the unknowable workings of the heart.

"I remember waiting for him to turn, so I could see him, see his face. It was so odd. In a way it was like an arranged match, where you wait with your heart fluttering to behold the face you will and must love.

"At last he turned. He was wrestling another boy. Even then, Xeo, Dienekes was unhandsome. You could hardly believe he was his brother's brother. But to my eyes he appeared *eueidestatos*, the soul of beauty. The gods could not have crafted a face more open or touching to my heart. He was thirteen then. I was nine."

The lady paused for a moment, gazing solemnly down at the spot of which she spoke. The occasion did not present itself, she declared, throughout her whole girlhood when she could speak in private with Dienekes. She observed him often on the running courses and in the exercises with his *agoge* platoon. But never did one share a moment with the other. She had no idea if he even knew who she was.

She knew, however, that his brother had chosen her and had been speaking with the elders of her family.

"I wept when my father told me I had been given to Iatrokles. I cursed myself for the heartlessness of my ingratitude. What more could a girl ask than this noble, virtuous man? But I could not master my own heart. I loved the brother of this man, this fine brave man I was to marry.

"When Iatrokles was killed, I grieved inconsolably. But the cause of my distress was not what people thought. I feared that the gods had answered by his death the self-interested prayer of my heart. I waited for Dienekes to choose a new husband for me as was his obligation under the laws, and when he didn't, I went to him, shamelessly, in the dust of the *palaistra,* and compelled him to take me himself as his bride.

"My husband embraced this love and returned it in kind, both of us over the still-warm bones of his brother. The delight was so keen between us, our secret joy in the marriage bed, that this love itself became a curse to us. My own guilt I could requite; it is easy for a woman because she can feel the new life growing inside her, that her husband has planted.

"But when each child was born and each a female, four daughters, and then I lost the gift to conceive, I felt, and my husband did too, that this was a curse from the gods for our passion."

The lady paused and glanced again down the slope. The boys, including my son and little Idotychides, had dashed out from the courtyard and now played their carefree sport directly below the site where we sat.

"Then came the summons of the Three Hundred to Thermopylae. At last, I thought, I perceive the true perversity of the gods' plan. Without a son, my husband cannot be called. He will be denied this greatest of honors. But in my heart I didn't care. All that mattered was that he would live. Perhaps for only another week or month, until the next battle. But still he would live. I would still hold him. He would still be mine."

Now Dienekes himself, his farm business completed within, emerged onto the flat below. There he joined playfully with the roughhousing boys, already obeying in their blood the instincts of battle and of war.

"The gods make us love whom we will not," the lady declared, "and disrequite whom we will. They slay those who should live and spare those who deserve to die. They give with one hand and take with the other, answerable only to their own unknowable laws."

Dienekes had now spotted Arete, watching him from above. He lifted the boy Idotychides playfully and made the lad's little arm wave up the slope. Arete compelled her own to answer.

"Now, inspired by blind impulse," she spoke toward me, "I have saved the life of this boy, my brother's bastard's son, and lost my husband's in the process."

She spoke these words so softly and with such sorrow that I felt my own throat catch and the burning begin in my eyes.

"The wives of other cities marvel at the women of Lakedaemon," the lady said. "How, they ask, can these Spartan wives stand erect and unblinking as their husbands' broken bodies are borne home to a grave or, worse, interred beneath some foreign dirt with nothing save cold memory to clutch to their hearts? These women think we are made of stauncher stuff than they. I will tell you, Xeo. We are not.

"Do they think we of Lakedaemon love our husbands less than they? Are our hearts made of stone and steel? Do they imagine that our grief is less because we choke it down in our guts?"

She blinked once, dry-eyed, then turned her glance to mine.

"The gods have played a game with you too, Xeo. But it may not be too late to steal a roll of the dice. This is why I have given you this pouch of 'owls.' "

Already I knew what her heart intended.

"You are not Spartan. Why should you bind yourself by her cruel laws? Haven't the gods stolen enough from you already?"

I begged her to speak of this no more.

"This girl you love, I can have her brought here. Just ask it."

"No! Please."

"Then run. Get out tonight. Go there."

I replied at once that I could not.

"My husband will find another to serve him. Let another die instead of you."

"Please, lady. This would be dishonor."

I felt my cheek sting and realized the lady had struck me. "Dishonor?" She spat the word with revulsion and contempt.

Down the slope the boys and Dienekes had been joined by the other lads of the farm. A game of ball had started. The boys' cries of *agon*, of contention and competition, pealed brightly up the slope to where the lady sat.

One could feel only gratitude for that which had sprung so nobly from her heart: the wish to grant to me that clemency which she felt *moira*, fate, had denied her. To grant to me and her whom I loved a chance to slip the bonds she felt herself and her husband imprisoned in.

I could offer nothing save that which she already knew. I could not go. "Besides, the gods would be there already. As ever, one jump ahead."

I saw her shoulders straighten then, as her will brought to heel the gallant but impossible impulse of her heart.

"Your cousin will learn where your body lies, and with what honor you perished. By Helen and the Twins, I swear this."

The lady rose from her bench of oak. The interview was over. She had become again a Spartan.

Now here on the morn of the march-out I beheld upon her face that same austere mask. The lady released her husband's embrace and gathered her children to her, resuming that posture, erect and solemn, replicated by the line of other Spartan wives extending fore and rear beneath the oaks.

I saw Leonidas embrace his wife, Gorgo, "Bright Eyes," their daughters, and his son, the boy Pleistarchus, who would one day take his place as king.

My own wife, Thereia, held me hard, grinding against me beneath her Messenian white robe, while she held our infants crooked in one arm. She would not be husbandless for long. "Wait at least until I'm out of sight," I joked, and held my children, whom I hardly knew. Their mother was a good woman. I wish I could have loved her as she deserved.

The final sacrifices were over, omens taken and recorded. The Three Hundred formed up, each Peer with a single squire, in the long shadows cast by distant Parnon, with the entire army in witness upon the shield-side slope. Leonidas assumed his place before them, beside the stone altar, garlanded as they. The remainder of the whole city, old men and boys, wives and mothers, helots and craftsmen, stood drawn up upon the spear-side rise. It was not yet daybreak; the sun still had not peeked above Parnon's crest.

"Death stands close upon us now," the king spoke. "Can you feel him, brothers? I do. I am human and I fear him. My eyes cast about for a sight to fortify the heart for that moment when I come to look him in the face."

Leonidas began softly, his voice carrying in the dawn stillness, heard with ease by all.

"Shall I tell you where I find this strength, friends? In the eyes of our sons in scarlet before us, yes. And in the countenances of their comrades who will follow in battles to come. But more than that, my heart finds courage from these, our women, who watch in tearless silence as we go."

He gestured to the assembled dames and ladies, singling out two matriarchs, Pyrrho and Alkmene, and citing them by name. "How many times have these twain stood here in the chill shade of Parnon and watched those they love march out to war? Pyrrho, you have seen grandfathers and father troop away down the Aphetaid, never to return. Alkmene, your eyes have held themselves unweeping as husband and brothers have departed to their deaths. Now here you stand again, with no few others who have borne as much and more, watching sons and grandsons march off to hell."

This was true. The matriarch Pyrrho's son Doreion stood garlanded now among the Knights; Alkmene's grandsons were the champions Alpheus and Maron.

"Men's pain is lightly borne and swiftly over. Our wounds are of the flesh, which is nothing; women's is of the heart—sorrow unending, far more bitter to bear."

Leonidas gestured to the wives and mothers assembled along the still-shadowed slopes.

"Learn from them, brothers, from their pain in childbirth which the gods have ordained immutable. Bear witness to that lesson they teach: nothing good in life comes but at a price. Sweetest of all is liberty. This we have chosen and this we pay for. We have embraced the laws of Lykurgus, and they are stern laws. They have schooled us to scorn the life of leisure, which this rich land of ours would bestow upon us if we wished, and instead to enroll ourselves in the academy of discipline and sacrifice. Guided by these laws, our fathers for twenty generations have breathed the blessed air of freedom and have paid the bill in full when it was presented. We, their sons, can do no less."

Into each warrior's hand was placed by his squire a cup of wine, his own ritual chalice, presented to him on the day he became a Peer and brought forth only for ceremonies of the gravest solemnity. Leonidas held his own aloft with a prayer to Zeus All-Conquering and Helen and the Twins. He poured the libation.

"In years six hundred, so the poets say, no Spartan woman has beheld the smoke of the enemy's fires."

Leonidas lifted both arms and straightened, garlanded, raising his countenance to the gods.

"By Zeus and Eros, by Athena Protectress and Artemis Upright, by the Muses and all the gods and heroes who defend Lakedaemon and by the blood of my own flesh, I swear that our wives and daughters, our sisters and mothers, will not behold those fires now."

He drank, and the men followed him.

TWENTY-ONE

His Majesty is well familiar with the topography of the approaches, defiles and the compressed battle plain wherein his armies engaged the Spartans and their allies at the Hot Gates. I will pass over this, addressing instead the composition of the Greek forces and the state of discord and disorder which prevailed as these arrived and took station, preparatory to defending the pass.

When the Three Hundred—now reinforced by five hundred heavy infantry from Tegea and a matching number from Mantinea, along with two thousand combined from Orchomenos and the rest of Arkadia, Corinth, Phlius and Mycenae, plus seven hundred from Thespiae and four hundred from Thebes—arrived at Opountian Lokris, ten miles from the Hot Gates, there to be joined by a thousand heavy infantry from Phokis and Lokris, they found instead the entire countryside deserted.

Only a few boys and young men of the neighborhood remained, and these occupied themselves in looting the abandoned homes of their neighbors and appropriating whatever stores of wine they could disinter from their compatriots' caches. They took to their heels at the sight of the Spartans, but the rangers ran them down. The army and populace of Lokris, the pimply pillagers reported, had taken to the hills, while the locals' chieftains were scurrying north toward the Persians as fast as their spindly shanks would bear them. In fact, the urchins claimed, their headmen had already capitulated.

Leonidas was furious. It was determined, however, in a hasty and decidedly ungentle interrogation of these farmyard freebooters, that the Lokrians of Opus had gotten the day of assembly wrong. Apparently the month called Karneius in Sparta is named Lemendieon in Lokris. Further its start is counted backward from the full moon, rather than forward from the new. The Lokrians had expected the

Spartans two days earlier and, when these failed to appear, determined that they had been left in the lurch. They bolted amid bitter oaths and maledictions, which the gales of rumor scattered swiftly into neighboring Phokis, in which country the Gates themselves are located and whose inhabitants were already in terror of being overrun. The Phokians had hightailed it too.

All along the march north, the allied column had encountered country tribes and villagers fleeing, streaming south along the military road, or what had now become a military road. Tattered clan groups fled before the Persian advance, bearing their pitiful possessions in shoulder sacks contrived from bedcovers or bundled cloaks, balancing their ragged parcels like water vessels atop their heads. Sunken-cheeked husbandmen wheeled handbarrows whose cargoes were more often flesh than furniture, children whose legs had given out from the tramp or bundled ancients hobbled with age. A few had oxcarts and pack asses. Pets and farm stock jostled underfoot, gaunt hounds cadging for a handout, doleful-looking swine being kicked along as if they knew they would be supper in a night or two. The main of the refugees were female; they trudged barefoot, shoes slung about their necks to save the leather.

When the women descried the allied column approaching, they vacated the road in terror, scrambling up the hillsides, clutching their infants and spilling possessions as they fled. There came always that moment when it broke upon these dames that the advancing warriors were their own countrymen. Then the alteration which overtook their hearts bordered upon the ecstatic. The women skittered back down the hardscrabble slopes, pressing tight about the column, some numb with wonder, others with tears coursing down their road-begrimed faces. Grandmothers crowded forward to kiss the young men's hands; farm matrons threw their arms about the necks of the warriors, embracing them in moments that were simultaneously poignant and preposterous. "Are you Spartans?" they inquired of the sun-blackened infantrymen, the Tegeates and Mycenaeans and Corinthians, Thebans, Philiasians and Arkadians, and many of these lied and said they were. When the women heard that Leonidas in person led the column, many refused to believe it, so accustomed had they become to betrayal and abandonment. When the Spartan king was pointed out to them and they saw the corps of Knights about him and at last believed, many could not bear the relief. They buried their faces in their hands and sank upon the roadside, overcome.

As the allies beheld this scene repeated, eight, ten, a dozen times a day, a grim urgency took possession of their hearts. All haste must be made; the defenders must at all costs reach and fortify the pass before the arrival of the enemy. Unordered, each man lengthened stride. The pace of the column soon outstripped the capacity of the train to keep up. The waggons and pack asses were simply left behind, to catch up as best they could, their necessaries transferred to the marching men's backs. For myself, I had stripped shoeless and rolled my cloak into a shoulder pad; my master's shield I bore in its hide case, along with his greaves and breastplate weighing something over sixty-five pounds, plus both our bedding and field kit, my own weapons, three quivers of ironheads wrapped in oiled goatskin and sundry other necessaries and indispensables: "fishhooks" and catgut; bags of medicinal herbs, hellebore and foxglove, euphorbia and sorrel and marjoram and pine resin; arterial straps, bindings for the hand, compresses of linen, the bronze "dogs" to heat and jam into puncture wounds to cauterize the flesh, "irons" to do the same for surface lacerations; soap, footpads, moleskins, sewing kit; then the cooking gear, a spit, a pot, a handmill, flint and firesticks; grit-and-oil for polishing bronze, oilcloth fly for rain, the combination pick and shovel called from its shape a *hyssax,* the soldier's crude term for the female orifice. This in addition to rations: unmilled barley, onions and cheese, garlic, figs, smoked goat meat; plus money, charms, talismans.

My master himself bore the spare shield chassis with double bronze facings, both our shoes and strapping, rivets and instrument kit, his leather corselet, two ash and two cornelwood spears with spare ironheads, helmet, and three *xiphe,* one on his hip and the other two lashed to the forty-pound rucksack stuffed with more rations and unmilled meal, two skins of wine and one of water, plus the "goodie bag" of sweetcakes prepared by Arete and his daughters, double-wrapped in oiled linen to keep the onion stink of the rucksack from invading it. All up and down the column, squire and man humped loads of two hundred to two hundred and twenty pounds between them.

The column had acquired a nonrostered volunteer. This was a roan-colored hunting bitch named Styx who belonged to Pereinthos, a Skirite ranger who was one of Leonidas' "king's selections." The dog had followed its master down to Sparta from the hills and now, having no home to return to, continued her attendance upon him. For an hour at a crack she would patrol the length of the column, all business, memorizing by scent the position of each member of the march, then returning to her Skirite master, who had now been nicknamed Hound, there to resume her tireless trot at his heel. There was no doubt that in the bitch's mind, all these men belonged to her. She was herding us, Dienekes observed, and doing a hell of a job.

With each passing mile, the countryside grew thinner. Everyone was gone. At last in the nation of the Phokians, nearing the Gates, the column entered country utterly denuded and abandoned. Leonidas dispatched runners into the mountain fastnesses to which the army of the locals had withdrawn, informing them in the name of the Hellenic Congress that the allies stood indeed upon the site and that it was their intention to defend the Phokians' and Lokrians' country whether these themselves showed their faces or not. The king's message was not inscribed upon the customary military dispatch roll, but scribbled on that kind of linen wrapper used to invite family and friends to a dance. The final sentence read: "Come as you are."

The allies themselves reached the village of Alpenoi that afternoon, the sixth after the march-out from Lakedaemon, and Thermopylae itself half an hour later. Unlike the countryside, the battlefield, or what would become the battlefield, stood far from deserted. A number of denizens of Alpenoi and Anthela, the north-end village that fronts the stream called Phoenix, had erected makeshift commercial ventures. Several had barley and wheat bread baking. One fellow had set up a grogshop. A pair of enterprising trollops had even established a two-woman brothel in one of the abandoned bathhouses. This became known at once as the Sanctuary of Aphrodite

Fallen, or the "two-holer," depending upon who was seeking directions and who proffering them.

The Persians, the rangers reported, had not yet reached Trachis either by land or sea. The plain to the north lay yet unpopulated by the enemy camp. The fleet of the Empire, it was reported, had put out from Therma in Macedonia either yesterday or the day before. Their thousand warships were even now traversing the Magnesia coast, the advance elements expected to reach the landing beaches at Aphetae, eight miles north, within twenty-four hours.

The land forces of the enemy had departed Therma ten days earlier; their columns were advancing, so fugitives from the north reported, via the coastal and inland routes, cutting through forests as they came. Their rangers were anticipated at the same time as the fleet.

Now Leonidas emerged to the fore.

Before the allied camps were even staked out, the king dispatched raiding parties into the country of Trachis, immediately north of the Gates. These were to torch every stalk of grain and capture or drive off every piece of livestock, down to hedgehogs and barn cats, which might make a meal for the enemy.

In the wake of these raiders, reconnaissance parties were sent out, surveyors and engineers from each allied detachment, with orders to proceed as far north as the landing beaches likely to be appropriated by the Persians. These men were to map the area, as best they could in the gathering darkness, concentrating upon the roads and trails available to the Persian in his advance to the Narrows. Although the allied force possessed no cavalry, Leonidas made certain to include skilled horsemen in this party; though afoot, they could best assess how enemy cavalry might operate. Could Xerxes get horsemen up the trail? How many? How fast? How could the allies best counter this?

Further the reconnaissance parties were to apprehend and detain any locals whose topographical knowledge could be of assistance to the allies. Leonidas wanted yard-by-yard intelligence of the immediate northern approaches and, most crucial recalling Tempe, an iron-clad assessment of the mountain defiles south and west, seeking any undiscovered track by which the Greek position could be outflanked and enveloped.

At this point a prodigy occurred which nearly broke the allies' will before they had even unshouldered their kits. An infantryman of the Thebans trod accidentally into a nest of baby snakes and received upon the bare ankle the full poison of half a dozen infant serpents, whose venom, all hunters know, is more to be feared than a full grown's because the young ones have not yet learned how to deal it out in doses, but instead inject it into the flesh in full measure. The infantryman died within the hour amid horrible sufferings, despite being bled white by the surgeons.

Megistias the seer was summoned while the stricken Theban writhed yet in the throes. The remainder of the army, ordered by Leonidas to assess at once the extension and reinforcement of the ancient Phokian Wall across the Gates, nonetheless amid their labors loitered with cold dread as the snakebitten man's life, emblematic all felt of their own, ebbed rapidly and agonizingly.

It was Megistias' son, at last, who thought to inquire the man's name.

This was, his mates reported, Perses.

At once all omen-spawned gloom dispelled as Megistias stated the prodigy's meaning, which could not have been plainer: this man, ill-starred in his mother's election of name, represented the enemy, who had in invading Greece stepped into a litter of serpents. Unfledged though these were and disunited, the fanged babes yet stood capable of delivering their venom into the foe's vital stream and bringing him low.

Night had fallen when this fortune-crossed fellow expired. Leonidas had him interred immediately with honor, then returned the men's hands at once to work. Orders were issued for every stonemason within the allied ranks to present himself, regardless of unit. Chisels, picks and levers were collected and more sent for from Alpenoi village and the surrounding countryside. The party set forth down the track to Trachis. The masons were ordered to destroy as much of the trail as possible, and also to chisel into the stone in plainest view the following message:

Greeks conscripted by Xerxes:
If under compulsion you must fight us your brothers,
fight badly.

Simultaneously work was begun on rebuilding the ancient Phokian Wall which blocked the Narrows. This fortification, when the allies arrived, was little more than a pile of rubble. Leonidas demanded a proper battle wall.

A wry scene ensued as various engineers and draughtsmen of the allied militias assembled in solemn council to survey the site and propose architectural alternatives. Torches had been positioned to light the Narrows, diagrams were sketched in the dirt; one of the captains of the Corinthians produced an actual drawn-to-scale blueprint. Now the commanders began wrangling. The wall should be erected right at the Narrows, blocking the pass. No, suggested another, better it should be set back fifty meters, creating a "triangle of death" between the cliffs and the battle wall. A third captain urged a setback distance of twice that, giving the allied infantry room to mass and maneuver. Meanwhile the troops loitered about, as Hellenes will, offering their own sage counsel and wisdom.

Leonidas simply picked up a boulder and marched to a spot. There he set the stone in place. He lifted a second and placed it beside the first. The men looked on dumbly as their commander in chief, whom all could see was well past sixty, stooped to seize a third boulder. Someone barked: "How long do you imbeciles intend to stand by, gaping? Will you wait all night while the king builds the wall himself?"

With a cheer the troops fell to. Nor did Leonidas cease from his exertions when he saw other hands joined to labor, but continued alongside the men as the pile of stones began to rise into a legitimate fortress. "Nothing fancy, brothers," the king guided the construction. "For a wall of stone will not preserve Hellas, but a wall of men."

As he had done at every engagement at which it had been my privilege to observe him, the king stripped and worked alongside his warriors, shirking nothing, but pausing to address individuals, calling by name those he knew, committing to memory the names and even nicknames of others heretofore unknown to him, often clapping these new mates upon the back in the manner of a comrade and friend. It was astonishing with what celerity these intimate words, spoken only to one man or two, were relayed warrior-to-warrior down the line, filling the hearts of all with courage.

It was now the changing of the first watch.

"Bring me the villain."

With these words Leonidas summoned an outlaw of the region who had fallen in with the column along the route and enlisted for pay to aid in reconnaissance. Two Skiritai brought the man forward. To my astonishment, I knew him.

This was the youth of my own country who called himself Sphaireus, "Ball Player," the wild boy who had taken to the hills following my city's destruction and had kicked about a man's stuffed skull as his sign of outlaw princeship. Now this criminal advanced into the margins of the king's fire, no longer a smooth-cheeked boy but a scarred and bearded man grown.

I approached him. The fellow recognized me. He was delighted to resume our acquaintance and vastly amused at the fate which had brought us, two orphans of fire and sword, to this, the very epicenter of Hellas' peril.

The outlaw stood in sizzling high spirits over the prospect of war. He would haunt its margins and prey upon the broken and the vanquished. War to him was big business; it was clear without words that he thought me a dunce for electing to serve, and for not a penny's pay or profit. "Whatever happened to that tasty bit of steam you used to tramp with?" he asked me. "What was her name—your cousin?" "Steam" was the salacious slang of my country for a female of fair and tender years.

"She's dead," I lied, "and you will be too for the price of another word."

"Easy, countryman! Back your oars. I'm only fanning the breeze."

The king's officers summoned the brigand away before he and I could speak further. Leonidas needed a buck whose soles knew how to grip the hardscrabble track of a goat trail, some stoutheart to scramble up the sheer three-thousand-foot face of Kallidromos which towered above the Narrows. He wanted to know what was up top and how dangerous it was to get there. Once the enemy took possession of the Trachinian plain and the northern approaches, could the allies get a party, even a single man, across the shoulder of the mountain and into their rear?

Ball Player appeared decidedly unenthusiastic about his participation in this hazardous venture. "I'll go with him." This from the Skirite Hound, a mountaineer himself. "Anything to get off building this miserable wall." Leonidas accepted this offer with alacrity. He instructed his paymaster to compensate the outlaw handsomely enough to get him to go, but poorly enough to make sure he came back.

Around midnight the Phokians and Lokrians of Opus began arriving from the mountains. The king welcomed the fresh allies warmly, making no mention of their near desertion but instead guiding them at once to that section of the camp which had been assigned to their use and in which hot broth and freshly baked loaves awaited them.

A terrific storm had sprung up, north along the coast. Bolts resounded furiously in the distance; though the sky above the Gates stood yet clear and brilliant, the men were getting spooked. They were tired. The six days' hump had taken the starch out of them; fears unspoken and demons unseen began to prey upon their hearts. Nor could the newly arrived Phokians and Lokrians fail to discern the slender, not to say suicidally small, numbers of the force which proposed to hold off the myriads of the enemy.

The native vendors, even the whores, had vanished, like rats evacuating to their holes presaging a quake.

There was a man among the loitering locals, a merchantman's mate, he said, who had sailed for years out of Sidon and Tyre. I chanced to be present, around a fire of the Arkadians, when this fellow began to fan the flames of terror. He had seen the Persian fleet firsthand and had the following tale to tell.

"I was on a grain galley out of Mytilene last year. We got taken by Phoenicians, part of the Great King's fleet. They confiscated our cargo. We had to trail them in under escort and unload it at one of his supply magazines. This was at Strymon on the Thracian coast. The sight I beheld there numbed the senses with awe."

More men began to cluster about the circle, listening gravely. "The dump was big as a city. One thought, coming in, that a range of hills stood beyond it. But when you got close, the hills turned out to be salt meat, towering in hogsheads of brine, stacked to the heavens.

"I saw weapons, brothers. Stands of arms by the tens of thousands. Grain and oil, bakers' tents the size of stadiums. Every article of war matériel the mind could imagine. Sling bullets. Lead sling bullets stacked a foot high, covering an acre. The trough of oats for the King's horses was a mile long. And in the middle of all rose one oilcloth-shrouded pyramid, big as a mountain. What in heaven could be under that? I asked the officer of marines guarding us. 'Come on,' he says, 'I'll show you.' Can you guess, my friends, what rose there, stacked to the sky beneath those covers?

"Paper," the ship's mate declared.

None of the Arkadians grasped the significance.

"Paper!" the Trachinian repeated, as if to drum the meaning into his hearers' thick skulls. "Paper for scribes to take inventory. Inventory of men. Horses. Arms. Grain. Orders for troops and more orders, papers for reports and requisitions, muster rolls and dispatches, courts-martial and decorations for valor. Paper to keep track of every supply the Great King is bringing, and every item of loot he plans on taking back. Paper to write down countries burned and cities sacked, prisoners taken, slaves in chains . . ."

At this moment my master chanced to arrive at the gathering's margins. He discerned at once the terror graven upon the listeners' faces; without a word he pressed forward into the firelight. At the sight of a Spartiate officer among his listeners, the ship's mate redoubled his fervor. He was enjoying the current of dread his tale had spawned.

"But the most fearsome remains yet to be told, brothers," the Trachinian continued. "That same day, as our gaolers marched us to supper, we passed the Persian archers in their practice. Not the Olympian gods themselves could have assembled such myriads! I swear to you, mates, so numerous were the multitudes of bowmen that when they fired their volleys, the mass of arrows blocked out the sun!"

The rumormonger's eyes burned with pleasure. He turned to my master, as if to savor the flame of dread his tale had ignited even in a Spartan. To his disappointment Dienekes regarded him with a cool, almost bored detachment.

"Good," he said. "Then we'll have our battle in the shade."

In the middle of the second watch came the first panic. I was still awake, securing my master's covered shield against the rain which threatened, when I heard the telltale rustle of bodies shifting, the alteration in the rhythm of men's voices. A terror-swept camp sounds completely different from a confident one. Dienekes rose out of a sound sleep, like a sheepdog sensing murmurs of disquiet among his fold. "Mother of bitches," he grunted, "it's starting already."

The first raiding parties had returned to camp. They had seen torches, cavalry brands of the Persians' mounted rangers, and had made their own prudent withdrawal before getting cut off. You could see the foe plainly now, they reported, from the shoulder of the mountain, two miles or less down the trail. Some of the forward sentries had made sorties on their own as well, and these had now returned to camp to confirm the report.

Beyond the shoulder of Kallidromos, upon the sprawling plain of Trachis, the advance units of the Persians were arriving.

TWENTY-TWO

Within minutes of the sighting of the enemy forerunners, Leonidas had the entire Spartan contingent on its feet and armed, with orders to the allies to marshal in succession and be ready to move forward. The remainder of that night, and all the next day, were consumed with ravaging in earnest the plain of Trachis and the hillsides above, penetrating along the coast as far north as the Spercheios and inland to the citadel and the Trachinian cliffs. Watch fires were set across the entire plain, not little rabbit-roasters as customary, but roaring bonfires, to create the impression of vast numbers of men. The allied units shouted insults and imprecations to one another across the darkness, trying to sound as cheerful and confident as possible. By morning the plain was blanketed end-to-end in fire smoke and sea fog, exactly as Leonidas wanted. I was among the final four parties, stoking bonfires as the murky dawn came up over the gulf. We could see the Persians, mounted reconnaissance units and marine archers of the foe's fast scout corvettes, upon the far bank of the Spercheios. We shouted insults and they shouted back.

The day passed, and another. Now the main-force units of the foe began streaming in. The plain commenced to fill with the enemy. All Greek parties withdrew before the Median tide. The scouts could see the King's officers claiming the prime sites for His Majesty's pavilions and staking out the lushest pasturage for his horses.

They knew the Greeks were here, and the Greeks knew they were.

That night Leonidas summoned my master and the other *enomotarchai*, the platoon leaders, to the low knoll behind the Phokian Wall upon which he had established his command post. Here the king began to address the Spartan officers. Meanwhile the commanders from the other allied cities, also summoned to council, began arriving. The timing of this was as the king intended. He wanted the allied officers to overhear the words he spoke seemingly for Spartan ears alone.

"Brothers and comrades," Leonidas addressed the Lakedaemonians clustered about him, "it appears that the Persian, despite our impressive showmanship, remains unconvinced of the prudence of packing his kit and embarking for home. It looks like we're going to have to fight him, after all. Hear, then, what I expect from each of you.

"You are the elect of Hellas, officers and commanders of the nation of Lakedaemon, chosen by the Isthmaian Congress to strike the first blow in defense of our homeland. Remember that our allies will take their cue from you. If you show fear, they will be afraid. If you project courage, they will match it in kind. Our deportment here must not differ from any other campaign. On the one hand, no extraordinary precautions; on the other, no unwonted recklessness. Above all, the little things. Maintain your men's training schedule without alteration. Omit no sacrifice to the gods. Continue your gymnastics and drills-at-arms. Take time to dress your hair, as always. If anything, take more time."

By now the allied officers had arrived at the council fire and were assuming their stations amid the already assembled Spartans. Leonidas continued as if to his own countrymen, but with an ear to the new arrivals as well.

"Remember that these our allies have not trained their whole lives for war, as we have. They are farmers and merchants, citizen-soldiers of their cities' militias. Nonetheless they are not unmindful of valor or they would not be here. For the Phokians and Lokrians of Opus, this is their country; they fight to defend home and family. As for the men of the other cities, Thebans and Corinthians and Tegeates, Orchomenians and Arkadians, Philiasians, Thespaians, Mantineans and the men of Mycenae, these display to my mind even nobler *andreia*, for they come uncompelled, not to defend their own hearths, but all Greece."

He motioned the new arrivals forward.

"Welcome, brothers. Since I find myself among allies, I am making a long-winded speech."

The officers settled in with an anxious chuckle. "I am telling the Spartans," Leonidas resumed, "what I now tell you. You are the commanders, your men will look to you and act as you do. Let no officer keep to himself or his brother officers, but circulate daylong among his men. Let them see you and see you unafraid. Where there is work to do, turn your hand to it first; the men will follow. Some of you, I see, have erected tents. Strike them at once. We will all sleep as I do, in the open. Keep your men busy. If there is no work, make it up, for when soldiers have time to talk, their talk turns to fear. Action, on the other hand, produces the appetite for more action.

"Exercise campaign discipline at all times. Let no man heed nature's call without spear and shield at his side.

"Remember that the Persian's most formidable weapons, his cavalry and his multitudes of archers and slingers, are rendered impotent here by the terrain. That is why we chose this site. The enemy can get no more than a dozen men at a time through the Narrows and mass no more than a thousand before the Wall. We are four thousand. We outnumber him four to one."

This produced the first genuine laughter. Leonidas sought to instill courage not by his words alone but by the calm and professional manner with which he spoke them. War is work, not mystery. The king confined his instructions to the practical, prescribing actions which could be taken physically, rather than seeking to produce a state of mind, which he knew would evaporate as soon as the commanders dispersed beyond the fortifying light of the king's fire.

"Look to your grooming, gentlemen. Keep your hair, hands and feet clean. Eat, if you have to choke it down. Sleep, or pretend to. Don't let your men see you toss. If bad news comes, relay it first to those in grade above you, never directly to your men. Instruct your squires to buff each man's *aspis* to its most brilliant sheen. I want to see shields flashing like mirrors, for this sight strikes terror into the enemy. Leave time for your men to sharpen their spears, for he who whets his steel whets his courage.

"As for your men's understandable anxiety concerning the immediate hours, tell them this: I anticipate action neither tonight nor tomorrow, nor even the day after. The Persian needs time to marshal his men, and the more myriads he is burdened with, the longer this will take. He must wait upon the arrival of his fleet. Beaching grounds are scarce and slender upon this inhospitable coast; it will take the Persian days to lay out roadsteads and secure at anchor his thousands of warships and transports.

"Our own fleet, as you know, holds the strait at Artemisium. Breaking through will require of the enemy a full-scale sea battle; preparing for this will consume even more of his time. As for assaulting us here in the pass, the foe must reconnoiter our position, then deliberate how best to attack it. No doubt he will send emissaries first, seeking to achieve by diplomacy what he hesitates to hazard at the cost of blood. This you need not concern yourselves with, for all treating with the enemy will be done by me." Here Leonidas bent to the earth and lifted a stone thrice the size of a man's fist. "Believe me, comrades, when Xerxes addresses me, he might as well be talking to this."

He spat upon the rock and slung it away into the dark.

"Another thing. You have all heard the oracle declaring that Sparta will either lose a king in battle or the city herself be extinguished. I have taken the omens and the god has answered that I am that king and that this site will be my grave. Be assured, however, that this foreknowledge will nowise render me reckless with other men's lives. I swear to you now, by all the gods and by the souls of my children, that I will do everything in my power to spare you and your men, as many as I possibly can, and still defend the pass effectively.

"Finally this, brothers and allies. Wherever the fighting is bloodiest, you may expect to discover the Lakedaemonians in the forefront. But convey this, above all, to your men: let them not yield preeminence in valor to the Spartans, rather strive to outdo them. Remember, in warfare practice of arms counts for little. Courage tells all, and we Spartans have no monopoly on that. Lead your men with this in mind and all will be well."

TWENTY-THREE

It was the standing order of my master on campaign that he be woken two hours before dawn, an hour prior to the men of his platoon. He insisted that these never behold him prone upon the earth, but awake always to the sight of their *enomotarch* on his feet and armed.

This night Dienekes slept even less. I felt him stir and roused myself. "Lie still," he commanded. His hand pressed me back down. "It's not even past second watch." He had dozed without removing his corselet and now creaked to his feet, all his scarred joints groaning. I could hear him crack the bones of his neck and hawk dry phlegm from the lungs he had seared at Oinoe, inhaling fire, which wound like the others had never truly healed.

"Let me help you, sir."

"Sleep. Don't make me tell you twice."

He snatched one of his spears from the stacked arms and shouldered his *aspis* by its sling cord. He took his helmet, seating it by its nasal into the warpack he now slung across his shoulders. He gimped off on his bad ankle. He was making for Leonidas' cluster among the Knights, where the king would be awake and perhaps wanting company.

Across the cramped confines the camp slumbered. A waxing moon stood above the strait, the air unseasonably chill for summer, dank as it is by the sea and made more raw by the recent storms; you could hear the breakers clearly, combing in at the base of the cliffs. I glanced across at Alexandros, pillowed upon his shield beside the snoring form of Suicide. Watch fires had banked down; across the camp the sleeping warriors' forms had stilled into lumpy piles of cloaks and sleeping capes that looked more like sacks of discarded laundry than men.

Toward the Middle Gate, I could see the bathhouses of the spa. These were cheerful structures of unmilled lumber, their stone thresholds worn smooth by the tread of bathers and summer visitors dating from centuries. The oiled paths meandered prettily under the oaks, lit by the olivewood lamps of the spa. A burnished wood plaque hung beneath each lamp, a snatch of verse carved upon it. I recall one:

As at birth the soul
steps into the liquid body
So step you now, friend, into these baths,
releasing flesh into soul,
reunited, divine.

I remembered something my master had once said about battlefields. This was at Tritaea, when the army met the Achaians in a field of seedling barley. The climactic slaughter had taken place opposite a temple to which in time of peace the deranged and god-possessed were conveyed by their families, to pray and offer sacrifice to Demeter Merciful and Persephone. "No surveyor marks out a tract and declares, 'Here we shall have a battle.' The ground is often consecrated to a peaceful purpose, frequently one of succor and compassion. The irony can get pretty thick sometimes."

And yet within Hellas' mountainous and topographically hostile confines, there existed those sites hospitable to war—Oenophyta, Tanagra, Koroneia, Marathon, Chaeronea, Leuktra—those plains and defiles upon and within which armies had clashed for generations.

This pass of the Hot Gates was such a site. Here in these precipitous straits, contending forces had slugged it out as far back as Jason and Herakles. Hill tribes had fought here, savage clans and seaborne raiders, migrating hordes, barbarians and invaders of the north and west. The tides of war and peace had alternated in this site for centuries, bathers and warriors, one come for the waters, the other for blood.

The battle wall had now been completed. One end abutted the sheer face of the cliff, with a stout tower flush to the stone, the other tailing off at an angle across the slope to the cliffs and the sea. It was a good-looking wall. Two spear-lengths thick at the base and twice the height of a man. The face toward the enemy had not been erected sheer in the manner of a city battlement, but left deliberately sloped, right up to the actual sallyports at the crest, where the final four feet rose vertical as a fortress. This was so the warriors of the allies could scamper rearward to safety if they had to, and not find themselves pinned and crushed against their own wall.

The rear face sloped up in stacked steps for the defenders to mount to the battlements, atop which had been anchored a stout timber palisade sheathed in hides which the standing watches could cast loose so that the tow arrows of the enemy would not set the palisade alight. The masonry was ragged stuff but sturdy. Towers stood at intervals, reinforcing redoubts right, left and center and secondary walls behind these. These strongpoints had been built solid to the height of the primary wall, then stacked with heavy stones to a man's height beyond. These loose boulders could be tumbled, should necessity dictate, into the breaches of the lower sallyports. I could see the sentries now atop the Wall and the three ready platoons, two Arkadian and one Spartan, in full *panoplia,* at each redoubt.

Leonidas was in fact awake. His long steel-colored hair could be distinguished clearly beside the commanders' fire. Dienekes attended him there among a knot of officers. I could make out Dithyrambos, the Thespaian captain; Leontiades, the Theban commander; Polynikes; the brothers Alpheus and Maron, and several other Spartan Knights.

The sky had begun to lighten; I became aware of forms stirring beside me. Alexandros and Ariston had come awake as well and now roused themselves and took station beside me. These young warriors, like myself, found their gaze drawn irresistibly to the officers and champions surrounding the king. The veterans, all knew, would acquit themselves with honor. "How will we do?" Alexandros put into words the anxiety that loitered unspoken in his youthful mates' hearts. "Will we find the answer to Dienekes' question? Will we discover within ourselves 'the opposite of fear'?"

Three days before the march-out from Sparta, my master had

assembled the warriors and squires of his platoon and outfitted a hunt at his own expense. This was in the form of a farewell, not to each other, but to the hills of their native country. None spoke a word of the Gates or of the trials to come. It was a grand outing, blessed by the gods with several excellent kills including a fine boar brought down in its charge by Suicide and Ariston with the javelin and the foot-braced pike.

At dusk the hunters, beyond a dozen with twice that number of squires and helots serving as beaters, settled in high spirits about several fires among the hills above Therai. *Phobos* took a seat as well. As the other huntsmen made merry around their separate blazes, diverting themselves with lies of the chase and good-fellow jesting, Dienekes cleared space beside his own station for Alexandros and Ariston and bade them sit. I discerned then my master's subtle intent. He was going to speak of fear, for these unblooded youths whom he knew despite their silence, or perhaps because of it, had begun in their hearts to dwell upon the trials to come.

"All my life," Dienekes began, "one question has haunted me. What is the opposite of fear?"

Down the slope the boar flesh was coming ready; portions were being shared out to eager hands. Suicide came up, with bowls for Dienekes, Alexandros and Ariston, and one apiece for himself, Ariston's squire Demades and me. He settled on the earth across from Dienekes, flanked by two of the hounds who had noses for the scraps and knew Suicide as a notorious soft touch.

"To call it *aphobia,* fearlessness, is without meaning. This is just a name, thesis expressed as antithesis. To call the opposite of fear fearlessness is to say nothing. I want to know its true obverse, as day of night and heaven of earth."

"Expressed as a positive," Ariston ventured.

"Exactly!" Dienekes met the young man's eyes in approval. He paused to study both youths' expressions. Would they listen? Did they care? Were they, like him, true students of this subject?

"How does one conquer fear of death, that most primordial of terrors, which resides in our very blood, as in all life, beasts as well as men?" He indicated the hounds flanking Suicide. "Dogs in a pack find courage to take on a lion. Each hound knows his place. He fears the dog ranked above and feeds off the fear of the dog below. Fear conquers fear. This is how we Spartans do it, counterpoising to fear of death a greater fear: that of dishonor. Of exclusion from the pack."

Suicide took this moment to toss several scraps to the dogs. Furiously their jaws snapped these remnants from the turf, the stronger of the two seizing the lion's share.

Dienekes smiled darkly.

"But is that courage? Is not acting out of fear of dishonor still, in essence, acting out of fear?"

Alexandros asked what he was seeking.

"Something nobler. A higher form of the mystery. Pure. Infallible."

He declared that in all other questions one may look for wisdom to the gods. "But not in matters of courage. What have the immortals to teach us? They cannot die. Their spirits are not housed, as ours, in this." Here he indicated the body, the flesh. "The factory of fear."

Dienekes glanced again to Suicide, then back to Alexandros, Ariston and me. "You young men imagine that we veterans, with our long experience of war, have mastered fear. But we feel it as keenly as you. More keenly, for we have more intimate experience of it. Fear lives within us twenty-four hours a day, in our sinews and our bones. Do I speak the truth, my friend?"

Suicide grinned darkly in reply.

My master grinned back. "We cobble our courage together on the spot, of rags and remnants. The main we summon out of that which is base. Fear of disgracing the city, the king, the heroes of our lines. Fear of proving ourselves unworthy of our wives and children, our brothers, our comrades-in-arms. For myself I know all the tricks of the breath and of song, the pillars of the *tetrathesis*, the teachings of the *phobologia*. I know how to close with my man, how to convince myself that his terror is greater than my own. Perhaps it is. I employ care for the men-at-arms serving beneath me and seek to forget my own fear in concern for their survival. But it's always there. The closest I've come is to act despite terror. But that's not it either. Not the kind of courage I'm talking about. Nor is beastlike fury or panic-spawned self-preservation. These are *katalepsis*, possession. A rat owns as much of them as a man."

He observed that often those who seek to overcome fear of death preach that the soul does not expire with the body. "To my mind this is fatuousness. Wishful thinking. Others, barbarians primarily, say that when we die we pass on to paradise. I ask them all: if you really believe this, why not make away with yourself at once and speed the trip?

"Achilles, Homer tells us, possessed true *andreia*. But did he? Scion of an immortal mother, dipped as a babe in the waters of Styx, knowing himself to be save his heel invulnerable? Cowards would be rarer than feathers on fish if we all knew that."

Alexandros inquired if any of the city, in Dienekes' opinion, possessed this true *andreia*.

"Of all in Lakedaemon, our friend Polynikes comes closest. But even his valor I find unsatisfactory. He fights not out of fear of dishonor, but greed for glory. This may be noble, or at least unbase, but is it true *andreia?*"

Ariston asked if this higher courage in fact existed.

"It is no phantom," Dienekes declared with conviction. "I have seen it. My brother Iatrokles possessed it in moments. When I beheld its grace upon him, I stood in awe. It radiated, sublime. In those hours he fought not like a man but a god. Leonidas has it on occasion. Olympieus doesn't. I don't. None of us here does." He smiled. "Do you know who owns it, this pure form of courage, more than any other I have known?"

None around the fire answered.

"My wife," Dienekes said. He turned to Alexandros. "And your mother, the lady Paraleia." He smiled again. "There is a clue here. The seat of this higher valor, I suspect, lies in that which is female. The words themselves for courage, *andreia* and *aphobia*, are female, whereas *phobos* and *tromos*, terror, are masculine. Perhaps the god we seek is not a god at all, but a goddess. I don't know."

You could see it did Dienekes good to speak of this. He thanked his listeners for sitting still for it. "The Spartans have no patience for such inquiries of the salon. I remember asking my brother once, on campaign, a day when he had fought like an immortal. I was mad to know what he had felt in those moments, what was the essence experienced within? He looked at me as if I had taken leave of sanity. 'Less philosophy, Dienekes, and more virtue.' "

He laughed. "So much for that."

My master turned sidelong then, as if to draw this inquiry to a close. Yet some impulse drew him back, to Ariston, upon whose features stood that expression of one of youthful years nerving himself to venture speech before his elders. "Spit it out, my friend," Dienekes urged him.

"I was thinking of women's courage. I believe it is different from men's."

The youth hesitated. Perhaps, his expression clearly bespoke, it smacked of immodesty or presumptuousness to speculate upon matters of which he possessed no experience.

Dienekes pressed him nonetheless. "Different, how?"

Ariston glanced to Alexandros, who with a grin reinforced his friend's resolve. The youth took a breath and began: "Man's courage, to give his life for his country, is great but unextraordinary. Is it not intrinsic to the nature of the male, beasts as well as men, to fight and to contend? It's what we were born to do, it's in our blood. Watch any boy. Before he can even speak, he reaches, impelled by instinct, for the staff and the sword—while his sisters unprompted shun these implements of contention and instead cuddle to their bosom the kitten and the doll.

"What is more natural to a man than to fight, or a woman to love? Is this not the imperative of a mother's blood, to give and to nurture, above all the produce of her own womb, the children she has borne in pain? We know that a lioness or she-wolf will cast away her life without hesitation to preserve her cubs or pups. Women the same. Now consider, friends, that which we call women's courage:

"What could be more contrary to female nature, to motherhood, than to stand unmoved and unmoving as her sons march off to death? Must not every sinew of the mother's flesh call out in agony and affront at such an outrage? Must not her heart seek to cry in its passion, 'No! Not my son! Spare him!' That women, from some source unknown to us, summon the will to conquer this their own deepest nature is, I believe, the reason we stand in awe of our mothers and sisters and wives. This, I believe, Dienekes, is the essence of women's courage and why it, as you suggested, is superior to men's."

My master acknowledged these observations with approval. At his side Alexandros shifted, however. You could see the young man was not satisfied.

"What you say is true, Ariston. I had never thought of it in that way before. Yet something must be added. If women's victory were simply to stand dry-eyed as their sons march off to death, this would not alone be unnatural, but inhuman, grotesque and even monstrous. What elevates such an act to the stature of nobility is, I believe, that it is performed in the service of a higher and more selfless cause.

"These women of whom we stand in awe donate their sons' lives to their country, to the people as a whole, that the nation may survive even as their own dear children perish. Like the mother whose story we have heard from childhood who, on learning that all five of her sons had been killed in the same battle, asked only, 'Was our nation victorious?' and, being told that it was, turned for home without a tear, saying only, 'Then I am happy.' Is it not this element—the nobility of setting the whole above the part—that moves us about women's sacrifice?"

"Such wisdom from the mouths of babes!" Dienekes laughed and rapped both lads affectionately upon the shoulder. "But you have not yet answered my question. What is the opposite of fear?

"I will tell you a story, my young friends, but not here or now. At the Gates you shall hear it. A story of our king, Leonidas, and a secret he confided to Alexandros' mother, Paraleia. This tale will advance our inquiry into courage—and will tell as well how Leonidas came to select those he did for the Three Hundred. But for this hour we must put a period to our salon or the Spartans, overhearing, will declare us effeminate. And they will be right!"

Now in camp at the Gates we three youths could see our *enomotarch*, responding to dawn's first glimmer, take leave of the king's council and return to his platoon, stripping his cloak to call the men to gymnastics. "On our feet, then." Ariston sprung up, snapping Alexandros and me from our preoccupations. "The opposite of fear must be work."

Drill-at-arms had barely begun when a sharp whistle from the Wall summoned every man to alert.

A herald of the enemy was advancing into view at the throat of the Narrows.

This messenger drew up at a distance, calling out a name in Greek, that of Alexandros' father, the *polemarch* Olympieus. When the herald was motioned forward, escorting a single officer of the enemy embassy and a boy, he cried further by name after three other Spartan officers, Aristodemos, Polynikes and Dienekes.

These four were summoned at once by the officer of the watch, he and all others in hearing astonished and by no means uncurious about the specificity of the enemy's request.

The sun was full up now; scores of allied infantrymen stood watching upon the Wall. Forward advanced the Persian embassy. Dienekes recognized its principal at once. This was the captain Ptammitechus, "Tommie," the Egyptian marine we had encountered and exchanged gifts with four years previous at Rhodes. The boy, it turned out, was his son. The lad spoke excellent Attic Greek and served as interpreter.

A scene of warm reacquaintance ensued, with abundant clapping of backs and clasping of hands. Surprise was expressed by the Spartans that the Egyptian was not with the fleet; he was, after all, a marine, a sea fighter. Tommie responded that he only, and his immediate platoon, had been detached to duty with the land armies, seconded to the Imperial Command at his own request for this specific purpose: to act as an informal ambassador to the Spartans, whose acquaintance he recalled with such warmth and whose welfare he wished above all to succor.

By now the crowd surrounding the marine had swelled to above a hundred. The Egyptian towered half a head over even the tallest Hellene, his tiara of pressed linen adding further to his stature. His smile flashed brilliant as ever. He bore a message, he declared, from King Xerxes himself, which he had been charged to deliver to the Spartans alone.

Olympieus, who had been senior envoy during the Rhodian embassy, now assumed that position in this parley. He informed the Egyptian that no treating would be done on a nation-by-nation basis. It was one for all among the Greeks, and that was that.

The marine's cheerful demeanor did not falter. At that moment the main body of Spartans, led by Alpheus and Maron, was running shield drills immediately before the Wall, working with and instructing two platoons of the Thespaians. Tommie observed the brothers for a number of moments, impressed. "I will alter my request, then," he said, smiling, to Olympieus. "If you, sir, will escort me to your king, Leonidas, I will deliver my message to him as commander of the Hellenic allies as a whole."

My master was plainly fond of this personable fellow and delighted to see him again. "Still wearing steel underpants?" he inquired through the boy interpreter.

Tommie laughed and displayed, to the further amusement of the assembly, an undergarment of white Nile linen. Then, with a gesture friendly and informal, he seemed to set aside his role as envoy and speak, for the moment, man-to-man.

"I pray that armor of mail need never be employed between us, brothers." He indicated the camp, the Narrows, the sea, seeming to include the defense as a whole in the sweep of his arm. "Who knows how this may turn out? It may all blow over, as it did for your force of Ten Thousand at Tempe. But if I may speak as a friend, to you four only, I would urge you thus: do not let hunger for glory, nor your own pride in arms, blinder you to the reality your forces now confront.

"Death alone awaits you here. The defenders cannot hope to stand, even for a day, in the face of the multitudes His Majesty brings against you. Nor will all the armies of Hellas prevail in the battles yet to come. Surely you know this, as does your king." He paused to let his son deliver the translation and to study the response upon the faces of the Spartans. "I beg you hearken to this counsel, friends, offered from my own heart as one who bears the most profound respect for you as individuals and for your city and its wide and well-deserved fame. Accept the inevitable, and be ruled with honor and respect—"

"You may stop there, friend," Aristodemos cut him off.

Polynikes put in with heat: "If that's all you came to tell us, brother, stick it between the creases."

The Egyptian maintained his level and amiable demeanor. "You have my word and His Majesty's upon it: if the Spartans will yield now and surrender their arms, none will exceed them in honor beneath the King's banner. No Persian foot will tread the soil of Lakedaemon now or forever, this His Majesty swears. Your country will be granted dominion over all Greece. Your forces will take their place as the foremost unit in His Majesty's army, with all the fortune and glory such prominence commands. Your nation has but to name its desires. His Majesty will grant them and, if I may claim to know his heart, will shower further gifts upon his new friends, in scale and costliness beyond imagining."

At this, the breath of every allied listener stoppered in his throat. Each eye stood fearfully upon the Spartans. If the Egyptian's offer was bona fide, and there was no reason to believe it wasn't, it meant deliverance for Lakedaemon. All she need do was forsake the Hellenic cause. What now would be these officers' response? Would they at once convey the envoy to their king? Leonidas' word would be tantamount to law, so preeminent stood his stature among the Peers and ephors.

Out of the blue, the fate of Hellas suddenly teetered upon the precipice. The allied listeners stood nailed to the site, awaiting breathlessly the response of these four warriors of Lakedaemon.

"It seems to me," Olympieus addressed the Egyptian with barely a moment's hesitation, "that if His Majesty truly wished to make the Spartans his friends, he would find them of far greater service with their arms than without."

"Further, experience has taught us," Aristodemos added, "that honor and glory are boons which cannot be granted by the pen but must be earned by the spear."

My glance scanned in this moment the faces of the allies. Tears stood in the eyes of not a few; others seemed so undone with relief that their knees threatened to give way beneath them. The Egyptian clearly discerned this. He smiled, gracious and patient, not abashed in the least.

"Gentlemen, gentlemen. I trouble you with matters which should and must be debated, not here in the marketplace so to speak, but in private before your king. Please, if you will, conduct me to him."

"He'll tell you the same, brother," Dienekes declared.

"And in far cruder language," put in another Spartan among the crowd.

Tommie waited for the laughter to subside.

"May I hear this response, then, from the king's own lips?"

"He'd have us whipped, Tommie," Dienekes put in with a smile.

"He'd tear the hide off our backs," spoke the same man who had interposed a moment earlier, "even to propose such a course of dishonor."

The Egyptian's eyes swung now to this speaker, whom he perceived to be an older Spartan, clad in tunic and homespun cloak, who now stepped into the second rank, at the shoulder of Aristodemos. For a moment the marine was taken aback to discover this graybeard, who clearly bore the weight of more than sixty summers, yet stood in infantryman's raiment among the other, far younger warriors.

"Please, my friends," the Egyptian continued, "do not respond out of pride or the passion of the moment but permit me to place before your king the wider consequences of such a decision. Let me set the Persian Majesty's ambitions in perspective.

"Greece is just the jumping-off point. The Great King already rules all Asia; Europe now is his goal. From Hellas His Majesty's army moves on to conquer Sikelia and Italia, from there to Helvetia, Germania, Gallia, Iberia. With you on our side, what force can stand against us? We will advance in triumph to the Pillars of Herakles themselves and beyond, to the very walls of Oceanus!

"Please, brothers, consider the alternatives. Stand now in pride of arms and be crushed, your country overrun, wives and children enslaved, the glory of Lakedaemon, not to say her very existence, effaced forever from the earth. Or elect, as I urge, the course of prudence. Assume with honor your rightful station in the forefront of the invincible tide of history. The lands you rule now will be as nothing beside the domains the Great King will bestow upon you. Join us, brothers. Conquer with us all the world! Xerxes son of Darius swears this: no nation or army will surpass you in honor among all His Majesty's forces! And if, my Spartan friends, the act of abandoning your Hellene brothers strikes you as dishonorable, King Xerxes extends his offer further, to all Greeks. All Hellenic allies, regardless of nation, will he set in freedom at your shoulder and honor second only to yourselves among his minions!"

Neither Olympieus nor Aristodemos nor Dienekes nor Polynikes lifted voice in response. Instead the Egyptian saw them defer to the older man in the homespun cloak.

"Among the Spartans any may speak, not just these ambassadors, as we are all accounted Peers and equals before the law." The elder now stepped forward. "May I take the liberty to suggest, sir, an alternative course, which I feel certain will find favor, not among the Lakedaemonians alone, but with all the Greek allies?"

"Please do," responded the Egyptian.

All eyes centered upon the veteran.

"Let Xerxes surrender to us," he proposed. "We will not fail to match his generosity, but set him and his forces foremost among our allies and grant to him all the honors which he so munificently proposes to shower upon us."

A laugh burst from the Egyptian.

"Please, gentlemen, we squander precious time." He turned away from the older man, not without a hint of impatience, and pressed his request again to Olympieus. "Conduct me at once to your king."

"No use, friend," answered Polynikes.

"The king is a crusty old bugger," Dienekes added.

"Indeed," put in the older man. "He is a foul-tempered and irascible fellow, barely literate, in his cups most days before noon, they say."

A smile now spread across the features of the Egyptian. He glanced to my master and to Olympieus.

"I see," said Tommie.

His look returned to the older man, who, as the Egyptian now discerned, was none other than Leonidas himself.

"Well then, venerable sir," Tommie addressed the Spartan king directly, dipping his brow in a gesture of respect, "since it seems I am to be frustrated in my desire to speak in person with Leonidas, perhaps, in deference to the gray I behold in your beard and the many wounds my eyes espy upon your body, you yourself, sir, will accept this gift from Xerxes son of Darius in your king's stead."

From a pouch the Egyptian produced a double-handled goblet of gold, magnificent in craftsmanship and encrusted with precious gems. He declared that the engravings thereupon represented the hero Amphiktyon, to whom the precinct of Thermopylae was sacred, along with Herakles and Hyllus, his son, from whom the race of the Spartans, and Leonidas himself, was descended. The cup was so heavy that the Egyptian had to hold it out with both hands.

"If I accept this generous gift," Leonidas addressed him, "it must go into the war treasury of the allies."

"As you wish." The Egyptian bowed.

"Then convey the Hellenes' gratitude to your King. And tell him my offer will remain open, should God grant him the wisdom to embrace it."

Tommie passed the goblet to Aristodemos, who accepted it for the king. A moment passed, in which the Egyptian's eyes met first Olympieus', then settled gravely upon my master's. An expression of solemnity, sober to the point of sorrow, shrouded the marine's eyes. Clearly he discerned now the inevitability of that which he had sought with such charity and concern to avert.

"If you fall in capture," he addressed the Spartans, "call my name. I will exert every measure of influence to see that you are spared."

"You do that, brother," Polynikes answered, hard as steel.

The Egyptian recoiled, stung. Dienekes stepped in swiftly, clasping the marine's hand warmly in his own.

"Till we meet," Dienekes said.

"Till then," Tommie replied.

BOOK SIX

DIENEKES

TWENTY-FOUR

They wore trousers.

Pantaloons of purple, bloused below the knee, topping calf-length boots of doeskin or some other precious product of the tannery. Their tunics were sleeved and embroidered, beneath mail jackets of armor shaped like fish scales; their helmets open-faced and brilliantly plumed, of hammered iron shaped like domes. Their cheeks they wore rouged and their ears and throats bedecked with ornament. They looked like women and yet the effect of their raiment, surreal to Hellene eyes, was not that which evoked contempt, but terror. One felt as if he were facing men from the underworld, from some impossible country beyond Oceanus where up was down and night day. Did they know something the Greeks didn't? Were their light skirmisher shields, which seemed almost ludicrously flimsy contrasted to the massive twenty-pound oak and bronze, shoulder-to-knee *aspides* of the Hellenes, somehow, in some undivinable way, superior? Their lances were not the stout ash and cornelwood eight-footers of the Greeks but lighter, slender, almost javelin-like weapons. How would they strike with these? Would they hurl them or thrust them underhand? Was this somehow more lethal than the overhand employed by the Greeks?

They were Medes, the vanguard division of the troops who would first assault the allies, though none among the defenders knew this for certain at the time. The Greeks could not distinguish among Persians, Medes, Assyrians, Babylonians, Arabians, Phrygians, Karians, Armenians, Cissians, Cappadocians, Paphlagonians, Bactrians nor any of the other five score Asiatic nations save the Ionian Hellenes and Lydians, the Indians and Ethiopians and Egyptians who stood out by their distinctive arms and armor. Common sense and sound generalship dictated that the commanders of the Empire grant to one nation among their forces the honor of drawing first blood. It made further sense, so the Greeks surmised, that when making trial of an enemy for the first time, a prudent general would not commit the flower of his troops—in His Majesty's case his own Ten Thousand, the Persian household guard known as the Immortals—but rather hold these elite in reserve against the unexpected.

In fact this was the selfsame strategy adopted by Leonidas and the allied commanders. These kept the Spartans back, choosing to honor, after much debate and discussion, the warriors of Thespiae. These were granted first position and now, on the morning of the fifth day, stood formed in their ranks, sixty-four shields across, upon the "dance floor" formed by the Narrows at the apex, the mountain wall on one side, the cliffs dropping to the gulf on the other and the reconstructed Phokian Wall at the rear.

This, the field of slaughter, comprised an obtuse triangle whose greatest depth lay along the southern flank, that which was anchored by the mountain wall. At this end the Thespaians were drawn up eighteen deep. At the opposing end, alongside the drop-off to the sea, their shields were staggered to a depth of ten. This force of the men of Thespiae totaled approximately seven hundred.

Immediately to their rear, atop the Wall, stood the Spartans, Philiasians and Mycenaeans, to a total of six hundred. Behind these every other allied contingent was likewise drawn up, all in full *panoplia*.

Two hours had elapsed since the enemy had first been sighted, half a mile down the track to Trachis, and still no motion had come. The morning was hot. Down the track, the roadway widened into an open area about the size of the agora of a small city. There, just after dawn, the lookouts had espied the Medians assembling. Their numbers were about four thousand. These, however, were only the foe who could be seen; the shoulder of the mountain hid the trail and the marshaling stations beyond. One could hear the enemy trumpets and the shouted orders of their officers moving more and more men into position beyond the shoulder. How many more thousands massed there out of sight?

The quarter hours crawled by. The Medes continued marshaling, but did not advance. The Hellenic lookouts began shouting insults down at them. Back in the Narrows, the heat and other exigencies had begun to work on the chafing, impatient Greeks. It made no sense to sweat longer under the burdens of full armor. "Dump 'em but be ready to hump 'em!" Dithyrambos, the Thespaian captain, called out to his countrymen in the coarse slang of his city. Squires and servants dashed forward among the ranks, each assisting his man in disencumbering himself of breastplate and helmet. Corselets were loosened. Shields rested already against knees. The felt undercaps which the men wore beneath their helmets came off and were wrung like bath linens, saturated with sweat. Spears were plunged at the position of rest, butt-spike-first, into the hard dirt, where they stood now in their numbers like an iron-tipped forest. The troops were permitted to kneel. Squires with skins of water circulated, replenishing the parched warriors. It was a safe bet that many skins contained refreshment more potent than that scooped from a spring.

As the delay grew longer, the sense of unreality heightened. Was this another false alarm, like the previous four days? Would the Persian attack at all?

"Snap out of those daydreams!" an officer barked.

The troops, bleary-eyed and sun-scorched, continued eyeing Leonidas on the Wall with the commanders. What were they talking about? Would the order come to stand down?

Even Dienekes grew impatient. "Why is it in war you can't fall asleep when you want to and can't stay awake when you have to?" He was just stepping forward to address a steadying word to his platoon when from out front among the foreranks rose a shout of such intensity that it cut his words off in midbreath. Every eye swung skyward.

The Greeks now saw what had caused the delay.

There, several hundred feet above and one ridgeline removed, a party of Persian servants escorted by a company of their Immortals was erecting a platform and a throne.

"Mother of bitches." Dienekes grinned. "It's young Purple Balls himself."

High above the armies, a man of between thirty and forty years could be descried plainly, in robes of purple fringed with gold, mounting the platform and assuming his station upon the throne. The distance was perhaps eight hundred feet, up and back, but even at that range it was impossible to mistake the Persian monarch's surpassing handsomeness and nobility of stature. Nor could the supreme self-assurance of his carriage be misread even at this distance. He looked like a man come to watch an entertainment. A pleasantly diverting show, one whose outcome was foreordained and yet which promised a certain level of amusement. He took his seat. A sunshade was adjusted by his servants. We could see a table of refreshments placed at his side and, upon his left, several writing desks set into place, each manned by a secretary.

Obscene gestures and shouted insults rose from four thousand Greek throats.

His Majesty rose with aplomb in response to the jeers. He gestured elegantly and, it seemed, with humor, as if acknowledging the adulation of his subjects. He bowed with a flourish. It seemed, though the distance was too great to be sure, as if he were smiling. He saluted his own captains and settled regally upon his throne.

My place was on the Wall, thirty stations in from the left flank anchored by the mountain. I could see, as could all the Thespaians before the Wall and every Lakedaemonian, Mycenaean and Philiasian atop it, the captains of the enemy, advancing now to the sound of their trumpets, in the van before the massed ranks of their infantry. My God, they looked handsome. Six division commanders, each, it seemed, taller and nobler than the next. We learned later that these were not merely the flower of the Median aristocracy, but that their ranks were reinforced by the sons and brothers of those who had been slain ten years earlier by the Greeks at Marathon. But what froze the blood was their demeanor. Their carriage shone forth, bold to the point of contemptuous. They would brush the defenders aside, that's what they thought. The meat of their lunch was already roasting, back down in camp. They would polish us off without raising a sweat, then return to dine at their leisure.

I glanced to Alexandros; his brow glistened, pale as a winding sheet; his wind came in strangled, wheezing gasps. My master stood at his shoulder, one pace to the fore. Dienekes' attention held riveted to the Medes, whose massed ranks now filled the Narrows and seemed to extend endlessly beyond, out of sight along the track. But no emotion disclarified his reason. He was gauging them strategically, coolly assessing their armament and the bearing of their officers, the dress and interval of their ranks. They were mortal men like us; was their vision struck, like ours, with awe of the force which stood now opposed to them? Leonidas had stressed again and again to the officers of the Thespaians that their men's shields, greaves and helmets must be bossed to the most brilliant sheen possible. These now shone like mirrors. Above the rims of the bronze-faced *aspides*, each helmet blazed magnificently, overtopped with a lofty horsehair crest, which as it trembled and quavered in the breeze not only created the impression of daunting height and stature but lent an aspect of dread which cannot be communicated in words but must be beheld to be understood.

Adding further to the theater of terror presented by the Hellenic phalanx and, to my mind most frightful of all, were the blank, expressionless facings of the Greek helmets, with their bronze nasals thick as a man's thumb, their flaring cheekpieces and the unholy hollows of their eye slits, covering the entire face and projecting to the enemy the sensation that he was facing not creatures of flesh like himself, but some ghastly invulnerable machine, pitiless and unquenchable. I had laughed with Alexandros not two hours earlier as he seated the helmet over his felt undercap; how sweet and boyish he appeared in one instant, with the helmet cocked harmlessly back upon his brow and the youthful, almost feminine features of his face exposed. Then with one undramatic motion, his right hand clasped the flare of the cheekpiece and tugged the ghastly mask down; in an instant the humanity of his face vanished, his gentle expressive eyes became unseeable pools of blackness chasmed within the fierce eye sockets of bronze; all compassion fled in an instant from his aspect, replaced with the blank mask of murder. "Push it back," I cried. "You're scaring the hell out of me." It was no joke.

This now Dienekes was assessing, the effect of Hellenic armor upon the enemy. My master's eyes scanned the foe's ranks; you could see piss stains darkening the trouser fronts of more than one man. Spear tips shivered here and there. Now the Medes formed up. Each rank found its mark, each commander his station.

More endless moments passed. Tedium stood displaced by terror. Now the nerves began to scream; the blood pounded within the recesses of the ears. The hands went numb; all sensation fled the limbs. One's body seemed to treble in weight, all of it cold as stone. One heard one's own voice calling upon the gods and could not tell if the sound was in his head or if he was shamefully crying aloud.

His Majesty's vantage may have been too elevated upon the overstanding mountain to descry what happened next, what stroke of heaven immediately precipitated the clash. It was this. Of a sudden a hare started from the cliffside, dashing out directly between the two armies, no more than thirty feet from the Thespaian commander, Xenocratides, who stood foremost in advance of his troops, flanked by his captains, Dithyrambos and Protokreon, all of them garlanded, with their helmets tucked under their arms. At the sight of this wildly sprinting prey, the roan bitch Styx, who had been already barking furiously, loose at the right flank of the Greek formation, now bolted like a shot into the open. The effect would have been comical had not every Hellene's eye seized upon the event at once as a sign from heaven and attended breathlessly upon its outcome.

The hymn to Artemis, which the troops were singing, faltered in midbreath. The hare fled straight for the Median front-rankers, with Styx hot on its heels and mad with pursuit. Both beasts appeared as screaming blurs, the puffs of dust from their churning feet hanging motionless in the air while their bodies, stretched to the full in the race, streaked on before them. The hare sped straight toward the mass of the Medians, at the approach to which it panicked and tore into a tumble, end over end, as it attempted a right-angle turn at top speed. In a flash Styx was on it; the hound's jaws seemed to snap the prey in two, but, to the astonishment of all, the hare burst free, unscathed, and in an eyeblink had regained full velocity in flight.

A zigzag chase ensued, in duration fewer than a dozen heartbeats, in which hare and hound traversed thrice the *oudenos chorion*, the no-man's-land, between the armies. A hare will always flee uphill; its forelegs are shorter than its rear. The speedster sprung now for the mountain wall, attempting to scamper to salvation. But the face was too sheer; the fugitive's feet skidded out from under; it tumbled, fell back. In an instant its form hung limp and broken within the Stygian jaws.

A cheer rose from the throats of four thousand Greeks, certain that this was an omen of victory, the answer to the hymn it had so serendipitously interrupted. But now from the ranks of the Medes stepped forth two archers. As Styx turned, seeking his master to show off the prize, a pair of cane arrows, launched from no farther than twenty yards and striking simultaneously, slammed into the beast's flank and throat, tumbling him head over heels into the dust.

A cry of anguish erupted from the Skirite whom all had come to call "Hound." For agonizing moments his dog flopped and writhed, pinioned mortally by the enemy's shafts. We heard the enemy commander cry an order in his tongue. At once a thousand Median archers elevated their bows. "Here it comes!" someone cried from the Wall. Every Hellene's shield was snatched at once to high port. That sound which is not a sound but a silence, a rip like that of fabric torn in the wind, now keened from the fisted grips of the enemy's massed bowmen as their string hands released and their triple-pointed bronzeheads sprung as one into the air, shafts singing, driving them forward.

While these missiles arced yet through the aether, the Thespaian commander, Xenocratides, seized the instant. "Zeus Thunderer and Victory!" he cried, tearing the garland from his brow and jerking his helmet down into position of combat, covering, save the eye slits, his entire face. In an instant every man of the Hellenes followed suit. A thousand arrows rained on them in homicidal deluge. The *sarpinx* bellowed. "Thespiae!"

From where I stood atop the Wall, it seemed as if the Thespaians closed to the foe within the space of two heartbeats. Their front ranks hit the Medes not with that sound of thunder, bronze upon bronze, which the Hellenes knew from collisions with their own kind, but with a less dramatic, almost sickening crunch, like ten thousand fistfuls of kindling stalks snapped in the vineyardman's fists, as the metallic facings of the Greeks' shields collided with the wall of wicker thrown up by the Medes. The enemy reeled and staggered. The Thespaians' spears rose and plunged. In an instant the killing zone was obscured within a maelstrom of churning dust.

The Spartans atop the wall held motionless as that peculiar bellowslike compression of ranks unfolded before their sight; the first three ranks of the Thespaians compacted against the foe and churned like a movable wall upon them; now the succeeding ranks, fourth, fifth, sixth, seventh, eighth and more, between whom an interval had opened in the rush, caught up, wave succeeding wave and compressing one upon the other, as each man elevated his shield to high port and planted it as squarely as his terror-unstrung limbs would permit into the back of the comrade before him, seating his left shoulder beneath the upper rim, and, digging his soles and toes into the earth for purchase, hurled himself with all his force into the melee. The heart stopped with the awe of it, as each warrior of the Thespaians cried out to his gods, to the souls of his children, to his mother, to every entity, noble or absurd, which he could imagine of aid, and, forgetting his own life, waded with impossible courage into the mob of murder.

What had been a moment earlier a formation of troops, discernible as ranks and files, even as individuals, transformed in the space of a heartbeat into a roiling mass of manslaughter. The Thespaian reserves could not contain themselves; they, too, hurled themselves forward, pressing the weight of their ranks into the backs of their brothers, heaving against the compacted mass of the enemy.

Behind these the Thespaians' squires danced like ants on a skillet, unranked and unarmored, some backpedaling in terror, others dashing forward, crying out to each other to remember their courage and not fail the men they served. Toward these servants of the train now sailed a second and third rainbow of arrows, loosed by the massed enemy archers stationed to the rear of their lancers and fired in arching fusillades directly over their comrades' plumed heads. The bronzeheads struck the earth in a ragged but discernible front, like a squall line at sea. One could see this curtain of death withdraw rearward as the Median archers fell back behind their lancers, maintaining an interval so they could concentrate their fire upon the mass of the Greeks assaulting them and not squander it, lobbing shafts over their heads. One Thespaian squire dashed recklessly forward to the squall line. A bronzehead nailed him right through the foot. He cavorted off, howling in pain and cursing himself for an idiot.

"Forward to Lion Stone!"

With a cry, Leonidas dismounted his post atop the Wall and advanced down the stone slope, which had been erected deliberately with a descendible incline, into the open before the Spartans, Mycenaeans and Philiasians. These now followed, as the "beaten zone" of the enemy's bronzeheads retreated under the furious push of the Thespaians, maintaining the dress of their lines, as they had rehearsed half a hundred times in the preceding four days, forming up in ready position on the level ground before the Wall.

Along the mountain face to the left, three stones, each at twice the height of a man so they could be seen above the dust of battle, had been selected as benchmarks.

Lizard Stone, so named for a particularly fearless fellow of that species who took his sun thereupon, stood farthest forward of the Phokian Wall, closest to the Narrows, perhaps a hundred and fifty feet from the actual mouth of the pass. This was the line to which the enemy would be permitted to advance. It had been determined by trial with our own men that a thousand of the foe, densely packed, could fit between this demarcation and the Narrows. A thousand, Leonidas had ordered, will be invited to the dance. There, at Lizard Stone, they will be engaged and their advance checked.

Crown Stone, second of the three and another hundred feet rearward of Lizard, defined the line at which each relief detachment would marshal, immediately before being hurled into the fray.

Lion Stone, rearmost of the three and directly in front of the Wall, marked the waiting line—the runners' chute, at which each relief unit would marshal, leaving enough space between itself and those actually fighting for the rear ranks of the combatants to maneuver, to give ground if necessary, to rally, for one flank to support another and for the wounded to be withdrawn.

Along this demarcation the Spartans, Mycenaeans and Philiasians now took their stations. "Dress the line!" the *polemarch* Olympieus bellowed. "Close up your interval!" He prowled before the front, disdaining the drizzle of arrows, shouting to his platoon commanders, who relayed the orders to their men.

Leonidas, out farther still before Olympieus, surveyed the roiling, dust-choked struggle ahead at the Narrows. The sound, if anything, had increased. The clash of sword and spear upon shield, the ringing bell-like toll of the bowl-shaped bronze, the cries of the men, the sharp cracking explosions as lances shivered under impact and snapped in two; all echoed and reverberated between the mountain face and the Narrows like some *theatron* of death circumvallated within its own stone amphitheater. Leonidas, still garlanded, with his helmet up, turned and signaled to the *polemarch*.

"Shields to rest!" Olympieus' voice boomed. Along the Spartan line, *aspides* were lowered and set upright upon the earth, top rims balanced against each man's thigh, with the shield's forearm sheath and gripcord ready to hand. All helmets were up, each man's face still exposed. Beside Dienekes, his captain-of-eight, Bias, was hopping like a flea. "This is it, this is it, this is it."

"Steady, gentlemen." Dienekes stepped forward to let his men see him. "Rest those cheeseplates." In the third rank Ariston, beside himself with agitation, yet clutched his shield at port. Dienekes reached through and whacked him with the flat of his lizard-sticker. "Are you showing off?" The youth snapped to, blinking like a boy awoken from a nightmare. For a full heartbeat you could see he had no idea who Dienekes was or what he wanted. Then, with a start and a sheepish expression, he recovered himself and lowered his shield to position of rest against his knee.

Dienekes prowled before the men. "All eyes on me! Here, brothers!" His voice penetrated, hard and throaty, carrying with the hoarse bark all combatants know when their tongue turns to leather. "Look at me, don't look at the fighting!"

The men tore their eyes from the flood and ebb of murder which was taking place a stone's lob in front of them. Dienekes stood before them, his back to the enemy. "This is what's happening, a blind man could tell just from the sound." Dienekes' voice carried despite the din from the Narrows. "The enemy's shields are too small and too light. They can't protect themselves. The Thespaians are carving them up." The men's glances kept tearing away toward the struggle. "Look at me! Put your lamps here, goddamn you! The enemy hasn't broken yet. They feel their King's eyes upon them. They're falling like wheat but their courage hasn't failed. I said, look at me! In the killing zone, you see our allies' helmets now, rising out of the slaughter; it seems as if the Thespaians are mounting a wall. They are. A wall of Persian bodies."

This was true. Distinctly could be beheld a rise of men, a wave of its own within the boiling melee. "The Thespaians will only last a few more minutes. They're exhausted from killing. It's a grouse shoot. Fish in a net. Listen to me! When our turn comes, the enemy will be ready to cave. I can hear him cracking now. Remember: we're going in for a boxer's round. In and out. Nobody dies. No heroes. Get in, kill all you can, then get out when the trumpets sound."

Behind the Spartans, on the Wall, which had been filled with the third wave of Tegeates and Opountian Lokrians twelve hundred strong, the wail of the *sarpinx* cut the din. Out front, Leonidas raised his spear and tugged his helmet down. You could see Polynikes and the Knights advance to envelop him. The Thespaians' round was over. "Hats down!" Dienekes bellowed. "Cheeseplates up!"

The Spartans came in frontally, eight deep, at a double interval, allowing the Thespaian rearmen to withdraw between their files, man by man, one rank at a time. There was no order to it; the Thespaians just dropped from exhaustion; the Lakedaemonian tread rolled over them. When the Spartan *promachoi*, the foreрankers, got within three shields of the front, their spears began plunging at the foe over the allies' shoulders. Many of the Thespaians just dropped and let themselves be trampled; their mates pulled them to their feet once the line had passed over them.

Everything Dienekes had said proved true. The Medes' shields were not only too light and too small, but their lack of mass prevented them from gaining purchase against the Hellenes' wide and weighty, bowl-shaped *aspides*. The enemy's targeteer shields slid off the convex fronts of the Greeks', deflecting up and down, left and right, exposing their bearers' necks and thighs, throats and groins. The Spartans struck overhand with their spears, again and again into the faces and gorges of the enemy. The Medes' armament was that of skirmishers, of lightly armed warriors of the plains, whose role was to strike swiftly, from beyond range of spear thrust, dealing death at a distance. This dense-packed phalanx warfare was hell on them.

And yet they stood. Their valor was breathtaking, beyond reckless to the point of madness. It became sacrifice, pure and simple; the Medes gave up their bodies as if flesh itself were a weapon. In minutes the Spartans, and no doubt the Mycenaeans and Philiasians as well, though I couldn't see them, were beyond exhaustion. Simply from killing. Simply from the arm's thrust of the spear, the shoulder's heave of the shield, the thunder of blood through the veins and the hammering of the heart within the breast. The earth grew, not littered with enemy bodies, but piled with them. Stacked with them. Mounded with them.

At the heels of the Spartans, their squires abandoned all thought of inflicting casualties with their own missile weapons, turning to nothing but dragging out trampled corpses of the foe to help their men maintain footing. I saw Demades, Ariston's squire, slit three wounded Medes' throats in fifteen seconds, slinging their carcasses back onto a mound already writhing with groaning men.

Discipline had broken among the Median forerankers; officers' bawled orders could not be heard amid the din, and even if they could, the men were so overwhelmed in the crush they could not respond to them. Still the rank and file had not panicked. In desperation they cast aside bows, lances and shields and simply grappled with bare hands onto the weapons of the Spartans. They clutched at spears, hanging on with both hands and struggling to wrest them from the Spartans' grips. Others of the foe flung themselves bodily onto the Lakedaemonians' shields, clasping the top rim and pulling the bowls of the *aspides* down, scratching and clawing at the Spartans with fingers and fingernails.

Now the slaughter in the forefront became man-to-man, with only the wildest semblance of rank and formation. The Spartans slew belly-to-belly with the murderously efficient thrust-and-draw of their short *xiphos* swords. I saw Alexandros, his shield torn from his grip, plunging his *xiphos* into the face of a Mede whose hands clawed and pounded at Alexandros' groin.

The middle-rankers of the Lakedaemonians surged into this bedlam, spears and shields still intact. But the Medes' capacity for reinforcement seemed limitless; above the fray, one could glimpse the next thousand reinforcements thundering into the Narrows like a flood, with more myriads behind, and yet more after that. Despite the catastrophic magnitude of their casualties, the tide began to flow in the enemy's favor. The weight of their masses alone began to buckle the Spartan line. The only thing that stopped the foe from swamping the Hellenes outright was that they couldn't get enough men through the Narrows quickly enough; that, and the wall of Median bodies that now obstructed the confines like a landslide.

The Spartans fought from behind this wall of flesh as if it were a battlement of stone. The enemy swarmed atop it. Now we in the rear could see them; they became targets. Twice Suicide drilled javelins right over Alexandros' shoulder into Medes lunging at the youth from atop the mound of corpses. Bodies were underfoot everywhere. I mounted atop what I thought was a stone, only to feel it writhe and wriggle beneath me. It was a Mede, alive. He plunged the stub end of a shattered *machaera* scimitar three inches into my calf; I bellowed in terror and toppled into the tangle of other gore-splattered limbs. The foe came at me with his teeth. He seized my arm as if to tear it from its socket; I punched him in the face with my bow still in my grip. Suddenly a foot planted itself massively upon my back. A battle-axe fell with a grisly swoosh; the enemy's skull split like a melon. "What are you looking for down there?" a voice bellowed. It was Akanthus, Polynikes' squire, spray-blasted with blood and grinning like a madman.

The enemy flooded over the wall of bodies. By the time I got to my feet I had lost sight of Dienekes; I couldn't tell which platoon was which or where my proper station was. I had no idea how long we had been in the fight. Was it two minutes or twenty? I had two spears, spares, lashed to my back, their iron sheathed in leather so that, should I tumble accidentally, the spearpoints would work no harm to our comrades. Every other squire bore the same burden; they were all as scrambled as I was.

Up front you could hear the Median lancers' shafts snapping as they clashed and shivered against the Spartan bronze. The Spartans' eight-footers made a different sound than the shorter, lighter lances of the foe. The flood was working against the Lakedaemonians, not from want of valor, but simply in consequence of the overwhelming masses of men which the enemy flung into the teeth of the line. I was frantic to locate Dienekes and deliver my spares. The scene was chaos. I could hear breakdowns right and left and see the rear-rankers of the Spartans buckling as the files before them gave way beneath the weight of the Median onslaught. I had to forget my master and serve where I could.

I dashed to a point where the line was thinnest, only three deep and beginning to swell into the desperate inverse bulge that precedes an out-and-out break. A Spartan fell backward amid the maw of slaughter; I saw a Mede lop the warrior's head clean off with a thunderous slash of a scimitar. The skull toppled, helmet and all, severed from its torso and rolling in the dust, with the marrow gushing and the bone of the spine showing grayish white and ghastly. Helmet and head vanished amid a storm of churning greaves and shod and unshod feet. The murderer loosed a cry of triumph, raising his blade to heaven; half an instant later a crimson-clad warrior buried an eight-footer so deep in the foeman's guts that its killing steel burst free, clear out the man's back. I saw another Mede pass out in terror. The Spartan couldn't haul the weapon back out, so he broke it right off, planting his foot on the still-living enemy's belly and snapping the ash shaft in two. I had no idea who this hero was, and never did find out.

"Spear!" I heard him bellow, the hellish eye sockets of his helmet spinning to the rear for relief, for a spare, for anything to call to hand. I tore both eight-footers off my back and thrust them into the unknown warrior's hands. Backward. He seized one and whirled, planting it with both hands into another Mede's throat, butt-spike-first. His shield's gripcord had been severed or snapped from within; the *aspis* itself had fallen to the dirt. There was no room to retrieve it.

Two Medes lunged toward the Spartan with lances leveled, only to be intercepted by the massive bowl of his rankmate's shield, dropping into place to defend him. Both enemy lances snapped as their heads drove against the bronze facing and oak bowlwork of the shield. In the rush, their momentum carried them forward, sprawling onto the ground atop and tangled with the first Spartan. He drove his *xiphos* into the first Mede's belly, rose with a cry of homicide and slashed the second hilt-deep across both eyes. The enemy clutched his face in horror, blood gushing between the fingers of his clenched and clawing hands. The Spartan seized with both hands his own fallen shield and brought its rim down like an onion chopper, with such force upon the enemy's throat that it nearly decapitated him.

"Re-form! Re-form!" I heard an officer shouting. Someone shoved me aside from behind. In an instant other Spartans, from another platoon, surged forward, reinforcing the membrane-thin front which teetered at the brink of buckling. This was fighting "scrambled." It stopped the heart to behold the gallantry of it. In moments, what had been a situation at the brink of catastrophe was transformed by the discipline and order of the reinforcing ranks into a strongpoint, a fulcrum of vantage. Each man who found himself in the fore, no matter what rank he had held in formation, now assumed the role of officer. These closed ranks and lapped shields, shadow-to-shadow. A wall of bronze rose before the scrambled mass, buying precious instants for those who found themselves in the rear to re-form and remarshal, surging into position in second, third, fourth ranks, and take on that station's role and rally to it.

Nothing fires the warrior's heart more with courage than to find himself and his comrades at the point of annihilation, at the brink of being routed and overrun, and then to dredge not merely from one's own bowels or guts but from one's own discipline and training the presence of mind not to panic, not to yield to the possession of despair, but instead to complete those homely acts of order which Dienekes had ever declared the supreme accomplishment of the warrior: to perform the commonplace under far-from-commonplace conditions. Not only to achieve this for oneself alone, as Achilles or the solo champions of yore, but to do it as part of a unit, to feel about oneself one's brothers-in-arms, in an instance like this of chaos and disorder, comrades whom one doesn't even know, with whom one has never trained; to feel them filling the spaces alongside him, from spear side and shield side, fore and rear, to behold one's comrades likewise rallying, not in a frenzy of mad possession-driven abandon, but with order and self-composure, each man knowing his role and rising to it, drawing strength from him as he draws it from them; the warrior in these moments finds himself lifted as if by the hand of a god. He cannot tell where his being leaves off and that of the comrade beside him begins. In that moment the phalanx forms a unity so dense and all-divining that it performs not merely at the level of a machine or engine of war but, surpassing that, to the state of a single organism, a beast of one blood and heart.

The foemen's arrows rained upon the Spartan line. From where I found myself, just behind the rear-rankers, I could see the warriors' feet, at first churning in disarray for purchase on the blood and gore-beslimed earth, now settle into a unison, a grinding relentless cadence. The pipers' wail pierced the din of bronze and fury, sounding the beat which was part music and part pulse of the heart. With a heave, the warriors' shield-side foot pressed forward, bows-on to the enemy; now the spear-side foot, planted at a ninety-degree angle, dug into the mud; the arch sank as every stone of the man's weight found purchase upon the insole, and, with left shoulder planted into the inner bowl of the shield whose broad outer surface was pressed into the back of the comrade before him, he summoned all force of tissue and tendon to surge and heave upon the beat. Like ranked oarsmen straining upon the shaft of a single oar, the unified push of the men's exertions propelled the ship of the phalanx forward into the tide of the enemy.

Up front the eight-footers of the Spartans thrust downward upon the foe, driven by each man's spear arm in an overhand strike, across the upper rim of his shield, toward the enemy's face, throat and shoulders. The sound of shield against shield was no longer the clash and clang of initial impact, but deeper and more terrifying, a grinding metallic mechanism like the jaws of some unholy mill of murder. Nor did the men's cries, Spartans and Medes, rise any longer in the mad chorus of rage and terror. Instead each warrior's lungs pumped only for breath; chests heaved like foundry bellows, sweat coursed onto the ground in runnels, while the sound which arose from the throats of the contending masses was like nothing so much as a myriad quarrymen, each harnessed to the twined rope of the sled, groaning and straining to drag some massive stone across the resisting earth.

War is work, Dienekes had always taught, seeking to strip it of its mystery. The Medes, for all their valor, all their numbers and all the skill they doubtless possessed in the type of open-plain warfare with which they had conquered all Asia, had not served their apprenticeship in this, Hellene-style heavy-infantry combat. Their files had not trained to hold line of thrust and gather themselves to heave in unison; the ranks had not drilled endlessly as the Spartans had in maintaining dress and interval, cover and shadow. Amid the manslaughter the Medes became a mob. They shoved at the Lakedaemonians like sheep fleeing a fire in a shearing pen, without cadence or cohesion, fueled only by courage, which, glorious though it was, could not prevail against the disciplined and cohesive assault which now pressed upon them.

The luckless foemen in front had nowhere to hide. They found themselves pinned between the mob of their own fellows trampling them from behind and the Spartan spears plunging upon them from the fore. Men expired simply from want of breath. Their hearts gave out under the extremity. I glimpsed Alpheus and Maron; like a pair of yoked oxen the brothers, fighting shoulder-to-shoulder, formed the tempered steel point of a twelve-deep thrust that drove into and split the Median ranks a hundred feet out from the mountain wall.

The Knights, to the twins' right, drove into this breach with Leonidas fighting in the van; they turned the enemy line into a flank and pressed furiously upon the foemen's unshielded right. God help the sons of the Empire seeking to stand against these, Polynikes and Doreion, Terkleius and Patrokles, Nikolaus and the two Agises, all matchless athletes in the prime of young manhood, fighting alongside their king and mad to seize the glory that now quavered within their grasp.

For myself, I confess the horror of it nearly overcame me. Though

I had loaded up double with two packed quivers, twenty-four ironheads, the demands of fire had come so fierce and furious that I was down to nothing before I could spit. I was firing between the helmets of the warriors, point-blank into the faces and throats of the foe. This was not archery, it was slaughter. I was pulling ironheads from the bowels of still-living men to reload and replenish my spent stock. The ash of a shaft drawn across my bow hand slipped from its notch, slimy with gore and tissue; warheads dripped blood before they were even fired. Overwhelmed by horror, my eyes clamped shut of their own will; I had to tear at my face with both hands to drive them open. Had I gone mad?

I was desperate to find Dienekes, to get to my station covering him, but the part of my mind which still owned its wits ordered me to rally myself here, contribute here.

In the crush of the phalanx each man could sense the sea change as the rush of emergency passed like a wave, replaced by the steadying, settling sensation of fear passing over, composure returning and the drill settling to the murderous work of war. Who can say by what unspoken timbre the tidal flow of the fight is communicated within the massed ranks? Somehow the warriors sensed that the Spartan left, along the mountain face, had broken the Medes. A cheer swept laterally like a storm front, rising and multiplying from the throats of the Lakedaemonians. The enemy knew it too. They could feel their line caving in.

Now at last I found my master. With a cry of joy I spotted his cross-crested officer's helmet, in the fore, pressing murderously upon a knot of Median lancers who no longer offered attack but only stumbled rearward in terror, casting away their shields as they fouled upon the desperate press of men behind them. I sprinted toward his position, across the open space immediately to the rear of the grinding, gnashing, advancing Spartan line. This strip of hinter ground comprised the only corridor of haven upon the entire field, in the overshot gap between the hand-to-hand slaughter of the line and the "beaten zone" of the Median archers' arrows, which they flung from the rear of their own lines over the clashing armies toward the Hellenic formations waiting in reserve.

The Median wounded had dragged themselves into this pocket of sanctuary, they and the terror-stricken, the possum players and the exhausted. Enemy bodies were everywhere, the dead and the dying, the trampled and the overrun, the maimed and the massacred. I saw a Mede with a magnificent beard sitting sheepishly upon the ground, cradling his intestines in his hands. As I dashed past, one of his own kinsmen's arrows rained from above, nailing his thigh to the turf. His eyes met mine with the most piteous expression; I don't know why, but I dragged him a half dozen strides, into the mainland of the pocket of illusory safety. I looked behind. The Tegeates and the Opountian Lokrians, our allies next up into the fray, knelt in their ranks, massed along the line below Lion Stone with their shields interleaved and elevated to deflect the deluge of enemy shafts. The expanse of earth before them bristled like a pincushion, as dense with enemy arrows as the quills of a hedgehog's spine. The palisade of the Wall was afire, blazing with the tow bolts of the enemy by the hundred.

Now the Median lancers cracked. Like a child's game of bowls, their stacked files toppled rearward; bodies fell and tumbled upon one another as those in the fore attempted to flee and those in the rear became entangled pell-mell with their flight. The ground before the Spartan advance became a sea of limbs and torsos, trousered thighs and bellies, the backs of men crawling hand over hand across their fallen comrades, while others, pinned upon their backs, writhed and cried out in their tongue, hands upraised, pleading for quarter.

The slaughter surpassed the mind's capacity to assimilate it. I saw Olympieus thrashing rearward, treading not upon ground, but upon the flesh of the fallen foe, across a carpet of bodies, the wounded as well as the dead, while his squire, Abattus, flanked him, sinking his lizard-sticker, punching the spiked shaft downward like a boatman poling a punt, into the bellies of the yet-unslain enemy as they passed. Olympieus advanced into plain view of the allied reserves in position along the Wall. He stripped his helmet so the commanders could see his face, then pumped thrice with his horizontally held spear. "Advance! Advance!"

With a cry that curdled the blood, they did.

I saw Olympieus pause bareheaded and stare at the foe-strewn earth about him, himself overcome by the scale of the carnage. Then he reseated his helmet; his face vanished beneath the blood-blasted bronze and, summoning his squire, he strode back to the slaughter.

To the rear of the routed lancers stood their brothers, the Median archers. These were drawn up in still-ordered ranks, twenty deep, each bowman in station behind a body-height shield of wicker, its base anchored to the earth with spikes of iron. A no-man's-land of a hundred feet separated the Spartans from this wall of bowmen. The foe now began firing directly into their own lancers, the last pockets of the valiant who yet grappled with the Lakedaemonian advance.

The Medes were shooting their own men in the back.

They didn't care if they slew ten of their brothers, if one lucky bolt could nail a Spartan.

Of all the moments of supreme valor which unfolded throughout this long grisly day, that which the allies upon the Wall now beheld surpassed all, nor could any who witnessed it place any sight beneath heaven alongside it as equal. As the Spartan front routed the last remaining lancers, its foreankers emerged into the open, exposed to what was now the nearly point-blank fire of the Median archers. Leonidas himself, at his age having survived a melee of murder whose physical expenditure alone would have pressed beyond the limits of endurance even the stoutest youth in his prime, yet summoned the steel to stride to the fore, shouting the order to form up and advance. This command the Lakedaemonians obeyed, if not with the precision of the parade ground, then with a discipline and order beyond imagining under the circumstances. Before the Medes had time to loose their second broadside, they found themselves face-to-face with a front of sixty-plus shields, the *lambdas* of Lakedaemon obscured beneath horrific layers of mud, gore and blood which ran in rivers down the bronze and dripped from the leather aprons pended beneath the *aspides*, the oxhide skirts which protected the warriors' legs from precisely the fusillade into which they now advanced. Heavy bronze greaves defended the calves; above each shield rim extended only the armored crowns of the helmets, eye slits alone exposed, while overtopping these waved the front-to-back horsehair plumes of the warriors and the transverse crests of the officers.

The wall of bronze and crimson advanced into the Median fire. Cane arrows ripped with murderous velocity into the Spartan lines. Possessed by terror, an archer will always shoot high; you could hear these overshot shafts hailing and clattering as they ripped at crown height past the Spartan foreranks and tore into the forest of spears held at the vertical; then the missiles tumbled, spent, among the armored ranks. Bronzehead bolts caromed off bronze-faced shields with a sound like a hammer on an anvil, their furious drumming punctuated by the concussive *thwock* of a dead-on shot penetrating metal and oak so the head lanced through the shield like a nail piercing a board.

I myself had planted shoulder and spine into the back of Medon, senior of the Deukalion mess, whose station of honor stood rearmost of the first file in Dienekes' platoon. The pipers were hunkered immediately in the lee of the formation, unarmed and unarmored, crouching for cover as close to the heels of the rear-rankers as they could without tripping them, all the while summoning breath to skirl out the shrill *aulos*'s beat. The densely packed ranks advanced not in a mobbed disordered charge shouting like savages, but dead silent, sober, almost stately, with a dread deliberateness in time to the pipers' keening wail. Between the fighting fronts, the hundred-foot gap had narrowed to sixty. Now the Medes' fire redoubled. You could hear the orders bawled by their officers and feel the air itself vibrate as the ranks of the foe loosed their fusillades in ever more furious succession.

A single arrow blazing past one's ear can turn the knees to jelly; the honed warhead seems to scream with malevolence, the hurdling weight of the shaft driving its death-dealing cargo; then come the fletched feathers communicating by their silent shriek the homicidal intent of the enemy. A hundred arrows make a different sound. Now the air seems to thicken, to become dense, incandescent; it vibrates like a solid. The warrior feels encapsulated as in a corridor of living steel; reality shrinks to the zone of murder in which he finds himself imprisoned; the sky itself cannot be glimpsed nor even remembered.

Now come a thousand arrows. The sound is like a wall. There is no space within, no interval of haven. Solid as a mountain, impenetrable; it sings with death. And when those arrows are launched not skyward in long-range arcing trajectory to beat upon the target driven by the weight of their own fall, but instead are fired point-blank, dead flush from the chute of the bowman's grip, so that their flight is level, flat, loosed at such velocity and at such close range that the archer does not trouble even to calculate drop into his targeting equation; this is the rain of iron, hellfire at its purest.

Into this the Spartans advanced. They were told later by the allies observing from the Wall that at this instant, as the spears of the Spartans' front ranks lowered in unison from the vertical plane of advance into the leveled position of attack and the serried phalanx lengthened stride to assault the foe at the double; at this moment, His Majesty, looking on, had leapt to his feet in terror for his army.

The Spartans knew how to attack wicker. They had practiced against it beneath the oaks on the field of Otona, in the countless repetitions when we squires and helots took station with practice shields, planted our heels and braced with all our strength, awaiting the massed shock of their assault. The Spartans knew the spear was worthless against the interlatticed staves; its shaft penetrated the wicker only to become imprisoned and impossible to extract. Likewise the thrust or slash of the *xiphos*, which caromed off as if striking iron. The enemy line must be struck, shock troop style, and overwhelmed, bowled over; it had to be hit so hard and with such concentrated force that its front-rankers caved and toppled, one rank backward upon another, like plateware in a cabinet when the earth quakes.

This is precisely what happened. The Median archers were drawn up not in a massed square front-to-back with each warrior reinforcing his comrades against the shock of assault, but honeycombed in alternating fronts, each rank at the shoulder of the one before it, so that the bowmen in the second could fire in the gaps left by the first, and on in this fashion rearward throughout the formation.

Moreover the enemy ranks were not stacked with the massed compaction of the Spartan phalanx. There was a void, an interval between ranks dictated by the physical demands of the bow. The result of this was precisely what the Lakedaemonians expected: the forerank of the enemy collapsed immediately as the first shock hit it; the body-length shields seemed to implode rearward, their anchoring spikes rooted slinging from the earth like tent pins in a gale. The forerank archers were literally bowled off their feet, their wall-like shields caving in upon them like fortress redoubts under the assault of the ram. The Spartan advance ran right over them, and the second rank, and the third. The mob of enemy mid-rankers, urged on by their officers, sought desperately to dig in and hold. Closed breast-to-breast with the Spartan shock troops, the foe's bows were useless. They flung them aside, fighting with their belt scimitars. I saw an entire front of them, shieldless, slashing wildly with a blade in each hand. The valor of individual Medes was beyond question, but their light hacking blades were harmless as toys; against the massed wall of Spartan armor, they might as well have been defending themselves with reeds or fennel stalks.

We learned that evening, from Hellenic deserters who had fled in the confusion, that the foe's rearmost ranks, thirty and forty back from the front, had been pressed rearward so resistlessly by the collapse of the men up front that they began tumbling off the Trachinian track into the sea. Pandemonium had apparently reigned along a section several hundred yards long, beyond the Narrows, where the trail ran flush against the mountain wall, with the gulf yawning eighty feet below. Over this brink, the deserters reported, hapless lancers and archers had toppled by the score, clinging to the men before them and pulling these down with them to their deaths. His Majesty, we heard, was forced to witness this, as his vantage lay almost directly above the site. This was the second moment, so the observers reported, when His Majesty sprung to his feet in dread for the fate of his warriors.

The ground immediately to the rear of the Spartan advance, as expected, was littered with the trampled forms of the enemy dead and wounded. But there was a new wrinkle. The Medes had been overrun with such speed and force that numbers of them, far from inconsiderable, had survived intact. These now rose and attempted to rally, only to find themselves assaulted almost at once by the massed ranks of the allied reserves who were already advancing in formation to reinforce and relieve the Spartans. A second slaughter now ensued, as the Tegeates and Opountian Lokrians fell upon this yet-unreaped harvest. Tegea lies immediately adjacent to the territory of Lakedaemon. For centuries the Spartans and Tegeates had battled over the border plains before, in the previous three generations, becoming fast allies and comrades. Of all the Peloponnesians save the Spartans, the warriors of Tegea are the fiercest and most skilled. As for the Lokrians of Opus, this was their country they were fighting for; their homes and temples, fields and sanctuaries, lay within an hour's march of the Hot Gates. Quarter, they knew, stood not within the invader's lexicon; neither would it be found in theirs.

I was dragging a wounded Knight, Polynikes' friend Doreion, to the safety of the field's shoulder when my foot slipped in an ankle-deep stream. Twice I tried to regain balance and twice fell. I was cursing the earth. What perverse spring had suddenly burst forth from the mountainside when none had shown itself in this place before? I looked down. A river of blood covered both feet, draining across a gouge in the dirt like the gutter of an abattoir.

The Medes had cracked. The Tegeates and Opountian Lokrians surged in reinforcement through the ranks of the spent Spartans, pressing the assault upon the reeling enemy. It was the allies' turn now. "Put the steel to 'em, boys!" one among the Spartans cried as the wave of allied ranks advanced ten deep from the rear and both flanks and closed into a massed phalanx before the warriors of Sparta, who at last drew up, limbs quaking with fatigue, and collapsed against one another and upon the earth.

At last I found my master. He was on one knee, shattered with exhaustion, clinging with both fists to his shivered blade-bereft spear which was driven butt-spike-first into the earth and from which he hung like a broken marionette upon a stick. The weight of his helmet bore his head groundward; he possessed strength neither to lift it nor to pull it off. Alexandros collapsed beside him, on all fours with the crown of his helmet, crest-first, mashed with exhaustion into the dirt.

His ribcage heaved like a hound's, while spittle, phlegm and blood dripped from the bronze of his cheekpieces in a frothing lather.

Here came the Tegeates and Lokrians, surging past us.

There they went, driving the enemy before them.

For the first interval in what seemed an eternity, the dread of imminent extinction lifted. The Lakedaemonians dropped to the earth where they stood, on knees first, then knees and elbows, then simply sprawling, on sides and on backs, collapsing against one another, sucking breath in gasping labored need. Eyes stared vacantly, as if blind. None could summon strength to speak. Weapons drooped of their own weight, in fists so cramped that the will could not compel the muscles to release their frozen grasp. Shields toppled to earth, bowl-down and defamed; exhausted men collapsed into them face-first and could not find strength even to turn their faces to the side to breathe.

A fistful of teeth spit from Alexandros' mouth. When he recovered strength sufficient to prise his helmet off, his long hair came out at the roots in wads, a tangled mass of salt sweat and matted blood. His eyes stared, blank as stones. He collapsed like a child, burying his face in my master's lap, weeping the dry tears of those whose shattered substance has no more fluid to spend.

Suicide came up, shot through both shoulders and oblivious with elation. He stood above the collapsed ranks of men, fearless, peering out to where the allies had now closed with the last of the Medes and were hacking them to pieces with such a grisly din that it seemed the slaughter was taking place ten paces away instead of a hundred.

I could see my master's eyes, pools of black behind the hooded eye slits of his helmet. His hand gestured feebly to the empty spear sheath across my back. "What happened to my spares?" his throat croaked hoarsely.

"I gave them away."

A moment passed while he waited for breath. "To our own men, I hope."

I helped him off with his helmet. It seemed to take minutes, so swollen with sweat and blood was his felt undercap and the tangled clotted mass of his hair. The water bearers had arrived. None among the warriors possessed the strength even to cup his hands, so the liquid was simply splashed upon rags and blouses which the men pressed to their lips and sucked. Dienekes swabbed the tangled hair off his face. His left eye was gone. Sliced through, leaving a ghoulish socket of tissue and blood.

"I know" was all he said.

Aristomenes and Bias and others of the platoon, Black Leon and Leon Donkeydick, now surfaced into view, gasping upon the earth, their arms and legs sliced and lacerated with innumerable slashes, glistening with mud and blood. They and other scrambled men from other scrambled units lay heaped upon one another like a frieze on a temple wall.

I knelt now at my master's side, pressing the water rag as a compress into the hollow where his eye had been. The fabric welled with fluid like a sponge.

Out front, where the enemy were falling back in wild disorder, the victors of the moment could see Polynikes, on his feet, alone, with his arms raised toward the fleeing foe. He wrenched his helmet from his skull, dripping blood and sweat, and flung it in triumph upon the earth.

"Not today, you sons of whores!" he bellowed at the foe in flight. "Not today!"

TWENTY-FIVE

I cannot state with certainty how many times on that first day each allied contingent took its turn upon the triangle bounded by the Narrows and the mountain face, the sea cliffs and the Phokian Wall. I can declare with conviction only that my master went through four shields, two whose oak underchassis were shattered by repeated blows, one whose bronze plexus was staved in and a fourth whose gripcord and forearm sheath were ripped right out of their sockets. Replacements were not hard to find. One had only to stoop, so many were the discards littered upon the field, with their owners dead and dying beside them.

Of the sixteen in my master's *enomotia* were slain on that first day Lampitos, Soöbiades, Telemon, Sthlenelaides, Ariston and grievously wounded Nikandros, Myron, Charillon and Bias.

Ariston fell in the fourth and final siege, that against His Majesty's Immortals. Ariston was that youth of twenty years, one of Polynikes' "broken noses," whose sister Agathe had been given as a bride to Alexandros. That made them brothers-in-law.

The retrieval party found Ariston's body around midnight, along the mountain wall. His squire Demades' form law sprawled atop Ariston's with his shield still in place seeking to protect his master, both of whose shins had been shattered by the blows of a *sagaris* battle-axe. The shaft of an enemy lance was broken off just beneath Demades' left nipple. Although Ariston had sustained more than twenty wounds upon his own body, it was a single blow to the head, apparently delivered with some kind of mace or battle sledge, which had ultimately slain him, crushing both helmet and skull directly above the eyeline.

The tickets of the dead were customarily held and distributed by the chief battle priest, in this case Alexandros' father, the *polemarch*

Olympieus. He himself had been killed, however, slain by a Persian arrow an hour before nightfall, just prior to the final clash with the Persian Immortals. Olympieus had taken shelter with his men on the rampart of the Wall, in the lee of the palisade, preparatory to arming himself for the day's final siege. Of all things, he was writing in his journal. The unburned timbers of the palisade protected him, he thought; he had stripped helmet and cuirass. But the arrow, guided by some perverse fate, pierced the single opening available to it, a space no wider than a man's hand. It struck Olympieus in the cervical spine, severing the spinal cord. He died minutes later, without regaining speech or consciousness, in his son's arms.

With that, Alexandros had lost father and brother-in-law in a single afternoon.

Among the Spartans, the most grievous casualties of the first day were suffered by the Knights. Of thirty, seventeen were either killed or incapacitated too severely to fight. Leonidas was wounded six times but walked off the field under his own power. Astonishingly Polynikes, fighting all day in the forefront of the bloodiest action, had sustained no more than the slashes and lacerations incidental to action, a number of them doubtless inflicted by his own errant steel and that of his mates. He had, however, severely strained both hamstrings and pulled his left shoulder, simply from exertion and the excessive demands made upon the flesh in moments of supreme necessity. His squire, Akanthus, had been killed defending him, lucklessly like Olympieus, just minutes before the cessation of the day's slaughter.

The second attack had commenced at noon. These were the mountain warriors of Cissia. None among the allies even knew where the hell this place was, but wherever it was, it bred men of ungodly valor. Cissia, the allies learned later, is a country of stern and hostile highlands not far from Babylon, dense with ravines and defiles. This contingent of the enemy, far from being daunted by the cliff wall of Kallidromos, took this obstacle in stride, clambering up and along its face, rolling stones down indiscriminately upon their own troops as well as the allies. I myself could not view this struggle directly, being stationed during that interval behind the Wall, all efforts consumed with tending my master's wounds and those of our platoon and looking to their and my own necessaries. But I could hear it. It sounded like the whole mountain coming down. At one point, from where Dienekes and Alexandros were, in the Spartan camp a hundred feet rearward of the Wall, we could see the ready platoons, in this rotation the Mantinean and the Arkadians, pouring up to the battlements of the Wall and there hurling javelins, spears and even dismantled boulders down upon the attackers, who, in the elation of the triumph they thought at hand, were keening a bloodcurdling wail which I can only replicate as "Elelelelele."

The Thebans, we learned that evening, were the ones who threw back the Cissian assault. These warriors of Thebes held the right flank, as the allies saw it, alongside the sea cliffs. Their commander, Leontiades, and the picked champions fighting alongside him managed to secure a breach in the mob of the enemy, about forty feet out from the cliffs. The Thebans poured into this break and began shoving the cutoff ranks of the foe, about twenty files in breadth, toward the cliffs. Again the weight of the allied armor proved irresistible. The enemy right were rooted backward by the press of their own failing comrades. They toppled into the sea, as before in the rout of the Medes, clutching at the trousers, sword belts and finally the ankles of their fellows, pulling them over with them. The scale and celerity of the slaughter had clearly been massive, made more so by the ghastly manner in which the slain perished, that is, tumbling eighty and a hundred feet to have their bodies broken upon the rocks below or, escaping that, to drown in armor in the sea. Even from our position an eighth of a mile away and above the din of battle, we could hear plainly the cries of the falling men.

The Sacae were the next nation elected by Xerxes to assault the allies. These massed below the Narrows around midafternoon. They were plainsmen and mountain men, warriors of the eastern empire, and the bravest of all the troops the allies faced. They fought with battle-axes and inflicted, for a time, the most grisly casualties upon the Greeks. Yet in the end their own courage was their undoing. They did not break or panic; they simply came on in wave after wave, clawing over the fallen bodies of their brothers to hurl themselves as if seeking their own slaughter upon the shields and iron spearpoints of the Greeks. Against these Sacae were arrayed at first the Mycenaeans, the Corinthians and the Philiasians, with the Spartans, Tegeates and Thespaians in ready reserve. These last were flung into battle almost at once, as the Mycenaeans and Corinthians spent themselves in the mill of murder and became too exhausted to continue. The reserves likewise became shattered with fatigue and themselves had to be relieved by the third rotation of Orchomenians and other Arkadians, these last having barely gotten out of the previous melee and had time to gnaw a hard biscuit and gulp down a snootful of wine.

By the time the Sacae broke, the sun was well over the mountain. The "dance floor," now in full shadow, looked like a field ploughed by the oxen of hell. Not an inch remained unchurned and unriven. The rock-hard earth, sodden now with blood and piss and the unholy fluids which had spilled from the entrails of the slain and the butchered, lay churned in places to the depth of a man's calf. There is a spring sacred to Persephone, behind the sallyport adjacent to the Lakedaemonian camp, where in the morning, immediately following the repulsion of the Median assault, the Spartans and Thespaians had collapsed in exhaustion and triumph. In that initial instant of salvation, however temporary all knew it must be, a flush of supreme joy had flooded over the entire allied camp. Panoplied men faced one another and slammed shields together, just for the joy of it, like boys rejoicing in the clamor of bronze upon bronze. I saw two warriors of the Arkadians standing face-to-face, pounding each other with fists upon the shoulders of their leathers, tears of joy streaming down their faces. Others whooped and danced. One warrior of the Philiasians grasped the corner of the redoubt with both hands and pounded his helmeted brow against the stone, bang bang bang, like a lunatic. Others writhed upon the ground, as horses will do sand-bathing, so overflushed with joy that they could discharge its excess in no other way.

Simultaneously a second wave of emotion coursed through the camp. This was of piety. Men embraced one another, weeping in awe before the gods. Prayers of thanksgiving were sung from fervent hearts, and none took shame to voice them. Across the expanse of the camp, one saw knots of warriors kneeling in invocation, circles of a dozen with clasped hands, knots of three and four with arms around each other's shoulders, pairs crouching knee-to-knee and everywhere individuals upon the earth in prayer.

Now, seven hours into the slaughter, all such observance of piety had fled. Men stared with hollow eyes upon the riven plain. Across this farmer's field of death lay sown such a crop of corpses and shields, hacked-up armor and shattered weapons, that the mind could not assimilate its scale nor the senses give it compass. The wounded, in numbers uncountable, groaned and cried out, writhing amid piles of limbs and severed body parts so intertangled one could not distinguish individual men, but the whole seemed a Gorgon-like beast of ten thousand limbs, some ghastly monster spawned by the cloven earth and now draining itself, fluid by fluid, back into that chthonic cleft which had given it birth. Along the face of the mountain the stone glistened scarlet to the height of a man's knee.

The faces of the allied warriors had by this hour clotted into featureless masks of death. Blank eyes stared from sunken sockets as if the divine force, the *daimon*, had been extinguished like a lamp, replaced by a weariness beyond description, a stare without affect, the hollow gaze of hell itself. I turned to Alexandros; he looked fifty years old. In the mirror of his eyes I beheld my own face and could no longer recognize it.

A temper toward the enemy now arose which had not been present before. This was not hatred but rather a refusal to reckon quarter. A reign of savagery began. Acts of barbarity which had been hitherto unthinkable now presented themselves to the mind and were embraced without a quibble. The theater of war, the stink and spectacle of carnage on such a scale, had so overwhelmed the senses with horror that the mind had grown numb and insensate. With perverse wit, it actually sought these and sought to intensify them.

All knew that the next attack would be the day's last; nightfall's curtain would adjourn the slaughter until tomorrow. It was also clear that whichever force the foe next threw into the line would be his finest, the cream saved for this hour when the Hellenes labored in exhaustion and stood the likeliest chance of being overthrown by fresh troops. Leonidas, who had not slept now in more than forty hours, yet prowled the lines of defenders, assembling each allied unit and addressing it in person. "Remember, brothers: the final fight is everything. All we have achieved so far this day is lost if we do not prevail now, at the end. Fight as you have never fought before."

In the intervals between the first three assaults, each warrior readying for the next engagement had striven to scour clean the face of his shield and helmet, to present again to the foe the gleaming terror-inspiring surface of bronze. As the threshing mill of murder progressed throughout the day, however, this housekeeping became honored increasingly in the breach, as each knurl and inlay on the shield acquired a grisly encrustment of blood and dirt, mud and excrement, fragments of tissue, flesh, hair and gore of every description. Besides, the men were too tired. They didn't care anymore. Now Dithyrambos, the Thespaian captain, sought to make a virtue of necessity. He ordered his men to cease from burnishing their shields, and instead to paint and streak them, and the men's own body armor, with yet more blood and gore.

This Dithyrambos, by trade an architect and by no means a professional soldier, had already distinguished himself with such magnificent courage throughout the day that the prize of valor, it was a foregone conclusion, would be his by acclamation. His gallantry had elevated him second only to Leonidas in prestige among the men. Dithyrambos now, stationing himself in the open in full view of all the men, proceeded to smear his own shield, which was already nearly black with dried blood, with yet more gore and guts and fresh dripping fluid. The allies in line, the Thespaians, Tegeates and Mantineans, ghoulishly followed suit. The Spartans alone abstained, not out of delicacy or decorum, but simply in obedience to their own laws of campaign, which command them to adhere without alteration to their customary disciplines and practices of arms.

Dithyrambos now ordered the squires and servants to hold their places, to refrain from sweeping the advance ground of enemy bodies. Instead, he sent his own men out onto the arena with orders to heap the corpses in display in the most ghoulish manner possible, so as to present to the next wave of the foe, whose marshaling trumpets could already be heard around the shoulder of the Narrows, the most ghastly and terrifying spectacle possible.

"Brothers and allies, my own beautiful dogs from hell!" he addressed the warriors, striding helmetless before the lines, his voice carrying powerfully even to those upon the Wall and marshaling in the ready-ground behind. "This next wave will be the day's last. Cinch up your balls, men, for one final surpassing effort. The enemy believes us exhausted and anticipates dispatching us to the underworld beneath his onslaught of fresh, rested troops. What he doesn't know is we're already there. We crossed the line hours ago." He gestured to the Narrows and its carpeting of horror. "We stand already in hell. It is our home!"

A cheer rose from the line, overtopped by wild profane shouts and whoops of hellish laughter.

"Remember, men," Dithyrambos' voice rose yet more powerfully, "that this next wave of Asiatic ass-fuckers has not seen us yet. Consider what they have seen. They know only that three of their mightiest nations have advanced against us wearing their testicles and come back without them.

"And I promise you: they are *not* fresh. They've been sitting on their dogblossoms all day, watching their allies carried and dragged back, hacked to pieces by us. Believe me, their imaginations have not been idle. Each man has conjured his own head cleaved at the neck, his own guts spilling into the dirt and his own cock and balls brandished before him on the point of a Greek spear! We're not the ones who are worn out, they are!"

Fresh shouting and tumult erupted from the allies, save the Spartans, while the Thespaians on the field continued their butchery. I glanced to Dienekes, who observed this all with a grim twist upon his features.

"By the gods," he declared, "it's getting ugly out there."

We could see the Spartan Knights, led by Polynikes and Doreion, taking their stations about Leonidas in the forefront of the line. Now a lookout came running back in from the forwardmost post. This was Hound, the Spartan Skirite; he sprinted straight to Leonidas and made his report. The news spread swiftly: the next wave would be Xerxes' own household guard, the Immortals. The Greeks knew that these comprised His Majesty's picked champions, the flower of Persian nobility, princes schooled from birth "to draw the bow and speak the truth."

More to the point, their numbers were ten thousand, while the Greeks had fewer than three thousand still fit to fight. The Immortals, all knew, derived their name from the custom of the Persians that replaced at once each royal guardsman who died or retired, thus keeping the number of Xerxes' finest always at ten thousand.

This corps of champions now advanced into view at the neck of the Narrows. They wore not helmets, but tiaras, soft felt caps topped with skull-crowns of metal glistening like gold. These half-helmets possessed no cover for the ears, neck or jaw and left the face and throat entirely exposed. The warriors wore earrings; some of their faces were painted with eye kohl and rouged like women. Nonetheless they were magnificent specimens, selected it seemed not merely, as the Hellenes well knew, for valor and nobility of family but for height and handsomeness of person as well. Each man looked more dashing than the fellow at his shoulder. They wore sleeved tunics of silk, purple rimmed with scarlet, protected by a sleeveless coat of mail in the shape of fish scales, and trousers atop calf-height doeskin boots. Their weapons were the bow, belt scimitar and short Persian lance, and their shields, like the Medes' and the Cissians', were shoulder-to-groiners made of wicker. Most astonishing of all, however, was the quantity of gold ornament each Immortal wore upon his person in the form of brooches and bracelets, amulets and adornments. Their commander, Hydarnes, advanced to the fore, the only mounted antagonist the allies had so far beheld. His tiara was peaked like a monarch's crown and his eyes shone brilliantly beneath kohled lashes. His horse was spooking, refusing to advance across the charnel sward of corpses. The foe drew up in ranks on the flat beyond the Narrows. Their discipline was impeccable. They were spotless.

Leonidas now strode forth to address the allies. He confirmed what each Hellenic warrior presumed by sight, that the division of the enemy now advancing into view was indeed Xerxes' own Immortals and that the number of their company, as nearly as could be estimated by eye, was the full ten thousand.

"It would appear, gentlemen," Leonidas' voice ascended powerfully, "that the prospect of facing the picked champions of all Asia should daunt us. But I swear to you, this battle will prove the most dustless of all."

The king used the Greek word *akoniti*, whose application is customarily to wrestling, boxing and the pankration. When a victor overthrows his opponent so swiftly that the bout fails even to raise the dust of the arena, he is said to have triumphed *akoniti*, in a "no-duster."

"Listen," Leonidas proceeded, "and I will tell you why. The troops Xerxes throws at us now are, for the first time, of actual Persian blood. Their commanders are the King's own kinsmen; he has brothers out there, and cousins and uncles and lovers, officers of his own line whose lives are precious to him beyond price. Do you see him up there, upon his throne? The nations he has sent against us so far have been mere vassal states, spear fodder to such a despot, who squanders their lives without counting the cost. These"—Leonidas gestured across the Narrows to the space where Hydarnes and the Immortals now marshaled—"these he treasures. These he loves. Their murder he will feel like an eight-footer in the guts.

"Remember that this battle at the Hot Gates is not the one Xerxes came here to fight. He anticipates far more momentous struggles to come, in the heartland of Hellas against the main force of our armies, and for these clashes he wishes to preserve the flower of his army, the men you see before you now. He will be frugal with their lives today, I promise you.

"As to their numbers: they are ten thousand, we are four. But each man we slay will sting like a regiment to their King. These warriors are to him like miser's gold, which he hoards and covets beyond all else in his treasury.

"Kill one thousand and the rest will crack. One thousand and their master will pull the remainder out. Can you do that for me, men? Can four of you kill one of them? Can you give me one thousand?"

TWENTY-SIX

His Majesty himself may best judge the precision of Leonidas' forecast. Suffice it to note, for this record, that darkness found the Immortals in shattered retreat, under His Majesty's orders as Leonidas had predicted, leaving the broken and dying upon the *orchestra,* the dance floor, of the Narrows.

Behind the allied Wall the spectacle was one of corresponding horror. A downpour had drenched the camp shortly after nightfall, drowning what few fires remained with none to tend them, all effort of squires, attendants and mates being required to succor the wounded and the maimed. Slides toppled from the wall of Kallidromos, sluicing the upper camp with rivers of mud and stone. Across this sodden expanse, slain and spared sprawled limb upon limb, many still in armor, the slumber of the exhausted so profound that one could not distinguish the living from the dead. Everything was soaked and muck-begrimed. Stores of dressings for the wounded had long since been depleted; the spa-goers' tents requisitioned by the Skiritai rangers as shelter now found their linen called to duty a second time, as battle compresses. The stink of blood and death rose with such palpable horror that the asses of the supply train bawled all night and could not be quietened.

There was a third unrostered member of the allied contingent, a volunteer other than the outlaw Ball Player and the roan bitch Styx. This was an *emporos*, a merchant of Miletus, Elephantinos by name, whose disabled waggon the allied column had chanced upon during its march through Doris, a day prior to arrival at the Gates. This fellow despite his misfortune of the road maintained the merriest of spirits, sharing a lunch of green apples with his hobbled ass. Upon the brow of his waggon rose a hand-painted standard, an advertisement as it were of his congeniality and eagerness of custom. The sign intended to declare, "The best service only for you, my friend." The tinker had misspelled, however, several words, chiefly "friend," *philos*, which his hand had inscribed *phimos*, the term in Doric for a contraction of the flesh which covers the male member. The waggon's banner declared roughly thus:

"The best service only for you, my foreskin."

The luster of this poesy rendered the fellow an instant celebrity. Several squires were detached to assist him, for which courtesy the tradesman expressed abounding gratitude. "And where, if one may inquire, is this magnificent army bound?"

"To die for Hellas," someone answered.

"How delightful!" Toward midnight the tinker appeared in camp, having tracked the column all the way to the Gates. He was welcomed with enthusiasm. His specialty lay in applying an edge to steel, and at this, he testified, he stood without peer. He had been sharpening farmers' scythes and housewives' cleavers for decades. He knew how to make even the meanest untempered trowel hold an edge, and moreover, he vowed, he would donate his services to the army in repayment of their kindness upon the highway.

The fellow employed an expression with which he spiked his conversation whenever he wished to emphasize a point. "Wake up to this!" he would say, though in his dense Ionian accent it came out as "Weck up to thees!"

This phrase was immediately and with high glee adopted by the entire army.

"Cheese and onions again, weck up to thees!"

"Double drill all day, weck up to thees!"

One of the two Leons in Dienekes' platoon, Donkeydick, rousted the merchant that succeeding dawn by brandishing before his slumber-dazed eyes a prodigious erection. "They call this a *phimos*, weck up to thees!"

The tradesman became a kind of mascot or talisman to the troops. His presence was welcomed at every fire, his company embraced by youths as well as veterans; he was considered a raconteur and boon companion, a jester and a friend.

Now in the wake of this first day's slaughter, the merchant appointed himself as well unofficial chaplain and confessor to the young warriors whom he had over the past days come to care for more intimately than sons. He passed all night among the wounded, bearing wine, water and a consoling hand. His accustomed cheerfulness he contrived to redouble; he diverted the maimed and mutilated with profane tales of his travels and misadventures, seductions of housewives, robberies and thrashings sustained upon the road. He had armed himself as well, from the discards; he would fill a gap tomorrow. Many of the squires, uncompelled by their masters, had taken upon themselves the same role.

All night the forges roared. The hammers of the smiths and foundrymen rang without ceasing, repairing spear and sword blades, beating out the bronze for fresh shield facings, while wrights and carpenters manned spokeshaves limning fresh spearshafts and shield carriages for the morrow. The allies cooked their meals over fires made from the spent arrows and shivered spearshafts of the enemy. The natives of Alpenoi village who a day earlier had peddled their produce for profit, now, beholding the sacrifice of the defenders, donated their goods and foodstuffs and hastened off with shuttles and handbarrows to bear up more.

Where were the reinforcements? Were any coming at all? Leonidas, sensing the preoccupation of the army, eschewed all assembly and councils of war, circulating instead in person among the men, transacting the business of the commanders as he went. He was dispatching more runners to the cities, with more appeals for aid. Nor was it lost upon the warriors that he selected always the youngest. Was this for speed of foot, or the king's wish to spare those whose share of remaining years was the greatest?

Each soldier's thoughts turned now toward his family, to those at home whom his heart loved. Shivering, exhausted men scribbled letters to wives and children, mothers and fathers, many of these missives little more than scratches upon cloth or leather, fragments of ceramic or wood. The letters were wills and testaments, final words of farewell. I saw the dispatch pouch of one runner preparing to depart; it was a jumble of paper rolls, wax tablets, potshards, even felt scraps torn from helmet undercaps. Many of the warriors simply sent amulets which their loved ones would recognize, a charm that had pended from the chassis of a shield, a good-luck coin drilled through for a neckband. Some of these bore salutations—"Beloved Amaris" . . . "Delia from Theagones, love." Others bore no name at all. Perhaps the runners of each city knew the addressees personally and could take it upon themselves to ensure delivery. If not, the contents of the pouch would be displayed in the public square or the agora, perhaps set out before the temple of the city's Protectress. There the anxious families would congregate in hope and trepidation, awaiting their turn to pore through the precious cargo, desperate for any message, wordless or otherwise, from those whom they loved and feared to behold again only in death.

Two messengers came in from the allied fleet, from the Athenian corvette assigned as courier between the navy below and the army up top. The allies had engaged the Persian fleet this day, inconclusively, but without buckling. Our ships must hold the straits or Xerxes could land his army in the defenders' rear and cut them off; the troops must hold the pass or the Persian could advance by land to the narrows of the Euripus and trap the fleet. So far, neither had cracked.

Polynikes came and sat for a few minutes beside the fires around which the remains of our platoon had gathered. He had located a renowned *gymnastes*, an athletic trainer named Milon, whom he knew from the Games at Olympia. This fellow had wrapped Polynikes' hamstrings and given him a *pharmakon* to kill the pain.

"Have you had enough of glory, Kallistos?" Dienekes inquired of the Knight.

Polynikes answered only with a look of surpassing grimness. He seemed chastened, out of himself for once.

"Sit down," my master said, indicating a dry space beside him.

Polynikes settled gratefully. Around the circle the platoon slumbered like dead men, heads pillowed upon each other and their yet-gore-encrusted shields. Directly across from Polynikes, Alexandros stared with awful blankness into the fire. His jaw had been broken;

the entire right side of his face glistened purple; the bone itself was cinched shut with a leather strap.

"Let's have a look at you." Polynikes craned forward. He located among the trainer's kit a waxed wad of euphorbia and amber called a "boxer's lunch," the kind pugilists employ between matches to immobilize broken bones and teeth. This Polynikes kneaded warm until it became pliable. He turned to the trainer. "You better do this, Milon." Polynikes took Alexandros' right hand in his own, for the pain. "Hang on. Squeeze till you break my fingers."

The trainer spit from his own mouth into Alexandros' a purge of uncut wine to cleanse the clotted blood, then with his fingers extracted a grotesque gob of spittle, mucus and phlegm. I held Alexandros' head; the youth's fist clamped Polynikes'. Dienekes watched as the trainer inserted the sticky amber wad between Alexandros' jaws, then gently clamped the shattered bone down tight upon it. "Count slowly," he instructed the patient. "When you hit fifty, you won't be able to prise that jaw apart with a crowbar."

Alexandros released the Knight's hand. Polynikes regarded him with sorrow.

"Forgive me, Alexandros."

"For what?"

"For breaking your nose."

Alexandros laughed, his broken jaw making him grimace.

"It's your best feature now."

Alexandros winced again. "I'm sorry about your father," Polynikes said. "And Ariston."

He rose to move on to the next fire, glancing once to my master, then returning his gaze to Alexandros.

"There is something I must tell you. When Leonidas selected you for the Three Hundred, I went to him in private and argued strenuously against your inclusion. I thought you would not fight."

"I know," Alexandros' voice ground through his cinched jaw.

Polynikes studied him a long moment.

"I was wrong," he said.

He moved on.

Another round of orders came, assigning parties to retrieve

corpses from no-man's-land. Suicide's name was among those detailed. Both his shot shoulders had seized up; Alexandros insisted on taking his place.

"By now the king will know about the deaths of my father and Ariston." He addressed Dienekes, who as his platoon commander could forbid him to participate in the retrieval detail. "Leonidas will try to spare me for my family's sake; he'll send me home with some errand or dispatch. I don't wish to disrespect him by refusing."

I had never beheld such an expression of balefulness as that which now framed itself upon my master's face. He gestured to a flat of sodden earth beside him in the firelight.

"I've been watching these little myrmidons."

There in the dirt, a war of the ants was raging.

"Look at these champions." Dienekes indicated the massed battalions of insects grappling with impossible valor atop a pile of their own fellows' fallen forms, battling over the desiccated corpse of a beetle.

"This one here, this would be Achilles. And there. That must be Hektor. Our bravery is nothing alongside these heroes'. See? They even drag their comrades' bodies from the field, as we do."

His voice was dense with disgust and stinking with irony. "Do you think the gods look down on us as we do upon these insects? Do the immortals mourn our deaths as keenly as we feel the loss of these?"

"Get some sleep, Dienekes," Alexandros said gently.

"Yes, that's what I need. My beauty rest."

He lifted his remaining eye toward Alexandros. Out beyond the redoubts of the Wall, the second watch of sentries was receiving their orders, preparatory to relieving the first. "Your father was my mentor, Alexandros. I bore the chalice the night you were born. I remember Olympieus presenting your infant form to the elders, for the 'ten, ten and one' test, to see if you were deemed healthy enough to be allowed to live. The magistrate bathed you in wine and you came up squawling, with your infant's voice strong and your little fists clenched and waving. 'Hand the boy to Dienekes,' your father instructed Paraleia. 'My son will be your protege,' Olympieus told me. 'You will teach him, as I have taught you.' "

Dienekes' right hand plunged the blade of his *xiphos* into the dirt, annihilating the Iliad of the ants.

"Now sleep, all of you!" he barked to the men yet surviving of his platoon and, himself rising, despite all protests that he, too, embrace the boon of slumber, strode off alone toward Leonidas' command post, where the king and the other commanders yet stood to their posts, awake and planning the morrow's action.

I saw Dienekes' hip give way beneath him as he moved; not the bad leg, but the sound. He was concealing from his men's sight yet another wound—from the cast of his gait, deep and crippling. I rose at once and hastened to his aid.

TWENTY-SEVEN

That spring called the Skyllian, sacred to Demeter and Persephone, welled from the base of the wall of Kallidromos just to the rear of Leonidas' command post. Upon its stone-founded approach my master drew up, and I hurrying in his wake overhauled him. No curses or commands to withdraw rebuffed me. I draped his arm about my neck and took his weight upon my shoulder. "I'll get water," I said.

An agitated knot of warriors had clustered about the spring; Megistias the seer was there. Something was amiss. I pressed closer. This spring, renowned for its alternating flows of cold and hot, had gushed since the allies' arrival with naught but sweet cold water, a boon from the goddesses to the warriors' thirst. Now suddenly the fount had gone hot and stinking. A steaming sulphurous brew spewed forth from the underworld like a river of hell. The men trembled before this prodigy. Prayers to Demeter and the *Kore* were being sung. I begged a half-helmetful of water from the Knight Doreion's skin and returned to my master, steeling myself to mention nothing.

"The spring's gone sulphurous, hasn't it?"

"It presages the enemy's death, sir, not ours."

"You're as full of shit as the priests."

I could see he was all right now.

"The allies need your cousin upon this site," he observed, settling in pain upon the earth, "to intercede with the goddess on their behalf."

He meant Diomache.

"Here," he said. "Sit beside me."

This was the first time I had heard my master refer aloud to Diomache, or even acknowledge his awareness of her existence. Though I had never, in our years, presumed to burden him with details of my own history prior to entering his service, I knew he knew it all, through Alexandros and the lady Arete.

"This is a goddess I have always felt pity for—Persephone," my master declared. "Six months of the year she rules as Hades' bride, mistress of the underworld. Yet hers is a reign bereft of joy. She sits her throne as a prisoner, carried off for her beauty by the lord of hell, who releases his queen under Zeus' compulsion for half the year only, when she comes back to us, bringing spring and the rebirth of the land. Have you looked closely at statues of her, Xeo? She appears grave, even in the midst of the harvest's joy. Does she, like us, recall the terms of her sentence—to retire again untimely beneath the earth? This is the sorrow of Persephone. Alone among the immortals the *Kore* is bound by necessity to shuttle from death to life and back again, intimate of both faces of the coin. No wonder this fount whose twin sources are heaven and hell is sacred to her."

I had settled now upon the ground beside my master. He regarded me gravely.

"It's too late, don't you think," he pronounced, "for you and I to keep secrets from one another?"

I agreed the hour was far advanced.

"Yet you preserve one from me."

He would have me speak of Athens, I could see, and the evening barely a month previous wherein I had at last—through his intercession—met again my cousin.

"Why didn't you run?" Dienekes asked me. "I wanted you to, you know."

"I tried. She wouldn't let me."

I knew my master would not compel me to speak. He would never presume to tread where his presence sowed distress. Yet instinct told me the hour to break silence had come. At worst my report would divert his preoccupation from the day's horror and at best turn it, perhaps, to more propitious imaginings.

"Shall I tell you of that night in Athens, sir?"

"Only if you wish."

It was upon an embassy, I reminded him. He, Polynikes and Aristodemos had traveled on foot from Sparta then, without escort, accompanied only by their squires. The party had covered the distance of 140 miles in four days and remained there in the city of the Athenians for four more, at the home of the *proxenos* Kleinias the son of Alkibiades. The object of the legation was to finalize the eleventh-hour details of coordinating land and sea forces at Thermopylae and Artemisium: times of arrival for army and fleet, modes of dispatch between them, courier encryptions, passwords and the like. Unspoken but no less significant, Spartans and Athenians wished to look each other in the eye one last time, to make sure both forces would be there, in their places, at the appointed hour.

On the evening of the third day, a salon was held in honor of the embassy at the home of Xanthippus, a prominent Athenian. I loved to listen at these affairs, where debate and discourse were always spirited and often brilliant. To my great disappointment, my master summoned me alone before table and informed me of an urgent errand I must run. "Sorry," he said, "you'll miss the party." He placed into my hands a sealed letter, with instructions to deliver it in person to a certain residence in the seaport town of Phaleron. A boy servant of the house awaited without, to serve as guide through the nighttime streets. No particulars were given beyond the addressee's name. I assumed the communication to be a naval dispatch of some urgency and so traveled armed.

It took the time of an entire watch to traverse that labyrinth of quarters and precincts which comprises the city of the Athenians. Everywhere men-at-arms, sailors and marines were mobilizing; chandlery waggons rumbled under armed escorts, bearing the rations and supplies of the fleet. The squadrons under Themistokles were readying for embarkation to Skiathos and Artemisium. Simultaneously families by the hundreds were crating their valuables and fleeing the city. As numerous as were the warcraft moored in lines across the harbor, their ranks were eclipsed by the ragtag fleet of merchantmen, ferries, fishing smacks, pleasure boats and excursion craft evacuating the citizenry to Troezen and Salamis. Some of the families were fleeing for points as distant as Italia. As the boy and I approached Phaleron port, so many torches filled the streets that the passage was lit bright as noon.

Lanes became crookeder as we approached the harbor. The stink of low tide choked one's nostrils; gutters ran with filth, backed up into a malodorous stew of fish guts, leek shavings and garlic. I never saw so many cats in my life. Grogshops and houses of ill fame lined streets so narrow that daylight's cleansing beams, I was certain, never penetrated to the floors of their canyons to dry the slime and muck of the night's commerce in depravity. The whores called out boldly as the boy and I passed, advertising their wares in coarse but good-humored tongue. The man to whom we were to deliver the letter was named Terrentaius. I asked the lad if he had any idea who the fellow was or what station he held. He said he had been given the house name alone and nothing more.

At last the boy and I located it, an apartment structure of three stories called the Griddle after the slop shop and inn which occupied its street-level floor. I inquired within for the man Terrentaius. He was absent, the publican declared, with the fleet. I asked after the man's ship. Which vessel was he officer of? A round of hilarity greeted this query. "He's a lieutenant of the ash," one of the tippling seamen declared, meaning the only thing he commanded was the oar he pulled. Further inquiries failed to elicit any additional intelligence.

"Then, sir," the boy guide addressed me, "we are instructed to deliver the letter to his wife."

I rejected this as nonsense.

"No, sir," replied the lad with conviction, "I have it from your master himself. We are to place the letter in the hands of the man's mistress, by name Diomache."

With but a moment's consideration I perceived in this event the hand, not to say the long arm, of the lady Arete. How had she tracked down and located, from the remove of Lakedaemon, this house and this woman? There must be a hundred Diomaches in a city the size of Athens. No doubt the lady Arete had maintained her intentions secret, anticipating that I, made aware of them in advance, would have found excuse to evade their obligation. In this, she was doubtless correct.

In any event my cousin, it was discovered, was not present in the apartments, nor could any of the seamen inform us as to her whereabouts. My guide, a lad of resourcefulness, simply stepped into the alley and bellowed her name. In moments the grizzled heads of half a dozen backstreet dames appeared above, among the hanging laundry of the lane-facing windows. The name and site of a harbor-town temple were shouted down to us.

"She'll be there, boy. Just follow the shore."

My guide set out again in the lead. We traversed more stinking sea-town streets, more alleys choked with traffic of the natives clearing out. The boy informed me that many of the temples in this quarter functioned less as sanctuaries of the gods and more as asylums for the cast-out and the penniless, particularly, he said, wives "put by" by their husbands. Meaning those deemed unfit, unwilling, or even insane. The boy pressed ahead in merry spirits. It was all a grand adventure to him.

At last we stood before the temple. It was nothing but a common house, perhaps home in former times to a middling-prosperous trader or merchant, sited upon a surprisingly cheerful slope two streets above the water. A copse of olives sheltered a walled enclave whose inner precinct could not be glimpsed from the street. I rapped at the gate; after an interval a priestess, if such a lofty title may be applied to a gowned and masked housewoman of fifty years, responded. She informed us the sanctuary was that of Demeter and Covert *Kore*, Persephone of the Veil. None but females might enter. Behind the shroud which concealed her face, the priestess was clearly frightened, nor could one blame her, the streets running with whoremongers and cutpurses. She would not let us in. No avenue of appeal proved of avail; the woman would neither confirm my cousin's presence nor agree to convey a message within. Again my boy guide took the bull by the horns. He opened his cheesepipe and bawled Diomache's name.

We were admitted at last to a rear courtyard, the lad and I. The house upon entry proved far more capacious, and a good deal cheerier, than it had appeared from the street. We were not permitted passage through the interior but escorted along an outer path. The dame, our chaperon, confirmed that a matron by name Diomache was indeed among those novices currently resident within the sanctuary. She was at this hour attending to duties in the kitchen; an interview, however, of a few minutes' duration might be granted, with permission from the asylum mother. My guide, the boy, was offered refreshment; the dame took him away for a feed.

I was standing, alone in the courtyard, when my cousin entered. Her children, both girls, one perhaps five, the other a year or two older, clung fearfully to her skirts; they would not come forward when I knelt and held out my hand. "Forgive them," my cousin said. "They are shy of men." The dame led the girls away to the interior, leaving me at last alone with Diomache.

How many times in imagination had I rehearsed this moment. Always in conjured scenarios, my cousin was young and beautiful; I ran to her arms and she to mine. Nothing of the sort now occurred. Diomache stepped into view in the lamplight, garbed in black, with the entire breadth of the court dividing us. The shock of her appearance unstrung me. She was unveiled and unhooded. Her hair was cropped short. Her years were no more than twenty-four yet she looked forty, and a hard-used forty at that.

"Can it really be you, cousin?" she inquired in the same teasing voice she had taken with me since we were children. "You are a man, as you were always so impatient to become."

Her lightness of tone served only to compound the despair which now seized my heart. The picture I had held so long before the eye of the mind was of her in the bloom of youth, womanly and strong, exactly as she had been the morning we parted at the Three-Cornered Way. What terrible hardships had been visited upon her by the intervening years? The vision of the whore-infested streets was fresh upon me, the crude seamen and the mean existence of these refuse-choked lanes. I sank, overcome with grief and regret, upon a bench along the wall.

"I should never have left you," I said, and meant it with all my heart. "Everything that has happened is my fault for not being at your side to defend you."

I cannot recall a word of what was spoken over the next several minutes. I remember my cousin moving to the bench beside me. She did not embrace me, but touched me with tender clemency upon the shoulder.

"Do you remember that morning, Xeo, when we set out for market with Stumblefoot and your little clutch of ptarmigan eggs?" Her lips declined into a sorrowful smile. "The gods set our lives upon their courses that day. Courses from which neither of us has had the option to stray."

She asked if I would take wine. A bowl was brought. I recalled the letter I bore and delivered it now to my cousin. Beneath its wrapper, it was addressed to her, not her husband; she opened and read it. Its contents were in the lady Arete's hand. When Diomache finished she did not show it to me, but tucked it away without a word beneath her robe.

My eyes, adjusted now to the lamplight of the court, studied my cousin's face. Her beauty remained, I saw, but altered in a manner both grave and austere. The age in her eyes, which had at first shocked and repelled me, I now perceived as compassion and even wisdom. Her silence was profound as the lady Arete's; her bearing spartan beyond spartan. I was daunted and even in awe. She seemed, like the goddess she served, a maiden hauled off untimely by the dark forces of the underworld and now, restored by some covenant with those pitiless gods, bearing in her eyes that primal female wisdom which is simultaneously human and inhuman, personal and impersonal. Love for her flooded my heart. Yet did she appear, inches from my grasp, as august as an immortal and as impossible to hold.

"Do you feel the city about us now?" she asked. Outside the walls, the rumble of evacuees and their baggage trains could clearly be heard. "It's like that morning at Astakos, isn't it? Perhaps within weeks this mighty city will be fired and razed, as our own was on that day."

I begged her to tell me how she was. Truly.

She laughed.

"I've changed, haven't I? Not the husband bait you always took me for. I was foolish then too; I thought as highly of my prospects. But this is not a woman's world, cousin. It never was and never will be."

From my lips blurted a course of passionate impulse. She must come with me. Now. To the hills, where we had flown once and been happy once. I would be her husband. She would be my wife. Nothing would ever harm her again.

"My sweet cousin," she replied with tender resignation, "I have a husband." She indicated the letter. "As you have a wife."

Her seemingly passive acceptance of fate infuriated me. What husband is he who abandons his wife? What wife is she taken without love? The gods demand of us action and the use of our free will! That is piety, not to buckle beneath necessity's yoke like dumb beasts!

"This is Lord Apollo talking." My cousin smiled and touched me again with patient gentleness.

She asked if she could tell me a story. Would I listen? It was a tale she had confided to no one, save her sisters of the sanctuary and our dearest friend Bruxieus. Only a few minutes remained to us. I must be patient and attend.

"Do you remember that day when the Argive soldiers shamed me? You knew I turned the hands of murder upon the issue of that violation. I aborted myself. But what you didn't know was that I hemorrhaged one night and nearly died. Bruxieus saved me as you slept. I bound him by oath never to tell you."

She regarded me with the same self-consecrated gaze I had observed upon the features of the lady Arete, that expression born of feminine wisdom which apprehends truth directly, through the blood, unobscured by the cruder faculty of reason.

"Like you, cousin, I hated life then. I wanted to die, and nearly did. That night in fevered sleep, feeling the blood draining from me like oil from an overturned lamp, I had a dream.

"A goddess stood above me, veiled and cowled. I could see nothing but her eyes, yet so vivid was her presence that I felt certain she was real. More real than real, as if life itself were the dream and this, the dream, life in its profoundest essence. The goddess spoke no words but merely looked upon me with eyes of supreme wisdom and compassion.

"My soul ached with the desire to behold her face. I was consumed with this need and implored her, in words that were not words but only the fervent appeal of my heart, to loose her veil and let me see the whole of her. I knew without thought that what would be revealed would be of supreme consequence. I was terrified and at the same time trembling with anticipation.

"The goddess unbound her veil and let it fall. Will you understand, Xeo, if I say that what was revealed, the face beyond the veil, was nothing less than that reality which exists beneath the world of flesh? That higher, nobler creation which the gods know and we mortals are permitted to glimpse only in visions and transports.

"Her face was beauty beyond beauty. The embodiment of truth as beauty. And it was human. So human it made the heart break with love and reverence and awe. I perceived without words that this alone was real which I beheld now, not the world we see beneath the sun. And more: that this beauty existed here, about us at every hour. Our eyes were just too blind to see it.

"I understood that our role as humans was to embody here, upon this shadowed and sorrow-bound side of the Veil, those qualities which arise from beyond and are the same on both sides, ever-sustaining, eternal and divine. Do you understand, Xeo? Courage, selflessness, compassion and love."

She drew up and smiled.

"You think I'm loony, don't you? I've gone cracked with religion. Like a woman."

I didn't. I told her briefly of my own glimpse beyond the veil, that night within the grove of snow. Diomache acknowledged gravely.

"Did you forget your vision, Xeo? I forgot mine. I lived a life of hell here in this city. Until one day the goddess's hand guided me within these walls."

She indicated a modestly scaled but superb statue in an alcove of the court. I looked. It was a bronze of Veiled Persephone.

"This," my cousin declared, "is the goddess whose mystery I serve. She who passes from life to death and back again. The *Kore* has preserved me, as the Lord of the Bow has protected you."

She placed her hands atop mine and drew my eyes to hers.

"So you see, Xeo, nothing has transpired amiss. You think you have failed to defend me. But everything you've done has defended me. As you defend me now."

She reached within the folds of her garment and produced the letter written in the lady Arete's hand.

"Do you know what this is? A promise to me that your death will be honored, as you and I honored Bruxieus and we three sought to honor our parents."

The housewoman appeared again from the kitchen. Diomache's children awaited within; my boy guide had finished his feed and stood impatient to depart. Diomache rose and held out both hands to me. The lamplight fell kindly upon her; in its gentle glow her face appeared as beautiful as it had to my eyes of love, those short years that seemed so long past. I stood too and embraced her. She tugged the cowl atop her cropped hair and slid the veil in place across her face.

"Let neither of us pity the other," my cousin spoke in parting. "We are where we must be, and we will do what we must."

TWENTY-EIGHT

Suicide shook me awake two hours before dawn. "Look what crawled in through the bunghole."

He was pointing to the knoll behind the Arkadian camp, where deserters from the Persian lines were being interrogated beside the watch fires. I squinted but my eyes refused to focus. "Look again," he said. "It's your seditious mate, Rooster. He's asking for you."

Alexandros and I went over together. It was Rooster, all right. He had crossed from the Persian lines with a party of other deserters; the Skiritai had him bound, naked, to a post. They were going to execute him; he had asked for a moment alone with me before they opened his throat.

On all sides the camp was rousing; half the army stood already on station, the other half arming. Down the track toward Trachis you could hear the enemy trumpets, forming up for Day Two. We found Rooster next to a pair of Median informers who had talked a good-enough game that they were actually being given breakfast. Not Rooster. The Skiritai had worked him over so hard that he had to be propped up, slumped against the post where his throat would be slit.

"Is that you, Xeo?" He squinted through eyeholes battered purple as a boxer's.

"I've brought Alexandros."

We managed to dribble some wine down Rooster's throat.

"I'm sorry about your father" were his first words to Alexandros. He, Rooster, had served six years as squire to Olympieus and saved his life at Oenophyta, when the Theban cavalry had ranged down upon him. "He was the noblest man of the city, not excepting Leonidas."

"How can we help you?" Alexandros asked.

Rooster wished to know first who else was still alive. I told him

Dienekes, Polynikes and some others and recited the names of the dead whom he knew. "And you're alive too, Xeo?" His features twisted into a grin. "Your crony Apollo must be saving you for something extraordinary."

Rooster had a simple request: that I arrange to have delivered to his wife an ancient coin of his nation, Messenia. This thumb-worn obol, he told us, he had carried in secret his whole life. He placed it into my care; I vowed to send it with the next dispatch runner. He clasped my hand in gratitude, then, lowering his voice in exigency, tugged me and Alexandros near.

"Listen closely. This is what I came to tell you."

Rooster spit it out quickly. The Hellenes defending the pass had another day, no more. His Majesty even now was offering the wealth of a province to any guide who could inform him of a track through the mountains by which the Hot Gates could be encircled. "God made no rock so steep that men couldn't climb it, particularly driven by gold and glory. The Persians will find a way around to your rear, and even if they don't, their fleet will break the Athenian sea line within another day. No reinforcements are coming from Sparta; the ephors know they'd only be enveloped too. And Leonidas will never pull himself or any of you out, dead or alive."

"You took that beating just to deliver this news?"

"Listen to me. When I went over to the Persians, I told them I was a helot fresh from Sparta. The King's own officers interrogated me. I was right there, two squares from Xerxes' tent. I know where the Great King sleeps and how to deliver men right to his doorstep."

Alexandros laughed out loud. "You mean attack him in his tent?"

"When the head dies, the snake dies. Pay attention. The King's pavilion stands just beneath the cliffs at the top of the plain, right by the river, so his horses can water before the rest of the army fouls the stream. The gorge produces a torrent coming out of the mountains; the Persians think it impassable, they have less than a company on guard. A party of half a dozen could get in, in darkness, and maybe even get out."

"Yes. We'll flap our wings and fly right over."

The camp had come fully awake now. At the Wall the Spartans

were already massing, if so grand a term may be applied to so meager a force. Rooster told us that he had offered to guide a party of raiders into the Persian camp in return for freedom for his wife and children in Lakedaemon. This was why the Skiritai had beaten him; they thought it a trick designed to deliver brave men into the enemy's hands for torture or worse. "They won't even relay my words to their own officers. I beg you: inform someone of rank. Even without me it can work. By all the gods I swear it!"

I laughed at this reborn Rooster. "So you've acquired piety as well as patriotism."

The Skiritai called to us sharply. They wanted to finish Rooster and get themselves into armor. Two rangers jerked him to his feet, to lash him upright to the post, when a clamor interrupted from the rear of the camp. We all turned and stared back down the slope.

Forty men of the Thebans had deserted during the night. A half dozen had been slain by sentries, but the others had made good their escape. All save three, who had just now been discovered, attempting to conceal themselves among the mounds of the dead.

This luckless trio was now hauled forth by a squad of Thespaian sentries and dumped into the open to the rear of the Wall, smack amid the marshaling army. Blood was in the air. The Thespaian Dithyrambos strode to the breach and took charge.

"What punishment for these?" he shouted to the encircling throng.

At this moment Dienekes appeared at Alexandros' shoulder, summoned by the commotion. I seized the instant to plead for Rooster's life, but my master made no answer, his attention held by the scene playing out below.

A dozen mortal punishments had been shouted out by the thronging warriors. Blows of homicidal intent were struck at the terrified captives; it took Dithyrambos himself, wading into the fray with his sword, to drive the men back.

"The allies are possessed," Alexandros observed with dismay. "Again."

Dienekes looked on coldly. "I will not witness this a second time."

He strode forward, parting the mob before him, and thrust himself to the fore beside the Thespaian Dithyrambos.

"These dogs must receive no mercy!" Dienekes stood over the bound and blindered captives. "They must suffer the most hateful penalty imaginable, so that no other will be tempted to emulate their cowardice."

Cries of assent rose from the army. Dienekes' raised hand quelled the tumult.

"You men know me. Will you accept the punishment I propose?"

A thousand voices shouted aye.

"Without protest? Without a quibble?"

All swore to abide by Dienekes' sentence.

From the knoll behind the Wall, Leonidas and the Knights, including Polynikes, Alpheus and Maron, looked on. All sound stilled save the wind. Dienekes stepped to the kneeling captives and snatched off their blinders.

His blade cut the prisoners loose.

Bellows of outrage thundered from every quarter. Desertion in the face of the enemy was punishable by death. How many more would flee if these traitors walked off with their lives? The whole army will fall apart!

Dithyrambos, alone among the allies, seemed to divine Dienekes' subtler intent. He stepped forward beside the Spartan, his raised sword silencing the men so that Dienekes could speak.

"I despise that seizure of self-preservation which unmanned these cravens last night," Dienekes addressed the thronging allies, "but far more I hate that passion, comrades, which deranges you now."

He gestured to the captives on their knees before him. "These men you call coward today fought shoulder-to-shoulder beside you yesterday. Perhaps with greater valor than you."

"I doubt it!" came a shouted cry, succeeded by waves of scorn and cries for blood pelting down upon the fugitives.

Dienekes waited for the tumult to subside. "In Lakedaemon we have a name for that state of mind which holds you now, brothers.

We call it 'possession.' It means that yielding to fear or anger which robs an army of order and reduces it to a rabble."

He stepped back; his sword gestured to the captives upon the ground.

"Yes, these men ran last night. But what did you do? I'll tell you. Every one of you lay awake. And what were the covert petitions of your hearts? The same as these." The blade of his *xiphos* indicated the pitiful wretches at his feet. "Like these, you yearned for wives and children. Like these, you burned to save your own skin. Like these, you laid plans to fly and live!"

Cries of denial struggled to find voice, only to sputter and fail before Dienekes' fierce gaze and the truth it embodied.

"I thought those thoughts too. All night I dreamt of running. So did every officer and every Lakedaemonian here, including Leonidas."

A chastened silence held the mob.

"Yes!" a voice cried. "But we didn't do it!"

More murmurs of assent, mounting.

"That's right," Dienekes spoke softly, his glance no longer lifted in address to the army but turned now, hard as flint, upon the trio of captives. "We didn't do it."

He regarded the fugitives for one pitiless moment, then stepped back so the army could behold the three, bound and held at swordpoint, in their midst.

"Let these men live out their days, cursed by that knowledge. Let them wake each dawn to that infamy and lie down each night with that shame. That will be their sentence of death, a living extinction far more bitter than that trifle the rest of us will bear before the sun sets tomorrow."

He stepped beyond the felons, toward that margin of the throng which led away to safety. "Clear a runway!"

Now the fugitives began to beg. The first, a beardless youth barely past twenty, declared that his poor farmstead lay less than half a week from here; he had feared for his new bride and infant daughter, for his infirm mother and father. The darkness had unmanned him, he confessed, but he repented now. Clasping his bound hands in supplication, he lifted his gaze toward Dienekes and the Thespaian. Please, sirs, my crime was of the moment. It is passed. I will fight today and none will fault my courage.

Now the other two chimed in, both men past forty, vowing mighty oaths that they, too, would serve with honor.

Dienekes stood over them. "Clear a runway!"

The crush of men parted to open a lane down which the trio might pass in safety out of the camp.

"Anyone else?" Dithyrambos' voice ascended in challenge to the army. "Who else feels like a stroll? Let him take the back door now, or shut his cheesepipe from here to hell."

Surely no sight under heaven could have been more baleful or infamous, so pitiful were the postures of the wretches and the slouching increments of their gait as they passed out along the avenue of shame between the ranks of their silent comrades.

I looked down into the faces of the army. Fled was the self-serving fury which had cried in false righteousness for blood. Instead in each chastened countenance stood graven a purged and pitiless shame. The cheap and hypocritical rage which had sought to vent itself upon the runaways had been turned inward by the intervention of Dienekes. And that rage, refired within the forge of each man's secret heart, now hardened into a resolution of such blistering infamy that death itself seemed a trifle alongside it.

Dienekes turned and stalked back up the knoll. Nearing myself and Alexandros, he was intercepted by an officer of the Skiritai, who clasped his hand in both his own. "That was brilliant, Dienekes. You shamed the whole army. Not one will dare budge from this dirt now."

My master's face, far from displaying satisfaction, instead stood darkened into a mask of grief. He glanced back toward the three miscreants, slouching miserably off with their lives. "Those poor bastards served their turn in the line all day yesterday. I pity them with all my heart."

The criminals had now emerged at the far end of the gauntlet of infamy. There the second man, the one who had groveled most shamelessly, turned and shouted back at the army. "Fools! You're all going to die! Fuck you all, and damn you to hell!"

With a cackle of doom he vanished over the brow of the slope, followed by his scampering mates, who cast glances back over their shoulders like curs.

At once Leonidas passed an order to the *polemarch* Derkylides, who relayed it to the officer of the watch: from here on, no sentries would be posted to the rear, no precautions taken to prevent further desertions.

With a shout the men broke up and marshaled to their ready stations.

Dienekes had now reached the compound where Alexandros and I waited with Rooster. The officer of the Skiritai was a man named Lachides, brother of the ranger called Hound.

"Give this villain to me, will you, friend?" Dienekes' weary gesture indicated Rooster. "He's my bastard nephew. I'll slit his throat myself."

TWENTY-NINE

His Majesty knows far better than I the details of the intrigue by which the ultimate betrayal of the allies was effected; that is, who the traitor was of the Trachinian natives who came forward to inform His Majesty's commanders of the existence of the mountain track by which the Hot Gates could be encircled, and what reward was paid this criminal from the treasury of Persia.

The Greeks drew hints of this calamitous intelligence first from the omens taken on the morning of the second day's fighting, corroborated further by rumors and reports of deserters throughout the day, and ultimately confirmed by eyewitness testimony upon that evening, the end of the allies' sixth in possession of the pass of Thermopylae.

A nobleman of the enemy had come over to the Greek lines at the time of the changing of the first watch, approximately two hours after the cessation of the day's hostilities. He identified himself as Tyrrhastiadas of Kyme, a captain-of-a-thousand in the conscripted forces of that nation. This prince was the tallest, best-looking and most magnificently appareled personage of the enemy who had thus far deserted. He addressed the assembly in errorless Greek. His wife was a Hellene of Hallicarnassus, he declared; that, and the compulsion of honor, had impelled him to cross over to the allied lines. He informed the Spartan king that he had been present before Xerxes' pavilion this very evening when the traitor, whose name I have learned but here and evermore refuse to repeat, had come forward to claim the reward offered by His Majesty and to volunteer his services in guiding the forces of Persia along the secret track.

The noble Tyrrhastiadas went on to report that he had personally observed the issuance by His Majesty of the orders of march and the marshaling of the Persian battalions. The Immortals, their losses replaced and now numbering again their customary ten thousand, had set out at nightfall under command of their general, Hydarnes. They were on the march at this very moment, led by their traitor guide. They would be in the allied rear, in position to attack, by dawn.

His Majesty, cognizant of the catastrophic consequence for the Greeks of this betrayal, may marvel at their response in assembly to the timely and fortuitous warning delivered by the noble Tyrrhastiadas.

They didn't believe him.

They thought it was a trick.

Such an irrational and self-deluding response may be understood only in the light not alone of the exhaustion and despair which had by that hour overwhelmed the allies' hearts but by the corresponding exaltation and contempt of death, which are, like the mated faces of a coin, their obverse and concomitant.

The first day's fighting had produced acts of extraordinary valor and heroism.

The second began to spawn marvels and prodigies.

Most compelling of all was the simple fact of survival. How many times amid the manslaughter of the preceding forty-eight hours had each warrior stood upon the instant of his own extinction? Yet still he lived. How many times had the masses of the foe in numbers overwhelming assaulted the allies with unstoppable might and valor? Yet still the front had held.

Three times on that second day the lines of the defenders teetered upon the point of buckling. His Majesty beheld the moment, immediately before nightfall, when the Wall itself stood breached and the massed myriads of the Empire clambered upon and over the stones, vaunting their victory cry. Yet somehow the Wall stood; the pass did not fall.

All day long, that second of battle, the fleets had clashed off Skiathos in mirrored reflection of the armies at the Gates. Beneath the bluffs of Artemisium the navies hammered each other, driving bronze ram against sheathed timber as their brothers contended steel against steel upon land. The defenders of the pass beheld the burning hulks, smudges against the horizon, and closer in, the flotsam of staved-in beams and spars, shivered oars and sailors' bodies facedown in the shore current. It seemed that Greek and Persian contended no longer as antagonists, but rather had entered, both sides, into some perverse pact whose aim was neither victory nor salvation, but merely to incarnadine earth and ocean with their intermingled blood. The very heavens appeared that day not as a peopled realm, assigning by their witness meaning to events below, but rather as a blank unholy face of slate, compassionless and indifferent. The mountain wall of Kallidromos overstanding the carnage seemed beyond all to embody this bereavement of pity in the featureless face of its silent stone. All creatures of the air had fled. No sign of green shoot lingered upon the earth nor within the clefts of rock.

Only the dirt itself possessed clemency. Alone the stinking soup beneath the warriors' tread proffered surcease and succor. The men's feet churned it into broth ankle-deep; their driving legs furrowed it to the depth of the calf, then they themselves fell upon it on their knees and fought from there. Fingers clawed at the blood-blackened muck, toes strained against it for purchase, the teeth of dying men bit into it as if to excavate their own graves with the clamp of their jaws. Farmers whose hands had taken up with pleasure the dark clods of their native fields, crumbling between their fingers the rich earth which brings forth the harvest, now crawled on their bellies in this sterner soil, clawed at it with the nubs of their busted fingers and writhed without shame, seeking to immure themselves within earth's mantle and preserve their backs from the pitiless steel.

In the *palaistrai* of Hellas, the Greeks love to wrestle. From the time a boy can stand, he grapples with his mates, dusted with grit in pits of sand or oiled with ooze in rings of mud. Now the Hellenes wrestled in less holy precincts, where the sluice pail held not water but blood, where the prize was death and the umpire spurned all calls for stay or quarter. One witnessed again and again in the battles of the second day a Hellenic warrior fight for two hours straight, retire for ten minutes, without taking food and gulping only a cupped handful of water, then return to the fray for another two-hour round. Again and again one saw a man receive a blow that shattered the teeth within his jaw or split the bone of his shoulder yet did not make him fall.

On the second day I saw Alpheus and Maron take out six men of the foe so fast that the last two were dead before the first pair hit the ground. How many did the brothers slay that day? Fifty? A hundred? It would have taken more than an Achilles among the foe to bring them down, not solely in consequence of their strength and skill but because they were two who fought with a single heart.

All day His Majesty's champions came on, advancing in wave after wave with no interval to distinguish between nations or contingents. The rotation of forces which the allies had employed on the first day became impossible. Companies of their own will refused to forsake the line. Squires and servants took up the arms of the fallen and assumed their places in the breach.

No longer did men waste breath to cheer or rally one another to pride or valor. No more did warriors exult or vaunt their hearts in triumph. Now in the intervals of respite these simply fell, wordless and numb, into heaps of the unstrung and the undone. In the lee of the Wall, upon every hollow of sundered earth, one beheld knots of warriors shattered by fatigue and despair, eight or ten, twelve or twenty, dropped where they fell, in unmoving postures of horror and grief. None spoke or stirred. Instead the eyes of each stared without sight into inexpressible realms of private horror.

Existence had become a tunnel whose walls were death and within which prevailed no hope of rescue or deliverance. The sky had ceased to be, and the sun and stars. All that remained was the earth, the churned riven dirt which seemed to wait at each man's feet to receive his spilling guts, his shattered bones, his blood, his life. The earth coated every part of him. It was in his ears and nostrils, in his eyes and throat, under his nails and in the crease of his backside. It coated the sweat and salt of his hair; he spat it from his lungs and blew it slick with snot from his nose.

There is a secret all warriors share, so private that none dare give it voice, save only to those mates drawn dearer than brothers by the shared ordeal of arms. This is the knowledge of the hundred acts of his own cowardice. The little things that no one sees. The comrade who fell and cried for aid. Did I pass him by? Choose my skin over his? That was my crime, of which I accuse myself in the tribunal of my heart and there condemn myself as guilty.

All a man wants is to live. This before all: to cling to breath. To survive.

Yet even this most primal of instincts, self-preservation, even this necessity of the blood shared by all beneath heaven, beasts as well as man, even this may be worn down by fatigue and excess of horror. A form of courage enters the heart which is not courage but despair and not despair but exaltation. On that second day, men passed beyond themselves. Feats of heart-stopping valor fell from the sky like rain, and those who performed them could not even recall, nor state with certainty, that the actors had been themselves.

I saw a squire of the Philiasians, no more than a boy, take up his master's armor and wade into the manslaughter. Before he could strike a blow, a Persian javelin shattered his shin, driving straight through the bone. One of his mates rushed to the lad to bind his gushing artery and drag him to safety. The youth beat back his savior with the flat of his sword. He hobbled upon his spear used as a crutch, then on his knees, into the fray, still hacking at the foe from the earth where he perished.

Other squires and servants seized iron pegs and, themselves unshod and unarmored, scaled the mountain face above the Narrows, hammering the pins into cracks of rock to secure themselves, from these exposed perches hurling stones and boulders down upon the foe. The Persian archers turned these boys into pincushions; their bodies dangled crucified from pitons or tumbled from their fingerholds to crash upon the roiling slaughter below.

The merchant Elephantinos dashed into the open to save one of these lads yet living, hung up on a ledge above the rear of battle. A Persian arrow tore the old man's throat out; he fell so fast he seemed to vanish straight into the earth. Fierce fighting broke out over his corpse. Why? He was no king or officer, only a stranger who tended the young men's wounds and made them laugh with "Weck up to thees!"

Night had nearly fallen. The Hellenes were reeling from casualties and exhaustion, while the Persians continued pouring fresh champions into the fray. Those in the foe's rear were being driven onward by the whips of their own officers; these pressed with zeal upon their fellows, driving them forward into the Greeks.

Does His Majesty remember? A violent squall had broken then over the sea; rain began sheeting in torrents. By this point most of the allies' weapons had been spent or broken. The warriors had gone through a dozen spears apiece; none yet bore his own shield, which had been staved in long since; he defended himself with the eighth and tenth he had snatched from the ground. Even the Spartans' short *xiphos* swords had been sundered from excess of blows. The steel blades held, but the hafts and grips had come undone. Men were fighting with stubs of iron, thrusting with shivered half-spears bereft of warhead and butt-spike.

The host of the foe had hacked their way forward, within a dozen paces of the Wall. Only the Spartans and Thespaians remained before this battlement, all others of the allies having been beaten back behind or upon it. The massed myriads of the enemy extended all the way from the Narrows, flooding at will across the hundred-yard triangle before the Wall.

The Spartans fell back. I found myself beside Alexandros atop the Wall, hauling one man after another up and over, while the allies rained javelins and shivered spears, stones and boulders and even helmets and shields down upon the onpressing foe.

The allies cracked and reeled. Back they fell in a disordered mass, fifty feet, a hundred, beyond the Wall. Even the Spartans withdrew in disorder, my master, Polynikes, Alpheus and Maron themselves, shattered by wounds and exhaustion.

The enemy literally tore the stones from the face of the Wall. Now the tide of their multitude flooded over the toppled ruins, skidding down the stadium steps of the Wall's rear onto the open earth before the unprotected camps of the allies. Vanquishment was moments away when for cause inexplicable, the foe, with victory before him in his palm, pulled up in fear and could not find courage to press home the kill.

The enemy drew up, seized by a terror without source or signature. What force had unmanned their hearts and robbed them of valor, no faculty of reason may divine. It may have been that the warriors of the Empire could not credit the imminence of their own triumph. Perhaps they had been fighting for so long on the foreside of the Wall that their senses could not embrace the reality of at last achieving the breach.

Whatever it was, the foe's momentum faltered. A moment of unearthly stillness seized the field.

Suddenly from the heavens a bellow of unearthly power, as that from the throats of fifty thousand men, pealed through the aether. The hair stood straight up on my neck; I spun toward Alexandros; he, too, held rooted, paralyzed in awe and terror, as every other man upon the field.

A bolt of almighty magnitude slammed overhead into the wall of Kallidromos. Thunder boomed, great stones blew from the cliff face; smoke and sulphur rent the air. On rolled that unearthly cry, nailing all in place with terror save Leonidas, who now strode to the fore with upraised spear.

"Zeus Savior!" the king's voice rose into the thunder. "Hellas and freedom!"

He cried the *paean* and rushed forward upon the foe. Fresh courage flooded the allies' hearts; they roared into the counterattack. Back over the Wall the enemy tumbled in panic at this prodigy of heaven. I found myself again atop its slick and sundered stones, firing shaft after shaft into the mass of Persians and Bactrians, Medes and Illyrians, Lydians and Egyptians, stampeding in flight below.

The ghastliness of the carnage that followed, His Majesty's own eyes may testify to. As the foreranks of the Persians fled in terror, the whips of their rearmen drove their reinforcing fellows forward. As when two waves, one crashing shoreward before the storm, the other returning seaward down the steep slope of the strand, collide and annihilate one another in spray and foam, so did the crash and wheel of the Empire's armies turn force upon force to trample by thousands those trapped within the riptide of its vortex.

Leonidas had earlier called upon the allies to build a second wall, a wall of Persian bodies. Precisely this now eventuated. The foe fell in such numbers that no warrior of the allies planted sole upon the earth. One trod upon bodies. On bodies atop bodies.

Ahead the Hellenic warriors could see the enemy stampeding into the whips of their own rearmen, charging them, slaying with spear and sword their own fellows in blood madness to escape. Scores and hundreds toppled into the sea. I saw the Spartan front ranks literally scaling the wall of Persian bodies, needing assistance from the second-rankers just to propel themselves over.

Suddenly the piled mass of the dead gave way. An avalanche of bodies began. In the Narrows the allies scrambled rearward toward safety atop a landslide of corpses, which fed upon itself, gaining momentum from its own weight as it tumbled with onrolling might upon the Persians, back down the track toward Trachis. So grotesque was this sight that the Hellenic warriors, unordered by command, but of their own instinct, pulled up where they stood and discontinued the press of their advance, looking on in awe as the enemy perished in numbers uncountable, swallowed and effaced beneath this grisly avalanche of flesh.

Now, in the night assembly of the allies, this prodigy was recalled and cited as evidence of the intercession of the gods. The nobleman Tyrrhastiadas stood beside Leonidas, before the assembled Greeks, urging them with what was clearly the passionate beneficence of his heart to retreat, withdraw, get out. The noble repeated his report of the ten thousand Immortals, even now advancing upon the mountain track to encircle the allies. Less than a thousand Hellenes remained still capable of resistance. What could these hope to effect against ten times their number striking from the undefended rear, while a thousand times their total compounded the assault from the fore?

Yet such was the exaltation produced by that final prodigy that the allies would neither listen nor pay heed. Men came forward in assembly, skeptics and agnostics, those who acknowledged their doubt and even disdain of the gods; these same men now swore mighty oaths and declared that this bolt of heaven and the unearthly bellow which had accompanied it had been none other than the war cry of Zeus Himself.

More heartening news had come in from the fleet. A storm, unseasonably spawned this prior night, had wrecked two hundred of the enemy's warships on the far shore of Euboea. One fifth of His Majesty's navy, the Athenian corvette captain Habroniches reported with exultation, had been lost with all hands; he had beheld the wreckage this day with his own eyes. Might not this, too, be the work of God?

Leontiades, the Theban commander, stepped forward, seconding and inflaming the derangement. What force of man, he demanded, may stand up before the rage of heaven? "Bear this in mind, brothers and allies, that nine-tenths of the Persian's army are conscripted nations, drafted against their will at the point of a sword. How will Xerxes continue to hold them in line? Like cattle as today, driven onward with whips? Believe me, men, the Persian's allies are cracking. Discontent and disaffection are spreading like pestilence through their camp; desertion and mutiny lie one more defeat away. If we can hold tomorrow, brothers, Xerxes' predicament will compel him to force the issue at sea. Poseidon who shakes the earth has already wreaked havoc once upon the Persian's pride. Perhaps the god may cut him down to size again."

The Greeks, inflamed by the Theban commander's passion, hurled harsh words at the Kymean Tyrrhastiadas. The allies swore it was not they who stood now in peril, but Xerxes himself and his overweening pride which had called forth the wrath of the Almighty.

I did not need to glance to my master to read his heart. This derangement of the allies was *katalepsis*, possession. It was madness, as surely the speakers themselves knew even as they spewed their grief- and horror-spawned rage at the convenient target of the Kymean noble. The prince himself bore this abuse in silence, sorrow darkening his already grave features.

Leonidas dismissed the assembly, instructing each contingent to turn its attention to the repair and refitting of weapons. He dispatched the Athenian captain, Habroniches, back to the fleet, with orders to inform the naval commanders Eurybiades and Themistokles of all he had heard and seen here tonight.

The allies dispersed, leaving only the Spartans and the nobleman Tyrrhastiadas beside the commander's fire.

"A most impressive testimony of faith, my lord," the prince spoke after some moments. "Such devout orations cannot fail to sustain your men's courage. For an hour. Until darkness and fatigue efface the passion of the moment, and fear for themselves and their families resurfaces, as it must, within their hearts."

The noble repeated with emphasis his report of the mountain track and the Ten Thousand. He declared that if the hand of the gods was at all present in this day's events, it was not their benevolence seeking to preserve the Hellenic defenders but their perverse and unknowable will acting to detach them from their reason. Surely a commander of Leonidas' sagacity perceived this, as clearly as he, lifting his glance to the cliff of Kallidromos, could behold there upon the rock the scores of lightning scars where over decades and centuries numerous other random bolts had in the natural course of coastal storms struck here upon this, the loftiest and most proximate promontory.

Tyrrhastiadas again pressed Leonidas and the officers to credit his report. The *demos* in assembly may elect to disbelieve him; they may denounce and even execute him as a spy; their reason may deceive itself and embrace a propitious prospect for the morrow. Their king and commander, however, cannot permit himself such luxury.

"Say," the Persian pressed, "that I am an agent of intrigue. Believe I have been sent by Xerxes. Say that my intention is in his interest, to influence you by guile and artifice to quit the pass. Say and believe all this. Yet still my report is true.

"The Immortals are coming.

"They will appear by morning, ten thousand strong, in the allied rear."

With a step the noble moved before the Spartan king, addressing him with passion, man-to-man.

"This struggle at the Hot Gates will not be the decisive one, my lord. That battle will come later, deeper into Greece, perhaps before the walls of Athens, perhaps at the Isthmus, perhaps within the Peloponnese, beneath the peaks of Sparta herself. You know this. Any commander who can read terrain and topography knows it.

"Your nation needs you, sir. You are the soul of her army. You may say that a king of Lakedaemon never retreats. But valor must be tempered with wisdom or it is merely recklessness.

"Consider what you and your men have accomplished at the Hot Gates already. The fame you have won in these six days will live forever. Do not seek death for death's sake, nor to fulfill a vain prophecy. Live, sir, and fight another day. Another day with your whole army at your back. Another day when victory, decisive victory, may be yours."

The Persian gestured to the Spartan officers clustered in the light of the council fire. The *polemarch* Derkylides, the Knights Polynikes and Doreion, the platoon commanders and the warriors, Alpheus and Maron and my master. "I beg you, sir. Conserve these, the flower of Lakedaemon, to give their lives another day. Spare yourself for that hour.

"You have proved your valor, my lord. Now, I beseech you, demonstrate your wisdom.

"Withdraw now.

"Get yourself and your men out while you still can."

BOOK SEVEN

LEONIDAS

THIRTY

There would be eleven in the party to raid His Majesty's tent.

Leonidas refused to hazard a greater number; he begrudged even this many, of the hundred and eight who remained of the Three Hundred yet in condition to fight, countenancing the inclusion of five Peers only, and that purely to give the party credibility among the allies.

Dienekes would lead, as the ablest small-unit commander. The Knights Polynikes and Doreion were included for their speed and prowess and Alexandros, over Leonidas' objections seeking to spare him, to fight beside my master as a *dyas*. The Skiritai Hound and Lachides would go. They were mountaineers; they knew how to scale sheer faces. The outlaw Ball Player would serve as guide up the cliff face of Kallidromos, and Rooster would take the company into the enemy camp. Suicide and I were included to support Dienekes and Alexandros and to augment with javelin and bow the party's striking power. The final Spartiate was Telamonias, a boxer of the Wild Olive regiment; after Polynikes and Doreion he was the fastest of the Three Hundred and the only one of the raiders unhampered by wounds.

The Thespaian Dithyrambos had been the force behind the adoption of the plan, conceiving of it on his own without prompting from Rooster, whom my master had not executed, after all, but instead ordered detained in camp throughout the second day with instructions to look to the wounded and the repair and replacement of weapons. Dithyrambos had lobbied strenuously with Leonidas in favor of the raid, and now, disappointed as he was not to be included himself, he stood to hand to wish the party well.

Night's chill had descended upon the camp; as the nobleman Tyrrhastiadas had predicted, fear now stood hard upon the allies; they were one rumor away from terror and one perceived prodigy from panic. Dithyrambos understood the militiamen's hearts. These needed some prospect to fix their hopes upon this night, some expectation to hold them steadfast till morning. Let the raid succeed or fail, it did not matter. Just send men out. And if indeed the gods have taken our part in this cause, well . . . Dithyrambos grinned and clasped my master's hand in farewell.

Dienekes divided the party into two units, one of five under Polynikes, the other of six under his own command. Each squad was to scale the cliff face independently, advancing across Kallidromos on its own to the rendezvous point beneath the cliffs of Trachis. This to increase the likelihood, in the event of ambush or capture, of at least one party getting through to strike.

When the men were armed and ready to move out, both parties presented themselves for final orders before Leonidas. The king spoke to them alone, without the allies or even the Spartan officers present. A cold wind had gotten up. The sky rumbled above Euboea. The mountain face loomed overhead; the moon, as yet only partially shrouded, could be glimpsed above the shreds of wind-torn fog.

Leonidas offered the parties wine from his personal store and poured the libations from his own plain cup. He addressed each man, squires included, not by his name, but by his nickname, and even the diminutive of that. He called Doreion "Little Hare," the Knight's play name from childhood. Dekton he addressed not as Rooster, but "Roo," and touched him with tenderness upon the shoulder.

"I've had your papers of manumission drawn," the king informed the helot. "They'll be in the courier's pouch for Lakedaemon tonight. They emancipate you as well as your family, and they free your infant son."

This was the babe whose life the lady Arete had saved, that night before the *krypteia;* the child whose being had made Dienekes under Lakedaemonian law the father of a living son and thus eligible for inclusion among the Three Hundred.

It was this infant whose life would mean Dienekes' death, and Alexandros' and Suicide's by their association with him. And mine as well.

"If you wish"—Leonidas' eyes met Rooster's in the gust-driven firelight—"you may change the name Idotychides, by which the babe is now called. It is a Spartan name, and we all know you bear scant affection for our race."

This name Idotychides, one may recall, was that of Rooster's father, Arete's brother, who had fallen in battle years before. The name the lady had insisted upon giving the babe, that night of the rump court behind the mess.

"You're free to call your son by his Messenian name," Leonidas continued to Rooster, "but you must tell me now, before I seal the papers and dispatch them."

I had seen Rooster whipped and beaten any number of times upon our chores and details in Lakedaemon. But never till this moment had I seen his eyes well and fill.

"I am struck with shame, sir," he addressed Leonidas, "to have extracted this kindness by extortion." Rooster straightened before the king. He declared the name Idotychides a noble one, which his son would be proud to bear.

The king nodded and placed his hand, warm as a father's, upon Dekton's shoulder. "Come back alive this night, Roo. I'll get you out to safety in the morning."

Before Dienekes' party had climbed half a mile above Alpenoi, heavy pellets of rain began to strike. The gentle slope had turned to cliff wall, whose composition was maritime conglomerate, chalky and rotten. When the downpour hit, the surface turned to soup.

Ball Player took the lead past the initial ascent, but it soon became apparent that he had lost his way in the dark; we were off the main track and into the bewildering network of goat trails that crisscrossed the steepening face. The party made up the trace as it went along, groping in the dark with one man taking his turn in the lead, unburdened, while the others followed bearing the shields and weapons. None wore helmets, just undercaps of felt. These became drenched and sodden, spilling cascades from their brimless fronts into the men's eyes. The climb became out-and-out mountaineering, traversing from toehold to handhold with each man's cheek mashed flat against the rotten face, while icy torrents sluiced upon him, accompanied by landslides of mud as the boulders and stones of the face released their hold, and all this in the dark.

For myself, my shot calf had cramped up and now burned as if a poker had been buried molten within the flesh. Each upward heave compelled exertion of this muscle; the pain nearly knocked me faint. Dienekes was laboring even more miserably. His old wound from Achilleion prevented him from raising his left arm above his shoulder; his right ankle was incapable of flexion. To top it off, the socket of his gouged eye had begun to bleed afresh; rainwater mingled with the dark blood, runneling through his beard and down onto the leathers of his corselet. He squinted across to Suicide, whose pair of shot shoulders made him slither like a snake, arms held low to his side as he writhed up the crumbling, mud-slick, rotting slope.

"By the gods," Dienekes muttered, "this outfit is a mess."

The party reached the first crest after an hour. We were above the fog now; the rain ceased; at once the night became clear, windy and cold. The sea rumbled a thousand feet below, blanketed an eighth of a mile deep in a marine fog whose cottony peaks shone brilliant white beneath a moon only one night shy of full. Suddenly Ball Player signed for silence; the party dropped for cover. The outlaw pointed out across a chasm.

Upon the opposite ridge, a third of a mile away, could be descried the tented throne of His Majesty, the one from upon which he had observed the first two days of battle. Servants were dismantling the platform and pavilion.

"They're packing up. For where?"

"Maybe they've had enough. They're heading home."

The party skittered down off the skyline to a shadowed ledge where it could not be seen. Everything the men bore was soaked. I wrung a compress and wound it fresh for my master's eye. "My brains must be leaking along with the blood," he said. "I can't think of another explanation for why I'm out here on this ass-fucked errand."

He had the men take more wine, for the warmth and to deaden the pain of their various wounds. Suicide continued squinting across to the far ridge and the Persian servants striking their master's theater seats. "Xerxes thinks tomorrow will be the end. Bet on it: we'll see him on horseback at dawn, in the Narrows, to savor his triumph at close hand."

The ridge saddle was broad and level; with Ball Player in the lead, the party made good time for the next hour, following game trails that wove among the scrub sumac and fireweed. The track ran inland now, the sea no longer in sight. We crossed two more ridges, then struck a wild watercourse, one of the torrents that fed the Asopus. At least that's what our outlaw guide guessed. Dienekes touched my shoulder, indicating a peak to the north.

"That's Oita. Where Herakles died."

"Do you think he'll help us tonight?"

The party reached a wooded upslope that had to be climbed hand over hand. Suddenly a swift crashing burst from the thicket above. Forms shot forth, invisible. Every hand flew to a weapon.

"Men?"

The sound receded swiftly above.

"Deer."

In a heartbeat the beasts were a hundred feet gone. Silence. Just the wind, tearing the treetops above us.

For some reason, this serendipitous find heartened the party tremendously. Alexandros pushed forward into the thicket. The earth where the deer had taken shelter was dry, crushed and matted where the herd had lain, flank-to-flank. "Feel the grass. It's still warm."

Ball Player assumed a stance to urinate. "Don't," Alexandros nudged him. "Or the deer will never use this nest again."

"What's that to you?"

"Piss down the slope," Dienekes commanded.

Odd as it sounds, the feeling within that cozy copse evoked a hearth of home, a haven. One could still smell that deery smell, the gamy scent of their coats. None of the party spoke, yet each, I will wager, was thinking the same thought: how sweet it would be, right now, to lie down here like the deer and close one's eyes. To allow all fear to depart one's limbs. To be, just for a moment, innocent of terror.

"It's good hunting country," I observed. "Those were boar runs we passed through. I'll bet there are bear up here, and even lion."

Dienekes' glance met Alexandros' with a glint. "We'll have ourselves a hunt here. Next fall. What do you say?"

The youth's broken face contorted into a grin.

"You'll join us, Rooster," Dienekes proposed. "We'll take a week and make an event of it. No horses or beaters, just two dogs per man. We'll live off the hunt and come home draped in lionskins like Herakles. We'll even invite our dear friend Polynikes."

Rooster regarded Dienekes as if he had gone mad. Then a wry grin settled into place upon his features.

"Then it's settled," my master said. "Next fall."

From the succeeding crest the party followed the watercourse down. The torrent was loud and discipline got careless. From out of nowhere arose voices.

Every man froze.

Rooster crouched in the lead; the party was strung out in column, the worst possible lineup to fight from. "Are they speaking Persian?" Alexandros whispered, straining his ears toward the sound.

Suddenly the voices froze too.

They had heard us.

I could see Suicide, two steps below me, silently stretch behind his shoulder, slipping a pair of "darning needles" from his quiver. Dienekes, Alexandros and Rooster all clutched eight-footers; Ball Player readied a throwing axe.

"Hey, fuckers. Is that you?"

Out of the darkness stepped Hound, the Skirite, with a sword in one hand and a dagger in the other.

"By the gods, you scared the shit out of us!"

It was Polynikes' party, pausing to gnaw a heel of dry bread.

"What is this, a picnic?" Dienekes slid down among them. We all clapped our mates in relief. Polynikes reported that the outroute his party had taken, the lower track, had been fast and easy. They had been in this clearing a quarter of an hour.

"Come down here." The Knight motioned to my master. "Take a look at this."

The whole party followed. On the opposite bank of the watercourse, ten feet up the slope, stretched a track wide enough for two men to pass abreast. Even in the deep shadow of the gorge, you could see the churned-up earth.

"It's the mountain track, the one the Immortals are taking. What else can it be?"

Dienekes knelt to feel the earth. It was freshly trodden, the passage no more than two hours old. You could glimpse on the uphill side the ridges where the marching soles of the Ten Thousand had caved the hill in, and the slides on the downslope from the weight of their passage.

Dienekes chose one of Polynikes' men, Telamonias the boxer, to retrace the track their party had taken and inform Leonidas. The man groaned with disappointment. "None of that," Dienekes snapped. "You're the fastest who knows the trail. It has to be you."

The boxer sprinted off.

Another of Polynikes' party was absent. "Where's Doreion?"

"Down the track. Taking a snoop."

A moment later the Knight, whose sister Altheia was Polynikes' wife, came loping into view from below. He was *gymnos*, naked for speed.

"What happened to your dog?" Polynikes greeted him merrily. "The little fellow has shriveled into an acorn."

The Knight grinned and snatched his cloak from where it hung upon a tree. He reported that the track ended about a quarter mile down. There an entire forest had been felled, probably this very evening, immediately after the Persians had learned of the track. The Immortals had no doubt marshaled there, on the freshly cleared ground, before setting out.

"What's there now?"

"Cavalry. Three, maybe four squadrons."

These were Thessalians, the Knight reported. Greeks whose country had gone over to the enemy.

"They're snoring like farmers. The fog is soup. Every nose is buried in a cloak, sentries too."

"Can we go around?"

Doreion nodded. "It's all pine. A carpet of soft needles. You can cross on a dead run and not make a sound."

Dienekes indicated the clearing in which the parties now stood. "This will be our rally point. We'll assemble here after. You'll guide us back from this point, Doreion, or one of your party, by the way you came, the fast way."

Dienekes had Rooster rebrief both parties on the layout of the enemy camp, in case something happened to him on the way down. The last of the wine was shared out. The skin in its sequence chanced to pass from Polynikes' hand to Rooster's. The helot seized this moment of intimacy before action. "Tell me the truth. Would you have killed my son that night with the *krypteia?*"

"I'll kill him yet," the runner answered, "if you fuck us up tonight."

"In that case," the helot said, "I look forward with even greater anticipation to your death."

It was time for Ball Player to depart. He had agreed to guide the party this far and no farther. To the surprise of all, the outlaw seemed torn. "Look," he offered haltingly, "I want to keep on with you, you're good men, I admire you. But I can't in good conscience without being compensated."

This struck the entire party as hilarious.

"Your scruples are stern, outlaw," Dienekes observed.

"You want compensation?" Polynikes clutched his own privates. "I'll save this for you."

Ball Player alone did not laugh.

"Goddamn you," he muttered, more to himself than to the others. With further grumbled curses, he took his place in the undermanned column. He was staying.

The party would no longer be divided; from here it would advance in teams of five, Ball Player attached to Polynikes' four to make up for Telamonias, but in tandem, each unit supporting the other.

The squads ghosted without incident past the snoozing Thessalians. The presence of this Greek cavalry was extremely good fortune. The way back, if there was one, would inevitably be in disorder; it would be of no small advantage to have a landmark as conspicuous in the dark as an acres-wide swath of felled forest. The Thessalians' horses could be stampeded to create confusion, and, if the party had to flee under fire through their camp, its shouts to one another in Greek would not betray it among the Greek-speaking Thessalians.

Another half hour brought the squads to the edge of a wood directly above the citadel of Trachis. The channel of the Asopus thundered beneath the city walls. It roared in torrent, deafening, with a sharp cold wind keening down the throat of the gorge.

We could see the enemy camp now.

Surely no sight beneath heaven, not Troy under siege, nor the war of the gods and Titans itself, could have equaled in scale that which now spread before our vision.

As far as the eye could see, three miles of plain extending to the sea, five miles across, with plain and more plain extending beyond sight around the shoulders of the Trachinian cliffs, thousands of acres square and all of it incandescent with the mist-magnified fires of the enemy.

"So much for them packing up."

Dienekes motioned Rooster to him. The helot laid it out as he remembered:

Xerxes' horses drink upstream of all, before the rest of the camp. Rivers are sacred to the Persians and must be preserved unprofaned. The whole upper valley is staked out as pasturage. The Great King's pavilion, so Rooster swore, stood at the head of the plain, within bowshot of the river.

The party dropped down, directly beneath the citadel walls, and entered the current. The Eurotas in Lakedaemon is mountain-fed; even in summer its snowmelt is bone-numbingly cold. The Asopus was worse. One's limbs went to ice within moments. It was so cold we feared for our safety; if you had to get out and run, you couldn't feel your own legs and feet.

Mercifully the torrent lessened a few hundred yards down. The party rolled its cloaks into bundles and floated them on shields turned bowls-up. Dams had been erected by the enemy to abate the torrent and facilitate the watering of horses and men. Pickets had been stationed atop these, but the fog and wind made conditions so inhospitable, the hour was so late and the sentries so complacent, deeming infiltration unthinkable, that the party was able to steal past, bellying over the spillways, then coasting swiftly into the shadows along the bank.

The moon had set. Rooster could not pick out His Majesty's pavilion. "It was here, I swear it!" He pointed across to a rise of land, upon which stood nothing but a street of grooms' tents snapping in the wind and a rope picket line shoulder-to-shoulder with horses standing miserably in the gale. "They must have moved it."

Dienekes himself drew his blade. He was going to open Rooster's throat on the spot as a traitor. Rooster swore by every god he could think of; he wasn't lying. "Things look different in the dark," he offered lamely.

Polynikes saved him. "I believe him, Dienekes. He's so fucking stupid, this is just the way he would screw it up."

The party slithered on, neck-deep in marrow-numbing rapids. At one point Dienekes' leg became snarled in a tangle of reeds; he had to submerge with his *xiphos* to cut himself free. He came up snorting.

I asked what he was laughing at.

"I was just wondering if it was possible to get any more miserable." He chuckled darkly. "I suppose if a river snake crawled up my ass and gave birth to quintuplets . . ."

Suddenly Rooster's hand nudged my master's shoulder. A hundred paces ahead stood another dam and spillway. Three linen pavilions abutted a pleasant beach; a lantern-lit walkway snaked up the slope, past a hide corral in which were confined a dozen blanket-draped war mounts of such magnificence that the worth of each alone must have equaled the produce of a small city.

Directly above rose a copse of oak, lit by iron cressets howling in the gale, and beyond, past a single picket line of Egyptian marines, could be glimpsed the pennanted kingposts of a pavilion so vast it looked like it housed a battalion.

"That's it." Rooster pointed. "That's Xerxes' tent."

THIRTY-ONE

The warrior's thoughts at the brink of action, my master had often observed (as the student of fear he ever declared himself to be), follow a pattern unvarying and ineluctable. There appears always an interval, often brief as a heartbeat, wherein the inward eye summons the following tripartite vision, often in the selfsame order:

First to the inmost heart appear the faces of those he loves who do not share his immediate peril: his wife and mother, his children, particularly if they are female, particularly if they are young. These who will remain beneath the sun and preserve within their hearts the memory of his passage, the warrior greets with fondness and compassion. To them he bequeaths his love and to them bids farewell.

Next arise before the inward eye the shades of those already across the river, they who stand awaiting upon the distant shore of death. For my master these comprised his brother, Iatrokles, his father and mother and Arete's brother, Idotychides. These, too, the warrior's heart greets in silent vision, summons their aid and then releases.

Lastly advance the gods, whichever a man feels have favored him most, whichever he feels himself most to have favored. Into their care he releases his spirit, if he can.

Only when this triple obligation has been requited does the warrior revert to the present and turn, as if arising from a dream, to those at his shoulder, they who in a moment will undergo with him the trial of death. Here, Dienekes often observed, is where the Spartans most hold advantage over all who face them in battle. Beneath what alien banner could one discover at his shoulder such men as Leonidas, Alpheus, Maron, or here in this dirt Doreion, Polynikes and my master, Dienekes, himself? These who will share the ferry with him, the warrior's heart embraces with a love surpassing all others granted by the gods to humankind, save only that of a mother for her babe. To them he commits all, as they all to him.

My own eyes now glanced to Dienekes, crouched upon the riverbank helmetless in his scarlet cloak which showed dead black in the darkness. His right hand was kneading the joints of his immobile ankle seeking to restore flexion, as he in compact phrase issued the instructions which would drive the men he commanded into action. At his shoulder Alexandros had scraped a fistful of sand from the bank and was scoring it along the haft of his eight-footer, abrading the surface for a grip. Polynikes with a curse worked his forearm into the sodden bronze and leather sleeve of his shield, seeking the point of balance and proper hold upon the gripcord. Hound and Lachides, Ball Player, Rooster and Doreion likewise completed their preparations. I glanced to Suicide. He was sorting swiftly through his darning needles, like a surgeon selecting his instrument, picking those three, one for his throwing hand, two for his free, whose heft and balance promised the truest flight. I moved in a crouch beside the Scythian, with whom I was paired in the assault. "See you in the ferry," he said, and tugged me with him toward the flank from which we would attack.

Would his be the last face I would see? This Scythian, mentor and instructor to me since I was fourteen. He had taught me cover and interval, dress and shadow; how to stanch a puncture wound, set a broken collarbone; how to take down a horse upon the open field, drag a wounded warrior from battle using his cloak. This man with his skill and fearlessness could have hired himself out as a mercenary to any army in the world. To the Persians if he wished. He would have been appointed captain-of-a-hundred, achieved fame and glory, women and wealth. Yet he chose to remain in the harsh academy of Lakedaemon, in service for no pay.

I thought of the merchant Elephantinos. Of all in camp, Suicide had taken most to this gay, ebullient fellow; the pair had become fast friends. On the evening before the first battle, when my master's platoon had settled, preparing the evening meal, this Elephantinos had appeared upon his rounds. He had traded away all his wares, bartered his waggon and ass, sold even his own cloak and shoes. Now on this night he circulated with a basket of pears and sweetmeats, distributing these treats to the warriors as they sat to their suppers. He stopped beside our fire. My master often sacrificed in the evenings; nothing much, just a crust of barley loaf and a libation, not praying aloud, just offering within his heart a few silent words to the gods. He would never reveal the contents of his prayer, but I could read it upon his lips and overhear the odd mumble. He was praying for Arete and his daughters.

"It is these young boys who should practice such piety," the merchant observed, "not you grisly veterans!"

Dienekes greeted the *emporos* warmly. "You mean 'grizzled,' my friend."

"I mean grisly, weck up to thees!"

He was invited to sit. Bias was still alive then; he joked with the merchant about his want of forethought. How will the old-timer get away now, without his ass and waggon?

Elephantinos made no reply.

"Our friend will not be leaving," Dienekes spoke softly, his gaze upon the earth.

Alexandros and Ariston arrived with a hare they had traded for with some boys from Alpenoi village. The old man smiled at the comradely ragging they endured from their mates over this prize. It was a "winter hare," so scrawny it wouldn't flavor a stew for two men, let alone sixteen. The merchant regarded my master.

"To see you veterans with gray in your beards, it is only right that you should stand here at the Gates. But these boys." His gesture indicated Alexandros and Ariston, including in its sweep myself and several other squires barely out of their teens. "How may I leave, when these babes remain?"

"I envy you comrades," the merchant continued when the emotion had cleared from his throat. "I have searched all my life for that which you have possessed from birth, a noble city to belong to." His smithy-scarred hand indicated the fires springing to life across the camp and the warriors, old and young, now settling beside them. "This will be my city. I will be her magistrate and her physician, her orphans' father and her fool."

He handed out his pears and moved on. One could hear the laughter he brought to the next fire, and the one after that.

The allies had been on station at the Gates for four nights then. They had observed the scale of the Persian host, on land and sea, and knew well the odds insuperable that faced them. Yet it was not until that moment, I felt, at least for my master's platoon, that the reality of the peril to Hellas and the imminence of the defenders' own extinction truly struck home. A profound soberness settled with the vanishing sun.

For long moments no one spoke. Alexandros was skinning the hare, I was grinding barley meal in a handmill; Medon prepared the ground oven, Black Leon was chopping onions. Bias reclined against the stump of an oak felled for firewood, with Leon Donkeydick upon his left. To the startlement of all, Suicide began to speak.

"There is a goddess in my country called Na'an," the Scythian broke the silence. "My mother was a priestess of this cult, if such a grand title may be applied to an illiterate countrywoman who lived all her life out of the back of a waggon. My mind is recalled to this by our friend the merchant and the two-wheeled cart he calls his home."

This was as much speech at one time as I, or any other, had heard Suicide give voice to. All expected him to halt right there. To their astonishment, the Scythian continued.

His priestess mother taught him, Suicide said, that nothing beneath the sun is real. The earth and everything upon it is but a forestander, the material embodiment of a finer and more profound reality which exists immediately behind it, invisible to mortal sense. Everything we call real is sustained by this subtler fundament which underlies it, indestructible, unglimpsed beyond the curtain.

"My mother's religion teaches that those things alone are real which cannot be perceived by the senses. The soul. Mother love. Courage. These are closer to God, she taught, because they alone are the same on both sides of death, in front of the curtain and behind.

"When I first came to Lakedaemon and beheld the phalanx," Suicide went on, "I thought it the most ludicrous form of warfare I had ever seen. In my country we fight on horseback. This to me was the only way, grand and glorious, a spectacle that stirs the soul. The phalanx looked like a joke to me. But I admired the men, their virtue, which was so clearly superior to that of every other nation I had observed and studied. It was a puzzle to me."

I glanced to Dienekes across the fire, to see if he had previously heard these thoughts articulated by Suicide, perhaps in the years before I had entered his service, when the Scythian alone stood as his squire. Upon my master's face was written rapt attention. Clearly this bounty from Suicide's lips was as novel to him as to the others.

"Do you remember, Dienekes, when we fought the Thebans at Erythrae? When they broke and ran? This was the first rout I had witnessed. I was appalled by it. Can there exist a baser, more degrading sight beneath the sun than a phalanx breaking apart in fear? It makes one ashamed to be mortal, to behold such ignobility even in an enemy. It violates the higher laws of God." Suicide's face, which had been a grimace of disdain, now brightened into a cheerier mode. "Ah, but the opposite: a line that holds! What can be more grand, more noble?

"One night I dreamt I marched within the phalanx. We were advancing across a plain to meet the foe. Terror froze my heart. My fellow warriors strode all around me, in front, behind, to all sides. They were all me. Myself old, myself young. I became even more terrified, as if I were coming apart into pieces. Then all began to sing. All the 'me's,' all the 'myself's.' As their voices rose in sweet concord, all fear fled my heart. I woke with a still breast and knew this was a dream straight from God.

"I understood then that it was the glue that made the phalanx great. The unseen glue that bound it together. I realized that all the drill and discipline you Spartans love to pound into each other's skulls were really not to inculcate skill or art, but only to produce this glue."

Medon laughed. "And what glue have you dissolved, Suicide, that finally allows your jaws to flap with such un-Scythian immoderation?"

Suicide grinned across the fire. Medon was the one, it was said, who had originally given the Scythian his nickname, when he, guilty of a murder in his country, had fled to Sparta, where he asked again and again for death.

"When I first came to Lakedaemon and they called me 'Suicide,' I hated it. But in time I came to see its wisdom, unintentional as it was. For what can be more noble than to slay oneself? Not literally. Not with a blade in the guts. But to extinguish the selfish self within, that part which looks only to its own preservation, to save its own skin. That, I saw, was the victory you Spartans had gained over yourselves. That was the glue. It was what you had learned and it made me stay, to learn it too.

"When a warrior fights not for himself, but for his brothers, when his most passionately sought goal is neither glory nor his own life's preservation, but to spend his substance for them, his comrades, not to abandon them, not to prove unworthy of them, then his heart truly has achieved contempt for death, and with that he transcends himself and his actions touch the sublime. This is why the true warrior cannot speak of battle save to his brothers who have been there with him. This truth is too holy, too sacred, for words. I myself would not presume to give it speech, save here now, with you."

Black Leon had been listening attentively. "What you say is true, Suicide, if you will forgive me for calling you that. But not everything unseen is noble. Base emotions are invisible as well. Fear and greed and lust. What do you say about them?"

"Yes," Suicide acknowledged, "but don't they feel base? They stink to heaven, they make one sick within the heart. The noble invisible things feel different. They are like music, in which the higher notes are the finer.

"This was another thing that puzzled me when I arrived in Lakedaemon. Your music. How much of it there was, not alone the martial odes or war songs you sing as you advance upon the foe, but in the dances and the choruses, the festivals and the sacrifices. Why do these consummate warriors honor music so, when they forbid all theater and art? I believe they sense that the virtues are like music. They vibrate at a higher, nobler pitch."

He turned to Alexandros. "That is why Leonidas chose you for the Three Hundred, my young master, though he knew you had never before stood among the trumpets. He believes you will sing here at the Gates in that sublime register, not with this"—he indicated the throat—"but with this." And his hand touched his heart.

Suicide drew up, suddenly awkward and abashed. Around the fire each face regarded him soberly and with respect. Dienekes broke the silence with a laugh.

"You're a philosopher, Suicide."

The Scythian grinned back. "Yes," he nodded, "weck up to thees!"

A messenger appeared, summoning Dienekes to Leonidas' council. My master motioned me to accompany him. Something had changed within him; I could sense it as we picked our way among the network of trails that crisscrossed the camps of the allies.

"Do you remember the night, Xeo, when we sat with Ariston and Alexandros and spoke of fear and its opposite?"

I said I did.

"I have the answer to my question. Our friends the merchant and the Scythian have given it to me."

His glance took in the fires of the camp, the nations of the allies clustered in their units, and their officers, whom we could see, like us approaching from all quarters the king's fire, ready to respond to his needs and receive his instructions.

"The opposite of fear," Dienekes said, "is love."

THIRTY-TWO

Two sentries covered the west, the rear of His Majesty's pavilion. Dienekes chose this side to attack because it was the dreariest and least prominent, the flank most exposed to the gale. Of all the fragmented images that remain from this brawl which was over no more than fifty heartbeats after it began, the most vivid is of the first sentinel, an Egyptian marine, a six-footer with a helmet the color of gold, decorated with stubby silver griffin's wings. These marines, as His Majesty knows, wear as a badge of pride brightly colored regimental sashes of wool. It is their custom on station to drape these pennants crosswise over the chest and belt them at the waist. This night this sentry had wound his over his nose and mouth to protect against the gale and the scoring of the driven dust, enwrapping ears and brow as well, with the merest slitted sliver held open for the eyes. His body-length wicker shield he bore before him at port, wrestling its unwieldly mass in the blow. It took little imagination to perceive his misery, alone in the cold beside a single cresset howling in the blast.

Suicide advanced undetected to within thirty feet of the fellow, snaking on his belly past the buttoned-up tents of His Majesty's grooms and the loudly snapping windbreaks of linen which shielded the horses from the gale. I was half a length behind him; I could see him mutter the two-word prayer—"Deliver him," meaning the foe—to his savage gods.

Blearily the sentry blinked up. Out of the darkness, tearing directly for him, he beheld the hurtling form of the Scythian clutching in his left fist a pair of dart-length javelins, with the bronze-sheathed killing point of a third poised in throwing position beside his right ear. So bizarre and unexpected must this sight have been that the marine did not even react with alarm. With his spear hand he tugged nonchalantly at the sash that shielded his eyes, as if muttering to himself at the obligation to respond to this sudden and unwonted irritation.

Suicide's first javelin drove so powerfully through the apple of the man's throat that its point burst all the way through the neck and out the spine, its ash extending crimson, half an arm's length beyond. The man dropped like a rock. In an instant Suicide was upon him, tearing the darning needle out with such a savage wrench that it brought half the man's windpipe with it.

The second sentry, ten feet to the left of the first, was just turning in bewilderment, clearly disbelieving yet the evidence of his senses, when Polynikes blindsided him on a dead sprint, slamming the man on his unshielded right a blow of such ferocious impact with his own shoulder-driven shield that the fellow was catapulted off his feet and hurled bodily through the air. The breath expelled from the guardsman's lungs, his spine crashed into the dirt; Polynikes' lizard-sticker punched through his breast so hard you could hear the bone shiver and crack even over the gale.

The raiders dashed to the tent wall. Alexandros' blade slashed a diagonal in the bucking linen. Dienekes, Doreion, Polynikes, Lachides, then Alexandros, Hound, Rooster and Ball Player blasted through. We had been seen. The sentries on either side bawled the alarm. It had all happened so swiftly, however, that the pickets could not at first credit the substance their eyes beheld. Clearly they had orders to remain at their posts and this they half did, at least the nearest two, advancing toward Suicide and me (the only ones yet outside the pavilion) with an abashed and befuddled tentativeness. I had an arrow nocked in my bow, with three more clutched in my left fist around the grip, and was raising to fire. "Hold!" Suicide shouted into my ear in the gale. "Give 'em a grin."

I thought he was mad. But that's just what he did. Gesturing like a crony, calling to the sentries in his tongue, the Scythian put on a performance, acting as if this were just some kind of drill which perhaps these sentries had missed at the briefing. It held them for about two heartbeats. Then another dozen marines roared from the pavilion's front. We turned and plunged into the tent.

The interior was pitch-black and filled with shrieking women.

The rest of our party was nowhere to be seen. We saw lamplight flare across the chamber. It was Hound. A naked woman had him about one leg, burying her teeth into the meat of his calf. The lamplight from the next chamber illuminated the Skirite's blade as he drove it like a cleaver, slicing through the gristle of her cervical spine. Hound gestured to the chamber. "Torch it!"

We were in some kind of concubines' seraglio. The pavilion as a whole must have had twenty chambers. Who the hell knew which was the King's? I dashed for the single lit lamp and jammed its flame into a closet of women's undergarments; in an instant the whole brothel was howling.

Marines were pouring in behind us, among the shrieking whores. We raced after Hound, in the direction he had taken down the corridor. Clearly we were all the way at the pavilion's rear. The next chamber must have been the eunuchs'; I saw Dienekes and Alexandros, shield by shield, blast through a pair of skull-shaved titans, not even pausing to strike but just bowling them over. Rooster disemboweled one with a swing of his *xiphos;* Ball Player chopped another down with his axe. Polynikes, Doreion and Lachides emerged ahead, from some kind of bedchamber, spearpoints dripping blood. "Fucking priests!" Doreion shouted in frustration. A Magus staggered forth, gutted, and dropped.

Doreion and Polynikes were in the lead when the party hit His Majesty's chamber. The space was vast, big as a barn and studded with so many ridgepoles of ebony and cedar that it looked like a forest. Lamps and cressets lit the vault like noon. The ministers of the Persians were awake and assembled in council. Perhaps they had risen early for the morrow, perhaps they had never gone to bed. I turned the corner into this chamber just as Dienekes, Alexandros, Hound and Lachides caught up with Polynikes and Doreion and formed in line, shield by shield, to attack. We could see the generals and ministers of His Majesty, thirty feet away across the floor, which was not dirt but platformed wood, stout and level as a temple, and carpeted so thick with rugs that it muffled all sound of onrushing feet.

It was impossible to tell which of the Persians was His Majesty, all were so magnificently appareled and all of such surpassing height and handsomeness. Their numbers were a dozen, excluding scribes, guards and servants, and every man was armed. Clearly they had learned of the attack only moments earlier; they clutched scimitars, bows and axes and seemed by their expressions not yet to believe the evidence of their eyes. Without a word the Spartans charged.

Suddenly there were birds. Exotic species by the dozen and the score, apparently brought from Persia for His Majesty's amusement, now clattered into flight at the feet of the onsurging Spartans. Some array of cages had either been spilled or trampled open, who knows by whom, perhaps one of the Spartans in the confusion, perhaps a quick-thinking servant of His Majesty, but at once and in the midst of the attack, a hundred or more shrieking harpies erupted into the interior of the pavilion, flying creatures of every hue, howling and churning the space to madness with the wild clatter and frenzy of their wings.

Those birds saved His Majesty. They and the ridgepoles which supported the vault of the pavilion like the hundred columns of a temple. These in combination, and their unexpectedness, threw off the rush of the attackers just enough for His Majesty's marines and those remaining household guards of the Immortals to secure with their swarming bodies the space before His Majesty's person.

The Persians within the tent fought just as their fellows had in the pass and at the Narrows. Their accustomed weapons were of the missile type, javelins, lances and arrows, and they sought space, an interval of distance from which to launch them. The Spartans on the other hand were trained to close breast-to-breast with the foe. Before one could draw breath, the locked shields of the Lakedaemonians were pincushioned with arrow shafts and lanceheads. One heartbeat more and their bronze facings slammed into the frantically massing bodies of the foe. For an instant it seemed as if they would utterly trample the Persians. I saw Polynikes bury his eight-footer overhand in the face of one nobleman, jerk its gore-dripping point free and plunge it into the breast of another. Dienekes, with Alexandros on his left, slew three so quickly the eye could barely assimilate it. On the right Ball Player was hacking like a madman with his throwing axe, directly into a shrieking knot of priests and secretaries cowering upon the floor.

The servants of His Majesty sacrificed themselves with stupefying valor. Two directly ahead of me, youths without even the start of a beard, tore in tandem a carpet from the floor, thick as a shepherd's winter coat, and, employing it as a shield, flung themselves upon Rooster and Doreion. If one had had time to laugh, the sight of Rooster's fury as he plunged his *xiphos* in frustration into that rug would have prompted gales of hilarity. He tore the first servant's throat out with his bare hands and caved in the second's skull with a lamp still aflame.

For myself, I had loosed with such furious speed all four of the arrows I clutched ready in my left hand that I was empty and groping to the quiver before I could spit. There was no time even to follow the shafts' flight to see if they had found their marks. My right hand was just clutching a fistful more from the sleeve at my shoulder when I raised my eyes and saw the burnished steel head of a hurled battle-axe pinwheeling straight for my skull. Instinct jerked my legs from beneath me; it seemed an eternity before my weight began to make me fall. The axehead was so close I could hear its whirling thrum and see the purple ostrich plume on its flank and the double-headed griffin imprinted on the steel. The killing edge was half an arm's length from the space between my eyes when a ridgepole of cedar, whose presence I had not even been aware of, intercepted the homicidal rush of its flight. The axehead buried palm-deep in the wood. I had half an instant to glimpse the face of the man who had flung the blade and then the whole wall of the chamber blew apart.

Egyptian marines poured through, twenty of them followed at once by twenty more. The whole side of the tent was now open to the gale. I saw the captain Tommie clash shield-to-shield with Polynikes. Those lunatic birds thrashed everywhere. Hound went down. A two-handed axe tore open his guts. An arrow shaft ripped through Doreion's throat; he reeled backward with blood spewing from his teeth. Dienekes was hit; he buckled rearward onto Suicide. In the fore remained only Alexandros, Polynikes, Lachides, Ball

Player and Rooster. I saw the outlaw stagger. Polynikes and Rooster were swamped by inrushing marines.

Alexandros was alone. He had singled out the person of His Majesty or some nobleman he took for him and now, with his eight-footer cocked overhand above his right ear, prepared to hurl the spear across the wall of enemy defenders. I could see his right foot plant, concentrating all force of leg and limb behind the blow. Just as his shoulder started forward, arm extended in the throw, a noble of the Persians, the general Mardonius I later learned, delivered with his scimitar a blow of such force and precision that it took Alexandros' hand off right at the wrist.

As in moments of extreme emergency time seems to slow, permitting the vision to perceive instant by instant that which unfolds before the eyes, I could see Alexandros' hand, its fingers still gripping the spear, hang momentarily in midair, then plummet, yet clutching the ashen shaft. His right arm and shoulder continued forward with all their force, the stump at the wrist now spraying bright blood. For an instant Alexandros did not realize what had happened. Discomfiture and disbelief flooded his eyes; he couldn't understand why his spear was not flying forward. A blow of a battle-axe thundered upon his shield, driving him to his knees. I was in too tight to use my bow to defend him; I dove for the fallen shaft of his eight-footer, hoping to thrust it back at the Persian noble before his scimitar could find the mark to decapitate my friend.

Before I could move, Dienekes was there, the huge bronze bowl of his shield covering Alexandros. "Get out!" he bellowed to all above the din. He hauled Alexandros to his feet the way a countryman yanks a lamb out of a torrent.

We were outside, in the gale.

I saw Dienekes cry an order from no farther than two arm's lengths and could not hear a word of it. He had Alexandros on his feet and was pointing up the slope past the citadel. We would not flee by the river, there was no time. "Cover them!" Suicide shouted into my ear. I felt scarlet-cloaked forms flee past me and could not tell who was who. Two were being carried. Doreion staggered from the pavilion, mortally wounded, amid a swarm of Egyptian marines. Suicide slung darning needles into the first three so fast, each seemed to sprout a lance in the belly as if by magic. I was shooting too. I saw a marine hack Doreion's head off. Behind him, Ball Player plunged from the tent, burying his axe in the man's back; then he, too, fell beneath a hail of pike and sword blows. I was empty. So was Suicide. He made to rush the enemy bare-handed; I clutched his belt and dragged him back screaming. Doreion, Hound and Ball Player were dead; the living would need us more.

THIRTY-THREE

The space immediately east of the pavilion stood occupied exclusively by the picketed mounts of His Majesty's personal riding stock and the service tents of their grooms. Through this open-air paddock the raiding party now fled. Linen windbreaks had been erected, dividing the enclosure into squares. It was like racing through the hanging laundry of a city's humble quarter. As Suicide and I overtook our comrades among the wind-numbed mounts, on a dead run and with the blood of terror pounding within our temples, we encountered Rooster at the party's rear, gesturing urgently to us to slow, to stop. Walk.

The party emerged into the open. Armored men advanced toward us by the hundreds. But these, as fortune or a god's hand would have it, had not been summoned to arms in response to the attack upon their King, but stood in fact in total ignorance of it. They were simply rising to the call of reveille, groggy yet and grumbling in the gale-pounded dark, to arm for the morning's resumption of battle. The marines' shouts of alarm from the pavilion were shredded in the teeth of the gale; their foot pursuit lost its way at once among the myriads in the dark.

The flight from the Persian camp became attended, as are so many moments in war, by a sense of reality so dislocated as to border upon, and even surpass, the bizarre. The party made good its escape neither sprinting nor flying, but limping and hobbling. The raiders trudged in the open, making no attempt to conceal themselves from the enemy but in fact approaching and even engaging him in converse. Irony compounded, the party itself helped spread the alarm of attack, helmetless as it was and bloodied, bearing shields from which the *lambda* of Lakedaemon had been effaced and carrying across its shoulders one desperately wounded, Alexandros, and one already dead, Lachides.

For all the world, the group appeared like a squad of overwhelmed pickets. Dienekes speaking in Boeotian Greek, or as near as he could come to the accent, and Suicide in his own Scythian dialect, addressed those officers whose arming men we passed through, spreading the word "mutiny" and gesturing back, not wildly but wearily, toward the pavilion of His Majesty.

Nobody seemed to give a damn. The great bulk of the army, it was clear, were grudging draftees whose nations had been conscripted into service against their will. These now in the dank and gale-torn dawn sought only to warm their own backsides, fill their bellies and get through the day's fighting with their heads still attached.

The raiding party even received unwitting aid for Alexandros from a squad of Trachinian cavalrymen, struggling to ignite a fire for their breakfast. These took us for Thebans, the faction of that nation who had gone over to the Persian, whose turn it was that night to provide inner-perimeter security. The cavalrymen provided us with light, water and bandages while Suicide, with the hands of experience surer than any battlefield surgeon's, secured the hemorrhaging artery with a copper "dog bite." Already he, Alexandros, was deep in shock.

"Am I dying?" he asked Dienekes in that sad detached tone so like a child's, the voice of one who seems to stand already at his own shoulder.

"You'll die when I say you can," Dienekes answered gently.

The blood was coming in surges from Alexandros' severed wrist despite the arterial clamp, sheeting from the hacked-off veins and the hundred vessels and capillaries within the pulpy tissue. With the flat of a *xiphos* gray-hot from the fire, Suicide cauterized and bound the stump, lashing a tourniquet about the pinion point beneath the biceps. What none was aware of in the dark and the confusion, not even Alexandros himself, was the puncture wound of a lancepoint beneath his second rib and the blood pooling internally at the base of his lungs.

Dienekes himself had been wounded in the leg, his bad leg with the shattered ankle, and had lost his own share of blood. He no longer had the strength to carry Alexandros. Polynikes took over, slinging the yet-conscious warrior over his right shoulder, loosening the gripcord of Alexandros' shield to hang it as protection across his back.

Suicide collapsed halfway up the slope before the citadel. He had been shot in the groin, sometime back in the pavilion, and didn't even know it. I took him; Rooster carried Lachides' body. Dienekes' leg was coming unstrung; he needed bearing himself. In the starlight I could see the look of despair in his eyes.

We all felt the dishonor of leaving Doreion's body and Hound's, and even the outlaw's, among the foe. The shame drove the party like a lash, impelling each exhaustion-shattered limb one pace more up the brutal, steepening slope.

We were past the citadel now, skirting the felled wood where the Thessalian cavalry were picketed. These were all awake now and armed, moving out for the day's battle. A few minutes later we reached the grove where earlier we had startled the slumbering deer.

A Doric voice hailed us. It was Telamonias the boxer, the man of our party whom Dienekes had dispatched back to Leonidas with word of the mountain track and the Ten Thousand. He had returned with help. Three Spartan squires and half a dozen Thespaians. Our party dropped in exhaustion. "We've roped the trail back," Telamonias informed Dienekes. "The climbing's not bad."

"What about the Persian Immortals? The Ten Thousand."

"No sign when we left. But Leonidas is withdrawing the allies. They're all pulling out, everyone but the Spartans."

Polynikes set Alexandros gently down upon the matted grass within the grove. You could still smell the deer. I saw Dienekes feel for Alexandros' breath, then flatten his ear, listening, to the youth's chest. "Shut up!" he barked at the party. "Shut the fuck up!"

Dienekes pressed his ear tighter to the flat of Alexandros' sternum. Could he distinguish the sound of his own heart, hammering now in his chest, from that beat which he sought so desperately within the breast of his protege? Long moments passed. At last Dienekes straightened and sat up, his back seeming to bear the weight of every wound and every death across all his years.

He lifted the young man's head, tenderly, with a hand beneath the back of his neck. A cry of such grief as I had never heard tore from my master's breast. His back heaved; his shoulders shuddered. He lifted Alexandros' bloodless form into his embrace and held it, the young man's arms hanging limp as a doll's. Polynikes knelt at my master's side, draped a cloak about his shoulders and held him as he sobbed.

Never in battle or elsewhere had I, nor any of the men there present beneath the oaks, beheld Dienekes loose the reins of self-command with which he maintained so steadfast a hold upon his heart. You could see him summon now every reserve of will to draw himself back to the rigor of a Spartan and an officer. With an expulsion of breath that was not a sigh but something deeper, like the whistle of death the *daimon* makes escaping within the avenue of the throat, he released Alexandros' life-fled form and settled it gently upon the scarlet cloak spread beneath it on the earth. With his right hand he clasped that of the youth who had been his charge and protege since the morn of his birth.

"You forgot about our hunt, Alexandros."

Eos, pallid dawn, bore now her light to the barren heavens without the thicket. Game trails and deer-trodden traces could be discerned. The eye began to make out the wild, torrent-cut slopes so like those of Therai on Taygetos, the oak groves and shaded runs that, it was certain, teemed with deer and boar and even, perhaps, a lion.

"We would have had such a grand hunt here next fall."

THIRTY-FOUR

The preceding pages were the last delivered to His Majesty prior to the burning of Athens.

The Army of the Empire stood at that time, two hours prior to sunset, some six weeks after the victory at Thermopylae, drawn up on line within the western walls of the city of Athena. An incendiary brigade of 120,000 men there dressed at a double-arms interval and advanced across the capital, putting all temples and shrines, magistracies and public buildings, gymnasia, houses, factories, schools and warehouses to the torch.

At that time the man Xeones, who had hitherto been recovering steadily from his wounds sustained at the battle for the Hot Gates, suffered a reverse. Clearly the witnessing of the immolation of Athens had distressed the man profoundly. In fever he inquired repeatedly after the fate of the seaport Phaleron wherein, he had told us, lay the temple of Persephone of the Veil, that sanctuary in which his cousin, the girl Diomache, had taken refuge. None could provide intelligence of the fate of this precinct. The captive began to fail further; the Royal Surgeon was summoned. It was determined that several punctures of the thoracic organs had reopened; internal bleeding had become severe.

At this point His Majesty stood unavailable, being on station with the fleet, which was drawing up in preparation for imminent engagement with the navy of the Hellenes, expected to commence with the dawn. The morrow's fight, it was anticipated eagerly by His Majesty's admirals, would eliminate all resistance of the enemy at sea and leave the unconquered remainder of Greece, Sparta and the Peloponnese, helpless before the final assault of His Majesty's sea and land forces.

I, His Majesty's historian, received at this hour orders summoning me to establish a secretaries' station to observe the sea battle at His Majesty's side and note, as they occurred, all actions of the Empire's officers deserving of valorous commendation. I was able, however, before repairing to this post, to remain at the Greek's side for most of the evening. The night grew more apocalyptic with each hour. The smoke of the burning city rose thick and sulphurous across the plain; the flames from the Acropolis and the merchant and residential quarters lit the sky bright as noon. In addition, a violent quake had struck the coast, toppling numerous structures and even portions of the city walls. The atmosphere bordered upon the primordial, as if heaven and earth, as well as men, had harnessed themselves to the engines of war.

The man Xeones remained lucid and calm throughout this interval. Intelligence requested by the captain Orontes had reached the medical pavilions to the effect that the priestesses of Persephone, presumably including the captive Xeones' cousin, had evacuated themselves to Troezen across the bay. This seemed to steady the man profoundly. He appeared convinced that he would not survive the night and was distressed only insomuch as this would cut short the telling of his tale. He wished, he said, to have recorded in what hours remained as much of the conclusion of the actual battle as he could dictate. He began at once, returning in memory to the site of the Hot Gates.

The upper rim of the sun had just pierced the horizon when the party began the descent of the final cliff above the Hellenes' camp. Alexandros' and Lachides' bodies were lowered by rope, along with Suicide, whose wound in the groin had robbed him of the use of his lower limbs. Dienekes needed a rope too. We crabbed down backward. Over my shoulder I could see men packing up below, the Arkadians and Orchomenians and Mycenaeans. For a moment I thought I saw the Spartans moving out too. Could it be that Leonidas, acknowledging the futility of defense, had given the order for all to withdraw? Then my glance, instinctively turning to the man beside me on the face, met the eyes of Polynikes. He could read the wish for deliverance so transparent upon my features. He just grinned.

At the base of the Phokian Wall, what remained of the Spartans, barely above a hundred Peers yet able to fight, had already completed their gymnastics and had themselves in arms. They were dressing their hair, preparing to die.

We buried Alexandros and Lachides in the Spartan precinct beside the West Gate. Both their breastplates and helmets, Alexandros' and Lachides', were preserved aside for use; their shields Rooster and I had already stacked among the arms at the camp. No coin for the ferryman could be located among Alexandros' kit, nor did my master or I possess a surrogate. Somehow I had lost them all, that purse which the lady Arete had placed into my safekeeping upon the evening of that final county day in Lakedaemon.

"Here," Polynikes offered.

He held out, still folded in a wrap of oiled linen, the coin his wife had burnished for himself, a silver tetradrachm minted by the citizens of Elis in his honor, to commemorate his second victory at Olympia. Upon one face was stamped the image of Zeus Lord of the Thunder, with winged Nike above his right shoulder. The obverse bore a crescent of wild olive in which was centered the club and lionskin of Herakles, in honor of Sparta and Lakedaemon.

Polynikes set the coin in place himself. He had to prise Alexandros' jaws apart, on the side opposite the "boxer's lunch" of amber and euphorbia which with steadfast loyalty yet held the fractured bone immobilized. Dienekes chanted the Prayer for the Fallen; he and Polynikes slid the body, wrapped in its scarlet cloak, into the shallow trench. It took no time to cover it with dirt. Both Spartans stood.

"He was the best of us all," Polynikes said.

Lookouts were hastening in from the western peak. The Ten Thousand had been spotted; they had completed their all-night encirclement and stood now in full force six miles in the Hellenes' rear. They had already routed the Phokian defenders on the summit. The Greeks at the Gates had perhaps three hours before the Persian Immortals could complete the descent and be in position to attack.

Other messengers were arriving from the Trachis side. His Majesty's lookout throne, as the raiding party had observed last night, had been dismantled. Xerxes upon his royal chariot was advancing in person, with fresh myriads at his back, to resume the assault on the Hellenes from the fore.

The burial ground stood a considerable distance, above half a mile, from the Spartan assembly point by the Wall. As my master and Polynikes returned, the contingents of the allies tramped past, withdrawing to safety. True to his word, Leonidas had released them, all save the Spartans.

We watched the allies as they passed. First came the Mantineans, in nothing resembling order; they seemed to slouch as if all strength had left their knees and hams. No one spoke. The men were so filthy they looked like they were made of dirt. Grit caked every pore and cavity of flesh, including the creases at the pockets of their eyes and the glue of sputum that collected uncleared in the corners of their mouths. Their teeth were black; they spit, it seemed, with every fourth step and the gobs landed black upon the black earth. Some had stuck their helmets upon their heads, cocked back without thought, as if their skulls were just convenient knobs to hang the bowls upon. Most had slung theirs, nasal foremost, across the bundles of their rolled cloaks which they bore as packs across their shoulders against the biting gripcords of their slung shields. Though the dawn was still chill, the men trudged in sweat. I never saw soldiers so exhausted.

The Corinthians came next, then the Tegeates and the Opountian Lokrians, the Philiasians and the Orchomenians, intermixed with the other Arkadians and what was left of the Mycenaeans. Of eighty original hoplites of that city, eleven remained yet able to walk, with another two dozen borne prone upon litters or strapped to pole-drags drawn by the pack animals. Man leaned upon man and beast upon beast. You could not tell the concussed and the skull-fractured, those who no longer possessed the sense of who or where they were, from their fellows stricken to numbness by the horrors and strain of the past six days. Nearly every man had sustained multiple wounds, most in the legs and head; a number had been blinded; these shuffled at the sides of their brothers, hands tucked in the crook of a friend's elbow, or else trailed alongside the baggage animals, holding the end of a tether attached to the pack frame.

Past the avenues of the fallen trudged the spared, each bearing himself neither with shame nor guilt, but with that silent awe and thanksgiving of which Leonidas had spoken in the assembly following the battle at Antirhion. That these warriors yet drew breath was not their own doing and they knew it; they were no more nor less brave or virtuous than their fallen fellows, just luckier. This knowledge expressed itself with a poet's eloquence in the blank and sanctified weariness inscribed upon their features.

"I hope we don't look as bad as you," Dienekes grunted to a captain of the Philiasians as he passed.

"You look worse, brothers."

Someone had set the bathhouses and the spa compound on fire. The air had stilled and the wet wood burned with acrid sullenness. The smoke and stink of these blazes now added their cheerless component to the already baleful scene. The column of warriors emerged out of smoke and sank again within it. Men threw the rags of their discarded kit, blood-begrimed cloaks and tunics, used-up packs and gear bundles; everything that would burn was flung willy-nilly upon the flame. It was as if the allies withdrawing intended to abandon not so much as a scrap to the enemy's use. They lightened their loads and marched out.

Men held out their hands to the Spartans as they strode by, touching palm to palm, fingers to fingers. A warrior of the Corinthians gave Polynikes his spear. Another handed Dienekes his sword. "Give them hell, fuckers."

Passing the spring, we came upon Rooster. He was pulling out too. Dienekes drew up and stopped to take his hand. No shame stood upon Rooster's face. Clearly he felt he had discharged his duty and more, and the liberty with which Leonidas had gifted him was in his eyes no more than his birthright, which had been denied him all his life and now, long overdue, had been fairly and honorably won by his own hand. He clasped Dienekes' hand and promised to speak with Agathe and Paraleia when he reached Lakedaemon. He would inform them of the valor with which Alexandros and Olympieus had fought and with what honor they had fallen. Rooster would make report to the lady Arete too. "If I may," he requested, "I would like to honor Alexandros before I go."

Dienekes thanked him and told him where the grave lay. To my surprise, Polynikes took Rooster's hand too. "The gods love a bastard," he said.

Rooster informed us that Leonidas had freed with honor all the helots of the battle train. We could see a group of a dozen now, passing out among the warriors of Tegea. "Leonidas has released the squires as well," Rooster declared, "and all the foreigners who serve the army." He addressed my master. "That means Suicide—and Xeo too."

Behind Rooster the train of allied contingents continued their march-out.

"Will you hold him now, Dienekes?" Rooster asked.

He meant me.

My master did not look in my direction but spoke in reply toward Rooster. "I have never compelled Xeo's service. Nor do I now."

He drew up and turned to me. The sun had fully risen; east, by the Wall, the trumpets were sounding. "One of us," he said, "should crawl out of this hole alive." He ordered me to depart with Rooster.

I refused.

"You have a wife and children!" Rooster seized my shoulders, gesturing with passion to Dienekes and Polynikes. "Theirs is not your city. You owe it nothing."

I told him the decision had been made years ago.

"You see?" Dienekes addressed Rooster, indicating me. "He never had good sense."

Back at the Wall we saw Dithyrambos. His Thespaians had refused Leonidas' order. To a man they disdained to withdraw, but insisted upon abiding and dying with the Spartans. There were about two hundred of them. Not a man among their squires would pull out either. Fully four score of the freed Spartan squires and helots stood fast as well. The seer Megistias had likewise scorned to retreat. Of the original three hundred Peers, all were present or dead save two. Aristodemos, who had served as envoy at Athens and Rhodes, and Eurytus, a champion wrestler, had both been stricken with an inflammation of the eyes that rendered them sightless. They had been evacuated to Alpenoi. The *katalogos*, the muster roll, of survivors marshaling at the Wall numbered just above five hundred.

As for Suicide, my master before departing to bury Alexandros had commanded him to remain here at the Wall, upon a litter. Dienekes apparently had anticipated the squires' release; he had left orders for Suicide to be borne off with their column to safety. Now here the Scythian stood, on his feet, grinning ghoulishly as his master returned, himself armored in corselet and breastplate with his loins cinched in linen and bound with leather straps from a pack mount. "I can't shit," he pronounced, "but by hell's flame, I can still fight."

The ensuing hour was consumed with the commanders reconfiguring the contingent into a front of sufficient breadth and depth, remarshaling the disparate elements into units and assigning officers. Among the Spartans, those squires and helots remaining were simply absorbed into the platoons of the Peers they served. They would fight no longer as auxiliaries but take their places in bronze within the phalanx. There was no shortage of armor, only of weapons, so many had been shivered or smashed in the preceding forty-eight hours. Two dumps of spares were established, one at the Wall and the second a furlong to the rear, halfway to a small partially fortified hillock, the most natural site for a beleaguered force to rally upon and make its last stand. These dumps were nothing grand—just swords stuck blade-first into the dirt and eight-footers jammed beside them, lizard-stickers down.

Leonidas summoned the men to assembly. This was done without so much as a shout, so few yet stood upon the site. The camp itself seemed suddenly broad and capacious. As for the dance floor before the Wall, its sundered turf lay yet littered with Persian corpses by the thousand as the enemy had left the second day's casualties to rot upon the field. Those wounded who had survived the night now groaned with their last strength, crying for aid and water, and many for the merciful stroke of extinction. For the allies the prospect of fighting again, out there upon that farmer's field of hell, seemed more than thought could bear.

This, too, was Leonidas' decision. It had been agreed among the commanders, the king now informed the warriors, no longer to fight in sallies from behind the Wall as in the previous two days but instead to put its stones at the defenders' backs and advance in a body into the widest part of the pass, there to engage the enemy, the allied scores against the Empire's myriads. The king's intent was that each man sell his life as dearly as possible.

Just as order of battle was being assigned, a herald's trumpet of the enemy sounded from beyond the Narrows. Under a banner of parley a party of four Persian riders in their most brilliant armor picked their way across the carpet of carnage and reined in directly beneath the Wall. Leonidas had been wounded in both legs and could barely hobble. With painful effort he mounted the battlement; the troops climbed with him; the whole force, what there was of it, looked down on the horsemen from atop the Wall.

The envoy was Ptammitechus, the Egyptian marine Tommie. This time his young son did not accompany him as interpreter; that function was performed by an officer of the Persians. Both their mounts, and the two heralds', were balking violently amid the underfoot corpses. Before Tommie could commence his speech, Leonidas cut him off.

"The answer is no," he called down from the Wall.

"You haven't heard the offer."

"Fuck the offer," Leonidas cried with a grin. "And yourself, sir, along with it!"

The Egyptian laughed, his smile flashing as brilliantly as ever. He strained against the reins of his spooking horse. "Xerxes does not want your lives, sir," Tommie called. "Only your arms."

Leonidas laughed. "Tell him to come and get them."

With a wheel-about, the king terminated the interview. Despite his carved-up legs he disdained help dismounting the Wall. He whistled up the assembly. Atop the stones the Spartans and Thespaians watched the Persian envoys rein their mounts about and withdraw.

Behind the Wall, Leonidas again took station before the assembly.

The triceps muscle in his left arm had been severed; he would fight today with his shield strapped with leather across his shoulder. The Spartan king's demeanor nonetheless could only be described as cheerful. His eyes shone and his voice carried easily with force and command.

"Why do we remain in this place? A man would have to be cracked not to ask that question. Is it for glory? If it were for that alone, believe me, brothers, I'd be the first to wheel my ass to the foe and trot like hell over that hill."

Laughter greeted this from the king. He let the swell subside, raising his good arm for silence.

"If we had withdrawn from these Gates today, brothers, no matter what prodigies of valor we had performed up till now, this battle would have been perceived as a defeat. A defeat which would have confirmed for all Greece that which the enemy most wishes her to believe: the futility of resistance to the Persian and his millions. If we had saved our skins today, one by one the separate cities would have caved in behind us, until the whole of Hellas had fallen."

The men listened soberly, knowing the king's assessment accurately reflected reality.

"But by our deaths here with honor, in the face of these insuperable odds, we transform vanquishment into victory. With our lives we sow courage in the hearts of our allies and the brothers of our armies left behind. They are the ones who will ultimately produce victory, not us. It was never in the stars for us. Our role today is what we all knew it was when we embraced our wives and children and turned our feet upon the march-out: to stand and die. That we have sworn and that we will perform."

The king's belly grumbled, loudly, of hunger; from the front ranks laughter broke the assembly's sober mien and rippled to the rear. Leonidas motioned with a grin to the squires preparing bread, urging them to snap it up.

"Our allied brothers are on the road to home now." The king gestured down the track, the road that ran to southern Greece and safety. "We must cover their withdrawal; otherwise the enemy's cavalry will roll unimpeded through these Gates and ride our comrades down before they've gotten ten miles. If we can hold a few hours more, our brothers will be safe."

He inquired if any among the assembly wished also to speak.

Alpheus stepped to the fore. "I'm hungry too so I'll keep it short." He drew up shyly, in the unwonted role of speaker. I realized for the first time that his brother, Maron, stood nowhere among the ranks. This hero had died during the night, I heard a man whisper, of wounds sustained the previous day.

Alpheus spoke quickly, unblessed by the orator's gift but graced simply with the sincerity of his heart. "In one way only have the gods permitted mortals to surpass them. Man may give that which the gods cannot, all he possesses, his life. My own I set down with joy, for you, friends, who have become the brother I no longer possess."

He turned abruptly and melted back into the ranks.

The men began calling for Dithyrambos. The Thespaian stepped forth with his usual profane glint. He gestured toward the pass beyond the Narrows, where the advance parties of the Persians had arrived and begun staking out the marshaling salients for the army. "Just go out there," he proclaimed, "and have fun!"

Dark laughter cut the assembly. Several others of the Thespaians spoke. They were more curt than the Spartans. When they finished, Polynikes stepped to the front.

"It is no hard thing for a man raised under the laws of Lykurgus to offer up his life for his country. For me and for these Spartans, all of whom have living sons, and who have known since boyhood that this was the end they were called to, it is an act of completion before the gods."

He turned solemnly toward the Thespaians and the freed squires and helots.

"But for you, brothers and friends . . . for you who will this day see all extinguished forever . . ."

The runner's voice cracked and broke. He choked and blew snot into his hand in lieu of the tears to whose issue his will refused to permit. For long moments he could not summon speech. He motioned for his shield; it was passed to him. He displayed it aloft.

"This *aspis* was my father's and his father's before him. I have sworn before God to die before another man took this from my hand."

He crossed to the ranks of the Thespaians, to a man, an obscure warrior among them. Into the fellow's grasp he placed the shield.

The man accepted it, moved profoundly, and presented his own to Polynikes. Another followed, and another, until twenty, thirty shields had traded hands. Others exchanged armor and helmets with the freed squires and helots. The black cloaks of the Thespaians and the scarlet of the Lakedaemonians intermingled until all distinction between the nations had been effaced.

The men called for Dienekes. They wanted a quip, a wisecrack, something short and pithy as he was known for. He resisted. You could see he did not wish to speak.

"Brothers, I'm not a king or a general. I've never held rank beyond that of a platoon commander. So I say to you now only what I would say to my own men, knowing the fear that stands unspoken in each heart—not of death, but worse, of faltering or failing, of somehow proving unworthy in this, the ultimate hour."

These words had struck the mark; one could read it plain on the faces of the silent, raptly attending men.

"Here is what you do, friends. Forget country. Forget king. Forget wife and children and freedom. Forget every concept, however noble, that you imagine you fight for here today. Act for this alone: for the man who stands at your shoulder. He is everything, and everything is contained within him. That's all I know. That's all I can tell you."

He finished and stepped back. At the rear of the assembly a commotion was heard. The ranks rustled; into view emerged the Spartan Eurytus. This was the man, stricken with field blindness, who had been evacuated to Alpenoi village, along with the envoy Aristodemos, felled by this same inflammation. Now Eurytus returned, sightless, yet armed and in armor, led by his squire. Without a word he steered himself into place among the ranks.

The men, whose courage had already been high, felt this now refire and redouble.

Leonidas stepped forth now and reassumed the *skeptron* of command. He proposed that the Thespaian captains take these final moments to commune in private with their own countrymen, while he spoke apart for the Spartans alone.

The men of the two cities divided, each to its own. There remained just over two hundred Peers and freedmen of Lakedaemon. These assembled, without regard to rank or station, compactly about their king. All knew Leonidas would address appeals to nothing so grand as liberty or law or the preservation of Hellas from the tyrant's yoke.

Instead he spoke, in words few and plain, of the valley of the Eurotas, of Parnon and Taygetos and the cluster of five unwalled villages which alone comprise that *polis* and commonwealth which the world calls Sparta. A thousand years from now, Leonidas declared, two thousand, three thousand years hence, men a hundred generations yet unborn may for their private purposes make journey to our country.

"They will come, scholars perhaps, or travelers from beyond the sea, prompted by curiosity regarding the past or appetite for knowledge of the ancients. They will peer out across our plain and probe among the stone and rubble of our nation. What will they learn of us? Their shovels will unearth neither brilliant palaces nor temples; their picks will prise forth no everlasting architecture or art. What will remain of the Spartans? Not monuments of marble or bronze, but this, what we do here today."

Out beyond the Narrows the enemy trumpets sounded. Clearly now could be seen the vanguard of the Persians and the chariots and armored convoys of their King.

"Now eat a good breakfast, men. For we'll all be sharing dinner in hell."

BOOK EIGHT

THERMOPYLAE

THIRTY-FIVE

His Majesty witnessed at close range, with His own eyes, the magnificent valor demonstrated by the Spartans, Thespaians and their emancipated squires and servants upon this, the final morning of defense of the pass. He has no need of my recounting the events of this battle. I will report only those instances and moments which may have escaped the notice of His Majesty's vantage, again, as he has requested, to shed light upon the character of the Hellenes he there called his enemy.

Foremost among all, and indisputable in claim to preeminence, may be only one man, the Spartan king, Leonidas. As His Majesty knows, the main force of the Persian army, advancing as it had on the previous two days along the track from Trachis, did not commence its assault until long after the sun was fully up. The hour of attack in fact was closer to midday than morning and came while the Ten Thousand Immortals had not yet made their appearance in the allied rear. Such was Leonidas' disdain for death that he actually slept for most of this interval. Snoozed might be a more apt description, so free from care was the posture the king assumed upon the earth, cushioned upon his cloak as a ground cloth, legs crossed at the ankles, arms folded across his breast, his eyes shaded by a straw sun hat and his head pillowed insouciantly upon the bowl of his shield. He might have been a boy, herding goats in some sleepy summer dale.

Of what does the nature of kingship consist? What are its qualities in itself; what the qualities it inspires in those who attend it? These, if one may presume to divine the meditations of His Majesty's heart, are the questions which most preoccupy his own reason and reflection.

Does His Majesty recall that moment, upon the slope beyond the Narrows, after Leonidas had fallen, struck through with half a dozen lances, blinded beneath his helmet staved in from the blow of a battle-axe, his left arm useless with its splintered shield lashed to his shoulder, when he fell at last under the crush of the enemy? Can His Majesty recall that surge within the melee of slaughter when a corps of Spartans hurled themselves into the teeth of the vaunting foe and flung them back, to retrieve the corpse of their king? I refer neither to the first time nor the second or third, but the fourth, when there stood fewer than a hundred of them, Peers and Knights and freedmen, dueling an enemy massed in their thousands.

I will tell His Majesty what a king is. A king does not abide within his tent while his men bleed and die upon the field. A king does not dine while his men go hungry, nor sleep when they stand at watch upon the wall. A king does not command his men's loyalty through fear nor purchase it with gold; he earns their love by the sweat of his own back and the pains he endures for their sake. That which comprises the harshest burden, a king lifts first and sets down last. A king does not require service of those he leads but provides it to them. He serves them, not they him.

In the final moments before the actual commencement of battle, when the lines of the Persians and Medes and Sacae, the Bactrians and Illyrians, Egyptians and Macedonians, lay so close across from the defenders that their individual faces could be seen, Leonidas moved along the Spartan and Thespaian foreranks, speaking with each platoon commander individually. When he stopped beside Dienekes, I was close enough to hear his words.

"Do you hate them, Dienekes?" the king asked in the tone of a comrade, unhurried, conversational, gesturing to those captains and officers of the Persians proximately visible across the *oudenos chorion*, the no-man's-land.

Dienekes answered at once that he did not. "I see faces of gentle and noble bearing. More than a few, I think, whom one would welcome with a clap and a laugh to any table of friends."

Leonidas clearly approved my master's answer. His eyes seemed, however, darkened with sorrow.

"I am sorry for them," he avowed, indicating the valiant foemen who stood so proximately across. "What wouldn't they give, the noblest among them, to stand here with us now?"

That is a king, Your Majesty. A king does not expend his substance to enslave men, but by his conduct and example makes them free. His Majesty may ask, as Rooster did, and the lady Arete, why one such as I whose station could most grandly be called service and most meanly slavery, why one of such condition would die for those not of his kin and country. The answer is, they were my kin and country. I set down my life with gladness, and would do it again a hundred times, for Leonidas, for Dienekes and Alexandros and Polynikes, for Rooster and Suicide, for Arete and Diomache, Bruxieus and my own mother and father, my wife and children. I and every man there were never more free than when we gave freely obedience to those harsh laws which take life and give it back again.

Those events of the actual battle I count as nothing, for the fight was over in its profoundest sense before it began. I had slept, sitting upright against the Wall, following Leonidas' example, while we waited that hour and the hour after and the hour after that for His Majesty's army to make its move.

In my doze I discovered myself again among the hills above the city of my childhood. I was no longer a boy but myself of grown years. My cousin was there, in years still a girl, and our dogs, Lucky and Happy, exactly as they had been in the days following the sack of Astakos. Diomache had given chase to a hare and was climbing, bare-legged with extraordinary swiftness, a slope which seemed to ascend to the heavens. Bruxieus waited atop, as did my mother and father: I knew, though I could not see them. I gave chase too, seeking to overtake Diomache with all my grown strength. I could not. However swiftly I mounted, she remained ever elusive, always an interval ahead, calling to me gaily, teasingly, that I would never run fast enough to catch her.

I came awake with a start. There awaited the massed Persians, less than a bowshot away.

Leonidas stood upon his feet, out front. Dienekes as always took his stance before his platoon, which was drawn up at seven-and-three, wider and shallower than on either previous day. My place was third in the second file, for the first time in my life without my bow but clutching instead in my right hand the heavy haft of the eight-footer which had last been Doreion's. Around my left forearm, braced tight against the elbow, stood wrapped the linen-cushioned bronze sleeve bolted through the oak and the bronze facing of the *aspis* which had been Alexandros'. The helmet I wore had belonged to Lachides and the cap beneath had been that of Ariston's squire, Demades.

"Eyes on me!" Dienekes barked, and the men as always tore their glance from the enemy, who marshaled now so near across the interval that we could see the irises beneath their lashes and the gaps between their teeth. There were ungodly numbers of them. My lungs howled for air; I could feel the blood pounding within my temples and read its pulse upon the vessels of the eyes. My limbs were stone; I could feel neither hands nor feet. I prayed with every fiber, simply for the courage not to faint. Suicide stood upon my left. Dienekes stood before.

At last came the fight, which was like a tide, and within which one felt as a wave beneath the storming whims of the gods, waiting for their fancy to prescribe the hour of his extinction. Time collapsed. Elements blurred and merged. I remember one surge carrying the Spartans forward, driving the enemy by the score into the sea, and another which propelled the phalanx rearward like boats lashed gunwale-to-gunwale driven before the irresistible storm. I recall my feet, planted solid with all my strength upon the earth slick with blood and urine, as they were driven rearward, in place before the push of the foe, like the fleece-wrapped soles of a boy playing upon the mountain ice.

I saw Alpheus take on a Persian chariot single-handedly, slaying general, henchman and both flank guardsmen. When he fell, shot through the throat by a Persian arrow, Dienekes dragged him out. He got up, still fighting. I saw Polynikes and Derkylides hauling Leonidas' corpse, each with a weaponless hand upon the shoulders of the king's shattered corselet, striking at the foe with their shields as they drew back. The Spartans re-formed and rushed, fell back and broke, then re-formed again. I killed a man of the Egyptians with the butt-spike of my shivered spear as he drove his own into the wall of my guts, then an instant later, falling under the blow of an axe, clawed free over a Spartan corpse, only to recognize, beneath its hacked-open helmet, the shattered face of Alpheus.

Suicide hauled me from the fray. At last the Ten Thousand Immortals could be seen, advancing in line of battle to complete their envelopment. What remained of the Spartans and Thespaians fell rearward from the plain, to the Narrows, pouring through the sally-ports of the Wall toward the final hillock.

The allies were so few now, and their weapons so spent and broken, that the Persians made bold to attack with cavalry, as they would in a rout. Suicide fell. His right foot had been chopped off. "Put me on your back!" he commanded. I knew without more words what he meant. I could hear arrows and even javelins thrumming into his yet-living flesh, shielding me as I bore him.

I saw Dienekes yet alive, slinging away one shattered *xiphos* and poring through the dirt for another. Polynikes churned past me, carrying Telamonias hobbled beside him. Half the runner's face had been sheared off; blood gushed in sheets from the opened bone of his cheek. "The dump!" he was calling, meaning that magazine of weapons which Leonidas had ordered placed in reserve behind the Wall. I felt the tissue of my belly tear and the intestines begin to spill. Suicide hung life-spent upon my back. I turned rearward toward the Narrows. Persian and Median archers in their thousands hailed bronzeheads down upon the retreating Spartans and Thespaians. Those who reached the dump were shredded like pennants in a gale.

The defenders staggered toward the knoll upon which the last stack of weapons had been cached. No more than sixty remained; Derkylides, astonishingly unwounded, rallied the survivors into a circular front. I found a strap and cinched my guts in. I was struck, for just a moment, with the impossible beauty of the day. For once no haze obscured the channel; one could make out individual stones upon the hills across the strait and track the game trails up the slopes, turn by turn.

I saw Dienekes reel beneath the blow of an axe, but had not

myself the strength to rally to him. Medes and Persians, Bactrians and Sacae, were not merely pouring over the Wall but dismantling it with a frenzy. I could see horses beyond. The officers of the foe no longer required whips to drive their men forward. Over the broken stones of the Wall thundered the horsemen of His Majesty's cavalry, followed by the bucking chariots of his generals.

The Immortals marshaled round about the hillock now, pouring bowfire point-blank into the Spartans and Thespaians crouched beneath the slender shelter of their shattered and staved-in shields. Derkylides led the rush upon them. I saw him fall, and Dienekes, fighting beside him. Neither had shields, nor for all that could be seen, weapons of any kind. They went down not like heroes of Homer crashing clamorously within the carapaces of their armor, but like commanders completing their last and dirtiest job.

The enemy stood, invincible in the might of their missile fire, but somehow the Spartans reached them. They fought without shields, with only swords and then bare hands and teeth. Polynikes went after an officer. The runner still had his legs. So swiftly did he cross the space at the base of the hillock that his hands found the foe's throat even as a storm of Persian steel tore his back apart.

The last few dozen upon the hillock, rallied now by Dithyrambos, both of whose arms had been shredded by enemy fire and hung now useless at his sides, pincushioned with bolts, sought to form a front for a final rush. Chariots and Persian horsemen stampeded pell-mell into the Spartans. A battle waggon, afire, rolled over both my legs. Before the defenders, completely encircling the hillock, the Immortals had formed now in bowmen's ranks. Their bolts thundered upon the last unarmed and shattered warriors. From their rear, more archers hurled volleys over the heads of their comrades to rain upon the last survivors among the Hellenes. Backs and bellies bristled with the fletched spines of arrow butts; shot-to-pieces men sprawled in rag piles of bronze and scarlet.

The ear could hear His Majesty bawling orders, so near at hand ranged he upon his chariot. Was he calling in his foreign tongue for his men to cease fire, to capture the final defenders alive? Were those to whom he cried the marines of Egypt, under their captain, Ptammitechus, who spurned their monarch's order and rushed in to gift what Spartans and Thespaians they could reach with the final boon of death? It was impossible to see or hear within the tumult. The marines parted toward the flanks. The fury of the Persian archers redoubled as they sought with the numberless shafts of their fusillades to extinguish at last the stubborn foe who had made them pay so dearly for this mean measure of dirt.

As when a hailstorm descends unseasonably from the mountains and hurls from the sky its icy pellets upon the husbandman's newly sprouted crop, so did the bolts of the Persians in their myriads thunder down upon the Spartans and Thespaians. Now the farmer assumes his anxious station in the doorway, hearing the deluge upon the tiles of the roof, watching its bullets of ice clatter and rebound upon the stones of the walk. How fare the sprouts of spring barley? One here and there survives, as if by miracle, and holds yet its head aloft. But the planter knows this state of clemency cannot endure. He turns his face away, in obedience to the laws of God, while without, beneath the storm, the final shaft breaks and falls, overwhelmed by the insuperable onslaught of heaven.

THIRTY-SIX

Such was the end of Leonidas and the defenders of the pass at Thermopylae, as related by the Greek Xeones and compiled in transcription by His Majesty's historian Gobartes the son of Artabazos and completed the fourth day of Arahsamnu, Year Five of His Majesty's Accession.

This date, in the bitter irony of God Ahura Mazda, was the same upon which the naval forces of the Persian Empire suffered the calamitous defeat at the hands of the Hellenic fleet, in the Straits of Salamis, off Athens, that catastrophe which sent to their deaths so many valiant sons of the East and, by its consequences for the supply and support of the army, doomed the entire campaign to disaster.

That oracle of Apollo delivered earlier to the Athenians, which declared,

"The wooden wall alone shall not fail you,"

had revealed its fateful truth, the timbered stronghold manifesting itself not as that ancient palisade of the Athenian Acropolis so speedily overrun by His Majesty's forces, but as a wall of ships' hulls and the sailors and marines of Hellas who manned them so superbly, dealing the death blow to His Majesty's ambitions of conquest.

The magnitude of the calamity effaced all consideration of the captive Xeones and his tale. Care of the man himself was forsaken amid the chaos of defeat, as every physician and tender of the Royal Surgeon's staff made haste to the shore opposite Salamis, there to minister to the myriad wounded of the imperial armada, washed up amid the charred and splintered wreckage of their vessels of war.

When darkness at last brought surcease from the slaughter, a greater terror seized the Empire's camp. This was of the wrath of His Majesty. So many officers of the court were being put to the sword, or so my notes recall, that the Historian's staff cried quits to the task of recording their names.

Terror overran the pavilions of His Majesty, heightened not only by the great quake which shook the city precisely at the hour of sunset but also by the apocalyptic aspect of the siting of the army's bivouac, there within the razed and still-smoldering city of the Athenians. Midway through the second watch the general Mardonius sealed His Majesty's chamber and debarred entry to any further officers. His Majesty's Historian was able to procure only the scantiest of instructions as to the disposition of the day's records. Upon dismissal, I inquired purely as an afterthought for orders concerning the Greek Xeones and his papers.

"Kill him," the general Mardonius replied without hesitation, "and burn every page of that compilation of falsehoods, whose recording has been folly from the first and the merest mention of which at this hour will serve only to drive His Majesty into further paroxysms of rage."

Other duties held me several hours. These at length completed, I proceeded in search of Orontes, captain of the Immortals, whose responsibility it must be to carry out these orders of Mardonius. I located the officer upon the shore. He was clearly in a state of exhaustion, overwrought both with the grief of the day's defeat and with his own frustration as a soldier at being unable, other than by pulling dying sailors out of the water, to aid the valiant mariners of the fleet. Orontes composed himself at once, however, and turned his attention to the matter at hand.

"If you'd like to find your head still upon your shoulders tomorrow," the captain declared when he had been informed of the general's order, "you will pretend you never heard or saw Mardonius."

I protested that the order had been issued in the name of His Majesty. It could not be ignored.

"It can't, can't it? And what will be the general's story tomorrow or a month hence, after his order has been carried out, when His Majesty sends for you and asks to see the Greek and his notes?

"I will tell you what will happen," the captain continued. "Even now in His Majesty's chambers, His chancellors and ministers press upon Him the necessity to withdraw the Royal Person, to take ship for Asia, as Mardonius has urged before. This time I think His Majesty will take heed."

Orontes declared his conviction that His Majesty would order the bulk of the army to remain in Hellas, under command of the general Mardonius and charged to complete the conquest of Greece in His name. That task accomplished, His Majesty will possess His victory. Today's calamity will be forgotten in that bright glow of triumph.

"Then in the delectation of conquest," Orontes continued, "His Majesty will call for these notes of the Greek Xeones, as a sweetcake to cap the banquet of victory. If you and I stand before Him empty-handed, which of us will point the finger at Mardonius, and who will believe our declarations of innocence?"

I asked then what we must do.

Orontes' heart was clearly torn. Memory recalled that he, as chief field commander of the Immortals beneath Hydarnes, their general, had strode in the van during the Ten Thousand's night envelopment of the Spartans and Thespaians at Thermopylae and had served with extraordinary valor in the final morning's assault, facing the Spartans hand-to-hand and securing for His Majesty the conquest of the foe. Orontes' own arrows had been among those fatal shafts flung at close range into the final defenders, perhaps into the flesh of the very men whose histories had been recounted within the captive Xeones' tale.

This knowledge, one could not help but read upon the captain's countenance, increased further his reluctance to deal harm to this man with whom he so clearly identified as a fellow soldier and even, one must at this point state, a friend.

All this notwithstanding, Orontes summoned himself to duty. He dispatched two officers of the Immortals with orders to remove the Greek from the Surgeon's tent and deliver him at once to the staff pavilion of the Immortals. After several hours attending to other more urgent business, he and I proceeded to that site. We walked in together. The man Xeones sat up conscious upon his litter, though drawn and gravely enfeebled.

Clearly he divined our purpose. His aspect was one of good cheer. "Come, gentlemen," he spoke before I or Orontes could give voice to our mission. "How may I assist you in your task?" His dispatch would not require the blade, he adjudged. "For the stroke of a feather, I feel, will be blow enough to finish the job."

Orontes inquired of the Greek Xeones if he grasped fully the magnitude of the victory his countrymen's navy had achieved this day. The man affirmed that he did. He expressed the opinion, however, that the war was far from over. The issue remained very much in doubt.

Orontes imparted his extreme reluctance to carry out the sentence of execution. In light of the present disorder within the Empire's camp, he declared it a matter of slender difficulty to spirit the fellow out unobserved. Did the man Xeones, Orontes inquired, possess friends or compatriots yet within Attika to whom we could deliver him? The captive smiled. "Your army has done an admirable job of driving any such off," he observed. "And besides, His Majesty will need all His men to bear more important baggage."

Yet did Orontes seek any excuse to postpone the moment of execution. "Since you ask no favor of us, sir," the captain addressed the prisoner, "may I request one of you?"

The man replied that he would gladly grant all that remained within his power.

"You have cheated us, my friend," Orontes declared with wry expression. "Deprived us of a tale of which your master, the Spartan Dienekes, so you said, promised to speak. This was around the fire during that last hunt of which you spoke, when he and Alexandros and Ariston addressed the subject of fear. Do you remember? Your master cut off the youths' discourse with a pledge that, when they reached the Hot Gates, he would tell them a tale of Leonidas and the lady Paraleia, on the subject of courage and of what criteria the Spartan king employed to select the Three Hundred. Or did Dienekes in fact fail to speak of this?"

No, the captive Xeones confirmed, his master had found occasion and did in truth impart this tale. But, the prisoner asked, absent His Majesty's imperative to continue documenting the events of this narrative, did the captain indeed wish to keep on?

"We whom you call foe are flesh and blood," Orontes replied, "with hearts no less capable of attachment than your own. Does it strike you as implausible that we in this tent, His Majesty's historian and myself, have come to care for you, sir, not alone as a captive relaying an account of battle but as a man and even a friend?"

Orontes requested, as a kindness to himself who had followed with keen interest and empathy the antecedent chapters of the Greek's tale, if the man would, as a comrade and so far as his strength permitted, relate to us now this final portion.

"What had the Spartan king to say of women's courage, and how did your master, Dienekes, in fact relate it to his young friends and proteges?"

The man Xeones propped himself with effort, and assistance from myself and the officers, upright upon his settle. Summoning his strength, he drew a breath and resumed:

I will impart this tale to you, my friends, as my master related it to me and to Alexandros and Ariston at the Hot Gates—not in his own voice, but in that of the lady Paraleia, Alexandros' mother, who recounted it in her own words to Dienekes and the lady Arete, only hours after its occurrence.

The time of the conveying of the lady Paraleia's tale was an evening three or four days before the march-out from Lakedaemon to the Hot Gates. The lady Paraleia had betaken herself for this purpose to the home of Dienekes and Arete, bringing with her several other women, all mothers and wives of warriors selected for the Three Hundred. None of the women knew what the lady wished to say. My master stood on the moment of excusing himself, that the ladies may have their privacy. Paraleia, however, requested that he remain. He must hear this too, she said. The ladies seated themselves about Paraleia. She began:

"What I tell you now, Dienekes, you must not repeat to my son. Not until you reach the Hot Gates, and not then, until the proper moment. That hour may be, if the gods so ordain, that of your own death or his. You will know it when it comes. Now attend closely, Dienekes, and you, ladies.

"This forenoon I received a summons from the king. I went at once, presenting myself within the courtyard of his home. I was early; Leonidas had not arrived from his business of organizing the march-out. His queen, Gorgo, however, awaited upon a bench in the shade of a plane tree, apparently intentionally. She welcomed me and bade me sit. We were alone, absent all servants and attendants.

" 'You are wondering, Paraleia,' she began, 'why my husband has sent for you. I will tell you. He wishes to address your heart, and what he imagines must be your feelings of injustice at being singled out, so to speak, to bear a double grief. He is keenly aware that in selecting for the Three Hundred both Olympieus and Alexandros he has robbed you twice, of son as well as husband, leaving only the babe Olympieus to carry on your line. He will speak to this when he comes. But first, I must confide in you from my own heart, woman-to-woman.'

"She is quite young, our queen, and looked tall and lovely, though in that shadowed light exceedingly grave.

" 'I have been daughter of one king and now wife to another,' Gorgo said. 'Women envy my station but few grasp its stern obligations. A queen may not be a woman as others. She may not possess her husband or children as other wives and mothers, but may hold them only in stewardship to her nation. She serves them, the hearts of her countrymen, not her own or her family's. Now you too, Paraleia, are summoned to this stern sisterhood. You must take your place at my shoulder in sorrow. This is women's trial and triumph, ordained by God: to abide with pain, to endure grief, to bear up beneath sorrow's yoke and thus to endow others with courage.'

"Hearing these words of the queen, I confess to you, Dienekes, and you, ladies, that my hands trembled so that I feared I may not command them—not alone with the foreknowledge of grief but of rage as well, blind bitter fury at Leonidas and the heartlessness with which he decanted the double measure of sorrow into my cup. Why me? my heart cried in anger. I stood upon the moment of giving voice to this outrage when the sound of the gate opening came from the outer court, and in a moment Leonidas himself entered. He had just come from the marshaling ground and bore his dusty footgear in his hand. Perceiving his lady and myself in intimate converse, he divined at once the subject of our intercourse.

"With apology for his tardiness he sat, thanking me for presenting myself so punctually and inquiring after my ailing father and others of our family. Though it was plain he bore a thousand burdens of the army and the state, not excepting the prescience of his own imminent death and the bereavement of his beloved wife and children, yet as he took his bench he dismissed all from his mind and addressed himself to me alone with undiverted attention.

" 'Do you hate me, lady?' These were his initial words. 'Were I you, I would. My hands would now be trembling with fury hard-suppressed.' He cleared a space upon his bench. 'Come, daughter. Sit here beside me.'

"I obeyed. The lady Gorgo moved subtly closer upon her settle. I could smell the king's sweat of his exercise and feel the warmth of his flesh beside me as, when a girl, I had known my own father's when he had called me to his counsel. Again the heart's surfeit of grief and anger threatened to take me out of hand. I fought this back with all my force.

" 'The city speculates and guesses,' Leonidas resumed, 'as to why I elected those I did to the Three Hundred. Was it for their prowess as individual men-at-arms? How could this be, when among champions such as Polynikes, Dienekes, Alpheus and Maron I nominated as well unblooded youths such as Ariston and your own Alexandros? Perhaps, the city supposes, I divined some subtle alchemy of this unique aggregation. Maybe I was bribed, or paying back favors. I will never tell the city why I appointed these three hundred. I will never tell the Three Hundred themselves. But I now tell you.

" 'I chose them not for their own valor, lady, but for that of their women.'

"At these words of the king a cry of anguish escaped my breast, as I understood before he spoke what further he would now say. I felt his hand about my shoulder, comforting me.

" 'Greece stands now upon her most perilous hour. If she saves herself, it will not be at the Gates (death alone awaits us and our allies there) but later, in battles yet to come, by land and sea. Then Greece, if the gods will it, will preserve herself. Do you understand this, lady? Well. Now listen.

" 'When the battle is over, when the Three Hundred have gone down to death, then will all Greece look to the Spartans, to see how they bear it.

" 'But who, lady, who will the Spartans look to? To you. To you and the other wives and mothers, sisters and daughters of the fallen.

" 'If they behold your hearts riven and broken with grief, they, too, will break. And Greece will break with them. But if you bear up, dry-eyed, not alone enduring your loss but seizing it with contempt for its agony and embracing it as the honor that it is in truth, then Sparta will stand. And all Hellas will stand behind her.

" 'Why have I nominated you, lady, to bear up beneath this most terrible of trials, you and your sisters of the Three Hundred? Because you can.'

"From my lips sprang these words, reproving the king: 'And is this the reward of women's virtue, Leonidas? To be afflicted twice over, and bear a double grief?'

"On this instant the queen Gorgo reached for me, to offer succor. Leonidas held her back. Instead, yet securing my shoulder within the grasp of his warm arm, he addressed my outburst of anguish.

" 'My wife reaches for you, Paraleia, to impart by her touch intelligence of the burden she has borne without plaint all her life. This has ever been denied her, to be simply bride to Leonidas, but always she must be wife to Lakedaemon. This now is your role as well, lady. No longer may you be wife to Olympieus or mother to Alexandros, but must serve as wife and mother of our nation. You and your sisters of the Three Hundred are the mothers now of all Greece, and of freedom itself. This is stern duty, Paraleia, to which I have called my own beloved wife, the mother of my children, and have now as well summoned you. Tell me, lady. Was I wrong?'

"Upon these words of the king, all self-command fled my heart. I broke down, weeping. Leonidas pulled me to him in kindness; I buried my face in his lap, as a girl does with her father, and sobbed, unable to constrain myself. The king held me firmly, his embrace neither stern nor unkind, but bearing me up with gentleness and solace.

"As when a wildfire upon a hillside at last consumes itself and flares no more, so my fit of grief burned itself out. A peace settled clemently upon me, as if gift not alone of that strong arm which clasped me yet in its embrace, but of some more profound source, ineffable and divine. Strength returned to my knees and courage to my heart. I rose before the king and wiped my eyes. These words I addressed to him, not of my own will it seemed, but prompted by some unseen goddess whose source and origin I could not name.

" 'Those were the last tears of mine, my lord, that the sun will ever see.' "

THIRTY-SEVEN

These were the final words spoken by the captive Xeones. The man's voice trailed off; his vital signs ebbed swiftly. Within moments he lay still and cold. His god had used him up and restored him at last to that station to which he yearned most to return, reunited with the corps of his comrades beneath the earth.

Immediately outside the captain Orontes' tent, armored elements of His Majesty's forces were clamorously withdrawing from the city. Orontes ordered the man Xeones' body borne without upon his litter. Chaos reigned. The captain was past due at his post; each succeeding moment heightened the urgency of his departure.

His Majesty will recall the state of anarchy which prevailed upon that morning. Numerous street youths and blackguards, the scum of the Athenian polity, that element of such mean station as not even to merit evacuation but who instead had been marooned by their betters and left to prowl the streets as predators, now made bold to penetrate the margins of His Majesty's camp. These villains were looting everything they could lay hands upon. As our party emerged onto that now-rubbled boulevard called by the Athenians the Sacred Way, a clutch of these felons chanced to be herded past by subalterns of His Majesty's military police.

To my astonishment the captain Orontes hailed these officers. He ordered them to release the miscreants to his charge and themselves begone. The malefactors were three in number and of the scurviest disposition imaginable. They drew themselves up before Orontes and the officers of the Immortals, clearly expecting to be executed upon the spot. I was commanded by the captain to translate.

Orontes demanded of these rogues if they were Athenians. Not citizens, they replied, but men of the city. Orontes indicated the coarsecloth wrap which draped the form of the man Xeones.

"Do you know what this garment is?"

The villains' leader, a youth not yet twenty, responded that it was the scarlet cloak of Lakedaemon, that mantle worn only by a warrior of Sparta. Clearly none of the criminals could summon explanation for the presence of the body of this man, a Hellene, here now in the charge of his Persian enemy.

Orontes interrogated the wretches further. Did they know the location, in the seaport precinct of Phaleron, of that sanctuary known as Persephone of the Veil?

The thugs replied in the affirmative.

To my further astonishment, and that of the officers as well, the captain produced from his purse three gold darics, each a month's pay for an armored infantryman, and held this treasure out to the reprobates.

"Take this man's body to that temple and remain with it until the priestesses return from their evacuation. They will know what to do with it."

Here one of the officers of the Immortals broke in to protest. "Look at these criminals, sir. They are swine! Place gold in their hands and they'll dump man and litter in the first ditch they come to."

No time remained for debate. Orontes, myself and the officers all must make haste to our stations. The captain held up, for the briefest of intervals, examining the faces of the three scoundrels before him.

"Do you love your country?" he demanded.

The villains' expressions of defiance answered for them.

Orontes indicated the form upon the litter.

"This man, with his life, has preserved it. Bear him with honor."

There we left him, the corpse of the Spartan Xeones, and in a moment were swept ourselves into the irresistible current of decampment and retreat.

THIRTY-EIGHT

There remain to be appended two final postscripts regarding the man and the manuscript which will at last round this tale into completion.

As the captain Orontes had predicted, His Majesty took ship for Asia, leaving in Greece under command of Mardonius the elite corps of the army, some 300,000 including Orontes himself and the Ten Thousand Immortals, with orders to winter in Thessaly and resume the conflict when campaigning weather returned in the spring. Come that season, so vowed the general Mardonius, the irresistible might of His Majesty's army would once and for all deliver into subjection the whole of Hellas. I myself remained, in the capacity of historian, upon station with this corps.

At last in the spring His Majesty's land forces faced the Hellenes in battle upon that plain adjacent to the Greek city of Plataea, a day's march northwest of Athens.

Across from the 300,000 of Persia, Media, Bactria, India, the Sacae and the Hellenes conscripted under His Majesty's banner stood 100,000 free Greeks, the main force comprised of the full Spartan army—5000 Peers, plus the Lakedaemonian perioikoi, armed squires and helots to a total of 75,000—flanked by the hoplite militia of their Peloponnesian allies, the Tegeates. The army's strength was completed by lesser-numbered contingents from a dozen other Greek states, foremost among whom stood the Athenians, to the number of 8000, upon the left.

One need not recount the particulars of that calamitous defeat, so grimly familiar are they to His Majesty, nor the details of the appalling losses to famine and disease of the flower of the Empire upon the long retreat to Asia. It may suffice to note, from the perspective of an eyewitness, that everything the man Xeones had forecast proved true. Our warriors beheld again that line of lambdas upon the interleaved shields of Lakedaemon, not this time in breadth of fifty or sixty as in the confines of the Hot Gates, but ten thousand across and eight deep, as Xeones had *described them, an invincible tide of bronze and scarlet. The courage of the men of Persia once again proved no match for the valor and magnificent discipline of these warriors of Lakedaemon fighting to preserve their nation's freedom. It is my belief that no force under heaven, however numerous, could have withstood their onslaught upon that day.*

In the hot-blood aftermath of the slaughter, the historian's station within the Persian palisade was overrun by two battalions of armed helots. These, under orders of the Spartan commander in chief, Pausanias, to take no prisoners, began butchering without quarter every man of Asia they could lay steel upon. In this exigency I thrust myself forward and began crying out in Greek, imploring the conquerors for mercy for our men.

Such, however, stood the Greeks' fear of the multitudes of the East, even in disarray and defeat, that none heeded or gave pause. Hands were laid upon my own person and my throat drawn back beneath the blade. Inspired perhaps by God Ahura Mazda, or in the instance by terror alone, I found my voice crying out from memory the names of those Spartans of whom the man Xeones had spoken. Leonidas. Dienekes. Alexandros. Polynikes. Rooster. At once the helot warriors drew up their swords.

All slaughter ceased.

Spartiate officers appeared and restored order to the mob of their armored serfs. I was hauled forward, hands bound, and dumped upon the earth before one of the Spartans, a magnificent-looking warrior, his flesh yet steaming with the gore and tissue of conquest. The helots had informed him of the names I had cried out. The warrior stood over my kneeling form, regarding me gravely.

"Do you know who I am?" he demanded.

I replied that I did not.

"I am Dekton, son of Idotychides. It was my name you called when you cried 'Rooster.' "

Scruple compels me here to state that what spare physical description the captive Xeones had supplied of this man failed in all ways to do him justice. The warrior who stood above me was a splendid specimen in the prime of youth and vigor, six feet and more in stature, possessed of a comeliness of person and nobility of bearing that belied utterly the mean birth and station from which, it was clear, he had in the interval arisen.

I now knelt within this man's power, pleading for mercy. I told him of his comrade Xeones' survival following the battle at Thermopylae, his resuscitation by the Royal Surgeon's staff and his dictation of the document by which I, its transcriber, had acquired knowledge of those names of the Spartans which I had, seeking pity, cried out.

By now a dozen other Spartiate warriors had clustered, encircling my kneeling form. As one, they scorned the document unseen and denounced me for a liar.

"What fiction of Persian heroism is this you have concocted of your own fancy, scribe?" one among them demanded. "Some carpet of lies woven to flatter your King?"

Others declared that they knew well the man Xeones, squire of Dienekes. How dare I cite his name, and that of his noble master, in craven endeavor to save my own skin?

Throughout this, the man Dekton called Rooster held silent. When the others' fury had at last spent itself, he put to me one question only, with Spartan brevity: where had the man Xeones last been seen?

"His body dispatched with honor by the Persian captain Orontes to that temple of Athens called by the Hellenes Persephone of the Veil."

At this the Spartan Dekton elevated his hand in clemency. "This stranger speaks true." His comrade Xeones' ashes, he confirmed, had been restored to Sparta, delivered months prior to this day's battle by a priestess of that very temple.

Hearing this, all strength fled my knees. I sank upon the earth, overcome by the apprehension of my own and our army's annihilation and by the irony of discovering myself now before the Spartans in that selfsame posture which the man Xeones had been compelled to assume before the warriors of Asia, that of the vanquished and the enslaved.

The general Mardonius had perished in the battle at Plataea, and the captain Orontes as well.

Yet now the Spartans believed me, my life was spared.

I was held at Plataea in the custody of the Hellenic allies, treated with consideration and courtesy, for most of the following month, then assigned as a captive interpreter to the staff of the Allied Congress.

This document, in the end, preserved my life.

. . .

An aside, as to the battle. His Majesty may recall the name Aristodemos, the Spartan officer mentioned on several occasions by the man Xeones as an envoy and, later, as among the Three Hundred at the Hot Gates. This man alone among the Peers survived, having been evacuated due to field blindness prior to the final morning.

Upon this Aristodemos' return alive to Sparta, he was forced to endure at the hands of the citizenry such scorn as a coward or tresante, *"trembler," that, now at Plataea, discovering the opportunity to redeem himself, he displayed such spectacular heroism, excelling all upon the field, as to eradicate forever his former disgrace.*

The Spartans, however, spurned Aristodemos for their prize of valor, awarding this to three other warriors, Posidonius, Philokyon and Amompharetus. The commanders adjudged Aristodemos' heroics reckless and unsound, striving in blood madness alone in front of the line, clearly seeking death before his comrades' eyes to expiate the infamy of his survival at Thermopylae. The valor of Posidonius, Philokyon and Amompharetus they reckoned superior, being that of men who wish to live yet still fight magnificently.

To return to my own lot. I was detained at Athens for two summers, serving in such capacities as translator and scribe as permitted me to witness firsthand the extraordinary and unprecedented transformation there taking place.

The ruined city rose again. With astonishing celerity the walls and port were rebuilt, the buildings of assembly and commerce, the courts and magistracies, the houses and shops and markets and factories. A second conflagration now consumed all Hellas, in particular the city of Athena, and this was the blaze of boldness and self-assurance. The hand of heaven, it seemed, had set itself in benediction upon each man's shoulder, banishing all timorousness and irresolution. Overnight the Greeks had seized the stage of destiny. They had defeated the mightiest army and navy in history. What lesser undertaking could now daunt them? What enterprise could they not dare?

The Athenian fleet drove His Majesty's warships back to Asia, clearing the Aegean. Trade boomed. The treasure and commerce of the world flooded into Athens.

Yet massive as was this economic recrudescence, it paled alongside the effects of victory upon the individuals, the commons of the populace themselves. A dynamism of optimism and enterprise fired each man with belief in himself and his gods. Each citizen-warrior who had endured trial of arms in the phalanx or pulled an oar under fire on the sea now deemed himself deserving of full inclusion in all affairs and discourse of the city.

That peculiar Hellenic form of government called democratia, *rule of the people, had plunged its roots deep, nurtured by the blood of war; now with victory the shoot burst forth into full flower. In the Assembly and the courts, the marketplace and the magistracies, the commons thrust themselves forward with vigor and confidence.*

To the Greeks, victory was proof of the might and majesty of their gods. These deities, which to our more civilized understanding appear vain and passion-possessed, riddled with folly and so prey to humanlike faults and foibles as to be unworthy of being called divine, to the Greeks embodied and personified their belief in that which was, if grander than human in scale, yet human in spirit and essence. The Greeks' sculpture and athletics celebrated the human form, their literature and music human passion, their discourse and philosophy human reason.

In the flush of triumph the arts exploded. No man's home, however humble, reascended from the ashes without some crowning mural, statue or memorial in thanksgiving to the gods and to the valor of their own arms. Theater and the chorus throve. The tragedies of Aeschylus and Phrynichus drew hordes to the precincts of the theatron, *where noble and common, citizen and foreigner, took their stations, attending in rapt and often transported awe to works whose stature, the Greeks professed, would endure forever.*

In the fall of my second year of captivity I was repatriated upon receipt of His Majesty's ransom, along with a number of other officers of the Empire, and returned to Asia.

Restored to His Majesty's service, I reassumed my responsibilities re-

cording the affairs of the Empire. Chance, or perhaps the hand of God Ahura Mazda, found me toward the close of the following summer in the port city of Sidon, there assigned to assist in the interrogation of a ship's master of Aegina, a Greek whose galley had been driven by storm to Egypt and there been captured by Phoenician warships of His Majesty's fleet. Examining this officer's logs, I came upon an entry indicating a sea passage, the summer previous, from Epidaurus Limera, a port of Lakedaemon, to Thermopylae.

At my urging, His Majesty's officers pressed their interrogation upon this point. The Aeginetan captain declared that his vessel had been among those employed to convey a party of Spartan officers and envoys to the dedication of a monument to the memory of the Three Hundred.

Also on board, the captain stated, was a party of Spartan women, the wives and relations of a number of the fallen.

No commerce was permitted, the captain reported, between himself and his officers and these gentlewomen. I questioned the man strenuously, but could determine neither by evidence nor by surmise if among these were included the ladies Arete and Paraleia, or the wives of any of the warriors mentioned in the papers of the man Xeones.

His vessel beached at the mouth of the Spercheios, the captain stated, at the eastern terminus of the very plain where His Majesty's army had encamped during the assault upon the Hot Gates. The memorial party there disembarked and proceeded the final distance on foot.

Three corpses of Greek warriors, the ship's master reported, had been recovered by the natives months earlier at the upper margins of the Trachinian plain, the very pastureland upon which His Majesty's pavilion had been sited. These remains had been preserved piously by the citizens of Trachis and were restored now with honor to the Lakedaemonians.

Though certainty remains ever elusive in such matters, the bodies, common sense testifies, can have been none other than those of the Spartan Knight Doreion, the Skirite "Hound" and the outlaw known as Ball Player, who participated in the night raid upon His Majesty's pavilion.

The ashes of one other body, that of a warrior of Lakedaemon returned from Athens, were borne by the Aeginetan vessel. The captain could provide no intelligence as to the identity of these remains. My heart, however, leapt at the possibility that they might be those of our narrator. I pressed the sea captain for further intelligence.

At the Hot Gates themselves, this officer declared, these final bodies and the urn of ashes were interred in the burial mound of the Lakedaemonian precinct, sited upon a knoll directly above the sea. Scrupulous interrogation of the captain as to the topography of the site permits me to conclude with near certainty that this hillock is the same whereupon the final defenders perished.

No athletic games were celebrated in memoriam, but only a simple solemn service sung in thanksgiving to Zeus Savior, Apollo, Eros and the Muses. It was all over, the ship's master stated, in less than an hour.

The captain's preoccupations upon the site were understandably more for the tide and the security of his vessel than with the memorial events transpiring. One instance, however, struck him, he said, as singular to the point of recollection. A woman among the Spartan party had held herself discrete from the others and chose to linger, solitary, upon the site after her sisters had reassembled in preparation to depart. In fact this lady tarried so late that the captain was compelled to dispatch one of his seamen to summon her away.

I inquired earnestly after the name of this woman. The captain, not surprisingly, had neither inquired nor been informed. I pressed the question, seeking any peculiarities of dress or person which might assist in mounting a supposition as to her identity. The captain insisted that there was nothing.

"What about her face?" I persisted. "Was she young or old? Of what age or appearance?"

"I cannot say," the man replied.

"Why not?"

"Her face was hidden," the ship's master declared. "All but her eyes obscured by a veil."

I inquired further as to the monuments themselves, the stones and their inscriptions. The captain reported what he recalled, which was little. The stone over the Spartans' grave, he recollected, bore verses composed by the poet Simonides, who himself stood present that day to assist in the dedication.

"Can you recall the epitaph upon the stone?" I inquired. "Or were the verses too lengthy for memory to retain?"

"Not at all," the captain replied. "The lines were composed Spartan style. Short. Nothing wasted."

So spare were they, he testified, that even one of as poor a memory as himself encountered no difficulty in their recollection.

O xein angellein Lakedaimoniois hoti tede
keimetha tois keinon rhemasi peithomenoi

These verses have I rendered thus, as best I can:

Tell the Spartans, stranger passing by,
that here obedient to their laws we lie.

ACKNOWLEDGMENTS

It goes without saying that a work which attempts to imagine vanished worlds and cultures owes everything to the original literary sources, in this case Homer, Herodotus, Plutarch, Pausanias, Diodorus, Plato, Thucydides, Xenophon, and on and on. They're the real stuff, without which nothing.

Almost as indispensable, however, have been the extraordinary scholars and historians of our own time, whose published wisdom I have looted shamelessly. I hope they will forgive the author of this work of far less rigorous scholarship than their own if he acknowledges with gratitude and by name a number of these distinguished classicists—Paul Cartledge, G. L. Cawkwell, Victor Davis Hansen, Donald Kagan, John Keegan, H. D. F. Kitto, J. F. Lazenby, E. V. Pritchett, W. K. Pritchett and, especially, Mary Renault.

In addition, I would like to thank two colleagues whose personal counsel and direction have been indispensable:

First, Hunter B. Armstrong, Director of the International Hoplology Society, for graciously sharing his expertise in hoplite weapons, tactics and practice and for his invaluable insights into, and imaginative reconstructions of, ancient battle. Himself an acclaimed weapons athlete, Mr. Armstrong's combatant's-eye-view assisted immeasurably in reimagining the experience of Greek heavy-infantry warfare.

Finally, my profound gratitude to Dr. Ippokratis Kantzios, Assistant Professor of Greek Language and Literature at the Richard Stockton College of New Jersey, for his generous and encyclopedic assistance through all aspects of this undertaking, acting not only as guide and mentor for historical and linguistic authenticity and as translator (free as well as exact) of the epigraph and of passages and terms throughout this book, but for numerous other sage and inspired contributions. There's not a page in the book that doesn't owe something to you, Hip. Thanks for your innumerable creative contributions, your unfailing encouragement and your ever-Olympian counsel.

WARS CHANGE. WARRIORS DON'T.

STEVEN PRESSFIELD, **the "master storyteller" *(Publishers Weekly)* and bestselling author, returns with a stunning, plausible near-future thriller about the rise of a privately financed and global military industrial complex.**

THE PROFESSION • A Thriller • $25.00 (Canada: $28.95) • 978-0-385-52873-3

"*The Profession* is chilling because it rhymes just enough with today to make us wonder whether this future will be, or only might be . . . A ripping read."

—NATHANIEL FICK, author of the *New York Times* bestseller *One Bullet Way*

"Pressfield dominates the military thriller genre."

—*LIBRARY JOURNAL*

Visit StevenPressfield.com, Facebook.com/StevePressfield, and Twitter.com/SPressfield for book updates and to share your thoughts.

Available wherever books and eBooks are sold.